# SERVE THE WORTHY

# SERVE THE WORTHY

Megan Formanek was born and raised in the often stormy Illawarra region of Australia. She has travelled the world following her obsession with history. Her desire to escape some brutally cold winters living abroad brought her to research archaeological sites, bringing characters to life through their belongings. She has been doing it ever since.
She, her partner, and her son now live in the wet tropics of Far North Queensland.
www.meganformanek.com

# SERVE THE WORTHY

## VIKING TRADING LANDS BOOK THREE

## MEGAN FORMANEK

For all the far-travelled wanderers, especially my sister Rebecca
and my closest friends Ellie and Rebecca. Friendships have such
an impact on our lives whether they last forever or for a moment,
even those which are relegated to our past continue to shape us.

# Place Names

The name given to any one place often changes with time. One location may be known by different names depending on the language spoken. This was no different in the Viking Age. In the 9th-century, and for many centuries after, spelling was inconsistent and largely phonetic. This can be problematic with accents affecting the pronunciation of place names and, thus, the way they are recorded.

Some readers will favour alternative references to those I have selected, but wherever possible, I have adopted the Old Norse designations consistent with the language spoken by the main character. Additionally, the spelling that has been adapted omits special characters that are especially difficult to pronounce for English speakers, let alone distinguish the sound without reference to an Old Norse dictionary. Further, as more archaeological evidence emerges, and our understanding of all things Viking improves, so does it change our perception of borders and the lands these names may refer to.

Abandoned

Paragon —        Lyubshanskaya Fortress, Russia.

Aldeigjuborg —   Staraya Ladoga, Russia.

Austmarr —       Baltic Sea.

Birka —          On the island of Björkö, Sweden.

Baghdad —        Part of the Abbasid Caliphate, modern-day
                 capital of Iraq.

Chernihiv —      Severian capital, now in Ukraine.

Gardarike —      The land of the Rus' (Rurikid dynasty), now
                 partially in both Ukraine and Russia.

Gnezdovo —       Krivichi settlement, now an archaeological site in
                 Russia.

Holmgardr —      Novgorod (Veliky), Russia.

Horodske —       Drevlian iron working and merchant settlement.

Iskorosten —     Drevlian capital, now known as Korosten,
                 Ukraine.

Itil —           Khazar capital from the 8th-10th century, also
                 known as Atil.

Karlstad —       Town in Sweden.

Khazaria —       Empire of the Khazars.

Kyiv —           City, now in Ukraine.

Malyn —          Prince Mal's court/settlement.

Miklagard —      Also known as Constantinople. Now Istanbul,
                 Turkey.

Serkland —       Abbasid Caliphate. A land that encompassed
                 much of the Middle East, western Asia, and
                 northeastern Africa.

Svealand —       Sweden.

Uppsala —        Significant sacred site in the Uppsala region,
                 Sweden.

Vytechev —       Rus' outpost and gathering point, now known as
                 Vitachiv, Ukraine.

# CHARACTERS

For a more comprehensive understanding of the relationships in this series, a family tree appears on page 375. It is recommended you do not look at it until you have read past chapter seventeen.

| | |
|---|---|
| Aeilar — | Mother of Astrid. |
| Ahmed Ibn Rashti — | Trader from Baghdad. |
| Alfrunr — | Niece of Oleg, Rus' princess. |
| Aslaug — | Friend of Estrid. |
| Astrid/Signe — | Main character, wool/sail merchant. |
| Björn — | Merchant from Birka. |
| Branka — | Woman who works in Astrid's warehouse in Kyiv (weaver). |
| Chestimir — | Husband of Mila. |
| Dir — | Bastard-born half-brother of Oleg. |
| Egbert/Toki — | Thrall belonging to Eskil. |
| Ellisif — | Daughter of Heilagr. |
| Eskil — | Previous hersir of Aldeigjuborg, warrior. |
| Estrid — | Wife of Heilagr, mother of Ellisif. |
| Eydis — | Sister of Astrid. |
| Freyja — | Astrid's daughter, born to Neflaug. |
| Frida — | Woman who works in Astrid's warehouse in Kyiv. |
| Frodi — | Oarsman from Birka. |
| Gudrun the Grey — | Wise woman of Gnezdovo. |

| | |
|---|---|
| Gunhild — | Wife of Hakon. |
| Gunnar — | Trader from Kyiv. |
| Harald — | Son of Heilagr and Estrid, brother of Ellisif. |
| Haskold — | Bastard-born half-brother of Oleg. |
| Helga — | Aldeigjuborg wool warehouse manager. |
| Helgi — | Son of Heilagr and Estrid, brother of Ellisif. |
| Heilagr — | Senior Druzhina, father of Ellisif. |
| Hemingr — | Hersir of Holmgardr. |
| Hilde — | Aldeigjuborg wool manager, mother of Helga. |
| Igor — | Son of Rurik, heir to the throne. Nephew to Oleg. |
| Inga — | Sister to Sveineld, betrothed to Harald. |
| Kari — | Thrall belonging to Sihtric. |
| Kjarr — | Husband of Astrid/Signe. |
| Kstianin — | Drevlian noble. |
| Leifr — | Husband of Ranveg, advisor to Oleg. |
| Licinia — | Thrall/maid of Ellisif. |
| Mal — | Prince of the Drevlians. |
| Mikel — | Carpenter in Aldeigjuborg, husband to Helga. |
| Mila — | Textile merchant from Gnezdovo, wife of Chestimir. |
| Mirca — | Wool merchant of Kyiv. |
| Neflaug — | Previous master of Astrid in Aldeigjuborg. |
| Niskinnin — | Drevlian noble. |

Odholf the Old —— Old Boyar, a close advisor of the previous prince, Rurik, and now Oleg.

Odrun —— Thrall belonging to Gunnar.

Oleg —— Grand Prince of the Rus' people, uncle to Igor.

Ostromyr —— Drevlian noble.

Ranveg —— Friend of Estrid, wife of Leifr.

Runolf —— Messenger of Oleg.

Rurik —— Deceased ruler of the Rus' people.

Sihtric —— Spice trader from Aldeigjuborg, captain of the *Bhobain*.

Svala —— Mother of Sven.

Sveineld the Younger —— Boyar and close advisor to Oleg.

Sven —— Best friend of Astrid, warrior.

Tarben —— Father of Astrid.

Tarkhan Tuvan (Tolze) —— Emissary from the Khazar Khagan.

Thorbjorn Hornklofi —— Norwegian skald, from the court of King Harald Fairhair

Thorsten —— Bone and antler craftsman.

Vrangi —— Captain of the *River-Raven*.

Volundr —— Norse blacksmith of Gnezdovo

# Norse Mythology

| | |
|---|---|
| Aesir — | Principal race of the norse gods which includes Freyja, Odin, Njord, Thor, and Bragi. |
| Asgard — | Home of the Aesir. |
| Baldr — | Son of Odin and Frigg. |
| Blót — | Ceremony of killing and offering an animal/being to the gods. |
| Bragi — | God of poetry. |
| Brisingamen — | Torc/necklace of Freyja. |
| Draugr — | Regarded as the undead who can be violent and cause damage. |
| Einherjar — | Those who die in battle and are brought to Valhalla by the Valkyries. |
| Eir — | Goddess of help and mercy. Possesses medical ability. |
| Freyja — | Goddess of love, fertility, war, and *seiðr*, among other things, and rules over her hall, Sessrúmnir in her field called Fólkvangr. |
| Frigg — | Goddess of motherhood, marriage, and prophecy. |

Hel —

Daughter of Loki and Angrboða. She rules the underworld of the same name.

Jól —

Midwinter celebration.

Jord —

Goddess of the earth, mother of Thor.

Jormungand —

*Jörmungandr.* The serpent who dwells in the sea encircling the earth. Son of Loki and Angrboða, brother of Hel.

Landvettr —

*Landvættir.* The land spirits who keep nature in good condition. If upset, they could be harmful, but the use of prow-beasts could scare them away.

Loki —

Often depicted as the trickster god.

Mani —

Moon god.

Nidhogg —

*Níðhǫggr,* the dragon/serpent who chews through one of the three roots of Yggdrasil, the world tree.

Njord —

God of the sea, seafaring, and wealth. Father of Freyja.

Norns —

Three deities who weave the fate of all mortals.

Odin —

God of death and war, sometimes referred to as the Allfather. He receives the *einherjar* in his hall at Valhalla.

Ragnarok —

*Ragnarök,* the Norse equivalent of the end of the world.

Seidr —

*Seiðr.* One type of magic, often associated with telling the future.

Skadi —

*Skaði,* born a Jotun (giant) and became a goddess by marriage to Njord. Associated with winter activities such as skiing and hunting.

Thor —

*Þórr,* god of storms, sacred groves, and strength.

Sol —

Sun goddess.

Svartalfheim —

Home of the dwarves (sometimes also referred to as dark elves).

Ullr —

God of oaths.

Valhalla —

*Valhǫll,* a hall ruled by Odin to receive warriors slain in battle for preparation for *Ragnarök.*

Valkyries —

Women who take the fallen warriors to Valhalla (*Valhǫll*) or Sessrúmnir.

Vanir —

Second group of gods.

Vetrnaetr —

Winter Nights festival marking the end of summer and the beginning of winter at which a sacrifice (*blót*) was made to the gods for the harvest and protection during the cold months.

Volundr —

*Vǫlundr.* Legendary blacksmith, also referred to as Wayland the Smith.

Völva —

Woman who practices *seidr,* and has the ability to foretell the future.

ALDEIGJUBORG
(STARAYA LADOGA)
Volkhov River
UPPSALA
HOLMGARDR
(RURIKOVO GORODISCHE)
KALRSTAD
BIRKA
OREBRO
Lovat River
Austmarr
(Baltic Sea)
GNEZDOVO
SMOLENSK
Dnieper River
KYIV
MIKLAGARD
(ISTANBUL)

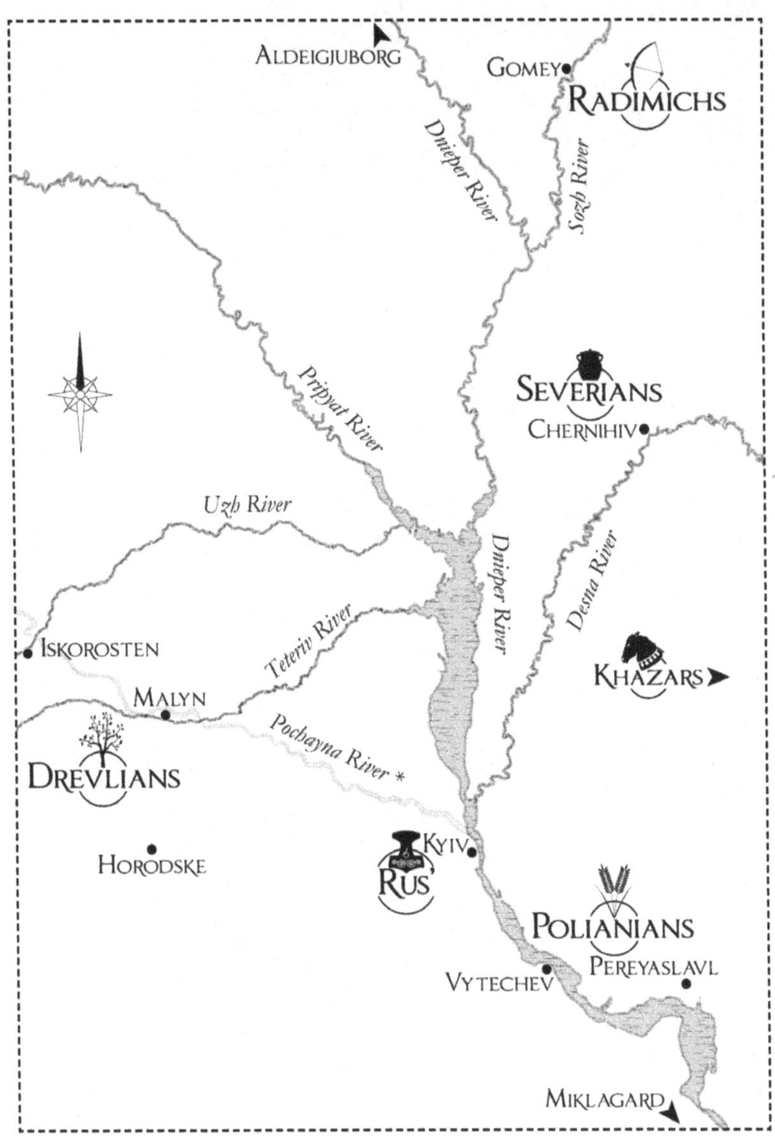


* The Pochayna River was separated from the Dnieper by a sand spit that submerged seasonally. Over time, the river changed course because of human intervention and, by the 18th century, was considered lost due to canal building. Today, a harbour is all the remains.

# PROLOGUE

## SPRING 877 CE KARLSTAD, SVEALAND

Hearth smoke, the smell of soured milk with stewed fruit, and my mother's voice woke me.

'Astrid!' Mother called, but I didn't want to rise. The bench inside my alcove was comfortable, and I wanted to sleep a little longer.

'Astrid!' Her voice was terse. That meant trouble. She shouldn't be kept waiting.

'Yes, Mother?' I responded, eyes closed against the assault of noise that prevented further slumber.

'Get up,' she ordered, words laced with unspoken threats.

It was after sunrise. I could tell, not because of any drenching of light, there was no window in our home. I knew because my mother was scrubbing her pots as she did every morning, even before the cows began lowing in the fields to be milked. The 'Cleanest cooking pots in the village,' she claimed and was proud of it, but I didn't want to help. To my mind, a cooking pot was a cooking pot, whether it was clean or seasoned with the many meals that went before it.

'Urgh,' I groaned, as I rolled over and peered above the blanket to judge how long it might be before my mother lost her patience with me.

My mother was busy on the other side, hanging her precious pot on the wall hook. Eydis, my sister, would be nearby, never far from my mother's skirts.

'Astrid, did you hear me?' Mother demanded, turning to glower in my direction. She glared through the bitter smoke that swirled around her like Nidhogg, the dragon gnawing on the roots of the world tree. I shuddered at the imagery.

'I heard you, Mother,' I responded and shifted from my bedding.

Though my mother was shorter than me, she was more intimidating, irritatingly stubborn, and vexed with my less-than-womanly attributes. Without the influence of my father, she remained completely unchecked and in charge; much to her delight.

My feet hit the floor, and I shuffled towards Mother who stood arms akimbo, looking a little less like a creature of the underworld and more like the striking woman men still glanced at. With her grey-blue eyes and golden hair worn long to cover her pointed ears, she looked younger than many other parents.

Eydis sat at the table, kneading rye flour and ale into a glossy ball of dough. She looked up at me and shook her flaxen head.

'What?' I demanded, but she looked away without meeting my stare again and punched the mass into a bowl.

'Eydis,' Mother breathed fire into the words, 'leave us. Take that bread and put it in the sun. Then tend to the animals. Don't come back until you see the door open.' Mother pointed to the door. My sister kept her pretty head bowed. A flash of golden hair rushed past as she scampered from the room into the bright sunlight, closing the door behind her.

It was now so dim that I could only make out my mother's form until my eyes adjusted to the small light filtering in through the smoke hole in the thatched roof. I sensed a lecture as my mother rounded on me, and I prepared my defence. Astrid, the ever-disappointing daughter. Eydis was the one my mother looked on with pride. She would have had two of her if Mother had her way. But Eydis was still young. Thirteen summers green. There was time enough for her to develop her mind. Even she might rebel. At least I hoped otherwise it would be a wonder how we were ever born to the same set of parents.

Mother wiped her hands down her apron and eyed me. 'Where were you last night?' she asked in the gloom. Her nose wrinkled, and her mouth twisted with words she didn't want to say aloud.

I smirked and pulled at the cuff of my *serkr*. 'Here, of course.'

'You were here this morning, but last night… last night you were out until the spirits stalked the forest,' she replied. Her clean hands smoothed over her dress, brushing off the dust that swirled in the low light.

'I was safe enough,' I answered.

She walked over to where Eydis had been and wiped the flour from the tabletop with a cloth. 'It is my job to protect you, even if that means I need to protect you from yourself.' She looked up with that infuriatingly knowing look.

'Mother. I did not return late,' I lied, handing her the scrubbing brush she gestured for.

'You did!' she raised her voice, and threw the brush across the room. 'I heard you come in well after Eydis, even though I asked you to return together. You probably came home well after the revelry had settled for the night. So, where were you? And this time, do not lie to me,' she commanded. The colour rose in her cheeks, and she stood with a glare that would send a shudder down the spine of Thor.

'The sky was so beautiful last night. I stayed to feel the gods' presence in the darkness, and to speak with father.'

'Your father is gone,' she said dully as she walked to collect the scrubbing brush.

I looked away from her. 'I know.'

'Astrid, he has left us alone, without protection. Tarben had scarce wealth and now I must look for another husband,' she complained while scouring the tabletop.

'He has gone to Valhalla, Mother.' I shrugged. 'And if you must take another husband, then you must, gods know your first attempt displeased you.'

She pulled the hand holding the brush back, and I thought she would throw it at me, but she hesitated. 'Your father was an excitable man but a failure as a provider,' she explained. 'I will not make the same mistake twice, nor will I allow you or Eydis to settle for anything less than I should have had.' She pushed away from the table empty-handed.

'Mother?' I did not like the way she spoke, nor the way she looked at me as if I were a saleable ewe with breeding hips and a back full of the finest fleece.

'It is time for both you and Eydis to marry.'

This wasn't the first time she had broached the subject. Three years prior, my mother had attempted to broker a marriage for me with a landowner in a nearby settlement. My father had intervened, knowing I was not ready, and she had bowed to her husband. But now, there was no one to stop her.

I pulled my *serkr* away from my skin. The room had grown hot. 'Mother, please do not make me marry someone I do not know.'

'It is not your choice. You have been too long a maid, and you have become wilful. You are indeed old to be first married, and you're fortunate to be asked, especially after your father was so indulgent with you.'

'I'm not old!' I argued. It was accurate enough that most girls my age were married, and many had at least one child, but I had not considered myself an aged bride. Marriage had not even crossed my mind until recently. 'What of Eydis?' I asked. 'She's too young.'

Eydis was three years my junior, and in her manner, she was scarcely more than a child. Though we had never been close, I felt protective of her being hastened to her marriage bed.

'She is grown enough. Astrid, both you and Eydis are women now. You are both ready for marriage and, unlike you, Eydis has not yet given me any cause to think she would take matters into her own hands.' Her eyes implied all I needed to know. My cheeks burned, and I knew what this confrontation was about. 'Eydis is a good girl. She will do as I bid her, marry who I tell her to, and make her husband happy. She knows it is her duty to bear children, keep her house, and support her husband. You are your father's daughter and have been too long without the discipline of a man.'

'Discipline of a man?' I asked, indignant, throwing my head back to scoff.

'Yes, and I intend for it to stop now,' she warned, walking towards me. 'I must keep you from dishonouring yourself and your family.' She brushed my hair from my shoulder with an uncharacteristic tenderness.

'Dishonouring? Mother! Please!' I folded my arms across my chest. She was making this far bigger than it needed to be. *I'll bow to her this time*, I thought, *just as I had so many times before, and she will forget this.*

'You are without control, Astrid. You do as you please and it has to stop! Tell me.' She paused. 'Were you alone last night when you were communing with the gods? Hmm? Were you alone searching the skies for answers?' She studied my face. 'Tell me, Astrid.' She squeezed my cheeks roughly in her hand, causing my lips to part and my jaw to ache. 'Who were you with?' Her pale eyes bored into me, willing my obstinance to break.

'Others,' I offered obtusely, forcing the muffled words out through bared teeth.

'Sven?' she asked, releasing her grip, and I massaged my smarting jaw.

I nodded. 'He was one of them,' I agreed, but did not tell her he was the only one. The rest of our friends had left not long after my sister. My heart fluttered as I recalled being alone with Sven under that glittering blanket of stars.

'Svala's boy, Sven?' she asked, confirming his mother's name.

'Yes.' My face grew hot, and I did not dare meet her gaze whilst my face was so readable.

'You weren't alone with him, were you?' She did not need to ask when she already knew the response. I feared her interrogation, and I had no confidence in my ability to hide the truth. 'Astrid,' she started, drawing my chin towards her, and forcing me to look into her eyes. 'Did you give yourself to him?'

'No, Mother. I swear,' I lied again.

'Swear it on what? Your life? A worthless scrap of cloth?' She prowled in circles, watching my face for a hint of betrayal. 'Your word means nothing if you won't swear the truth on anything you value.'

Sweat ran down my spine and beaded on my lip.

'You lie, I can tell,' she insisted.

Not only had Sven and I been together that night, but we had also promised ourselves to one another as though our union was ours alone to make.

'How far has it gone, Astrid?'

'Mother,' I started, then stopped to clear my throat and summon some courage. *What harm could the truth do now?* 'We are handfasted,' I declared defiantly to her gaping mouth and disbelieving eyes. 'Sven said he would come to you with his mother and ask for my hand.'

She shook her head. 'Astrid, how could you be so stupid?' Mother wavered on the spot before drawing in a great breath and with it, her eyes became as piercing as arrow points and their target was me. 'Of course a boy like him would say that!' she yelled, spittle flying from her mouth. 'He would tell you anything to get you on your back and in between your legs. There is little consequence for him. And now that you have given him what he wanted, he will find another, and another, until his mother grows tired of his behaviour and finds him a woman to wed. That woman will not be you.' She drove the words in like daggers. 'It will be someone who has not devalued herself.' She shook me by the shoulders.

'He would not do that to me. His mother is for the marriage. He told me so!' I insisted. I wanted to believe that Sven would not betray me, but how could my mother have found out if not from Svala? Tears threatened to spill, and I squeezed my eyes shut. She would not see me cry. *All her words are lies,* I told myself.

'Svala did not mention the union when she called on me this morning,' my mother explained and paused, 'to announce that they are moving away.'

'They're leaving?' I swallowed hard. Tears burned my eyes as I blinked them back.

Mother's voice softened. 'Everyone makes mistakes, Astrid.' She placed her hands on my shoulders. 'A single mistake can be overlooked if you put it behind you and move forward.' Her lip curled, *a smile perhaps.*

*She thinks she has won.* Her smug grin stoked the fire of defiance within me, and I couldn't help but taunt her in return. 'Oh, but Mother,' I began. 'It wasn't a single mistake.' Even at this moment, when I should have reined in my disobedience, I still wanted to shock my mother. 'It's been going on since…'

'You wilful little troll!' she screamed. Long, hurried strides took her to the wall on which a hazel rod hung. Mother kept it there to use on obstinate animals. She also used it to ward off evil spirits. I suppose at that moment she thought I might be either, or both. 'Put your arms around your head,' she commanded. 'You go to your new husband in three days, and I won't have you with sores on your face and hands.'

My hands slid over my face as she bid. 'I will marry no one but Sven.'

'That is not the life I have planned for you, Astrid,' she said as she delivered the first blow, a stinging strike, to my back. 'Do you want your life to be like this?' She motioned to the dark single room house we lived in. 'This is all we have! You could have more. You could have someone else to do all the work, just as I should have had.'

I yelped. 'Father would not have wanted it to be this way.'

'Your father was weak. He thought if we gave you more time, you would come to it on your own. But all you have brought me is trouble.' She drew her arm back again and struck me on the back of my thighs with a sickening whack.

'I swore myself to Sven,' I whimpered.

She bared her teeth. 'Then more the fool you are.' Mother's voice strained as she hit me, this time harder on the shoulder blade. 'You are lucky to be married before anyone hears of this, least of all your new husband,' she yelled. 'He lives a suitable distance from here, and is much older, and able to keep a pigheaded girl like you in line.' She struck me on the backside. 'Be a good wife. Once the babies come, they will keep you busy. There will be no time for any more of this nonsense.'

'I won't marry him,' I cried. She had beaten me before. I learned to clench my muscles tight to lessen the injury, but her anger thieved control and she delivered wickedly fast lashes against my skin.

'Let the pain serve as a reminder. Should you ever consider acting the fool again, think better of it. My role as your mother is not to coddle you. It's to beat these fantasies from you,' she shrieked as she beat me with the switch. 'What kind of mother would I be if I let you give yourself to someone with…' She stopped as she drew back her arm and whipped me on the thigh. 'With no wealth.' Another strike. 'No position.' She struck again, the stick cutting through the air with a whoosh before striking pink flesh.

'Mother!' I cried, shrinking away from her attack.

'Marrying *that* boy would bring you less than I had, and I regretted marrying your father every day of his life.'

'But I love him,' I confessed, hoping my declaration might stop her.

She slapped me across the face, skin stinging where her palm met my tender cheek. 'Love brings nothing but hardship,' she roared and brought the rod down on my back.

I cowered, hunching over to protect my bruised body. 'Mother, please.'

'Stand up,' she ordered. 'Meet your punishment like the woman you say you are.'

My body hurt, and my heart broke. Despite that, I stood against her bullying. Every part of me stung where the flesh had split and my *serkr* stuck to my bleeding wounds.

'Should I trust you have learned your lesson?' Mother asked breathlessly as she righted her clothing.

I bowed my head. 'Yes, Mother.'

She narrowed her eyes, assessing my words, gaze raking my body for a hint of remaining rebellion. Then her eyes widened. 'Just in case,' she hissed, and drew back her hand and struck me with such force that it propelled me into the hearth post. My head hit the wood. I stumbled around dizzily, my hand gingerly feeling the mound that grew on my forehead. Blood trickled down my cheek as I slid onto the ground, the room darker than before.

'I told you to cover your face!' Mother shrieked. 'Now I'll have to delay the wedding! Auden won't want an old, battered, and soiled sow!' She looked down at me, then turned on her heel and went to open the door, a signal to my sister it was safe to return.

I sobbed into the earth floor and whispered his name. 'Sven.'

And Eydis carried her bowl of dough inside, ignorant of the fate that also awaited her.

# Part One

## The River Road

# ONE

## SPRING 883 CE HOLMGARDR, GARDARIKE

My face hurt.

I nursed my wound and turned away from anyone who looked in my direction. It had been a heavy blow, and my skin had ripped like water parted by the prow of a ship, bruising with deep hues of purple and blue. Every time I touched it, memories of my mother striking me came flooding back, and I had to remind myself that this was a war wound sustained in the Battle of the Abandoned Paragon. Though long years had passed, fresh hurts had a way of making old injuries raw again. This time, instead of being sent to my new husband as an unwilling bride, I was journeying from Aldeigjuborg to Kyiv to reunite with Kjarr, my handfasted husband who allowed me my freedom, my dreams, and understood my nightmares.

I exhaled my impatience. We were only days into a much longer journey and if I could not calm my hammering heart, the passing time would be torturous. I lay back on the bench as the strakes groaned and the *Bhobain* rocked gently on the lapping tide. Birds flew high overhead in a blue sky rippled with white tufts. Graceful wings taking them somewhere new, just as we should have been. Instead, I was guarding Sihtric's ship, the *Bhobain*, and had made a poor bed on the inflexible rowing benches, waiting for the men to return from whatever mischief they were making in the fortress. I could have gone with them but had opted to stay with the ship, where fewer people stared at my battered face. A battle injury on a man was obvious, and people nodded their heads and said no more. As a woman, they either assumed I was a roughly treated slave, or a wife seeking to divorce her husband for his violent ways. So, I avoided the horrified looks of the children being swept away by their mothers, by staying aboard the *Bhobain*, where only the evil spirits of the water would recoil in fear from my appearance.

Earlier, I frightened the fish when I tried to glimpse my reflection on the water's surface. They scattered. Even those goggle-eyed creatures were repulsed, and, I hoped, it was not a sign that the water gods would also look away from our crew, taking their favour with them. I closed my eyes against the encroaching thoughts, but it did nothing to dampen the surrounding din.

Holmgardr's harbour was busy. Men filled and emptied their ship's hold from sunup to sundown. Merchants shouted greetings at each other, guards came to take payment, and ship's hulls thudded into mooring poles around us as we waited. Sihtric had docked the *Bhobain* the afternoon before, and most of our crew disembarked to attend to business they said would keep them no longer than midday the following day. I slowly opened my eyes, using my hand to shield against the bright light above me. Judging by the sun's position, now passing its peak, they were late.

Those who had gone ashore spent the night there, and I regretted my decision to stay when I remembered it meant another night sleeping on its deck between the benches. The constant squawking of birds and the rancid odour of rotting fish did nothing to assuage my annoyance. Then boredom set in.

But I wasn't alone. Ahmed Ibn Rashti, the traveller from the Abbasid Caliphate who I met in Aldeigjuborg, had also volunteered to stay onboard. Frodi, the shipmaster, also remained, if only to sleep below the sails and escape any heavy lifting, and Gunnar left his female thrall, Odrun, in our keeping.

From the aft deck, Ahmed stirred from his writing. He tapped his books with his immaculately trimmed nails. 'Trouble,' his steady, deep voice spoke, rich with foreign inflection.

'Huh?' I sat up and looked towards the docks where he had glanced before.

'Looks like trouble,' he repeated, before returning to his notebook, obviously leaving it to me to resolve the issue.

Skara, my axe, was lying on the deck. I picked her up by her handle and placed her on the bench by me. A comforting thud of well-used metal on oak. If anything was going to happen, I wanted her close.

The rest of our weapons were stowed in a barrel in the hold. Visitors could not go into the fortress armed. Only Holmgardr's forces carried swords or axes within its walls. And, just as Ahmed had mentioned, *trouble* in the form of two men dressed in Holmgardr's colours of red and brown were striding across the dock. But they weren't looking at us. They stopped by a ship from Ribe, got in, and started rifling through the contents of her bilge, much to the horror of the young man aboard.

I reclined on the bench again, toying with the armring I wore on my forearm. 'They're not coming for us,' I mumbled, tracing its design. 'Ulf won't be pleased when he learns they've been rummaging through his trade for a second time. Probably someone down here hiding stolen goods.'

Ahmed arched a dark eyebrow at me. 'Everyone here has stolen goods.'

I levelled him with a smirk. 'You know what I mean.'

Ahmed was unperturbed, nodding towards the two guards. 'They're for us, mark my words.'

There was no reason to worry. We had paid our levy, committed no foul, and disturbed no one. 'We are small fish, my friend,' I replied to Ahmed.

Odrun popped up from between two chests in the storage hold, where she had been sleeping alongside Frodi, who was snoring his head off. 'What's happening?' she asked, pulling her heavy wadmal cape around her neck despite the strong sun.

'Guards coming to question us,' Ahmed answered.

'They are not,' I insisted, waving away the threat as if it were a tendril of smoke.

Odrun made a face. 'As long as it's not Gunnar, the weasel turd,' she cursed, twisting the words awkwardly as she wrestled with a language that was not hers. Like most female thralls, Odrun was not overfond of her master.

'Ahmed, you might be right,' I conceded, keeping the red and brown-clad guards in my sight. 'It seems like they're coming for us. Heads up, Frodi!' I called, stirring the sleeping man.

He grunted and sat up abruptly. 'What is it?' he asked, scratching his scalp under his lank and greying hair.

I swung my legs on the bench to sit. 'Guards headed this way. Wake up. I might have need of you.'

Frodi rubbed his dark eyes and shielded them from the light. 'What do they want with us?' he asked, straightening up, though he looked like someone had slapped him across the head with a sail. 'What have the boys done?' He reached into the hold, grasping his axe from the barrel.

'Nothing,' I replied. 'At least I don't think they've done anything,' I corrected myself.

Frodi draped himself over a chest and snorted in reply, closing his eyes. Two heartbeats later, he was snoring. Odrun shook the small man.

'I'm awake,' he grumbled, swatting her away with his calloused hands.

'Barely,' she complained, glaring at him with her amber eyes full of distrust.

The guards were near now. 'Oi! You there!' One of them beckoned in our direction.

'Us?' I called back, raising my hand against the sun.

He swirled his red cape over his right shoulder and grabbed the prow of the *Bhobain* with his hand. 'You said you'd go on the next tide, but it looks like you're still tethered to our moorings,' the man whined. His companion stood halfway down the length of our hull, peering over the side.

'I thought we'd be gone too,' I muttered under my breath. 'It seems some of us aren't keen on keeping to their word.' Whatever was delaying our crew, it had better be for a good reason. '*Drengr*,' I began, offering the compliment to placate their annoyance, 'surely you are not so desperate to need this particular pole, nor this position in your harbour, right at this very moment, are you?'

'We are! We need this very one at this very moment,' he snarled. 'Got a line of ships waiting for a mooring round the bend and if we don't offer it to them, they could sail on.'

I doubted they would pass Holmgardr. A merchant wasn't likely to sail past a profitable trading town. They would more likely beach their boat or find somewhere else to moor and walk the distance. It was clear the guards were starved of entertainment and thought our ignorance might line their coin pouches.

'In that case. Let me offer you my sincere apology and promise we will leave as soon as the rest of our crew returns.' I looked behind me for support. Ahmed shrugged and Frodi must have determined it was safe because he had laid down once again and was already snoring, his axe discarded on the deck. 'And perhaps a few coins to lessen the inconvenience?'

'A few coins?' the broad man asked. 'You think we would take a few coins and look the other way? You need to get gone.'

'Fine men,' Ahmed began in a calming voice, 'is that any way to address a great warrior?'

The guards cast a glance first at me, then at each other, and guffawed. 'Who are you?' the broad man addressed my companion. 'And why does she have a face like a smashed beet?' The smaller of the two turned to address me. 'Did your husband pummel you for being a mouthy wench?'

'Odin's beard,' I groaned, as I pitched the bridge of my nose. Pain seared fresh from the touch.

Ahmed closed his notebook and lay it on the bench before him. 'Who am I? Me?' he asked. 'I am Ahmed Ibn Rashti, a traveller to these parts, that have, so far, been found lacking in hospitality. And the woman who stands before you is the great Signe of Aldeigjuborg, who fought in the Battle of the Abandoned Paragon.'

'Is that right?' the smaller man questioned, 'the Abandoned Paragon?'

'Mm-hmm,' Ahmed confirmed, his lips a tight line of disapproval over their boorish behaviour.

'Svein and I were there also,' the broader man answered, gesturing to his shorter friend. 'Didn't see no great woman warrior. In fact, I'd wager you weren't even there, not that I was looking. I was too busy fighting the actual battle from the shield-wall.'

*Thugs*, I thought as I stood and walked from the bench to the gunwale. 'From where I was, at the top of the Abandoned Paragon's ramparts protecting the archers,' I began, leaning towards them, my hair hanging over the bruised half of my face. 'I never saw our men form a shield-wall. Not unless you were fighting for the enemy. They certainly had one, and that was protected by a lethal spear thrower who my archers brought down.' My mouth quirked with a smug smile.

'Ummm,' Svein stammered. 'We were obviously with Hemingr's men.'

I toyed disinterestedly with the pouch tied to my belt. 'Which half? The ones who came in the first ship, or the idiots who came in the second and missed their mark and almost drowned?'

It had been a terrible mistake. Half of the Holmgardr force had landed right before the old fortress and hardly made it out of the vessel before a third of them were slaughtered. The joint arrival of Hemingr's contingent and the fury of Aldeigjuborg were the only things that saved them.

Ahmed chortled behind me as the guards' faces blanched.

'I killed three men!' the broad man claimed, looking towards Svein for reassurance.

His friend nodded and added, 'And I killed four!'

I laughed. 'We outnumbered the rebels at least two to one. A man would have been lucky to get one kill in. If you killed seven of the bastards, you'd be hailed as heroes, not relegated to harrying ships that outstay their welcome.'

The two guards released their grips on the *Bhobain*. 'You've got 'til the next tide,' Svein said, trying to sound authoritative.

'We'll be gone,' I promised, though it was nothing more than hope until the rest of our crew returned.

The guards shuffled off, but didn't go far. Now they would look for easier prey.

I rounded on Ahmed. 'What was that?' I demanded, gesturing vaguely to the docks.

He shrugged. 'They didn't know who you were,' he said without looking up from his writing. 'And I am yet to find out what happens when *al-Rus* outstays the welcome of the *Saqaliba*.'

'For your notebooks?' I asked, trying to peer at his book, not that it would have enlightened me. His scribbles were not anything I could read, though Ahmed had enthusiastically begun teaching me his language.

'*Bita bietalil hali*,' he replied sagely, his moss-green eyes full of that rare intelligence he possessed.

I crossed my arms against my chest. 'Hmm, well, I think your *natural curiosity* is just boredom. You're as tired of waiting for the rest of them as I am.'

Ahmed shrugged, neither confirmation nor denial.

In the distance, sauntering down the grassy hill from the town's fortress, came Sven, Björn, and Gunnar, each carrying a recent purchase. 'At least three of them are on their way back,' I said, nodding in their direction.

'Finally,' Ahmed added.

'Traipsing around Holmgardr doing whatever it is they've been doing. Perhaps, next time you feel like causing trouble, I'll show you what it's like for a Saracen to overstay their welcome,' I teased, grinning at his amused chuckle. 'Then you might apply that same knowledge to your *al-Rus* and *Saqaliba* situation,' I added, using a deep voice to imitate his own.

Ahmed scribbled something in his book and looked up. 'I'm weary of their questions every time I walk within their walls. I ache for home. The food here is tasteless, the music too shrill and jaunty, and I miss the call of prayer.' He'd been away a long time.

I chewed on my bottom lip and felt my sadness at being separated from Kjarr. 'One day soon you'll be home, Ahmed. One day soon.'

Heavy boots thudded along the wooden platforms. Gunnar reached the *Bhobain* first and pushed past the guards that now stood idly on the docks. 'Problems?' Gunnar demanded of them.

'Just wondering why you haven't moved on yet,' Svein, the smaller guard, asked.

Gunnar hopped over the side of the *Bhobain* and confidently inspected the steering oar as if he were suddenly an expert shipmaster. 'We're waiting on Eskil, who has disappeared somewhere with your hersir. Don't think Hersir Hemingr would take too kindly to his friend being abandoned if you make us cast off, do you? He might want to know who forced us to leave without him.' Gunnar stared them down with a malevolence he radiated with ease. His sky-blue eyes dared them to step one more foot in his direction.

Neither spoke. Both pretended to inspect a nearby ship's stern line, ignoring Gunnar's challenge.

'Last I saw him, he was down at the slave market,' Sven chimed in, awkwardly mounting the gunwale and slipping down onto the bench next to me. 'Did you miss me, *minn Svanr?*' he asked, nudging my shoulder.

I shook my head. 'I hope you slept more comfortably than me.'

He winked. 'Bought a small barrel of ale from the tavern where we lost Gunnar for a while.'

'Don't worry, we found him!' Björn grinned his gappy smile. He wobbled his silver-speckled mane and raked his fingers through it before shoving on his cap.

'Obviously,' I responded.

'Between the legs of the alewife!' Björn roared with laughter.

I raised my eyebrows at Sven, who shrugged and scooped a mug of ale for me from the barrel.

'Had to!' Gunnar grumbled, thumb motioning behind him. 'Odrun's a spiteful cow with a sour face. Every time I take her to bed…'

My hand shot up to stop his diatribe.

'Anyway, I tried to sell her to Eskil, but he wasn't up for it. Thought about selling her here, but she might prove useful on the journey to Kyiv if she would smile once in a while.' He grabbed the girl by the jaw and forced her lips upward.

Gunnar was a pig. It was he who was spiteful with a disgusting toad-like face. Odrun had every reason to hate him. She'd been purchased from a slaver and from then been used for men's entertainment. Her current master carted her from the marketplace he bought her to Birka, and, most recently, Aldeigjuborg. Now, she was travelling to Kyiv by which time Gunnar was likely to be tired of her and no doubt sell her on. From Kyiv, Gunnar might take her to the exotic marketplaces of Miklagard, where men would marvel at the foreign beauty of her golden eyes and angular features.

'Leave her alone, Gunnar,' I called across the benches.

Björn drew the ale into more cups and held one towards him. 'Come and drink.'

The offer enticed Gunnar enough to release his grip on Odrun's jaw. She rubbed her face and shot me a look that could have almost been thanks, before burying herself once more between the trunks in the storage hold.

'Eskil is with Hemingr?' I asked, turning to Sven.

'Hmm,' he agreed.

'Frodi,' Björn called to his Sámi friend. 'Wake up! Ale! Ahmed?' Björn offered, waving a mug at the man.

'You know I don't,' he answered, not unkindly. Ahmed never partook in drinking, not even with meals.

Frodi clambered from his sleeping place and assumed his seat next to Björn, accepting the proffered drink. If there was anything Frodi liked more than his sleep, it was ale. He'd once told me it had been ale that saved his life; a story I might have not believed had he not detailed the long winter he spent in the far north lands of Norway, when all he had were two flasks of the stuff and a will to survive. The ordeal had left him with a permanent reminder; a toe lost to the bite of the frost.

'Where are Sihtric and Kari?' I asked, searching the faces moving along the docks.

'They shouldn't be too far behind. Kari was carrying a small chest, and Sihtric said he had one more thing to deal with,' Sven answered, sipping from his mug.

Björn sat forward. 'Wonder what's in it, eh?' he asked. 'It's not a big one, but it might be heavy with fancy trinkets.' He whistled through the space where teeth used to be.

As if the mention of their names had summoned their appearance, Sihtric, and his thrall strode across the platform. Sihtric waved as he parted his way through the other merchants standing about. 'Who are we waiting for?' he asked, breathing hard.

'Eskil, of course!' Gunnar complained as he refilled his cup. 'Thinks he can keep us while he does whatever he likes.'

'Easy!' Sven warned. 'If you drink too much now, we will have little to share on the journey and nowhere to pull in for supplies.' Sven put his arm protectively across the barrel.

Gunnar rolled his eyes and produced a coloured cloth for gameplay, inviting Björn to join him.

Sven laughed suddenly. 'Thorsten. We've all forgotten about Thorsten. Could you imagine if we rowed away without him?'

'He'd find passage on another vessel,' Sihtric replied.

'Probably for free,' I added with a chuckle. 'He could charm his way onto a boat, regale them with his stories all the way to Kyiv, and the men aboard would love him for it. Was he with you at the tavern?' I questioned Sven.

He shook his head. 'He went to the market this morning to see if he could sell a few pieces.'

'I saw him haggling for a nice set of reindeer antlers, but I dinnae ken where he went after that,' Sihtric said, as he handed Kari, who was inside the boat, the small chest.

'What's in it?' I asked.

'Gold.' He grinned, keeping his hand firmly over the lid.

Björn's head shot up, and Gunnar stopped his prattling at the mention of the metal.

Sihtric laughed. 'You dinnae think I would trust you lot with something so precious? It's salt you *braw reivers*. A *wheen* of it too. The folk of Kyiv will have good need of it for preserving their harvest time kill.'

'Surely that small chest won't go far?' I asked as he placed it in a larger one and locked it.

'Course not! The rest is on its way down now. Look.' He pointed as four men, rolling a lead-lined barrel each, lumbered down the hill. They stowed the cargo in the hold and as they were leaving, Thorsten ran down the hill holding a fine pair of antlers aloft. His fire-blonde hair bounced as he made his way towards us.

'I got them!' he screamed joyfully. 'For a good price, too! This'll make combs a plenty for the women of Kyiv to wear on their hips. By this time next year, I'll have a fortune,' he dreamed aloud.

I ran my hand over one side of the antlers, smooth and unblemished. 'How fast can you work?' I asked.

'Ha! Not fast enough, Signe, not fast enough.' Thorsten clambered onto the ship and squeezed Sven on the shoulder. 'Am I the last? Oh! Sorry.'

A few of the men shrugged or shook their heads.

'Still waiting on Eskil,' I replied.

'Gods know when we'll be setting off then,' Thorsten joked, running his thick fingers through his shining locks.

Sven nudged me again. 'You in a hurry to get back to your husband?' he asked.

'Just sick of being around in a ship going nowhere and everything hurts.' I brushed my neck, and then the side of my head and yelped with pain.

'You've got to stop doing that,' Sven chided me as he wiped my face with the edge of his sleeve. 'Smearing the ointment all through your hair, and now you've rubbed dirt into the mix. Weren't you supposed to be keeping it clean so it can heal?'

During the Battle of the Abandoned Paragon, the blow I suffered to the right side of my face could have taken my eyesight. Instead, it caused substantial swelling that was only just beginning to subside. But the bruising remained, and so did a small rupture of the skin that was slowly knitting back together. I had covered the wound on my eyebrow and temple with an ointment made from the wax of honeybees and a bunch of sweet-smelling herbs as prepared by the healer. She had instructed me to keep it protected. I might have ignored the injury, but the healer's prediction, that should I leave it unprotected, the wound would fester, pucker, and scab and leave me with an awful scar that would permanently disfigure my face, had scared me. I wasn't vain, but if I could avoid having a face, "Like a smashed beet," as the guard had called it, I would. And Sven had threatened to apply the balm every night as I slept if I did not comply with the healer's instructions, so I accepted.

'Stick a piece of cloth over it. That should stop you from smudging the sticky stuff everywhere. It might even stop everything else from being stuck to your face. You're beginning to look like a dung heap!' Sven chuckled as he dabbed a rag into the water and dragged it down my face.

'Ow! It still hurts, be careful!' I recoiled from his touch.

'Of course it does! Your face is still black and blue.' He dabbed the last of it away. 'Hand me the jar.'

I passed him the small pot. He held it under his nose and gave it a whiff. 'Smells like something you'd smother over roast meat.' He chuckled. 'You'll smell delicious!' He could barely contain his laughter.

I narrowed my eyes and frowned. 'Just put it on my face, would you?'

He smeared some over my eyebrow and temple, then covered it with a square of linen. 'There,' he said, putting the stopper back on the jar. 'The healer said to change it every other day.' He examined the residue on his fingers. 'I wonder...' He chanced a lick. 'Ew! No! It doesn't taste like something I'd want on my food!' He spat over the side of the ship.

My hands gripped my stomach as I doubled over in hysterics. 'Serves you right for trying it.'

Ahmed's shoulders silently heaved with laughter on the deck.

Gunnar and Björn had struck up a conversation with Svein and the other guard as Eskil and Hemingr came down the steep hill to the docks. Behind them was a wiry man carrying a sack of something.

'Looks like Eskil got himself a slave,' Gunnar grinned. 'Didn't have the coin for a pretty one, I see.' The merchant laughed.

'He kens the rules,' Sihtric cut Gunnar's tittering short as the hersir approached the ship. 'Hersir Hemingr.' Sihtric nodded. 'I trust you've been keeping our Eskil out of trouble.'

'Pffft,' Eskil replied, scratching at his chin. 'I don't need any bloody help,' he scowled at Sihtric, then turned to Hemingr. 'But it was good to see you again and talk of battle.'

'My men needed the fight,' Hemingr replied, gripping the bigger man on the side of his arm. 'Nothing makes a warrior fat and lazy like having nothing to do. We were glad when you needed us to ride out and save your arses.'

Eskil opened his mouth to reply.

'What have you got there?' Gunnar asked, pointing at the man behind the two warriors.

'Someone to carry our goods on the overland sections,' Eskil responded.

Gunnar's mouth twitched up in the corner, his head cocked to the side. 'Not exactly what you said you were looking for,' he teased.

Eskil refused to be intimidated by the merchant. 'Realised a woman would be bloody useless. Needed a man with some energy, didn't I?'

The man behind him was small and taut with a sinewy strength that could be lethally fast in hand-to-hand fighting. He wore a long filthy tunic over similarly dirty pants, belted around the middle with a knotted cord. On his head was a cap in the same colour as the tunic and it covered most of his dark brown hair.

'What's your name?' I asked Eskil's slave, who was staring at his bare toes.

He looked up with wide, brown eyes. 'Egb...' he began, but Eskil cut him off.

'Toki,' Eskil answered forcefully.

'Toki?' I asked, shaking my head.

'Wait! Isn't that the same name you gave the one you had before?' Sven asked. 'You know, the one that ran away to warn the rebels but was captured before…'

'Shut up, Sven. His name is Toki,' Eskil insisted as he shoved the smaller man into the boat.

Sven helped him down and showed him to the seat next to us.

'My name is Egbert,' the small brown-haired man whispered to me.

'Don't talk to her,' Eskil bellowed at Egbert.

'You expect us all to be on this ship and for him to speak to no one?' I asked.

'And you! Don't talk to him,' Eskil commanded, pointing aggressively towards me.

'You might own him, Eskil, but you certainly don't own me,' I snapped, shooting him a reproving glare.

'If you talk to him, I'll beat him, and if he talks to you, I'll bloody beat him again,' he warned.

'Eskil,' Sihtric hissed, 'you ken the rules.'

Sihtric's mission was to get me to Kyiv alive. If Eskil laid even a finger on me, he would have Kjarr to answer to. I wondered if that threat caused any fear in the big man's chest.

Eskil folded his arms. 'Humph.'

'An ill-treated slave has nae place on this ship,' Sihtric responded.

'It's bad luck,' Sven, Thorsten, and Björn answered in unison.

'Lucky Hemingr isn't travelling with us then.' Eskil laughed. 'Apparently, Mokosh does nothing but moan and cry.'

Mokosh was the girl who had been a deity to the rebels defeated at the Abandoned Paragon. When we overthrew them, Hemingr took her as spoils of war.

'She'll calm down, eventually,' Hemingr assured his friend. 'It's the wife that causes the real trouble. She doesn't much like the young thing. I'm not sure I do either.' He scratched the stubble on his cheek.

My stomach turned. 'Free her then,' I suggested.

'Never,' he answered gruffly, 'not after everything her men did. The wife will put her to use in the kitchen soon once I'm done with her.'

'Maybe she'll calm down then,' Eskil smiled and grasped the hersir's arm. 'Farewell, then.'

Frodi stood from the bench. 'Ready to cast off?' he asked Sihtric.

Sihtric nodded. 'Eskil, get in.'

'To oars,' Björn bellowed.

'Give me a bloody moment, will you?' Eskil complained. He grabbed the stern line, throwing it aboard as he launched himself over the side. 'Which one's mine?' He looked between the few vacant seats that remained.

I pointed to the bench up the back, next to Gunnar. Frodi was perched at the steering oar.

'I see how it is,' Eskil grumbled as he took his position.

'Arseholes in the back where they ought to be,' Sven sniggered. 'Order of importance.'

'If you're the last one to return, you don't get to pick where you sit,' Björn answered.

'Give us a push out?' Eskil asked Hemingr.

Hemingr ordered his guard, Svein, to retrieve the bowline, which Sihtric expertly coiled and stowed. Then they shoved the boat out and stood tall, watching us manoeuvre out of the tight moorings.

'My regards to the Grand Prince,' Hemingr shouted as we began rowing, 'make sure he knows who saved your skins out there!'

'Don't you worry,' I mumbled, 'we will make sure they get the entire story.'

# Two

The afternoon sun cast extended shadows over the landscape.

Long days on the Lovat had been without event while we coasted under sail where the water road ran wide. A few more days and those tranquil times would be behind us. The closer we came to the end of the river, marked by the great pools that went no further south, the more difficult our journey would become. We would remove the *Bhobain* from the water no less than three times to join waterway veins that flowed towards the beating heart of Gnezdovo, where we would stop for supplies. But today, we did not need to worry about jagged rocks lurking beneath the surface threatening to tear at the *Bhobain's* hull, or chuckling rapids that capsized vessels and sent their contents into the bubbling cauldron. For now, there was a gentle breeze guiding us to our destination, and we looked for somewhere to spend the night before the hard work ahead.

'Ready the stone anchor,' Frodi bellowed.

Thorsten and Sven grappled with the great rock that would keep us in place through the dark hours.

Frodi tilted his head and peered at the sky. 'On the deck, be ready when we beach her.'

The men nodded.

'Here?' I asked Sihtric, looking at the gentle slope of the western bank. To me, it appeared as good a place as any to rest.

He shook his tawny head. 'Not here, *bhana charaid*. There's a spot a bit further along.' Sihtric's bronzed forearms braced against the forward gunwale while Frodi manoeuvred the *Bhobain* around the bend with a gentle hand on the steering oar, barely a quiver felt down the keel. 'The river splits in two, and there is a *wee* island that's perfect for us,' Sihtric explained.

I stood next to him on the bow deck. 'How can you recall such a place?' It was a long journey between Aldeigjuborg and Kyiv, and a lot of the landscape was indistinguishable to me.

He smiled, complete contentment as he stared ahead. 'I've sailed this riverway so many times, I can almost smell it before I see the change in the land.' A gentle breeze blew through his hair.

Eskil watched over the flat terrain as we drifted past. 'Who rules here?'

Gunnar sat up, ever eager to impart his knowledge. 'Slovenes or Krivichs. They may pay us tribute by now.' Tribute to the Grand Prince of Kyiv, he meant.

'They're peaceful enough,' Sihtric added. 'We'll nae be bothered, but we'll keep a watch just in case.'

'Whose turn is it to be on sentry tonight?' Gunnar asked.

'Not mine,' Ahmed called from his bench.

'Think it's mine,' Sven answered from behind, 'and Sihtric. Is that right?'

'Aye,' Sihtric agreed.

Eskil furrowed his brow, squinting into the distance where the forest met the river. 'Any Khazars in these parts?'

Gunnar snorted at the warrior's discomfort. 'Not here, friend.' He stumbled over to Eskil and knuckled the larger man's shoulder. 'You're not worried, are you?' The man fed off other's fear.

Eskil glanced up at him. 'Only a bloody fool wouldn't be.'

'Aye,' Sihtric agreed. 'You never ken where they will be exactly. They don't collect tribute here. So, unless they take a sudden desire to extract tariffs from these grassland people, we may never meet them.'

Eskil eased himself down onto the rowing bench. 'I'd wager it's a bit bloody far for their greedy fingers to reach,' he mumbled to soothe his anxieties.

'We dinnae need to worry until we've passed Gnezdovo,' Sihtric explained.

Gunnar plonked onto a chest. 'There is usually a convoy of vessels to meet there who will head onto Kyiv,' he added.

'Safety in numbers, huh?' Eskil asked, nerves shifting finally.

Gunnar sent a sideways glance towards Eskil. 'But we left late,' he began. 'We will be on our own.' He couldn't resist stirring the pot.

Björn cleared his throat. 'There's always someone lagging.'

Gunnar grinned. 'But then we might have the Pechenegs to worry about as well.'

Sihtric gave the merchant a long look.

'Rashti?' Eskil raised his voice, causing Ahmed Ibn Rashti to look up from his book. 'What do you say?'

He shrugged. 'Some say they are like kin to one another.'

'And your caliph has sent emissaries to both of them,' Gunnar prodded, now setting his sights on the trader from Baghdad.

'Gunnar,' I chided.

'What?' He pretended at shock, his hand pressed against his chest and his mouth slightly open.

'Let's fret about getting through these portages, and then worry about the Khazars, or anyone else, later.' Sihtric stood with his face in the wind. 'Then we'll need to be careful.'

Gunnar resumed his position on the bench as I watched the flat green land pass as we lazily coasted by. Great clumps of woodland covered the plateau and, further in the distant west, was a rise that was as bare as a newborn babe's backside. It was like this for most of the day; great expanses of fields, and gatherings of trees in alternation. Nothing else to see save for a stream here or there, and the occasional mound.

'If there was anyone, they would have built a bloody gigantic fortress up on that hill,' Eskil said, slowly convincing himself there was no threat.

'You'll see someone up there from time to time,' Sihtric confessed, 'but all they do is watch.'

If anyone stood out on that bare hill to watch us sail up the river, we would see them. Which was fine if they meant us no harm. Sihtric was unperturbed, but Eskil, ever the man of war, still watched the land pass with caution.

'Through those trees is the settlement of Gorodok,' Sihtric explained. 'It's only lively during the travelling season, but I'll have to go there and pay my dues.'

'I'll accompany you,' Ahmed offered.

Sihtric nodded. 'You and me, then,' he agreed. 'Nae far now,' Sihtric started, standing a little taller and gesturing ahead.

'To oars,' Frodi yelled.

We sprang into our positions. Everyone, even Toki and Odrun, crammed their backsides onto a plank next to a rowlock, or helped the man nearest to them. Two palms on the oar handle, the blade kept high and out of the water. Sihtric raised his hand. Frodi didn't need him to speak. The two of them were so in tune that I knew we were in expert hands. The words Sihtric spoke benefited the rest of us. 'Steady,' he warned.

We kept the oars high.

Frodi, with a gentle push of the steering oar against the current, guided us towards the grassy slope ahead that ramped onto the island.

'Now,' Sihtric instructed.

'Row,' Björn bellowed, and we pulled hard on those long shafts of wood.

The *Bhobain* lurched through the shallows and onto the bank, where her hull shuddered to a stop on the shore. She was half-in, half-out, but the hard part was done. Thorsten and Sven grunted as they lifted the anchor stone over the gunwale and hurled it into the water, breaking the surface with a *plunk* before it plunged into the riverbed.

Frodi beamed, springing up from his squat. 'Well done!'

Björn lumbered over trunks and benches from the aft. 'Better than last time.'

'And in one attempt.' Frodi loosened the strap on the steering oar, letting it flap with the pull of the water, and when he was satisfied he had done his job, launched himself over the stern into the knee-deep river. He tugged on the anchor stone. 'She's secure,' he called back to Björn, 'won't be going anywhere tonight.'

'Get what we need ashore, then we'll collect a bit of wood for a fire,' Sihtric instructed.

Eskil shouldered a few bedrolls. 'Send Toki and Odrun off to get it,' he suggested.

Not needing to be told twice, Egbert and Odrun climbed out, Thorsten helping them down and before we were all ashore, the two thralls had disappeared to complete their task.

'I'll see if there is anything about for eating,' Björn offered. He fished in his bag for a length of dried cow gut and fastened an iron hook to one end, casting it over the side of the *Bhobain* before kicking up his heels.

'You sure you want to send them off together?' Thorsten asked Eskil, as they walked up the rise away from the water.

Gunnar pushed between Thorsten and Eskil. 'What trouble can two thralls get up to? This island is the size of most villages and is ringed by water. They're not going anywhere except to fetch what they've been asked for.'

'Unless they can swim,' Thorsten quipped.

'What if… they…?' Eskil intimated with a rise and fall of his full brows.

Gunnar grunted. 'Then Odrun might come back with a smile on her face for once,' he said while tying off the mooring line to a tree. Gunnar glanced over his shoulder towards Eskil, 'But I'd geld that thrall of yours!'

Eskil chuckled awkwardly in reply and continued trudging up the rise, laden with camp supplies. We were used to the process by now. Each of us understood what needed to be done and how to do it in as little time as possible. The faster the work was done, the more time for talking, dice games, drinking, and, most importantly, sleep.

'Leave the sail tonight. We've nae need for a tent,' Sihtric commanded. 'It'll be safe enough unfurled and we'll leave at first light.'

I gazed up at the square of woven wool and smiled. It was creating sails that helped me make my fortune, and made Helga and Hilde's lives all the better. If I could convince the women of Gnezdovo and Kyiv to invest their time in weaving sails, I knew their incomes would improve, too.

'So, it's under the stars tonight,' Sven beamed.

'A fine night,' Sihtric agreed.

Sven turned to me. 'Want me to set you up?' he asked, dragging my rolled bedding to the front of the *Bhobain*.

My hand grazed his as I tightened the strap. 'Thank you,' I muttered. 'I think I'll go and find Odrun and Egbert.'

'Don't let Eskil hear you calling his thrall by that name,' Sven warned gently.

'Calling him Toki doesn't feel right,' I added. It wasn't the man's name, but I didn't want to make his life harder than it already was. 'Set me up away from the snorers,' I mumbled as I slung my legs over the gunwale and dropped over the side.

The fall from the *Bhobain* to the shore wasn't so bad. The shin-deep water seeped into my boots and soaked the hem of my dress, but it would dry quickly in the afternoon sun. After removing my shoes, I wandered off into the thicket to gather dry branches to keep us warm through the night. Plenty was lying about. Odrun and Egbert needn't have strayed far, but the two had vanished.

'Can't blame them,' I mumbled to myself. 'If I was a slave and asked to wander off into the trees to find sticks, I'd take my sweet time.'

*Could either of them swim?* I wondered. *Would anyone brave the breadth of the Lovat for a chance of freedom?* The thought pricked at me, drawing a worried panic that had me calling out their names. 'Odrun!' I called out. 'Egbert,' I shouted in a whisper, not wanting to alert any of the crew. 'Odrun! Egbert' I repeated, continuing as the pine trunks grew denser, tighter together, and I had to squeeze through to pass. There came no answer. Not that I really expected one.

The island was the perfect place for river travellers to rest, just as Sihtric had said. A small mound of land, hugged by a wide moat of flowing water. No one would come for us here. I kept walking until I could see the river once again through the trees and realised I had walked the entire length of the landmass and still failed to find Odrun and Egbert. My bare foot caught a tree root, and a branch cracked as I stumbled backwards. It was dry here and parched wood made the best kindling, so I stopped to collect some.

Soft voices singing muddled words reached my ears. The lilt was familiar. Perhaps I knew the tongue, I wasn't sure. Another voice sang sweetly, joining with the melody. A man and a woman. It sounded like…

'Odrun?' I gasped as I walked into the glade.

Fair Odrun turned, mouth open. A simple cream kerchief covered her head. Beside her, Egbert was on his knees in the dirt, his hands clasped together just as Odrun's were steepled under her chin.

'There's no need to worry,' I tried to assure them.

Egbert got to his feet and Odrun snatched the covering from her head as they looked at each other.

'I won't tell anyone,' I promised, edging towards them.

Odrun levelled me with an unsmiling gaze. 'What is it you think you've seen?' she asked, voice haughty as usual.

Skara was at my belt, but I held my hands forward to show them I would bring no harm. 'You were singing,' I said, looking at Egbert.

The wiry man glanced at Odrun, mouth a straight line and eyes wide.

'Was it a Frankish song?' I chanced.

His eyes lit up and before Odrun could stop him, he responded, 'You speak our language?'

'Fool,' I caught Odrun muttering under her breath as she pulled on the edge of her thick woollen cape draped around her neck.

'Just a few words,' I replied, striding more confidently to where they stood. The merchant Eryk of Aldeigjuborg had taught me the spoken language when I was under his tutelage, though I proved a poor student in its written form.

'It was just singing,' Odrun added with a huff, turning her nose up and pretending to study the trees overhead.

'Your song was lovely, and both your voices sounded beautiful.'

Encouraged by my compliment, Egbert stumbled over roots towards me. 'It's a prayer.'

Odrun raced forward and put her hand on his forearm. 'No more,' she cautioned with a glare.

He pursed his lips, placed his hand over hers, and turned away from me.

'You're both Christians?' I asked.

But they would say no more.

'A promise is a promise,' I began. 'I won't tell anyone what I've seen here. You have my word.'

Odrun watched me with narrowed eyes and empty arms.

'Can I make one suggestion?' I ventured, tipping my head to the side and smiling sweetly. 'You've been sent out to collect wood for the fire. Unless you want the others to be suspicious, I'd come back with an armful each.' I paused, casting an eye over them. 'Unless you're planning to take your chances in these foreign lands?'

Odrun shook her head solemnly. Egbert echoed the response.

'I'll let them know you're not far behind me,' I finished, as I turned to leave.

They said nothing as I walked away, neither moving, and once I was out of earshot, I didn't listen for them again. It was hardly surprising to learn Odrun and Egbert were Christians, if that's what they were.

My assumption was based on what I had seen others, such as my friend Helga, do when they worshipped the baby god. They kneeled, just as Egbert had, and hands pressed firmly together. To hear Odrun singing brought no shock either. Everyone sang. Whether it be for worship or entertainment. What alarmed me was her association with Egbert. Odrun was one to hold her head aloft despite the fact she was not free and yet, she had grown close enough to Egbert to wander into the forest with him, though they'd only known each other for a few weeks. That they spoke the same language was astonishing enough, and I wondered what it had taken Odrun to trust Egbert when she was closed to everyone else. She merely tolerated me, which was fine. She could do what she wished. Though, I was convinced what I had witnessed meant something more than I could presently piece together. But solve the puzzle, I must, and before anyone else.

Bronze rays, low on the horizon, twinkled through the branches as I carried my pile of dry twigs back to the camp. Everyone else was laying out beds, or sat around a fallen tree partaking in a game of *taflkast*.

'You were gone a while,' Gunnar commented, rolling one die. 'Where is Odrun?' His legs were spread out wide, and his hand lay against his inner thigh as he looked up at me.

I grimaced. 'She won't be far behind.' It was hard to ignore the slimy invisible hand his words raked down my spine.

'And, Toki?' Eskil asked. He chuckled at Gunnar's poor roll and scooped up the dice, rattling them within his fist.

I dumped the wood on the ground. 'He went in the opposite direction,' I lied, and was not sure why I did. 'He'll be back soon.'

'Were they together?' Gunnar questioned. A smile crept across his toad-like face as he saw his winning dice roll. 'They've been gone long enough to warrant concern.'

'Everything is fine, Gunnar. You've no cause for unease.' I handed kindling sticks to Sven, who was busy building a stone ring for the firebed.

'I shouldn't have let her out of her manacles. She's probably parading around out there, or chanced her escape across the river,' he grumbled but wasn't troubled enough to move and search for her.

'If she's gone, then Toki would have followed,' Eskil worried, scrambling to his feet.

'Didn't you hear me? I said they'll be back soon! Where would they have gone, anyway?' I asked. 'The island is tiny, and I doubt either of them could swim to save themselves.'

Sihtric was lying on the ground, his man Kari mending a shirt behind him. 'If you dinnae want them to run away, perhaps you should take better care of them,' Sihtric spoke, and I saw his own man smile. He could do little more than that. When Kari was taken from his native island, his captors had severed the tongue from his mouth, leaving him unable to speak, though he could grunt and gesture enough to get his meaning across.

Gunnar thumped the tree trunk with his fist. 'So, where are they?' he demanded.

Sick of his incessant questioning, I bared my teeth at him. 'Do I look like their keeper? What is the point of having a thrall if you want everyone else to chase around after them?'

Eskil shot me a furious glare. 'Is he bloody coming back or not?'

I shrugged. 'How would I know? Maybe he has run off, like the last one.'

My mocking tone broke his anger and amusement slid across his features. 'Tell me you've seen him.'

'That's what I said, isn't it?' I agreed, as I bent down to help Sven pile up branches. 'He was on the other side of the island and had a stack of wood for the fire. They'll be back, Eskil.'

The big man let out a great sigh. 'Are you sure Kjarr will want her back?' Eskil teased, pretending to question Sihtric.

'For certain, though sometimes I'm nae sure why.' He winked at me.

'You can all choke on a fish bone!' I exclaimed. 'Why am I on the receiving end of this vitriol?' I need not have asked. It was clear everyone was on edge, and I was an easy target who always took the bait.

There was a rustle as Odrun and Egbert staggered through the trees with sticks piled high in their arms. Gunnar shoved Odrun down by the fire. Eskil sent Egbert to help Björn gut the salmon he caught for dinner, while Sven and I secured a cauldron of water over the fire.

'He's asked you to come all of this way,' Sven mumbled as he hoisted the large vessel onto the hook.

'What are you talking about?' I replied, picking wild herb leaves from stems and throwing them into the pot.

'Kjarr. He sent for you! He'd be mad to turn you away.'

I took my knife and chopped the stems finely on a small board of wood. 'You heard what Eskil said.'

Sven handed me a withered leek to slice into chunks. 'Ignore him. He's all tangled up since the battle, after he left his position as Hersir of Aldeigjuborg. He doesn't know who he is anymore.'

Fat rings of leeks slid off the board into the simmering broth. 'And, Kjarr? What is he going to do, divorce me for wearing pants?' I scoffed.

'You know, he could.'

A growl escaped my lips. 'Well, I haven't worn them since I left Aldeigjuborg, so unless you or any of the other louts tell him, he won't know.'

Björn brought the gutted fish uphill and laid them on the board before Sven, who cut the flesh and slid the pink slabs into the now bubbling stew. It wasn't long before the meat was cooked through, and we feasted on our first hot meal in days.

After our bellies were filled, the sun dipped low on the horizon. Sihtric yawned.

'Are you sure you're fit for sentry duty?' I asked him. 'Why don't you sleep, and I'll take this one? Go to bed.'

He stood and stretched his back. 'Cannae, remember? I'm waiting for someone to take us to the settlement.'

'That means you'll want me to take your place, then?' I wondered.

'Aye, if you would, Signe,' he agreed.

'I guess I'll sleep on the deck while you row tomorrow.'

He stretched lazily, his neck giving a satisfying crack as he pulled it to one side. 'You sure you'll be all right on your own with Sven?'

'Mmm, I'll be all right.'

He walked away, but hesitated. 'You should talk it over, *bhana charaid.* Before we get to Kyiv. Before Kjarr sees you like this.'

'Why does everyone think my face is such a cause for concern?' I complained.

'Nae your face, you *grossart.* I ken Kjarr well. He's as stalwart as they come. He'll have you in his mind the same as before. You need to decide what you want before he sees you or he'll see it before you tell him. You know it'll be…'

'Written on my face,' I finished for him.

'Aye. One of the things I like about you, *bhana charaid*. You cannae lie. Nae well, anyway,' he said with a gentle smile. 'Good night, Signe, lass.' He patted me on the shoulder. 'Here they are now.' Sihtric pointed to the small rowing vessel lapping its way across the river.

The two men did not step from the boat as they flung a rope to Sihtric and he pulled them towards the shore. Wary eyes watched Ahmed and Sihtric as they approached, but the unease was short-lived. After a package of furs, coupled with Sihtric's charm, they were all smiling and on their way to Gorodok.

# THREE

It was late into the evening once the crew settled into their beds after a night of drinking, eating, and music. Thorsten had provided us with a dinnertime serenade as he played his bone flute. Lithe fingers deftly tapped at the small holes as his steady breath pushed out a mellow tune.

Now, a chorus of snores filled the night while I stayed by the fire, staring into its red flickering light. Sven had wandered down the rise to do another inspection of the shore and the *Bhobain*, ensuring it remained where we left it, leaving me alone with the thoughts that plagued me with uncertainty. Kjarr, Kyiv, and Grand Prince Oleg.

Almost a year had passed since I last saw my husband. Before that, trade had taken him from me for another season entirely, interrupted by only the briefest of visits. My mind clung to those short days, raking over the details of Kjarr's voice, his face, and the smell of him. Kjarr had been called away by the leader of the Rus', the Grand Prince. For what reason, he could not say. Sihtric, my husband's best friend, assured me Kjarr had gone unwillingly. Yet, he was still absent, and it was a nagging canker, fuelled by the ongoing secrecy.

All I knew was that Kjarr had gone to serve Oleg. The only message he sent was for me to join him in Kyiv, an arduous and dangerous journey to take with no explanation. In all this time, had I sent Kjarr a word of reply? Not exactly. When I had been ill, perhaps preparing to leave Midgard altogether, Sven had dispatched a missive to Kjarr. Whether he ever received the missive was unknown. I certainly did not receive a reply. But it was the only communication I had attempted in our long separation. Perhaps it was my way of punishing him for abandoning me when I needed him the most. With each passing day, the uncertainty of my position as Kjarr's wife in Kyiv drew nearer, and more unclear. As we navigated the waterways flowing south, I approached a life and a court I did not understand, and I didn't know how to prepare for it.

*Are you sure Kjarr will want her back?* I replayed Eskil's words in my head and chided myself for letting them get to me. They teased me because they could. Because I bit. Their fun was watching me rise to their baiting, and they had nothing better to do than repeat the game until I lashed out.

The fire hissed and spat bronze sparks into the night, fizzling out on the damp grass. I shook off the smothering thoughts. It was too warm by the flames, so I followed the cool breeze to the shore where Sven sat. His back was towards me as I approached. His shirt was wide at the neck to expose the ink that swirled from his shoulder to the space behind his ear, illuminated by the faint glow of the fire.

'What happened to Sihtric's rule?' said Sven without moving as I slipped onto the ground next to him, overlooking the river. From this position, we could see any oncoming danger from the water, close enough to camp to hear if anyone stirred.

'Which one?'

Sihtric had so many.

He shifted. 'Not leaving us on watch together.'

I cleared my throat and swallowed hard. 'Ah. Well, Sihtric has gone off on business again and needed someone to take his place,' I explained.

The rule had come at my insistence; I didn't want to repeat that night by the hearth.

I shrugged. 'It's all right, I'm sure we won't get into too much trouble.'

Sven laughed lightly as he turned over a small object in his hands. 'Hope he offered you something worthwhile.'

*An opportunity to talk things over with you,* I thought, but decided against saying anything.

'He'd take your place if you needed him to,' Sven added. He took a whittling knife and chipped away at the edge of the wood figure he had in his palm, though I couldn't make out any details.

'What's that?' I asked.

He held it up to the dim light. 'It's a carving I've been working on.'

'In the dark?' I questioned, craning to see better.

Sven held the creature aloft. 'Not now. I've already stabbed myself in the thumb twice. At this rate, I'll slice it right off if I don't stop. It'll have to wait until morning,' he replied, setting it into my open hand.

The shape was recognisable as my fingers traced each carved line. The outer curve of the head, an inner swirl for the open mouth with its tongue extended to scare away the evil spirits of the land, or bring fear to sea monsters intent on dragging us to their murky lairs. 'It's a prow-beast,' I exclaimed, as I marvelled at his fine work.

He nodded, saying no more. His hand reached for the beast, and he dropped it on the grass beside him. 'How many days do we have left?' Sven asked, as if he didn't count the days like the rest of us.

'To Kyiv?' Instinctively, I shifted a little closer. It was dark now, even the firelight wasn't bright enough to show the movement of his head, though I knew he nodded. 'Björn said it was six weeks from Aldeigjuborg to Kyiv, give or take. We are only ten.' I paused. 'Or eleven days in, so…'

'Still got a while to go,' he finished for me.

'Even then, if the crew intended to continue, we would be halfway to our ultimate destination,' I continued, mind racing ahead.

Sven hummed dreamily. 'To Miklagard.'

'I'm in no hurry to get to Kyiv.' Every day we passed on our journey made the feeling of discomfort more impossible to ignore.

'I can tell,' Sven spoke softly, turning towards me.

'Here I was, thinking I was hiding it so well,' I joked. 'Curse my readable face!'

Sven's voice was solemn in its reply. 'It's not your face, it's just you. You've been different since we left Aldeigjuborg.'

'Everything has been different since we left. There was the battle at the Abandoned Paragon, my illness, Freyja…' I trailed off. The night air blew through my hair as I unbound it.

'Hmmm,' he agreed. 'Is that what you're worried about?'

I took my comb from my belt and started running it from root to end. 'About telling him everything?'

'Mm-hmm.'

There was so much my husband had missed in the years we had been apart. We had lost our daughter, our home, Aldeigjuborg had been under attack, and Kjarr had almost lost me to illness.

'What if he hears it all and decides he does not want me anymore?' I asked, putting away my comb.

Sven grunted. 'About before… I'm sorry. I shouldn't have even said it in jest. There's been this darkness hanging over you ever since…'

The small carving lay on the grass between us. I picked it up and turned it over in my hands. 'It's almost like I don't know why I'm doing any of this.'

Sven asked, 'The journey?'

I shook my head. 'When I married Kjarr, there was a reason.' *A baby*, I recalled. Now, that child was dead. 'All the reasons are gone, and I'm left wondering if he wants to be free of the arrangement.'

'Free of you?' Sven wondered. 'Why would he? Sihtric says the man is wild for you.'

'Wild,' I scoffed, stifling a laugh. 'No one would describe Kjarr as wild.' Perhaps it wasn't so ridiculous. The last time Kjarr had come to Aldeigjuborg, he rode three days to see me for a moment; and just to turn around and ride three more days back to his duties. The one time he had abandoned caution. Those two days, we fell into place as if it had always been that way. 'Sven, I love him,' I admitted.

'So you say,' he responded. His voice was flat and I could hear the snap of a blade of grass being torn in two as he plucked it from the ground.

My voice came out strangled as I continued, 'Is love enough? Are my feelings enough to weather whatever storm I am walking into when I arrive in Kyiv?'

He blew out a deep breath. 'I can't answer that for you.'

'You wouldn't, even if you thought it was,' I responded, a little more rudely than I meant to.

He stopped and reached for my arm. 'Why would you say that?'

I turned my face towards him. 'You're telling me you would help me decide, even if that means making a choice you disagreed with?'

'Of course.' He was close, so dangerously close. I could feel his breath on my cheek.

'You don't have a history of providing good counsel when you're conflicted,' I jibed, drawing back from him.

'Ouch!' He recoiled from my sharp words, then nudged me with his shoulder. 'Are you trying to wound me?' he teased.

I pursed my lips and looked at the sky. 'It's true!'

'All right. I deserved that. But you can't tell me you're not conflicted either.'

My hands cradled my head. 'I can't,' I agreed. 'My decision is made. I'm going to Kjarr with no intention of seeking a divorce. He is a good husband to me, and if he feels the same, we will remain married and face whatever is coming. Together.'

The fire crackled behind us, starved of fuel. Without its heat, the night was cool. Colder now that the sun had disappeared completely, and the land was carpeted black. We broke our conversation to lay some bigger logs down, prodding the small flames with long sticks until they once again licked at the wood with their autumnal hues. Sven and I settled closer to its heat. Far enough from the sleeping men that we would not wake them but at the top of the rise so we could see the river, land, and the *Bhobain*.

Sven waited for me to join him on the ground before he spoke again. 'Are we going to talk about what happened?'

I bit my lip. 'Sihtric said we should.'

'He knows?' Sven asked, aghast, running his hand through his dusty blonde hair.

The light was better near the fire. I could see his face and, just like me, he wasn't good at hiding how he felt. 'I never told him, but somehow Sihtric knows,' I confessed.

'That man has a shrewd mind and seeing eyes. He's been wary of me.'

I picked a wildflower and plucked each yellow petal one at a time. 'He's Kjarr's best friend, and he's making sure his wife returns to him unscathed,' I replied flatly. 'You can't keep anything from him, and it's not like you've tried to hide it.'

Sven hunched forward, reaching for a blade of grass. 'You could have warned me.'

'Would you have listened?'

Amber flames danced in his grey-green eyes, and he chuckled. 'No.'

'What happened should not have happened,' I began.

The twinkle in his eyes vanished. 'Not like it did,' he agreed. 'You didn't want to, and…'

'I didn't say that. I wanted to…' I was saying too much.

His gaze was intent as he waited for me to speak again. The words died in my throat. That night, I had lost my senses. Grief overran me. Sven and I had tumbled onto my hearth floor, and it had almost gone too far. Until the searing crack of an overboiled pot dripping into the fire had put an end to our foolishness. When the heat of our encounter cooled, Sven had surprised me by issuing an ultimatum. Though he might long for us to be together, he would never allow it until it was my free decision.

The yellow flower in my hands was ruined. Its petals lay discarded, the stem ripped in half and still, my fingers pulled at its greenery. 'Kjarr is going to find out.' I threw the remnants of the stem on the ground and plucked another flower from the patch.

Sven gritted his teeth and sucked in a breath. 'How big is this husband of yours? Handy with a sword? Who would win in a fight?' he rambled.

'Stop it,' I warned, pushing his shoulder with my hand. 'I have to tell him.'

'He's going to kill me.' Sven grabbed my arm. 'Will he challenge me himself, or send someone else to do it?'

I ignored his questions. 'Kjarr and I promised to be honest with each other.'

Sven's hand grasped my knee. 'How honest has he been with you?'

That was a question I had asked myself, over and over. When I had last seen Kjarr, he had been guarded, refusing to offer any information about his position in Oleg's retinue. 'He might be keeping something from me,' I conceded.

'Tell him about your illness, the battle, about Freyja, but why tell him about us?' He paused and realised there must have been something more than what I was saying. 'Does he know about us before?'

I nodded. His palm was still on my knee.

'Gods! You told him everything? He is going to kill me!' His free hand traced the line along his jaw.

'But you're a big powerful warrior, Sven,' I teased, pushing him off my leg. 'Kjarr is a merchant that can wave a sword about if need be.'

'How are you going to explain that I found you in Aldeigjuborg after everything that passed before, and then tell him what happened after?'

'Odin's beard, Sven. Kjarr isn't a jealous man!' I tried to calm him.

Sven shifted in agitation. 'So you keep telling me. Maybe he'll just hate me forever, then.'

I glared at him in the dim light. *Why did men have to be so difficult?* 'That will be between you and him. It seems you've already decided to dislike him.'

'Kjarr?' he asked with sandy eyebrows raised. 'Oh! I won't like him. First, because he left you on your own, and secondly...'

'Sven!' I warned.

Sven huffed before he spoke. 'He is your husband. I suppose I'll have to tolerate him while he remains so.' He paused, looking out at the water sparkling in the moonlight. 'Do you think Kjarr won't take what happened as a slight to his honour?'

Many men would. 'Nothing happened between you and me, not really.'

'If you say so.' He tossed a small stone into the river. We heard the *plunk* as it broke the surface and sank to the riverbed. 'What if he wants to divorce you over it?'

'He wouldn't,' I replied, and for a moment, I wondered what my reaction would be if Kjarr had done the same.

'How well do you know him?' Sven asked, breaking my thoughts.

Years before, when I married Kjarr, I would have said I knew him well. I could trust him and there was some kindred adventuring spirit between us. Since then, we had been apart longer than in each other's company.

'It's your choice, Astrid.' My name was barely a whisper.

No one in our crew knew my real name, and the further I went from Aldeigjuborg, the more distance I needed to put between myself and my identity as Signe. Astrid so desperately wanted to resume her place in the world.

'Why does it have to be my choice?' I whined. *The Norns had a lot to answer for.*

Sven chuckled to himself. 'You won't have a decision to make if Kjarr divorces you,' he goaded.

I threw my petalless stem at him.

'It's not up to you. The Norns have already decided. So, smile and go along for the ride.'

'Is that your answer for everything?' I asked, turning again to look at him.

He spread his broad hand on the ground and leaned into me. 'Want me to decide for you?'

Our noses were almost touching. My breath caught in my throat as I searched for the words. 'What should I do?'

We stared at each other for what felt like an eternity before Sven spoke. 'Don't go back to him. Bypass Kyiv, we'll go overland if we must. Let's travel to Miklagard, together.' He had that dark look in his eyes that made me shift under his gaze.

But I was stronger now. The world I lived in was not full of fantasy. Conflict had taught me to question motives. Loss had cautioned me against hasty actions. So, I waited until his intensity faded before I countered his move.

'In doing so, Sihtric abandons us without means of getting to our destination. It'll just be you and me, basking in the golden daytime sun, and at night we will make love under the stars. We'll live like forest spirits until babies come, and what then, Sven? Will we make stews from mud and river stones to fill us? Will we construct our hut from twigs and dried muck? You'll hunt wild boar for dinner, and one day the beast will bury its sharp tusk in your belly and I'll be alone with two screaming babes. What will we have then, other than our dream that was left unfulfilled?'

He didn't recoil when I killed his hope; he surprised me by smiling. 'You have thought about it.'

Sven was frustratingly consistent. 'Of course, I have,' I confessed.

'But I have nothing and Kjarr can give you a better life,' Sven whispered. He reached for my fingers.

'It's not like that.'

'But does he dream about you, Astrid? Did he care for you when you were dying? He sent one message. One! It was to order you to his side. What kind of man is that?'

'Honestly, I do not understand what it is he is facing,' I tried to explain, leaving my hand clasped between his palms.

'Maybe the gods show me a fate that isn't mine,' he muttered, releasing my hand and looking towards the opposite bank.

I sat back, letting a breath loose. 'You still have those dreams?'

He looked at me sideways. 'The one where the Norns whisper your name to me? Where they tell me you are my fate, and I can be nothing without you?'

'Do they?' I asked, a flutter in my chest.

'No.' He glanced over at the water.

I wasn't sure how to react, so I said, 'Oh.'

'You almost sound disappointed. Of course, I do, *minn Svanr*. They never stop.' He took up another stone, and this time threw it further. His jaw was clenched tight, and his mouth was a grim line.

'How can you dream such a thing each night and wake up to a world that is not the same?'

He grunted as he picked up a new rock. 'It's difficult, but I manage. Not well, as you can see, but I try.'

'And you believe someday things will change?' It was my turn to throw a stone, and it plopped into the shallows with a *clunk* as it hit the rocks there.

'Don't we all,' he agreed.

It felt like our words butted against each other all night, but it was the catharsis we needed. As the first streaks of colour stained the grey-black sky, still we sat. Sven, who had resumed his whittling of his enigmatic prow-beast, and I with my walrus tusk comb, raking it through my unbound hair over and over, though my hair was free of tangles. It kept both our hands busy.

'You're fantastic at that.' I pointed to the carving taking shape within his calloused palms.

'Thorsten has been teaching me how to etch faces.' He held it close so I might see the detail he was achieving. 'Wood differs from ivory, but the technique is similar.'

I ran my finger down the protruding tongue. 'What do you think Kyiv will be like?' I asked him. 'Will it be like Birka?' It was the biggest settlement either of us had been to, years before, when I had left Svealand for Aldeigjuborg. It was a great walled town, cradled by high defences, and ringed with the raging ocean.

He shrugged and said, 'We will find out soon enough.'

'Gunnar said the town spreads from the harbour right into the shadows of the great rocks that tower over it and that the land is clefted by great ravines that soar above the river.' There wasn't much I liked about Gunnar, but he had a way of capturing the essence of a place.

'We might not see much of one another. You'll be in your place, and I'll be in mine with Eskil and the other men,' Sven grumbled.

'I'll have to enjoy the freedom while I have it.' I lay back on the grass and tied my comb back onto my belt. 'Sven. I just wanted to say that I'm glad it wasn't your fault all those years ago.'

'Hmm,' he mumbled.

'But it's too late now,' I added, my eyes growing heavy.

'I know,' he replied. 'It's all right.'

But we both knew it wasn't. All those years ago, we promised ourselves to one another, but happiness had been stolen. For better or worse, the damage had been done and there was no going back.

'Your scar is looking better,' he said, lifting the cloth from my temple, and gently cleaning it in the river water.

'Do you think so? I was hoping by the time we got to Kyiv it would be gone.'

'I don't think that's likely. You'll most certainly have a scar until you die.' He dabbed the cloth on my face. Sadness marked his features above me.

'Until I die?' I laughed at the thought, pressing the damp cloth against my scar.

'You know what I mean,' he replied as he finished his work and lay down next to me. We stared into the morning light, still half-hidden by dark clouds. 'Have you had any more of those dreams about your father?' he asked.

'Nothing so nice. It's mostly been my mother and those awful nightmares.'

'Want to talk about it?' he asked, brushing my arm with an extended finger.

'Not really.' My eyes were tired and my head hurt, but sleep would still be some time away and I wasn't keen on talking over troubled dreams. 'When we get to Kyiv, what will you do?'

'Aside from keeping you out of trouble, and annoying your husband with my presence?' At least he sounded amused.

'I hope you don't.'

'You know I will. I won't make it easy.' He nudged me with his knee.

'Perhaps you should find someone when you're there,' I suggested, though the thought gripped my chest uncomfortably.

His voice was strained as he replied, 'You wouldn't mind?'

'Mind? You are free, Sven.'

He changed the subject, 'Sihtric suggested I should carve him a new prow-beast for the *Bhobain*, and I think I might.'

'That's why you've been practising on this little thing.' I grasped the small carving, examining its wide-open eyes. 'The carvings you did during winter were great, but you've attempted nothing that big.'

'Wielding a chisel is going to differ from whittling this small thing, that's for sure,' he agreed.

'If you fail and make something truly horrendous, it'll still scare the crap out of everyone, and that's half the job.'

He snorted. 'If I fail, Sihtric has threatened to throw me overboard.'

'I wouldn't let him,' I said sleepily as I reached for his hand lying on the grassy rise. 'Sven, I'm so glad you found me.' I turned to face him, and he did the same.

'You told me that,' Sven replied, his mouth curving at the edges.

'I hadn't realised I needed you so much.'

His eyes widened. 'You needed me?'

'You were right when you said the Norns had woven our fate together, but the god who whispers in your dreams is almost certainly Loki.' A blink went a moment too long, and I felt like I was falling. I desperately wanted to sleep, but I forced my eyes open again. 'Our destiny may be entwined but…' I rambled, trying to explain.

'What?' He looked at me, eyes heavy with tiredness. 'What are you trying to say?'

'You were right, Sven. We are meant to be together.' I squeezed his hand and let go. *Together in the same place. By each other's side. Just not in the way you wanted.* I was too tired to continue talking.

His eyes were closed, and his breathing deepened. Mere moments away from the bliss of slumber. His mouth curved into a contented smile. 'Say it again.'

# Four

Soft ground cradled my weary body, threatening to swallow me whole. My heavy limbs ached from the day's work. No reprieve would come with the morning. Tomorrow's passage would be even more arduous. I couldn't think of that yet. Not now. Sihtric had told us many men had dragged a ship across land and we would follow in their footsteps. I didn't want to follow anyone. All I wanted was to remain prone, forget the world, and let sleep engulf me in her yawning mouth.

That morning, we had arrived at the basin of the Lovat, and came ashore to make preparations for the next part of our journey. The *Bhobain* was to rise from the Lovat, follow a path carved through the expansive forest, and descend into another waterway that would eventually lead us to the Western Dnieper route. Björn, Frodi, and Sihtric knew what to do. Ahmed Ibn Rashti had seen it before. Even Gunnar believed it was possible. The rest of us stood bewildered, looking between the dense covering of pine trees and the *Bhobain*, peacefully floating in her natural place.

'Who do you think was the first man to think of dragging a ship overland?' I asked Sven, as Sihtric explained what needed to be done.

'Someone mad,' Sven replied.

'It's nae madness, Sven. It's a dream brought to life,' Sihtric responded wistfully, his profile shadowed in the afternoon light.

'A mad dream,' I came back with a laugh.

Sihtric tutted me. 'A boatless man goes nowhere, *bhana charaid*.'

It was true. A man without means of travelling could not expect the scenery to change. Here we were, about to do what many without a vessel would consider a far-fetched imagining, if not absolutely impossible.

'Back home,' Frodi interjected, 'we carry our ships all the time.'

Björn nodded in agreement. 'But, it's short distances there. Just between one river and the next, eh?'

'You can usually see both rivers,' Frodi added, twiddling a lock of his grey-speckled dark hair between his forefinger and thumb.

'It may seem impossible, but dinnae fret,' Sihtric assured us. 'All we need is a few good straight logs and, as you can see, we've nae shortage of that.' He waved his hand at the towering birches.

At his direction, Eskil, and Sven set about felling the trees we required. I offered Skara for the task, and Sven used her to hack at the trunk with a glorious *whack*. Each chop was as rhythmic as a beating drum until he and Eskil had created a sizable wedge in the tree's base. With pouring sweat and plenty of grunting, the men made their back-cut. The trunk creaked and splintered, and with a deafening crack, the birch trembled.

'Out of the bloody way,' Eskil bellowed, and we ran to higher ground.

The forest shuddered as the tree met the ground, and the process began again. Eskil and Sven felled the rest we had marked, and we stripped the trunks, chipping them until smooth. Axe and *knifr* ran back and forth over uneven logs. Wood chips flew, and bark curled until it covered the forest-floor and our arms burned and backs ached. Still, the daylight held. Sol smirked as she watched us toil, goading us to do more. The sweat that beaded on my brow stung my wound until it was hot and raw. We worked hard until Sol's brother, Mani, chased her from the sky. Then it was time to rest.

Or at least I thought it was, until Sihtric started issuing more instructions, 'Bring the two longest logs to the waterfront.' He wiped the perspiration dripping from his chin, a girthy flax rope coiled over his shoulder.

While Eskil and Sven had dealt with the trees, Frodi, Sihtric, Thorsten, and Björn had spent the morning taking down the mast of the *Bhobain* and stowing her sail. Now, I watched as Sihtric and Thorsten tied the thick line to a plank behind the prow, leaving a length on each side that flopped over the gunwale and fell to the ground. All four men removed their shirts, exposing sweat-slicked muscles.

'Anyone volunteering to pull?' Thorsten shouted, as he brushed back his sodden hair.

Sven groaned. Eskil belched.

Sihtric laughed at the men's eagerness. 'If you're nae pulling, you'll be pushing,' he warned before straightening his trousers.

It seemed no one was getting out of the heavy lifting. No one volunteered for the task.

Sihtric heaved a great sigh of annoyance. 'Gunnar and Eskil.' He pointed at the two he named. 'You're on ropes,' he commanded.

Gunnar glowered indignantly at his captain. 'Me? Why me?'

'Why?' Sihtric began, taking a few steps towards the sandy-haired merchant. 'Because you're a handsome and well-built lad! We need our strongest men at the fore.' He grasped Gunnar by the shoulders and shook him roughly.

Gunnar bristled against his handling but didn't decline, especially as Sihtric had challenged his manliness. And, though Eskil had not been forthcoming, there was no complaint from him either. That left Sven, Egbert, and me to roll two logs down to the river, while Gunnar and Eskil took up the ropes.

Frodi crouched by my side, as he did when he sat at the steering oar. 'Now, we need to get them under the hull,' Frodi said, gesturing to the underside of the ship.

'The hull?' Sven asked, tone full of disbelief.

'Gotta shimmy them under the ship, get 'em straight, then we'll haul on this rope and drag the *Bhobain* out of the water and onto land,' Frodi explained, gesticulating wildly.

It was easier than I had imagined. After positioning the birch poles on land, and digging them in so they wouldn't roll away, we pushed on one side of the hull until it lifted off the ground. Then we pushed the log beneath it and repeated the process on the other side and we had made a makeshift ramp. The hull of the *Bhobain* would slide on the two rails until it was completely free of the river.

'The spruce poles,' Björn yelled as he grabbed a well-crafted rod, perfectly shaped to fit through the round openings in the ship's strakes. He slotted one into the oar hole from the outside, and passed it through until it met the opposite one, skewering the *Bhobain* like a roast piglet at a Jol feast. He repeated the same on the next two sets of oar holes behind the first, the spruce poles running in the same direction as the rowing benches. It was ingenious. Piercing the *Bhobain* with the rods made it easier to carry and push. The configuration bore a resemblance to a stretcher used to carry an injured warrior from the battlefield, and I wondered if that was where the idea had come from.

'Right!' Sihtric began, calling us to attention. 'Signe, and Frodi on the first set,' he pointed to the poles sticking out of the oarlocks. 'Odrun and Toki on the second. Sven and me on the aft in the water. Eskil! You've got a good grip on that rope?' he asked.

The big man nodded, face red and chin on his chest, ready to go.

'Is everyone ready?' Sihtric called out.

Björn and Thorsten angled additional rods, smaller and more flexible, under the hull to help pry her from the river that sucked to her underbelly like calflings at their mother's udders.

'Keep her straight!' Sihtric yelled from his vantage. 'Heave,' he encouraged us, 'haul!' He sang the words over and over while we dragged and drove the *Bhobain* onto the sandy soil. A triumphant cry rang out. The jubilation of success withered with exhaustion as we manoeuvred her along the ground. It was slow going. Each foot the *Bhobain* shifted was hard-won at first, but once she was moving, the momentum was easier to maintain. Thankfully, there was not far to go on that first night. Once we were out of the water, somewhat through the clearing, we stopped to make camp for the night as the sun disappeared from the sky. Finally, the moon god, Mani, shone his silver light into the sheet of darkness. We threw handfuls of bark stripped from the birch trees onto the fire. The flames caught fast, greedily consuming the curls of wood as the shards popped in the heat.

'You said two days to drag this ship to the next waterway?' Gunnar asked Sihtric unenthusiastically.

'That's how long it usually takes, eh?' agreed Björn.

Sihtric nodded as he chewed on a lump of dried meat. 'Aye, it's two long days. We've done the hardest part, but it'll nae be easy to drag her across the sandy soil.'

'Back hurts just thinking about it.' Björn raised his bushy eyebrows. 'Would be easier with a tiny rowing boat.' He held his hands out to the fire's warmth, each finger gnarled at the knuckles.

'An *ushkui*?' Gunnar suggested, tugging his tunic off. The heat of the day had dissipated, the night bringing with it cool air.

Sihtric shook his head and spat out a piece of gristle. 'Might be a touch lighter, but they cannae carry much cargo, and only a few men. And who's going to transport the thing?' he asked.

Gunnar would not be dissuaded. 'They're not as heavy, so it would be easier.'

'If they have fewer people, fewer will bear the weight,' Sihtric repeated.

Gunnar slapped his thigh in frustration. 'But it's lighter.'

'Fewer men, lighter ships. It's the same.' Sihtric clipped the words as he spoke. 'Is it really any easier? Do you ken my meaning?' He stared at Gunnar disbelievingly.

Gunnar stayed silent, petulantly puckering his mouth and crossing his arms over his chest.

Björn chuckled at the discomfort. 'S'pose not,' he answered for the merchant. He rubbed his calloused hand along the leathery skin of his face. 'Once we get the *Bhobain* rolling along the logs, it'll be easier to keep her moving,' he offered.

'Aye,' Sihtric pitched in, 'it's nae so difficult.' He threw Björn a grateful look.

'Most troublesome part is getting her started,' Frodi added. 'But that's for tomorrow.' He lay down, wrapped his cloak around him, and was snoring the next moment. Nothing got between Frodi and his love of slumber. The small, dark-eyed man from the north could sleep anywhere, but he hated being cold.

Gunnar had put Sihtric in a bad mood and he knew it. He wasn't part of our crew for any other reason than he needed to get to Kyiv, and if Sihtric grew tired of his irascibility, he might just hand him back his payment and leave him at the next settlement. The merchant narrowed his gaze but kept his mouth shut while Sihtric excused himself and set up his bedroll next to Kari's at the edge of the camp.

Björn and Thorsten, on tonight's guard duty, wandered off to make rounds of the area. Egbert and Odrun were tasked with stripping the birch bark into manageable strips and stacking them neatly into watertight containers, so we might use them later as fire starters. That left Ahmed and Sven for company, and Gunnar for continued belligerence.

'Ahmed,' I whispered to the trader across the fire. 'Will you tell us one of your stories so I don't have to listen to any more of Gunnar's drivel?'

'Pfft,' Gunnar protested, shrinking against a tree trunk. 'Still think it would be easier with a lighter ship.'

'Let it go, Gunnar,' Sven mumbled from his slumped position against a log, his cap pulled down to cover his eyes.

Gunnar left the campfire in a huff, dragging his feet along the ground, grumbling all the while about everyone's stupidity and his superior intellect.

Ahmed shook his head, but edged closer. 'All right, Signe. Which tale will it be? Do you want to hear about my home or my travels this time?'

I thought for a moment. 'Tell me about your home.'

'Again?' he asked with amusement, one dark eyebrow arched beneath the coil of cloth that covered his head.

The night birds hooted in the distance as I nestled myself against a rock. 'You might have left something out last time.'

Ahmed closed his book and lay it on the ground, never far from his side. 'You have an insatiable thirst for the unknown, Signe,' he replied.

Sven peeked out from under his cap. 'Even if you tell her the same story thirty times over, she'll want to hear it again.'

I shot him a reproachful glare and laughed through my nose.

'All right,' Ahmed agreed, tugging at the end of his shirt and straightening up. 'The Medina al-Salam,' he began.

'The City of Peace?' I confirmed the translation. My hand cupped the side of my face as I listened on in wonder, eyes closed to imagine the descriptions Ahmed gave.

'The City of Peace,' he agreed. 'It is the greatest city in the world.'

'But don't tell Gunnar that. He's bound to disagree,' Sven interjected.

I opened one eye and quietly giggled.

Ahmed continued, 'Shaped like the full moon. The River Tigris flows right by it, and from it, water flows via aqueducts to the houses and lush gardens within the city walls. Streets are kept clean and free of debris, and at night lamps that cast pinpricks of light onto the stone paths illuminate the entire city.'

I squeezed my eyes tighter. *Stone.* That part always amazed me. Not the board paths I had sometimes encountered, not packed earth, and certainly not the dirt sludge that came after the downpour of rain.

Ahmed went on, 'It is an important part of the world. With places of learning, for the care of the body, and at the very centre is the Golden Gate Palace and the Grand Mosque.'

His face always lit up when he explained the way the doorways arched, so I sat up and watched him as he recounted the paintings, colours, and decorations in excruciating detail. Only painful because I feared I would never see it for myself.

'Tell me about the Khizanat al-Hikma,' I pleaded, not for the first time.

He looked at me with the patient expression of a father entertaining the whims of a child. 'Do you never tire of it?' he asked.

'Never,' I replied, shaking my head. 'How can I ever imagine such a place? I've never seen a…' I searched for the right word.

'Library,' Sven offered.

Ahmed looked at my friend in amazement. 'Very good, Sven. Yes. Library. The Khizanat al-Hikma is a building of countless books, of study, and of learning.'

Sven pulled his cap back from his eyes, and I saw the smug grin that spread as he noticed the surprise on mine. 'I've heard the description as many times as you have.'

Ahmed ran his fingertips through his bushy beard. 'And do you find them just as fascinating?'

Sven threw a green twig onto the fire. It cracked and sizzled in the flames. 'How can such a place exist when we struggle to build fortifications from wood?' he wondered aloud.

'You don't believe the Medina al-Salam is real?' Ahmed questioned in his temperate manner.

My friend took a strip of bark from the pile and began teasing threads away. 'I'm not saying it doesn't exist,' he conceded. 'I just don't understand how. You say it was built in four years? From stone? And it has water that runs to houses, clean streets, and places filled with bound volumes?'

'Books,' Ahmed corrected. 'Yes. The difference is knowledge,' he began, waving his hand before the fire. 'For many years, our people have sought learning from all over the world and brought it to Medina al-Salam where we translate important texts from many other languages into one our scholars know well. We have men who teach, many who learn, and this flow of understanding allows us to build such a wonder.'

Sven threw his arms up. 'Now, you are here in the middle of nowhere with a group of Odin worshippers.'

Ahmed lowered his head and shuddered slightly. His lips moved in silent prayer.

'You've no comfort at all,' Sven continued.

'All of life is a lesson. No education should ever be wasted,' Ahmed replied in the customary style of his riddling.

But I was still lost in the pictures of my mind. 'I must see it.'

The trader lifted his notebook from the ground. 'You will, Signe. I believe you will.'

Sven slumped back against the log. 'One day they will call her an adventurer.'

Ahmed smiled. 'They will call you Signe the Far-Travelled,' he said, waving his book towards me.

'Ahmed?' Sven croaked, coughing on the smoke from the fire. 'Why do you need a building just for words?'

'Hmm, how do I explain this?' He gestured to the pages. 'These are not just scratchings of ink on parchment. It is wisdom. Everything I have learned on my travels. Things that might be useful to our understanding of the world. A library keeps all of that learning together and someone who can read these words can access what others have inscribed before them.'

Sven scratched his hair under his cap. 'Our folk pass stories down from father to son, mother to daughter, lawspeaker to lawspeaker, Jarl to Jarl, always spoken and remembered,' Sven explained.

Ahmed clicked his tongue and inhaled. 'Memory is fallible, Sven. People die before they impart everything that they have to give. In writing it down, you can build on what has come before you.'

Sven considered the notion. 'Then why don't we have libraries?' he wondered, directing the question at me.

'Can you read, Sven?' I asked, knowing the answer already.

He slumped his shoulders. 'No. Nor can I write.'

'Who do you know who can read and write?'

'Aside from you and Ahmed,' he began.

'Sihtric,' I added.

'No one,' Sven finished. He scrunched his nose as he thought.

'What value is a place of books and words, when our people can not understand what is written on their pages?' I looked at Ahmed for support.

'So, we can have all of this knowledge, as Ahmed calls it,' Sven answered.

Ahmed chuckled lightly. 'You cannot gain the answers simply from touching the pages or from glimpsing the sketches. You must be able to understand the markings. Only then can you read what has taken lifetimes to accumulate.'

'If it is written, it can never be lost,' I mumbled.

'Unless it's sacked and burned,' Sven added.

Ahmed folded his hands over his closed book. 'Spoken like a true heathen,' he replied with a hint of mockery. 'We seek peace by learning. The knowledge contained in the Khizanat al-Hikma is more than any man could read in all his years, yet it is one of our most precious possessions. One could say it is just as important as our places of worship. Perhaps more valuable than gold, gems, or spice, for knowledge is power,' he finished, and stifled a yawn.

'Power,' Sven repeated, turning the word over in his mouth as he did with the piece of bark in his hand.

'I must retire for the night. All this talk of home has made me tired,' Ahmed said, a finger rubbing his eyes.

There was another hoot in the distance. It was time for the night birds to hunt the small creatures that scuttled in the undergrowth. Time for us to retire to our bedrolls and rest before the back-breaking day ahead.

'Power,' Sven repeated next to me, as he threw the last shard of birch bark onto the fire and it hissed like Jormungand.

'Goodnight, Ahmed,' I farewelled. 'May your dreams be filled with visions of your beautiful city.'

'And of my little daughters, who, no doubt, will be much grown upon my return. Whenever that might be,' he concluded, his tone and mouth somewhat downturned.

'Next time, I would like to hear of your daughters, Ahmed, if you want to speak about them. Perhaps I could write a message to them as part of my lessons?' I suggested, looking up at the trader.

'As you like, Signe. Woman who will travel to the ends of the earth.'

# FIVE

The next day began and ended with the same laborious task - dragging the *Bhobain* through the pine and birch forest, over a sandy soil that crunched underneath the well-greased logs, slicked with fat from barrels we had brought along for this exact purpose. The ship creaked and rattled as she slid oak over pine, her prow naked, for we did not want to scare the spirits of the land. Ropes blistered flesh, causing tomorrow's callouses. We were all splattered head to toe with dirt, sand, and whatever else the forest deigned to spit at us, as globs of earth catapulted from under the ship's hull. Each of us stank, some worse than the others. Sweat, dirt, and grease. A delightfully rank combination.

'Ergh!' Thorsten grunted as he was pelted with a thick wad of mud. 'That one got me in the eye!' He wiped it away with his forearm. His usually immaculately groomed red-gold hair was now tinted dark from filth.

'Keep going,' Sihtric bellowed out in front.

Frodi was at the rear. Egbert, Odrun, Gunnar, Thorsten, Kari, and Sven were at the rods that penetrated the oar holes. Ahmed and I walked alongside the ship, with the unenviable job of bringing the logs around from the rear to the front to keep the ship gliding on oiled rollers, as well as keeping watch. Ambush was an ever-present threat in foreign territory. So far, we had encountered no one. The next basin was infamously difficult to pass without some sort of confrontation, or so Gunnar advised. Sihtric, however, assured us he knew someone, as he often did, and no one would disturb us. I thanked the gods for Sihtric and his impressive connections. For the time being, we were very distracted by pushing and pulling the great mass of wooden strakes along a terrain it was never meant to sail upon.

'Heave!' Sihtric called through gritted teeth. 'Heave!' He lumbered along with the rope over his shoulder.

Faces glowed red with exertion as the *Bhobain* creaked and inched forward. As Björn had said the night before, the hardest part was getting the ship moving. Once she was, it was a simple forward motion that kept the momentum. Our group followed a trail cleared through the woodlands by those who came before. To carve our own path would have taken time we didn't have and expended precious energy.

As the sun passed through the sky, we took our turns at rods, ropes, or rollers. No task was preferable to the others. It was all exhausting work that needed to be done. By midday, we stopped to rest. Bodies covered in sweat. Skin prickling under thick fabric, irritated by the hot rays of sunlight that shot through the forest. Most of the men, except Ahmed and Egbert, removed their shirts and continued working in their trousers, bare chests glistening with perspiration. I was down to my *serkr*, past caring if the scant clothing was immodest.

My stomach grumbled loudly. 'I can't decide if I want to sleep or eat,' I mumbled as I flopped onto the ground next to Sven.

He handed me a waterskin. I drained it before handing it back. Sven refilled it from the barrel aboard the *Bhobain*. 'Who's on sentry tonight?' he asked, hanging off the side of the ship.

'Not me,' I responded swiftly, 'but if it is, I'm calling in my debt with Sihtric.' My mouth salivated as Sven passed me a strip of smoked meat. 'Did Gunnar or Eskil feed their thralls?'

'Not that I saw,' Sven answered. 'They'll need it.' He massaged his calf as he chewed away on something.

'Where are they?'

Sven shrugged and stretched his leg.

I grabbed a few scraps of meat and wandered towards the fringes of the forest to search for Egbert and Odrun. They took any chance they had to fade into the forest. No one thought it strange so long as they returned with whatever they were sent off to gather. But the crew had not seen what I had that day I found them on the island. Hands steepled under chins, kneeling to their Lord in prayer. I'd told no one, just as I promised. Mostly because I had given my word, but also because I had no idea what any of it meant. *The gods play tricks, and* perhaps they sought to entertain themselves with fickle humans in wretched circumstances. I wouldn't put it past them.

Odrun and Egbert had not gone far. *Who had the energy to waste?* When I found them, they were seated next to one another on a tree fallen sideways, speaking in low voices. Egbert held a stick, drawing symbols on the dusty soil.

'I come with food,' I announced, startling them. Odrun glanced up wide-eyed, and Egbert hastily disposed of his stick by throwing it sideways.

It was Egbert who took my offering first, holding out his hand and muttering, 'Thank you.' His eyes travelled to the ground as he dragged his foot through the etchings there, covering the lines of disturbed earth.

'What were you doing?' I asked, trying to sound innocent.

Odrun pressed her hands into her lap. She had accepted nothing to eat. 'Resting,' she answered. Her hair was damp, and her skin was pink from the heat of the day, but still, she wore her wadmal cape. She never took it off.

I edged forward, placing a few strands of dried beef on Odrun's knee. 'Can I join you?'

Neither protested. A gnarled root served well as a stool to sit upon as I waited for one of them to speak.

Odrun surprised me by being the first, 'Why haven't you told anyone what you saw on the island?' she asked, amber eyes narrowed with distrust, and underlined by dark circles.

'Who you pray to is your business,' I responded with a shrug. I crossed my ankles and reclined against a tree trunk.

She shifted on the log. 'It would be Gunnar's business too if he found out,' she said in a tight voice. 'I'm not allowed to be anything other than what Gunnar wants me to be.'

I uncrossed my heels and leaned forward. 'If you haven't noticed,' I began, meeting her eye, 'I'm not in the habit of placating Gunnar, nor do I care to make your life more difficult.'

Odrun took a nibble of her food. Egbert sat next to her.

Sitting back again, I said, 'I don't keep slaves, Odrun.'

She chuckled softly, something I'd never seen her do before. 'Have you ever been gifted one?'

I knew what she was implying. She thought I was not wealthy enough to buy a thrall, but she was wrong. If I wanted to, I could easily afford it, and after my reunion with Kjarr, I would have sufficient funds to purchase even the most expensive bodies from the most exotic of places. A notion that repulsed me fully.

But I wanted to be honest with her, 'I have.'

She tilted her pretty head and assessed me with her sharp eyes. 'What did you do about that?'

'Her name was Isla. A gift from my first husband and I tried to make her life there as good as possible. Owning a person is not something that sits well with me. Unfortunately, it was not in my power to free her,' I explained.

Odrun swiped her nose with an elegant finger. 'Because you are a woman,' she added. For the first time, there was a kernel of understanding that passed between us.

I nodded. 'I am ashamed to say, I do not know what became of her after my husband's death as I left with nothing more than I could carry.'

Odrun dropped the piece of meat into her lap. 'You say I can trust you,' she began, lips pursed and mangling the words with foreign inflection.

Egbert sat silently, watching his fellow thrall.

I unleashed a deep exhale. 'I won't plead with you to tell me more, Odrun. People who shout their virtues the loudest rarely possess them at all, I find.'

Egbert nodded enthusiastically, his first contribution to the discussion.

I twisted my mouth before continuing, 'You would think ill of me otherwise.'

Her eyes narrowed again. 'You care what I think of you?' she asked, genuine shock in her voice.

My shoulders shook with a silent chuckle. 'Not really.'

Her face blanched.

'Don't take it personally. I try not to care what anyone thinks. If I did, I wouldn't do half of the things I've done in my life.'

She sat back a little and resumed chewing. Egbert glanced at Odrun, who shook her head at his unasked question.

'Water?' I asked, handing them Sven's refilled skin. 'You'll need it to keep going. Egbert,' I looked at the wiry man, 'whatever you do, don't let them know you can write.'

His eyes widened. 'Huh? How do you…'

Odrun handed back the pouch of liquid, half-empty. 'Believe it or not, but I can make markings too. Though, perhaps they're not as good as yours,' I explained as he looked at me with mild shock. There was a stick lying by my foot and I picked it up, carving runes into the dirt. 'See.'

Impressed or not, they said nothing more. I left them to their writing, their planning, and, no doubt, to the trouble they were making for themselves. If they chanced an escape, it wouldn't surprise me, not nearly as much as if they made it. *We cannot control the fate of others*, I told myself; *the Norns had that in hand.* It was Gunnar and Eskil's problem if they were too stupid to see their thralls were plotting behind their backs, and not my place to enlighten them.

'Everything all right?' Sven asked as I flung myself on the grass beside him once I had reached the clearing again. He offered me a fistful of hazelnuts purchased by Sihtric in Gorodok. 'Forest sprites causing chaos?'

'Something like that,' I agreed noncommittally, crunching on the cob.

Thorsten played his flute merrily while the others chatted and ate.

He watched me, waiting for further explanation as he flicked a nut into his mouth. 'Any chance these *landvettr* will help us drag this lump through the forest?'

I offered him a wry smile. He wasn't as clueless as he sometimes pretended to be. 'Hmm, I'd say they're about as willing as the rest of us.'

'Come on, you weaklings,' Eskil goaded as he dragged himself to his feet.

Rest time was over.

Sven pulled me to stand. 'You're on logs again.'

I threw my head back and groaned. 'Not the logs!'

'Better than the poles,' he offered.

I looked at him with a long face. 'Nothing is worse than the logs.'

Sihtric turned his face to the sky. 'Looks like rain,' he predicted. Glimpses of the sky visible through the canopy of trees were not enough for me to see clouds.

'What do we do if it comes?' I asked.

Sihtric glanced at me and smiled. 'We keep going, *bhana charaid*, and hope we make it out the other side before the ground turns to mush.'

Now, I contemplated something worse than being on the logs; being on the logs in the mud.

The rest of the day was a blur of shifting gigantic logs from the *Bhobain's* stern to bow, heaving at tight ropes until my hands cracked and bled, and marching alongside the vessel as my head lolled and one eye shut.

When evening blessedly arrived and sleep was near, I couldn't hold it off. Even if the world had burst into flames and the frost giants came to do battle, calling the *einherjar* to Ragnarok, I would have been deaf to the horn's call. Nott came and dragged me violently into the depths of her realm, where visions of the future raged. Whether real or imagined, I could not quite tell. Dreams full of danger. Shadows chasing me through unfamiliar places. One wrong turn led to unknown paths until I lost myself entirely.

When I woke with the rising of the morning sun, I knew this foreboding was the gods' way of cautioning me against losing sight of the destiny woven for me. Sven and I might have made our peace, but there was an entire labyrinth to hazard with Kjarr, and whatever came along with that.

Sihtric passed out the meagre offerings for breakfast. We were all holding out for something fresh and warm once we got to Gnezdovo. 'Today,' he began, 'we dinnae have far to go, but it's easier going than yesterday so long as the rain continues to hold off.'

'I don't like the "but",' Gunnar grumbled.

Eskil sniggered.

The rest of the group groaned. Eskil loved his bodily humour.

'We go up before we go down,' Sihtric continued. 'Then, the *Bhobain* will be on the water and we'll be on our way to the Dnieper.'

'Via a coupl'a more portages,' Björn put in.

Sihtric silenced the man with his hand. 'Let's get through this day.'

Björn nodded, but there was glee in the smirk he offered to our suffering. 'Eat well. You'll need your strength.'

There was nothing else for it. If we wanted to reach the next waterway before nightfall, all the grunting and complaining wouldn't get us there any faster. All we could control was how we approached the task; with a grin or a grimace. *The gods would be more entertained if I sang my way through it*, I thought, and I struck up a tune to amuse the Aesir. Gunnar met the day with a toad-like scowl. Odrun with a sneer. Eskil with a howl of laughter, and Frodi…Well, Frodi hadn't woken up yet.

Björn hollered, 'Frodi! Wake up, or we'll be leaving you here!'

His small friend staggered to his feet, wrestling between wakefulness, and dreaming. 'I'm awake,' he claimed, eyes clamped shut. Somehow, he found his place and was ready to go before Thorsten had finished packing his bedroll.

Gunnar sauntered forward, taking up the pole at the front-left side. 'Get to work!' he yelled.

I started my song again, 'On the oars we pull to lands unknown. Call to Ran, the way to be shown.'

No one joined in.

Sihtric offered me a sympathetic smile before turning to the other. 'Cheer up, lads. We're over halfway!'

# Six

By early afternoon, the heat of the day waned, and a cool breeze whispered through the trees. A small falcon issued her shrill call from the treetops and I wondered if it was a sign of rain, or if she simply anticipated dusk when she might hunt the tiny insects that zipped about.

Mercifully, Sihtric hadn't been lying when he said we were over halfway. By the time we reached the edge of the forest, his predictions of rain hadn't eventuated but, now I could see a moody sky filled with dark clouds.

The land's inclination had been gradual. It was hard work pushing the *Bhobain* uphill, but at least it wasn't a sudden and steep rise before the final descent. Our overland journey was almost complete and the sight from the top was sweet; a glittering expanse of water sparkling in the dwindling sunlight below us.

Thorsten stood on the crest, smiling down at the sight. 'So close,' he said, his fair skin freckled with mud.

It was *so close*, but the way down presented its own challenges. The ship might pass the hill easily, with its weight being the driving force. Controlling that momentum, and keeping the vessel straight, was Sihtric's most pressing concern. To slow the *Bhobain*, we would need to use our strength, and that, I found, was more difficult than dragging the *bloody thing*, as Eskil had taken to calling the ship.

We dug in rolling logs as a guide, pointing toward the water, to help the *Bhobain* down the slope. I hoped the soil would stay parched, as that would slow our progress.

In four words, Sihtric dashed that hope. 'The rain is coming,' he shouted, holding a hand out to feel for droplets. 'The *Bhobain's* got to get in the water, now!'

Thunder cracked overhead, and, from the dark tufts, the gods rained down their tears. It didn't take long to realise why Sihtric had been worried all this time. The ground, dry as it had been, was thirsty for the downpour. Impossible to drink it all, puddles formed, causing boggy ground that slurped at our bare feet.

'Once we're on that water, it's nae problem at all,' Sihtric tried to offer comfort. 'In fact, a *braw* drenching will help us on our way, though it increases the danger to us now.'

Eskil bellowed, 'This hill is as slick as a whore's….'

'Don't finish that!' I interjected, as he shot me a disappointed frown.

Ropes strained as we began.

'Keep her steady,' Sihtric encouraged, wrapping the rope around his fist.

A great glob of sludgy earth splattered onto one of the rolling logs. The *Bhobain* passed down the rungs and, when it got to the slick roller, jolted horribly.

Thorsten ran around the side, looking at the under-belly of the ship. 'It's slipping,' he cried.

Now the rain was pelting down. Thor's anger struck the sky. Bolts of light cracked through the darkening spectre. We were already soaked through. The ground was a bog. No doubt the bilge of the *Bhobain* was filling with water and would soon make her heavier.

Sihtric looked frantic. 'We need her to slow!' he yelled.

Sven and I did the only thing we thought might help. We grasped the spruce poles still protruding from the ship's oar holes, hoping to pull it back into line.

'No!' Gunnar screamed.

But it was too late. Seeing what we meant to do, Ahmed and Egbert had taken up the poles behind us. It might have worked had the spruce poles not splintered as the *Bhobain* shuddered, weight bearing against the thin rails of wood. Egbert and Ahmed's pole snapped in half, the ship listed right, and slipped off the birch rollers right into the slick mud.

Sihtric cursed. I knew we were in trouble then.

Frodi sprang forward, slipping in the knee-deep mire. 'Ropes,' he commanded.

Whoever was near enough to grab one did. Despite being covered in mud, we pulled on slick ropes with our chafed hands.

There was a scream from the other side of the *Bhobain*. A deep, fearful bellow that was silenced far too quickly for my liking. The rain pelted down, a deafening deluge as we brought the ship under control. The ropes strained against the vessel, forcing her back onto the rollers and away from the uncontrolled descent.

I doubled over, trying to catch my breath, hair plastered to my face and clothes clinging to my body. 'Who screamed?' I called out.

We counted heads. Eskil was there, holding the ship steady with the flax rope. Gunnar was there, too. Egbert was looking sorry for himself but unharmed, Odrun as well. Björn, Frodi, Sihtric, and Kari, I could see. I stood on my toes. There was Ahmed. 'Where is Sven?' I asked, and felt the panic rising. 'SVEN?' My heart hammered. I couldn't breathe. I slipped through the muck, fear riving my body. 'Sven!'

There was a muffled response as I rounded the aft. My feet slid from beneath me and my backside hit the ground. Sven was beside the keel. 'He's here. I found him,' I cried, a flood of relief calming my earlier distress. 'Are you hurt?' My hands ran over his face, smearing him with dirt that was quickly streaked clean with the falling rain.

He pulled my hands away, unable to hear me above the downpour. I shook him. Sven squinted at me. 'It's Thorsten. He's under the *Bhobain*,' he screamed, all the while digging with his hands. Only the bone craftsman's head and torso were visible.

As fast as I could, I ran to the others and bid them to follow me.

'Eskil, hold the best you can,' Sihtric began. 'Gunnar and Signe, grab Thorsten and pull him when I say so.' He turned to Egbert. 'Secure that rope to the fattest trunk you can find. Tight, you hear?'

Egbert nodded, nostrils flared. He skidded and slipped, lumbering with the thick rope. We had to trust he would tie it off well. We didn't have time to waste.

'The rest of you,' Sihtric continued, screaming into the rain, 'push against the hull. Just as we did when we got her out of the water. Ready? On my count. Three, two, one.'

I pulled on Thorsten's arms as hard as I was able. He groaned, eyes closed, but didn't move.

'Again,' Sihtric commanded.

The men leaned into the strakes, pushing with all their might. It moved enough for Gunnar and me to free Thorsten, and he emerged with a squelching slurp. Mud caked his clothing. Unable to see if his limbs were damaged, I fumbled with his string belt to remove his trousers as Sihtric pulled the man away from the ship.

A hand stilled mine. 'We don't know each other that well, Signe,' Thorsten mumbled with a chuckle.

'You're alive,' Sihtric marvelled. 'You had me worried that I'd never hear a fine tune again, Thorsten.'

'Lucky bastard,' Eskil shouldered the craftsman. 'Bet you'll want out of the rest of the work today.'

Thorsten tried to walk. 'I'm a bit sore. The ground almost swallowed me whole, Eskil! I don't think there is any lasting damage. When I tell this story, I expect you all to say I single-handedly saved this ship from sliding to its destruction.'

Eskil laughed.

'I should write a song about it,' Thorsten added. The rain was easing up now. 'But I couldn't sing and play the flute at the same time.'

'If anyone could, it would be you,' Eskil joked.

Thorsten grasped my arm as he lumbered past. 'The gods must love you,' I said with a relieved smile.

Frodi untied the rope Egbert had fastened just moments before, ready to finish the job. 'After today, we'll need to give the gods something special.'

Sihtric looked to the sky. No rain fell now. 'There's a place I ken where they dwell. We can make our offerings there.'

Before the sun set, we lowered the *Bhobain* into the basin that would lead us to the Western Dnieper. There were more portages to come, shorter overland sections. I refused to think about that. Not yet, not now. By the time the ship was floating again, spruce poles removed and replaced by oars, mast erected, and sail unfurled, we were all aching and exhausted. Just like Aldeigjuborg, the settlements here also were influenced by the north. Their inhabitants were a mix of those who came as settlers and those who were born in  the land. Over time, each group, isolated though they might be, had developed a different way of speaking and of doing things. Each wanted their cut from the traders who passed through their territory.

Sihtric pointed to the western bank and told us he would visit a small settlement there. 'Failure to do so,' he said, 'would result in their oarsmen harrying us, and probably robbing our crew. Best to pay the levy.' As always, Sihtric knew someone there, and assured us it wouldn't be a problem so long as he went by morning.

That night we slept aboard the *Bhobain*. It was the first time I did not find the rowing benches hard under my back. I was unbothered by the light rain that fell, and did not even wake to fill my belly that growled with vicious hunger. All I cared about and all I did was sleep.

For once, my body hurt more than my face or my heart did.

# SEVEN

'Sven,' I whispered into the night. My strangled voice was high as it wrung from my throat.

It was the same dream that night as it had been so many nights since my injury at the Abandoned Paragon; my mother striking me furiously with her hazel switch, until I fell and struck my head. I always woke up at the same point; when I fell to the ground, blood seeping from my brow, *his* name spoken from my lips, 'Sven.'

A hand reached across the darkness and covered my mouth with its rough skin. 'Shh,' Sven urged.

Somewhere between dreaming and reality, I mumbled against his palm. His grip became firmer as he muffled my voice.

'If you go on like that, they'll think something is going on,' Sven warned, nodding his head towards our sleeping comrades.

The camp was still. No one else had awoken, but there was an unsettling sense that I had woken up for a reason. 'Sven, be quiet,' I hushed him, pushing his hand away. 'Did you hear something?'

He shifted closer. 'Aside from you moaning my name in your sleep?' he asked groggily. 'Nothing.'

We lay as still as possible, straining ears for the cracking of a twig, rustle of a leaf, or a whisper from the tree-line. Nothing came.

Sven shifted in his bedding, rolling onto his side before he questioned me. 'Bad dreams again?'

'Mmm,' I agreed, rubbing sleep from my eyes.

'That skull bash must have been hard to bring it all back,' he said, 'the bad and the good,' he continued, his voice lighter as he tried to lift me from my dwindling nightmare.

'There is nothing good in those dreams,' I replied curtly and stretched languidly under my furs.

He breathed, disappointed, 'Hmmpf,' and whispered teasingly, 'and here I was thinking you called my name after a pleasant dream.'

'Sven,' I stopped him. 'The day my mother said you'd left, she beat me until I agreed to marry Auden,' I began.

Most of the time, I woke myself up before anyone was the wiser, but this time, I had the distinct feeling of being overheard.

Where we camped on the western bank of the River Dyna was too dangerous to light a fire in case hostile folk might discover us with our guard down, which was almost certain because Frodi was on sentry duty. He was likely asleep when he ought to be awake.

Nightjars sounded in the distance, their strange call emanating from their nests in the bushy undergrowth of the birch-wood forests to the nearby east. With the moon so full, they would hunt the insect prey who dared scurry about the base of the trees in the dark hours. In turn, the nightjars would be hunted by the foxes that dozed in burrows during the day, or the silver-grey wolves who howled in the night. We heard them each evening since we departed the friendlier lands on the banks of the Lovat. Each cry caused a shiver down my spine, no matter how far off they might be.

The *Bhobain* bobbed placidly on the calm and glittering waters, the small islands there providing shelter enough to anchor. Nearby, the intersecting Kasplya, wound a path through lush land. Sihtric guessed it all belonged to the Krivichs, or once did. Whether that tribe had sworn allegiance to Grand Prince Oleg or remained in the stiff embrace of the Khazars, we had yet to learn, and none were keen to discover the answer with weapons drawn.

Sven drew me back from my thoughts when he spoke. 'I wish there had been a way to tell you.' His words pierced the silence.

'Would it have changed anything?' I asked, staring up at the star-studded sky.

He shrugged, his shoulder nudging mine with the movement. 'Like you said, it's too late now.'

A distinct clink of metal sounded behind us. My hand shot out to quieten him. 'Sven. Did you hear that?'

He lay on his back still, listening. 'Nothing,' he replied, softer than before.

'Shhh! Stop talking.'

There it was again; a small noise and a whisper, too.

He reached over to take my hand beneath the blankets while his other hand searched for his weapons. I did the same. Skara was never far away, and I grasped her smooth handle that fit so well within my hand. Sven had his sword, Hjarta-Gaddar; Heart-Piercer, which he drew and held before him as we got to our feet and edged towards our sleeping crewmates. No one had stirred, every man tucked under their cloaks or furs, sleeping soundly.

I found Frodi propped up against a rock, slumping to his right as he faced the forest, snoring loudly. 'Useless sentry you are,' I grumbled and kicked the sleeping man's foot.

He jerked awake and grunted. 'Why'd you do that?'

'Because you're supposed to be awake and keeping watch,' Sven growled.

I knelt beside him. 'There was a noise,' I added.

Frodi scrunched up his already wrinkled face and struggled to his feet as we looked around. Sihtric lay prone, one arm over Kari. Thorsten was muttering something about trade in his sleep, and Ahmed was on his back, motionless with his arms crossed against his chest. Björn was face down, dribbling into the dirt, one hand wrapped around his knife, and beside him, Eskil, spread out with his limbs splaying in different directions as a boorish snore erupted from his open maw. Next to him should have lain Egbert, but the thrall was missing. And, as I picked my way across to Gunnar, I realised Odrun was absent, too. Between the trader's arms was a sack stuffed with furs, roughly the size of the woman slave.

I turned back to Sven and Frodi. 'It's Odrun and Egbert,' I whispered.

He sheathed his sword. 'Trying their luck with escape?' he wondered.

More likely that than causing us any harm, and if the two of them had left their masters living, they weren't intent on slaughtering the rest of us.

'Should we wake everyone?' he asked.

'We will face their ire if we don't,' I responded reluctantly, glancing around to see if the escapees had taken anything. The *Bhobain* still bobbed on the weak current and nothing about the camp seemed disturbed. If Odrun and Egbert took anything, it was almost certainly only food.

'What are you three blathering about?' Sihtric groaned as he smoothed his bed hair. 'I hope it's important or I'll box your ears in for waking me.'

Frodi stared up at Sven and me, wearing his slapped-about-the-face expression.

There was a screech from behind us as Eskil hollered, 'Toki! What the bloody…?'

Sihtric stood beside us now, jaw set. 'What is going on?' he demanded. Kari, ever his shadow, stood behind and gave a small grunt.

Eskil strode over, fastening his sword-belt around his ample waist. 'Toki is gone,' Eskil growled.

'Odrun, too,' Sven added as Eskil came to stand beside him. 'And, with your bellowing, everyone else will be awake.'

'As they should be,' Eskil complained. 'Where has the idiot gone? He'll fall into a hole or something, lose a leg.' His eyes glowered in the moon's dim light.

Sihtric and Sven tried to calm the big man, who commanded them to pursue the lost thralls into the forest. Surely, they had not got far. *What were they thinking? Unarmed and in enemy territory was not a recipe for survival.*

A garbled noise came from Gunnar's throat as he finally woke, no doubt shocked to be holding a sack instead of a woman. 'My seax!' he screamed, considerably more shrill than I had ever heard from his mouth.

*Armed and in enemy territory*, I amended my earlier thought. Odrun was a smart woman, I knew. I'd wager Egbert would never have dared an escape if not for her. Together, they might have a chance.

Gunnar continued his strange high-pitched squeal as he freed himself from his bedroll.

Sven snorted a laugh. 'He sounds like a Frisian rutting a pig.'

Eskil was offended on his friend's behalf. 'What in bloody Midgard are you laughing at?' His hand was on his hilt in an instant, menacing glare alive in his eyes. Never had he directed such anger at Sven.

Eskil was the broader and taller of the two, though Sven would be undoubtedly quicker. It was not a fight I wanted to witness, not if we had any hope of finding Odrun and Egbert before they ventured too far. The longer we waited, the further they slipped away from us and I almost thought about letting them. Surely the best thing I could do for them was to let them go, but something nagged at me. A creeping feeling that all would not be right. Night birds issued their haunting echoes, and I took it for the sign it was. We would not be safe this night. Not because the thrall masters scented blood. There was danger afoot. I could feel it.

'You don't seem to have much luck with thralls,' Sven teased Eskil further.

'Don't', I warned, but Eskil was already irate.

The enormous warrior shoved Sven roughly. 'What do you mean by that?'

Sven didn't respond. The answer was obvious; *they all ran away.* Sven's silence rankled the big warrior, and he half-drew his sword from its scabbard.

Sihtric stopped Eskil with one look. 'Put your weapon away until we have need of it,' he warned.

A *whoosh* disturbed the confrontation, as Gunnar hurtled into the forest, howling Odrun's name indignantly. He disappeared into the dense shrubbery at the edge of the birch forest.

'We have to find them before Gunnar does,' I spoke, suddenly desperate to free them from the madman's fury. Gunnar might kill Odrun. He had the legal right to do so, and I couldn't let that happen.

Sven ran to fetch his bow and arrows. Hastily, he strung it and slung it over his shoulder. 'Is everyone armed?' he asked.

'Frodi, you remain to keep watch,' Sihtric ordered. He glanced at his own thrall. 'Kari, stay with Frodi. You ken where the extra weapons are?'

Kari nodded once.

'Use them if you have to. All else,' Sihtric said, turning to address us, 'with me.'

Eskil, Sven, and I joined Sihtric as we followed Gunnar's cries, creeping through the undergrowth as the sky lightened to grey in that time, somewhere between the middle of the night and the approaching of dawn. Sunrise would not come for hours, but at least we could see where we trod now. The Harpa moon shone bright enough to keep each other in sight as we stumbled over roots, mist rolling around gnarled plants, shrouding trunks in Niflheim haze.

'Why not let them go?' Sven asked, still clutching at my elbow.

'If I thought they'd survive, I wouldn't have woken anyone. But they'll die out here. Odrun isn't used to hard work, and I suspect Egbert is a holy man,' I explained.

He stopped, incredulous eyes wide. 'How do you know that?'

I pulled back from the others. 'A few weeks ago when we portaged the *Bhobain* between the Lovat and the Western Dnieper, I caught him writing in the dirt. Some symbols I recognised as the ones Eryk taught me. They were Frankish.'

Sven opened his mouth to ask a question.

'I couldn't read them all,' I answered before he asked.

Sven took my hand, and we walked on, lifting our feet high as we progressed. 'Why didn't you tell anyone?'

'Because I feared what they would do to Odrun and Egbert,' I confessed, releasing his hand, 'and you mustn't tell anyone.'

He nodded in promise, looking ahead to keep Sihtric and Eskil in sight. 'Why do you think Egbert is a holy man?'

One hand grasped Skara tight, and the other reached beneath the neck of my dress to rub my Valkyrie pendant between my fingers for luck. 'They're always writing, aren't they?'

Sven shrugged with one shoulder as he held his sword in front of him. 'Could he not be one of those people who can read books, as Ahmed said? A learned man.'

It seemed I had to divulge more. 'There was another time I discovered them. They were praying.'

'Ah,' he breathed, stopping to look down at me. He bit the side of his lip and smiled. 'You've always been trouble, *minn Svanr.*' He shook off a thought and trudged on. 'All right. We have a Christian, perhaps a Frankish man of God. So, what is Odrun?' he asked.

'Odrun is a hazelnut,' I answered, looking ahead. Sihtric and Eskil were far in front now, mere shadows in the burgeoning morning light.

'A hazelnut?' Sven repeated. 'She's a woman. A fine-looking woman, but…'

'She's difficult to crack,' I jested, speeding up my steps and throwing my hair behind my shoulder. 'I haven't quite figured her out yet.' I reached back for Sven's hand, pulling him forward. 'And I'll not have the chance unless we find them.'

No one had located the thralls once we caught up with Sihtric and Eskil, who had subdued Gunnar from his rage. Another hundred paces through the dense woodlands took us into the forest's heart, and we were hesitant to go any further. With their honour at stake, Gunnar, and Eskil goaded us to continue our hunt, vexed that the people they called property continued to evade us.

'We must keep going,' Gunnar seethed.

Eskil, annoyed at our trepidation, galloped ahead alone into a clump of dense foliage. Beyond that was an open pasture surrounded by a smattering of copses. He ran to the nearest gathering of trees, squeezing between two ghostly birch trunks. 'There,' he called back to us, 'up ahead. I saw something.' He pointed to another grouping of trees and sprinted from sight.

'Wait,' Sihtric shouted back, but the big man had gone.

The early morning fog rolled over the clearing, separating Eskil's last position from ours.

'The *gyte reiver*!' Sihtric cursed. 'He dinnae ken where he is or what's out there.' He threw his hands up in frustration. Sihtric steeled himself with a great breath. 'Gods protect us.'

Gunnar turned to Sihtric, the corner of his mouth quirking up. 'You're not scared, are you?' Though Gunnar, too, had hung back with the rest of us instead of galloping alongside his friend.

'Aye, I am,' Sihtric replied with scorn. 'And if you're not, then you're just as stupid as the big man.'

'We can't just let him go ahead,' Gunnar complained.

'Then you follow him,' Sven suggested. 'I'm not about to wander into...'

Ahead, somewhere in the distance, someone yelped.

'Eskil,' I whispered. It had to be him.

Gunnar tittered, 'Probably fell into a ditch.' Emboldened, Gunnar trotted over fallen branches, keeping his knees high. 'You poor lamb,' he called to Eskil. 'Gunnar will rescue you.'

'Nae. Gunnar. Stop!' Sihtric tried, but failed to stop the trader as he made his way up the small rise of a hill in the near distance. Then, the swirling mist swallowed the two men.

Sihtric, Sven, and I had no desire to continue. I thought about leaving Eskil and Gunnar to their folly and returning to camp, but there was a *clacking* sound, a grumble, and a snort that sounded strangely like a…

'Horse,' Sven whispered beside me.

A mask of terror covered Sihtric's face. 'Its rider is nae a friend to us,' he managed, voice shaking. Sihtric ushered us towards the nearest copse and we pushed our bodies hard against the trees. 'Whoever it is, we dinnae want them to see us before we get a good look at them.' Sihtric peered through the gloom, I on his left, and Sven holding fast to my other arm.

My heart beat like a drum, making it hard to speak. 'We need to get closer.'

Sihtric and Sven turned to face me in unison.

'I didn't say I wanted to get closer, but we have to.' *If we wanted to save the fools who went before us.*

Sven went first, sprinting the stretch between our position and the next thicket. I held my breath as I watched Sihtric follow, and, when it was my turn, the silence around filled my veins with red-hot anxiety that I thought would be punctured with an arrow point at any moment.

Daylight was coming, and as the forest warmed, so too did the mist clear. We could see further, and it was not the sight I had wished for. In the foreground, Eskil stood in a strange position; his head bowed and fists together. He had not fallen, as Gunnar said he might have. Eskil had walked right into enemy riders who had bound his hands and looped a lead rope around his neck. Two men restrained him, both wearing some kind of vest that shone like fish scales in the wan light. Each donned a helmet from which either feathers or horse's tail streamed. It was difficult to tell from such a distance.

Eskil strained against the rope as the two men tied it to the horse's tail, and he screamed obscenities at them. There was a third man mounted, and it was he who pointed in our direction. We froze, unsure if he had seen us or was alerted by a noise there. It wasn't us he had noticed, but Gunnar lying just in front of the gathering of trees.

'Gunnar, get back,' Sihtric whispered and was greeted with a look of sheer horror as the man edged backwards into the trees' protection.

The warrior on horseback called something to his companions, and they stopped their work.

'Are there any more of them?' Sven asked.

I glanced around the clearing. 'Not that I can see. Gunnar?'

He breathed steadily, trying to compose himself enough to answer, 'Three is all I've seen.'

'So, we outnumber them,' Sven replied, licking his dry lips. 'But we're at a disadvantage. They have a horse.'

'I only count spears,' I added, assessing what weapons they were armed with.

The enemy scouts seemed to determine us as a minor threat. They had captured one of our numbers and were making ready to depart with their captive.

'They've nae arrows that I can see,' Sihtric spoke quietly. 'Sven, you'll aim for the rider. Take him down and it'll give us precious time to get the big man,' he instructed.

Thank the gods Sven had the sense to grab his bow.

Sihtric continued. 'We'll do our best to distract them and stay alive.'

The two men holding Eskil lowered their spears in our direction, but kept him under close guard.

'Kill them!' Eskil screamed, thrashing against his bonds in desperation.

The rider kicked his horse on, and Eskil lurched, hands forward, chafing against the cord.

In front of me, Gunnar patted himself down. He groped at his belt, and I realised, with Odrun taking his seax and his hasty departure from camp, he was unarmed. The realisation hit Gunnar at the same time, and his face blanched.

'Take mine,' I said, shoving my fine knife into his empty hand.

Sihtric and Gunnar slid out from the tree's protection, using the dark shadows of the forest to obscure their movement.

Sven drew me close and planted a kiss on my left temple before I could protest. 'I won't miss,' he promised, as he grasped the Valkyrie pendant around my neck and kissed that, too. 'Now, show the gods what you can do, *minn Svanr*,' he commanded with a wink before he drew his bowstring and took aim.

Sihtric sprinted forward, sword drawn, and I was tempted to stand back to see if he had any skill with it, but the danger was too real. This wasn't some practice yard match. It was life and death, and Eskil's assailants seemed too well-adorned to be novice fighters.

It began before I could question any of it. Sihtric moved against one of the foot soldiers. Sword against spear. The spearman jabbed at Sihtric's chest, his reach much longer than that of Sihtric's sword, but my friend nimbly jumped out of the way.

I sprinted, launching myself at the man engaged with Sihtric. Too distracted by the spice merchant, the spearman didn't have time to see Skara as she arced overhead, splintering the wood between his hands. A sickening *crack* like bone, and a shudder ran through my arm upon contact. The second scout, a thick bristled moustache sticking out under the cheek plates of his helmet, grunted and drove his spear towards my arm. I tried to chop through his spear-shaft too, but all I hit was the iron rings that gave it strength and the rivets that held it together. Skara sang a metallic tune I didn't like, and I knew her to be dulling. She was sharp enough to hack, but her bite would be jagged.

I almost felt sorry for the moustached scout who lunged at me, too close to stab with his spear. He fumbled at his belt for his short-sword, but was too late. Skara, blade blunt, cleaved the space between his helmet and his plate shirt in three hewing strikes. Blood spurted from the wound in a crimson cascade, and his hands pawed at the flow.

Gunnar darted forward like a hare through heather and stabbed at the remaining spearman with the broken shaft. The scout whacked Gunnar with the pole and the trader seemed momentarily stunned. As the enemy drew closer, I saw a flash of seax point as it disappeared under the plated metal, into his groin. My knife in Gunnar's grip, he twisted it and wrenched the blade upwards, as the man attempted to use his tipless spear to whack the merchant. A well-timed arrow whipped through the air. I heard it hit flesh as the horse shrieked, kicking its hind legs and thrashing its hooves to rid itself of the pain. The arrow had hit true, burying deep into the mare's flank.

Eskil cried out as the horse's solid hoof walloped his guts. He fell to the ground, clutching his middle, and groaned horribly. Then the horse fell, narrowly missing the big man but trapping the mounted rider's legs.

Seeing my chance, I leapt over the flailing horse and pinned the horseman's hand under my boot as he groped for his weapon, too far away.

'Who are you?' I shouted at him.

Dark eyes stared from beneath his helm and he shook his head, refusing to speak. His plumed helmet rolled off, exposing thick black hair that glistened like tar.

I screamed the same question in Frankish, for I did not know what language he might speak. Nothing. I tried the Slavic dialects Hilde had taught me. At this, he grinned with his blackened teeth, but did not reply. Then he spat, sticking out his spiteful tongue. I twisted my heel into his wrist. His response was to caterwaul, his mewling more like an infant than a hardened warrior. His eyes bulged, and he gritted his teeth in pain. I suspected the weight of his dying horse might now be crushing his spine.

Sihtric and Gunnar came over to see if the horse still lived. Sihtric pulled the arrow out of her belly. 'It went too deep to save her. What about him?' he asked, pointing to the rider under my foot.

I prodded him with the toe of my axe. 'Can't get any sense out of him. He won't answer.'

'Let me try,' Gunnar offered. He crouched down low to the man and pressed my seax to his bearded neck. He spoke in an unfamiliar language, later translating his question as, 'Are there more of you?'

The man stared up at Gunnar, muttered something, and nodded.

'What did he say?' Sven asked as he ran to join us, breathing hard.

I removed my foot from the warrior's hand and looked at Gunnar.

'Says they're everywhere,' he replied.

'Close by,' Sven worried, unstringing his bow and placing it in the bag over his shoulder with the arrows.

Gunnar sank lower and questioned the man, yelling foreign words at him until the warrior spoke. 'Perhaps losing a finger would make your mouth move,' Gunnar said, for our benefit. He grunted as he poked the seax through bone and flesh.

'Is there immediate danger?' I asked, eyes searching the forest.

Gunnar translated my question and responded, 'He says they're part of a scouting party and there are more of them in the hills looking for straggling ships.'

'Were there more of them? Could one have escaped without us seeing?' Sven asked.

Gunnar shook his head. 'I was on the ground for some time before you all came along, and there was no one else. He says it's usual for them to scout in threes. One rider, two spearmen, sometimes all are mounted.

That's the Khagan's direct command. There are others in the area and we cannot rule out them hearing,' he explained. 'Normally, they watch for crews in their groups, then take the information back to the camp that lies hidden near the tributaries. They wait there, or near the overland sections, to spring the traps. Then they capture crews for slaves and take their trading goods.'

Sihtric eyed Gunnar warily. 'He told you all that, did he?'

'No,' Gunnar replied with a snort. 'He told me there were more of them, but I already knew where they like to attack, just as you do, Sihtric. As you know, we're a few days away from it. That means they'll be more of these cretins and, while I'd love to sit here and pick him apart finger by finger, his screeching might attract his friends.' He pierced the warrior's palm with the point of the seax and stomped it through sinew right into the ground. 'I think we've got all we can out of him.'

He looked at Sihtric, who nodded.

Then, with a feral grin, he rammed my seax through the scout's neck. The man died quickly, choking on his lifeblood. We left him there, pinned under his horse.

Gunnar walked towards me, wiping the blade on a scrap of fabric he had torn from the guard's garment. 'Fine blade you have there, Signe,' he ground the words out. 'Almost too good for a woman.' Gunnar held the weapon forth, laboured breath in sync with my own as he ran a predatory eye over my body. It was the look of a man drunk on battle joy, hungering for a way to ebb the flow of ecstasy.

I stepped back. He pressed the knife, handle first, into my palm as his face was less than a hand span from mine. 'Thanks,' I said, snatching it.

Sihtric wrapped his arm across Gunnar's shoulder and steered him away. 'Let's see what they've left us. Come on,' he ordered.

Eskil, back on his feet, was clutching his guts. Unsteady, he needed Sven and me to shoulder him as he limped on. It was clear he needed treatment and unless we happened upon someone on our travels, he would not get it until we reached Gnezdovo in a few days.

'Should I have aimed for the rider rather than the horse?' Sven asked me as we lumbered along. 'If I did, you might not be in such a terrible state,' he said by way of apology.

'I'll be all right,' Eskil groaned.

Sihtric and Gunnar stripped the dead men of their plate mail shirts, their weapons, and anything else of value. They had some food on them, and there was a clutch of arrows Sven could use, but we only had so many hands to carry the stuff. Some had to be left behind.

A wolf howled far in the distance, echoed by its pack.

'Maybe the wolves will eat the rest of those feathered cap brutes,' Sven growled.

'I heard they kill them and wear their pelts as a status symbol,' Gunnar interjected as we stumbled back towards the river.

By now, the sky was lightening. There was no colour show this morning as small rain threatened and puffs of grey clouds filled the sky. It would be a wet day as we made our way onto the Udra via one of its many tributary rivers. *Not far until we reached Gnezdovo*, I reminded myself, *not far*. Then we would walk among people who would rather take our coin for goods and services than our lives. At least, I hoped that would be the reception we received.

Ahead, there was a commotion. Familiar voices were shouting in tongues we could understand.

Eskil leaned more heavily on our shoulders. Sven worried. 'You don't think there are more of them, do you?'

Gunnar appeared beside me and asked to borrow my seax once more. 'It's coming from our camp,' I said, waving my hand towards the noise.

Amid the discarded bedrolls, Frodi pulled Odrun's hair, tugging her backwards. Egbert was scrambling on the ground in his dirty robes, Björn's boot on his chest. Ahmed was attempting to placate them all with reason.

'It is not for us to decide their fate,' we could hear him speaking forcefully.

'They ran away and should be beaten!' Frodi yelled, wrenching Odrun so hard she fell on her backside. When she saw us, she scrambled to her feet, eyes wide with fear.

Ahmed's hands were before him, spread open. 'Stay calm, friends.'

'Where did you go?' I asked before I could stop myself.

Björn raced to our group to explain, 'They snuck back here to take the food once they saw you scarper off into the trees. Then they tried to take the ship.' He took his foot off Eskil's slave, but the big man was in no shape to punish his thrall.

Gunnar slammed his foot into Egbert's middle, winding the small man who gasped for air in the dirt. 'You're fortunate that Eskil is injured, and

I have Odrun to deal with or I would have tied you to a tree and left you for the Khazars,' he threatened.

'Bloody thralls,' was all that Eskil could manage as we helped him to sit on a log.

Kari came forward, presenting Sihtric with his bedding, tied neatly with its strap. Sihtric nodded. 'Make ready,' he commanded. 'We leave now before anyone notices those scouts missing.'

Sven and I hastily packed our things.

Once Gunnar had released Odrun from Frodi's grasp, he dragged her to his furs. 'Why do you cause me such misery?' he screamed in her face.

She held her nose up, refusing to look at him.

Then he slapped her across the face, and yelled, 'You will submit to me, whore!'

Odrun closed her eyes as Gunnar ripped her dress at the neckline, splitting it to her navel. She stood tall and defiant, breasts exposed, and I looked away. There was no getting involved. Gunnar was just as likely to take out his anger on anyone else, and though I hated to admit it, Odrun had caused this mess.

'You want me to take you in front of the men? I will,' he glowered. 'Lie down.'

Her voice was barely a squeak as she answered, 'No.'

'What did you say?'

They stood nearly eye to eye, and though Gunnar was physically larger, Odrun commanded herself well. 'No,' she said, more forcefully this time. 'Even if you tried, you're not able to do the job. You've not been able to do it for weeks. Gunnar,' she said his name with such scorn it sounded like a curse, 'you are no man.'

He backhanded her around the jaw so hard she spat blood. But as Gunnar walked away, sullenly boarding the ship without another word, Odrun looked at me, and for the first time, it wasn't with disgust or scorn. It was an image of victory. She smiled as she covered her body and tugged on the edge of her wadmal shawl.

Odrun had conquered her master when she questioned his manhood. That small win would cost her greatly, but there was no question, that Odrun was a woman who would not rest until the war was won. And she wanted her freedom.

# EIGHT

Scouts, danger, and Eskil's fate were all a constant source of conjecture as we navigated the winding rivers towards Gnezdovo.

Ahmed shocked us all by recounting what future awaited fighting men captured by the scouts that likely belonged to the Khazars.

'He'd become part of the slave army,' the trader explained matter-of-factly, surprised that no one knew what he spoke of. 'You've never heard the tales?' His usually smooth forehead was wrinkled in consternation.

At our oars, we all shook our heads.

'Sihtric? You've never heard of the heathen armies of Itil?' Ahmed asked, black brows knitted together as he addressed our leader.

Sihtric stared back. 'Never.'

Ahmed gave a small nod before continuing. 'Whenever they capture trained warriors, they give them a choice; swear loyalty to the Khanate and go there to be part of the great heathen army kept on the western embankment of the city.'

Eskil's hand lay protectively over his stomach. 'Or what?' he asked.

'It's either fight for them, or die,' Ahmed answered.

A shudder ran down Eskil's spine, and he grimaced with the pain it caused. The injury wasn't the only thing worrying him. The thought of the fate we'd saved him from stalked his nightmares.

Sven grumbled, 'Some choice.'

But Ahmed, sitting at the front of the *Bhobain* in his usual spot, shrugged. 'They say they treat the warrior slaves well.'

'They'd have to. If the men rebelled, they'd have a hard time subduing them,' I added with a snigger.

Ahmed nodded in agreement. 'While they live in Itil, they are well fed, given women, allowed plunder whilst on campaign, and most live happy lives. Even when they earn their release, some choose to stay.'

'Because they're in the middle of nowhere and do not know how to get home,' I ground out, looking away from the trader. The evenness of his voice irritated me, though I knew he merely recounted what he'd learned on his travels.

When I glanced back, he met my gaze with his always sharp moss-green eyes, seeing more than I wanted him to. One of his eyebrows arched, and his mouth crooked at the corner. 'Show me a rich land and I shall show you the backs of the men who made it so,' he quipped sagely.

I had nothing to say in response. It had been the way of things for many generations. Those who can take will, and those who are taken, must make the best of the unpleasant situation.

Ahmed opened his book and began scribbling notes as he often did, and I turned around in my seat, taking Skara onto my lap for a long overdue polish with a scrap of coarse wool. The wind filled our sail, and it was only out of habit we sat at our benches while rowing was unnecessary.

Sven watched me as I worked. His nose wrinkled and eyes narrowed. 'What is it?' I asked.

He bent closer to examine my axe. 'There's something wrong there,' he said, pointing to Skara's bite.

A divot had appeared on the blade's edge. A thin crack ran from that defect back to the handle. One hard strike and the entire thing might fracture.

My heart sank. 'Do you think I sharpened her to an in-curve?' I lamented.

Sven shook his head. 'Was it there before we fought the scouts?'

'Odin's beard!' I cursed. 'It must have happened when I struck those spear-shafts. One of them had an iron ring, and I recall hearing a noise but...' I slumped onto the bench, one hand under my chin and my mouth frowning hard.

'There's a *smedr* in Gnezdovo, he might fix Skara' Sven tried to comfort me, but I was unreachable in my bad mood.

Rain fell lightly, and I scowled up at the black clouds that gathered. Thor's thunder rumbled, and water poured down, heavier by the moment. Soaked, bleak, and dispirited, I took it as an omen from the gods. If I had thought the journey so far had been difficult, they laughed and said, *It's not about to get any easier.*

Days later, we rowed the coiling paths of water toward the Udra. With constant downpours, our clothes were sodden, our bodies sweat grimed and filthy; everyone was desperate to bathe and change into dry clothing.

Sihtric smiled into the sun as he said, 'I ken a place.'

Our crew laughed.

Thorsten, who entertained us with gentle music that morning, chuckled against his bone flute. 'Of course you do,' he answered before returning to the tune.

Unbothered by the taunt, Sihtric went on, 'We can wash there; our clothes and our bodies. This afternoon the sun'll be warm enough to dry it all before we set off, and, by morning, we'll have reached the settlement.'

Gunnar grumbled, still sulking from his conflict with Odrun, though he made sure to glare at her every time she moved. 'Have to keep a close eye on these two,' he seethed, tossing his head towards the thralls in the back, where they had been, morning and night, since the incident.

'I can watch her while she bathes,' Frodi offered, lips wet with spittle and eyes already devouring the poor girl.

'No, you won't,' I spoke up. 'She will go with me and she won't be out of my sight. I'll promise you that,' I swore to Gunnar. 'And you've been too long on the water.' I prodded Frodi.

'Too long without the loving arms of a woman,' he corrected me as he wrapped his limbs around himself and stroked his arms as a lover might.

Odrun's mouth tightened, and she flared her delicate nostrils. I wasn't sure if she was grateful or calculating her chances of escaping my watchful eye.

Sihtric clapped gleefully. 'Och! Don't you fret! There's plenty of lovely women in Gnezdovo's taverns, Frodi.'

Gunnar grunted and folded his arms, leaning against the gunwale. 'Plus a few that aren't so lovely but are within your budget.'

Frodi ignored the jibe and whooped loudly. Eskil grabbed the smaller man by the shoulder to steady himself as he tottered over to the side and urinated into the wind. He winced as he was splattered with his own piss.

'You all right, Eskil?' Gunnar worried. His friend was just about the only thing he cared about other than himself.

Eskil looked down at his shirt, now sprayed a light pink. 'I'm pissing blood,' he groaned, tying his belt before he sat back down on the bench. 'That's not a good sign.'

Sihtric jumped down from the bow deck and squeezed the big man on his muscular shoulder. 'There'll be a healer in Gnezdovo. Dinnae ken what can be done, but there'll be something.'

Eskil nodded, staring across the landscape with a pinched expression, one hand grasping his midsection.

'A good soak might help,' Gunnar suggested lamely, but it looked like he, too, wondered if we should head directly to Gnezdovo without delay. But Eskil didn't press. He seemed content to spend the afternoon resting, and come morning, would find a wise woman to heal his wounded guts.

The river narrowed and twisted, dancing through densely forested areas of mostly flat terrain save for a rise here and there. We anchored the *Bhobain* where the river looped in a near-perfect circle and took turns scuttling up the nearby hill to a small lake to bathe. Sihtric told us it was deep, but there was a small pool there too, where you could stay in the shallow waters if you couldn't swim.

Ahmed continued ahead, while the rest of us washed outer garments and hung them over the ship's side to dry in the bright sunshine. Ahmed returned with a joyous smile, face tilted towards the sun's light.

'You're in a better mood,' I called to him as he ambled down the overgrown path. He'd changed into clean clothing, and the moss-green of his tunic complimented his similarly coloured eyes.

'Little else feels as good as clean does,' he replied, waving a greeting. Ahmed was fastidious about his hygiene, partaking in regular ritualistic cleaning. He could not pray to his god without washing first, and so he did, morning, noon, and night, and then some. 'Who goes next?' he asked.

'Frodi, Björn, and Thorsten will go while we finish up here,' Sihtric answered. 'Then Sven, Eskil, Kari, and Toki will go. I'll go with the girls and keep watch while they bathe.'

'Can we swap?' Sven asked.

Even I thought he was joking at first.

'I'd like to swap too.' Björn put his hand up, much to everyone's amusement.

Sihtric narrowed his eyes at Sven. 'But I'll nae look at them when they're naked,' he replied stoically.

Sven took a step back and straightened his stance. 'Neither will I.'

Sihtric looked at me for confirmation, but I just shrugged in response.

'You swear it?' Sihtric asked, weighing up Sven's promise.

'On my life,' he agreed.

The first of the men departed while I waited for my turn. Every single one of them came back in various states of undress, holding their clean but dripping clothing over their nakedness, unless they had other garments to wear. Some found secluded bluffs, surrounded by shrubs on which to dry their clothes, and basked in the afternoon's warmth like lizards on a rock.

'Are you ready?' I asked Odrun as Sihtric, and Eskil returned with their slaves.

She nodded swiftly, but said nothing. Not a word had left her lips in days.

'Gunnar,' I called to her master. 'I'll need the key to her manacles.'

'Why? She can wear it in the water,' he replied caustically. Since she'd tried to escape, Gunnar had shackled her night and day, never once removing the heavy iron ring from around her neck.

'It'll rust,' I shouted back, but he waved me off. 'Wouldn't you rather she was clean when she came back to you? She can't do that if she cannot move and wash herself.'

With a growling exhale, he capitulated and handed me the key.

Odrun and I made our way up the path, scattering birds as we went. Sven followed at a respectful distance.

'You two take the pool. There is a big rock where you can lay your clothes to dry. I'll stay around the corner, out of sight, unless you need me,' Sven uttered softly, and left us to walk the further distance to the bathing pool. 'I'll whistle if I see anyone approaching.'

As soon as we were alone, Odrun cleared her throat and spoke for the first time in days. 'Why do you insist on helping me?'

The branches of a bare tree hung over the path. I pushed them aside. 'Am I helping you?' I answered her question with my own. 'Was I wrong to come with you instead of Frodi?'

She levelled me with an unimpressed scowl and pursed her lips. 'You told them nothing of what you saw,' she replied, stumbling over each word. 'Tell me why.'

The water glittered, inviting us into its cool depths. I sat on a rock to remove my boots.

'Why would I tell them?' I asked. 'Gunnar is no friend of mine.'

Off my shoulders, I slipped my *serkr* and bent down to scrub it clean. Bare as the day I was born, save for the Valkyrie pendant around my neck and the armring my father had given me years before, on my forearm.

'And, nor am I,' Odrun replied, fumbling with the crude stitches that held her ripped dress in place.

'Let me take off your neck-cuff,' I offered, producing the key Gunnar had provided.

She stepped out of her repaired shift and slipped off her wadmal cape, rough on the fair skin of her neck and shoulders. Red-raw lines gleamed where the manacle had chafed at her flesh.

'Is that why you always wear that thick woollen cape?'

She nodded. 'And I always will. Until I am no longer a slave.'

My ears pricked at such a statement.

She continued without my interruption. 'Then I will wear something else to cover the scar.'

Odrun was a strange woman. Still, I couldn't fault her for having dreams of freedom, dangerous though, that might be.

We washed our clothing in silence until Odrun worked up the courage to speak of what gnawed at her. Fists crumpled her damp fabric as she chose the words, 'I need your help.'

'Don't ask me to help you escape again,' I responded without looking.

The water that ran off my *serkr* was grey. Odrun passed me the rough rock she'd been using to scour her drab garment.

'That did not go as planned,' she admitted. 'No. I need you to get parchment for Egbert.'

My eyes widened, and I took in a sharp breath. 'That almost sounds like a command, Odrun,' I replied as I scrubbed my underdress. 'How am I meant to get parchment, huh?'

She flopped her sodden dress back into the water before wringing it. 'I don't know.'

We laid our clothes on a bush by the lake to dry.

'What is Egbert going to write in this letter?' I wondered aloud.

Odrun lowered her head, tipping it to one side, and looked up at me through her fair lashes. 'How do you know it would be a letter?'

'What else is he going to do with it? Draw me a nice little picture?' I scoffed, dipping my toe into the shallows.

Parchment and ink were expensive commodities. There was only one member of our crew who carried it. If I was going to get any, I either had to ask Ahmed or I would need to purchase some in Gnezdovo. Else, I would need to wait another couple of weeks before we arrived in Kyiv, where it would undoubtedly be easier for me to obtain the items, but my access to Egbert and Odrun would be removed.

Odrun was ahead of me, paddling into the deeper water before she disappeared beneath its surface. When she bobbed up, she seemed calmer.

'You'll need a messenger,' she added, calling out as I swam to her.

'Odin's beard, Odrun,' I exclaimed, and she recoiled at the mention of my gods. 'Are you going to tell me who this letter is going to?'

She shook her head, wet hair draped back in a curtain of golden-brown. 'Eventually, I'll have to, but the less you know now, the better.'

Sighing heavily, I floated on my back and said nothing more while we drifted on the dark surface. I closed my eyes and considered all Odrun had said. *If she was me, would she do the same?* I wondered, but in the end decided it didn't matter. I did what I thought was right. 'You promise you'll tell me?' I asked her.

'All I ask is that you trust me now.'

'Because you are trustworthy?' I derided, remembering my rule that the ones that exclaimed their virtue the loudest did not hold them in their possession at all.

'No,' she replied, swimming to the edge of the lake to get out. I swam behind her. She turned back to me. 'Because I have no other choice.'

Desperation. It was there in her eyes and I had so many times before mistaken it for defiance.

'You might not,' I agreed, stepping out of the water and onto the rock where I'd left my weapons earlier, 'but I do.'

A metallic tang sounded off the rocks as I brought Skara down on Odrun's chains. Anger pulsed through my hands, urging me to smash the axe against her offcast restraints. Whether it was for hatred of that slimy token-toter Gunnar, the bubbling anxiety of seeing Kjarr again, or because something in Odrun had reminded me of myself, I wasn't sure. All I knew was the compulsion to destroy the very symbol of oppression.

'What are you doing?' Odrun cried, swimming towards me, hair spreading like molten metal behind her.

There was a deafening clang as Skara bit into the rusting iron again, warping the weaker metal. I struck again and again until the ring broke in two and Skara hit the rock beneath and when she did; she splintered. My hardworking axe, a gift from my father, finally fractured. I ran my thumb over the chipped bite and scooped up the pieces.

Odrun was standing in the shoal, open-mouthed, hair hanging limply over her chest. 'Why?' she asked, brow furrowed in confusion.

'We'll tell Gunnar they broke,' I grumbled, knowing very well he wouldn't believe me.

*He also won't do anything about it,* I thought, *not when my husband is Sihtric's best friend.* There was already discord between the merchants. Gunnar had tried, blind with rage after Odrun's denouncing, to cleave open Sihtric's small chest secured on board the *Bhobain*, sure it contained gold, or gems beyond his imagining. Sihtric and Frodi had held him overboard by the ankles, face dipping into the choppy waters, until he swore to rein himself in on threat of abandonment at the next village. No, I could do this knowing Gunnar would not dare step a foot out of line to challenge me.

'Your axe,' she cried, looking down at the bits of iron that had contained her.

I ignored her protests. 'Gunnar can't make you wear them if they're smashed. For two days at least, you'll walk unfettered,' I explained, offering her the remnants of the manacle. 'You'll enter Gnezdovo without a chain around your neck, walk without the shackles, sleep without the metal biting your flesh,' I seethed.

There were tears in her eyes. Odrun was a woman who had learned to trust no one, just as I had. 'Your axe, Signe.'

'Skara was finished,' I muttered tonelessly. 'Damaged beyond repair,' I added, as if it wasn't the second most important thing my father had ever given me.

We stared at each other for longer than was comfortable before I spoke, my voice far calmer than I felt. 'I'll get you ink and parchment, Odrun. Something tells me that whatever it costs me, it'll be worth it.'

# NINE

## SPRING 883 CE GNEZDOVO

Gnezdovo would be a fascinating place, or so Sihtric said.

Set on the Dnieper, the inhabited section was on the raised right bank which was as tall as a man, and protected Gnezdovo's people from the rising water levels. He described how the river rose fast here and often. At times the river claimed the land, turning it into vast waterlogged zones. Right after the thaw, when snow melted at a rapid pace, the Dnieper would swell to the greatest levels all year, flooding this pasture. It was only when the summer wore on, sun drinking up the excess, that the field would be used again. The cycle repeated itself year after year.

'So, it's a bog,' I asked Sihtric, after he explained the process.

'I've never seen it so, but I suppose it might be sometimes,' he conceded. 'The flooding must be worse on the left bank. There's a small patch of farmland there, but it's tiny compared to what's on the other side.'

It was a day of travelling under oars. The going was easy as the current guided us along. Sihtric had taken Sven's position behind me, letting my friend snatch some much-needed sleep after being on sentry duty the night before. Sven snored soundly, curled up on the deck near my feet. By this point, most of us were accustomed to sleeping through all the noise and movement.

I looked back over my shoulder at Sihtric. 'They abandon it every summer with the rising river?'

'Aye, I'd think so. Last time I was there was just after river run. Mila, the woman I'll introduce you to, told me the water was at its highest,' he explained, referring to his contact in Gnezdovo. 'They'd harvested the winter barley and cleared out. Suspect they plant a *wee* bit before the frost and harvest straight after the snow melts. I'm nae a farmer, but even I ken that's the only thing'll be grown there.'

Nothing but grasses and reeds grew in the marshy areas surrounding a river, sometimes worse in the waterlogged flat lands. Desperate farmers often attempted to plant crops before they realised how wet the soil would get. As the Dnieper expanded, all the crops would be destroyed. Months of hard work for nothing, and dreams of an easy winter, were dashed as the burgeoning crops were ruined.

'With their left bank so temperamental, does the settlement only exist on one side then?' I probed further.

He nodded. 'Unless they've built something recently, they all lived on the dry side last I was there.'

I extended my arms, pushing the oar in the rowlock. 'How much longer?' I asked, feeling my back crack and relief flooding between my shoulders.

'Always with the questions,' Frodi croaked from behind us at the steering oar, his dark greying hair hanging over his eyes. His mood seemed directly linked to the emptiness of our ale barrel. We would refill in Gnezdovo, but that meant Frodi had to last the day without a drink.

Sihtric stretched, twisting his torso. 'Before noon.'

'Urgh,' Frodi groaned.

The rest of the crew were sullenly silent, all waiting eagerly to see something other than forests and fields. The *Bhobain* creaked as we made our way, her earthy scent hardly diminished by the musky odour of the river. Soon, we would walk the land instead of the small space of her belly, if only for a few days.

I looked around at the surly expressions and decided they needed something to cheer them up, so I sang, 'Oh! Njord. Your breath is our breeze.'

Sven perked up at the ditty. 'Fill our sails with wind, and we'll be down on our knees!' he joined in, but was making up the lyrics. As usual, he didn't know the words.

'Shut up, you two,' Gunnar grumbled. He disliked anything that brought pleasure to another. 'It sounds more like a lament than any song a god would want to hear.'

He was still in a foul mood and my destruction of Odrun's chains had done little to improve it, though he had merely sulked off and ordered me to finance their repairs. I agreed, of course, but he could hardly blame me if the manacle came back made of inferior slag. He never said he wanted them ironclad.

'I reckon more like a curse,' Björn added with a snigger. A proper shipmaster, Björn knew all the best songs. 'The way you're singing is all wrong.'

Sven chuckled, rubbing his nose with his fist. 'Come on, then, Björn. Give us a sample of those skaldic kennings of yours.'

The shipmaster tried to wave him away. Understanding Sven would not be dissuaded, Björn cleared his throat and began, 'Oh! Njord. Your breath is our breeze. Bring wealth to us, and our enemies appease.' His song squeaked out through a strangled voice, pitchy and high, but at least the words were correct.

Frodi guffawed. 'Sounds like someone lifted your breaches into your arse crack.'

Thorsten swatted imaginary tears from his cheek with the hem of his tunic. 'Just beautiful, Björn. Stunning.'

'Sew your mouth shut, the both of you! Not everyone can have a honey-sweet tongue like Fire-Head over there.' Björn waved a fist in Thorsten's direction. A mock threat between friends.

Sihtric stood suddenly, face peaceful as he turned it towards the sun. 'Och! The wind,' he breathed, as a fresh blast filled the cloth of the mast.

It was welcome to be under sail again. Rowing had been challenging after yet another portage, this one between the Dyna and back to the Dnieper. More arduous, given the absence of Eskil's brawn. The poor fellow could only lay useless inside the *Bhobain* and groan every time the vessel jostled. His pain was agonising. His condition had worsened and, by the time we left the bathing lake, he was begging Sihtric for a healer, which we were sure to find in Gnezdovo. Since then, he'd assumed a horizontal position and slept in the hold.

'Not much further,' I offered in sympathy to the big man.

Nothing but a grunt came in response.

*Gnezdovo, a funny name for a settlement*, I thought. Sihtric informed me it was also known as Syrnes, which I liked much better. Still, it was a strange thing to call a place after a swine. Sihtric explained it was named for the brook that carved through the settlement, called the Svinnas, swine brook.

'Why name it for a pig?' I had asked, eyes flicking up to the sky, searching for answers.

He offered a paltry explanation. 'Perhaps the meeting of the two rivers looks like a *svinfylking*?'

My eyebrows arched at that. 'A swine's head?'

'More its tusks,' he answered. 'You'll see, *bhana charaid*.'

Just as Sihtric had told me, I saw the settlement was sprawling. At its heart was a walled rampart with a garrison manned by northern people, though the settlement itself was not considered part of Grand Prince Oleg's lands. Gnezdovo belonged to the Krivichs, paying tribute to Oleg in exchange for the valuable warriors that guarded their fortifications. Only one in four inhabitants were foreigners, the rest were Krivichs and neighbouring Slav groups, and together they lived in peaceful harmony. As much as that was ever possible and surprising given the conflict we'd faced in Aldeigjuborg. Somehow, the people of Gnezdovo had realised the benefit each offered to the other and were keen to keep that relationship flourishing.

'There she is,' Sihtric beamed, pointing to the farms on the right bank.

As far as my eye could take in, the land was richly green and fertile. Animals roamed, munching on grasses. Crops sprouted from the ground in neat, well-planned rows. Even the houses looked to be in excellent repair, thatch straight and thick, not mouldered or broken as they might have been in poorer settlements. Men in the field appeared strong, a well-fed round belly straining at their belts. Life was evidently good here.

We rowed into the harbour where the water was deep enough for an anchorage, protected from the onward flow of the river.

'Further along, where the Olsha intersects the Dnieper, there's another fort,' Sihtric began explaining, 'it overlooks the river in both directions. There is a smaller settlement within easy walking distance of Gnezdovo. I hear there's a garrison there in the fort on Olsha Hill protecting the folk here, too.'

I raised an impressed eyebrow and cast a look to my crewmates, many of whom stared open-mouthed at the floodplain terraces before the sprawling Gnezdovo complex that stretched the distance between the Dnieper and Svinnas, almost all the way to the Olsha.

'It's much bigger than Aldeigjuborg,' I said, at which every man aboard bobbed his head in agreement.

Sihtric grinned, eyes glinting with the optimism of a practised merchant, seeing opportunities in all things. 'If Oleg keeps the river road safe, Gnezdovo will continue to expand.'

With fruitful fields, a naturally defensible position, and easy access to the riverway, it was no wonder why people were drawn here and no mystery why the Grand Prince was eager to keep it in his fold.

On the breeze, I caught a whiff of tar pits. The sticky substance was used for waterproofing vessels, and many a ship's crew would call in at the settlement for restocking and repair. Also competing against the tar smell was the pungent aroma of lime. Though it was not yet the slaughter season, the tanners must have been busy treating some animal skins, removing hair and fat, before preparing the skins for leather working. That gave me an idea. Odrun had asked for parchment and ink so Egbert might write a letter. When I had agreed, I had no notion of how I might accomplish it. After smelling the lime on the midday breeze, I recalled Father Niall of Aldeigjuborg telling me of the skill required to produce it, and I wondered if that was a competency Egbert possessed. The opportunity to get parchment had arrived, and I would take it. But first, the crew's most pressing concern was Eskil.

Sihtric tied off the *Bhobain* to a mooring, while Thorsten and Sven dropped the anchor stone into the water's depths.

'Gudrun will help you,' the wharf-man said, 'for a fee. She is expensive, but she's good. Gudrun the Grey, we call her. As old as those there mounds full of rich Krivichi voivodes well before my time, mind.'

Gunnar was sceptical.

'What other choice do we have?' Thorsten asked.

Everyone knew Eskil's condition was only getting worse. If we waited any longer, there might be no hope of saving him.

The wharf-man whistled through his teeth as Sihtric questioned him. 'Aye, she knows her craft,' the old man replied. He was inspecting mooring lines, tying off the vessels, hoping to be flicked a morsel by the grateful.

'How far away did you say?' Gunnar's contempt was bright as day as he addressed the wizened fellow.

He pointed with a dry and cracked finger beyond the water, over the settlement into the distance. 'She lives on the far side of them farms, to the north and then some.' His nose was dripping as he pulled on his cap. 'Gudrun cured my daughter of a nasty skin malady so she could be married.'

Gunnar laughed coldly. 'A glowing endorsement. If she's a daughter of yours, she wouldn't be much to look at in the first place.'

The man scratched his hair beneath his cap. 'Aye, you're not wrong there. Unsightly she was a plenty before Gudrun the Grey laid her hands upon my girl. For a week, she kept my daughter in that dark hovel of hers. When she stepped out, my girl was clear-skinned and ruddy, a better sight than when she went in after which a decent man took her to wife,' he detailed, eyes round at the retelling.

'A witch,' Gunnar groaned under his breath. 'Is there no one else?' he asked, glancing back at his oafish friend lying beneath the benches.

'Not in these parts,' the wharf-man replied. 'There's a woman for birthing, but that'll be of no use to you. Gudrun is the wisest with herbs and…'

'Spells?' I wondered.

'As you say, perhaps. I'd never dare ask. Don't ask, just pay and she'll find a way,' the man answered as he tied off another flax rope. 'For lodgings, if you're looking, that'd be the Stinkhorn. Mind you stay away from the Rusty Hauberk. Unless you're looking for trouble.' He raised his greying brows that met in the middle of his forehead and leaned over the gunwale.

'The Stinkhorn?' I repeated.

'Aye,' Sihtric answered, 'it's a mushroom that grows in these parts. Dinnae go eating it, though.'

The wharf-man nodded effusively. 'It's also the pet name for the tavern-keeper's wife. No idea why, but she makes a mean plate of spring pork in mustard sauce with leek. If you have coin to spare,' he added, holding a hand out to receive payment for information he had proffered. I flicked him a veksha. 'And she'll remember you.' He pointed at Sihtric. 'She's not forgotten that black spice you gave her when last you were here.'

We carried a little coin, usually veksha and some dirhams, and a mix of hack. Silver dirhams were considered superior currency. Each piece weighed the same amount, as prescribed under Islamic law, therefore ensuring its value. Compromising that came with a penalty of death and, as it circulated through the trading routes far outside the Arabic world, it was lauded for its consistency so much so that traders preferred to be paid in that manner. This was not always possible and when that occurred, hack silver could be proffered. But as the name suggested, hack silver was pieces of metal broken from various objects such as jewellery, plate, or other coins and you were never sure just what you were getting. Even weighing it did not bring certainty, as scales could be falsely weighted, and silver could be plated, containing inferior metals beneath its glittering surfaces. Locally, and for smaller purchases, veksha, hryvnia, or a good barter was acceptable, but never preferred.

Gunnar obtained more detailed directions from the man after producing another coin as payment, while Eskil was lifted out of the *Bhobain*, groaning in pain. We made a stretcher from the spruce poles and tied cloth to it to form a crude bed. His head tossed while we awkwardly carried his enormous body as we made our way along the wharf.

Sihtric stopped to deal with the guard who came to exact their fee and customs.

Unencumbered by the stretcher, he caught up. 'The healer is on the western side, to the north of the Svinnas,' he explained breathlessly, grasping the pole behind me. He grimaced. It was not the weight of the body that worried him. Anyone with eyes could see he was seriously injured. Eskil's face was brave enough. If pissing blood wasn't bad enough, he now defecated it, too. Not much, Eskil had assured us, but enough that even he was worried. The horse's kick had caught him square in the belly, and though there was no wound, there was a mighty bruise that had coloured his skin black and blue.

'I've made the gods angry,' Eskil grumbled, helpless on the fabric. He stared into the clear blue sky.

Sihtric gripped his hand, difficult to do when he was trying to bear the man's weight. 'We'll give them an offering soon enough.'

Eskil grimaced. 'Not me!'

'Nae. Not your body,' he replied with a laugh. 'We'll give them goods worthy of your recovery.'

That placated Eskil enough for him to cease his moving and allow us to carry him for so long that our arms burned and shoulders ached far more than rowing the *Bhobain* had ever wearied us. A small hovel came into view. It couldn't have been any more than one room, with a low thatched roof that reeked of mildew. A leather curtain covered the doorway, blocking the dark interior from prying eyes, but the healing woman sat outside the house on a low stool, grinding something in a small bowl.

She looked up as we approached. Her grey eyes peered from beneath sagging eyelids. 'Come inside,' she croaked. The woman struggled to her feet, stooped with age and moving as if all her joints had stiffened. Inside, she motioned to a small pallet against the far wall. 'Put him there.'

We slid Eskil from the stretcher onto the pallet bed, dislodging a layer of dust from the surface as if no one had slept there for months. The hovel was dark and musty but unusually well-ordered, with neat rows of jars and clean cooking vessels hanging from the walls.

Gudrun ambled over, looking down at Eskil with a startling lack of interest. 'What's it that ails him, then?' she asked, as if she thought the answer would bore her.

She prodded the big man with a gnarled finger, her eyes narrowed as she regarded the hapless man before her.

'We're hoping you might tell us,' Sven offered. He was the only one thus far to find his voice.

She cocked her head to one side, thinning silver hair falling over her shoulder. 'The wound?'

'A horse kicked him in the guts,' Sven answered, still shouldering the guilt that it was his arrow that caused the horse to buck.

Gudrun clicked her tongue and said, 'Nasty one, that. Such force inside does not do him well.'

*Would she help Eskil?* I wondered. She hadn't said as much, and watching her now, as she pottered over to her hearth where a pot of soup simmered, I didn't think she was so inclined. The broth's pungent aroma filled the room with the smell of leeks, onion, and wild herbs.

'Hand me that cup,' Gudrun commanded me, gesturing to a shelf where a cluster of earthenware drinking vessels were stacked. 'He'll drink it and we should know if the wound has spread elsewhere.'

I handed her a small cup and sighed. 'So, you'll help him?'

She shrugged, her threadbare cloak dipping low on her shoulder. 'How else'll I make coin if not helping men that gladly run to danger?' Gudrun ladled in steaming broth and shuffled back to Eskil's bedside, gesturing for the men to incline Eskil enough that he might drink.

'Does he piss blood?' she asked, frowning as she pressed the cup to Eskil's mouth.

'Aye,' Sihtric confirmed, squatting by the pallet.

Gudrun tutted, pressing the cup more forcefully to Eskil's lips. 'Are his breeches marked by blood also?'

Sihtric nodded.

'Hmm,' she grumbled, and I didn't like the sound. Gudrun motioned for Gunnar to take charge of Eskil's drinking before she asked, 'Coughing it up, too?'

Sihtric shook his head this time. 'Nae, but he weakens.'

'He's a big strong one, though,' Gudrun mumbled, and her lips quaked into an eerie smile as she watched Eskil garble and splutter like a force-fed youngling.

The liquid flowed down his gullet, then when he had stopped his flailing, the healer sniffed his midsection, down to his arse.

'He'll live,' she announced, much to our relief.

Back in the middle of the room, Gudrun tipped the unused contents of the cup back into the bubbling pot. 'He has a tear inside the body. With the right treatment, it will heal.' She turned her lined face towards me and spoke, 'Grab the two jars there on the shelf, girl.'

The rows of containers had captured my attention, each marked with a unique symbol. 'Which ones?' I asked. Her pointing had been too vague to narrow down my options.

The healer squinted at me and wrinkled her brow. 'The ones you want, or the ones he needs?' she riddled, throwing her head toward Eskil, now lying flat on the pallet.

My cheeks burned hot. I had intended to make a purchase of my own, but did not want the crew to know. 'Peasant's eye?' I chanced, knowing it was common in healing swelling.

'And broadleaf. That one there,' she said, pointing to the jar beside the one she indicated was peasant's eye.

I plucked it from the shelf and handed it to her.

'You know how to crush leaves?' she asked.

I nodded. The men had edged out of the hovel, one by one, until I found only myself, Eskil, and Sihtric remained in Gudrun's company.

'Do it well, and I'll give you the herbs you need,' she promised. 'Leave him here with me for three days,' she continued, turning back to Sihtric.

'Three days?' he exclaimed, mind busily thinking over what this might mean for our journey.

'Three days,' Gudrun confirmed with a nod. 'I'll tend him as he needs. After the third night, he'll be strong enough to travel.'

Sihtric stood dumbfounded for a moment while the healer shook bits of bark and leaf into her small bowl. He found his voice. 'You'll be paid well,' he agreed.

She held out her hand and wiggled her fingers for coins. 'The rest when you return,' she ordered and dismissed him from her house. 'And, you,' she turned to me, 'be wanting muggi, am I right?' Her stone-grey eyes assessed me with a coolness that crept down my spine.

I swallowed my discomfort. 'That and clove, if you have it.'

'Clove is expensive,' she mused, blinking her eyes against the hearth fire smoke. Her gaze fell on my scar, and she sucked on her teeth.

'I'll need more ointment for my face, too.'

Gudrun approached, moving aside a lock of my fair hair, and sniffed the wound. 'Easy enough,' she said and turned away. 'Clove for a toothache, girl? Or are you wanting to warm your body for a babe?'

My hands held the bowl she'd proffered, crushing the green leaves within into a lumpy paste.

'No,' she growled. 'Not for a baby. Not if you're also wanting muggi.'

I stopped pounding with the pestle. 'Do you need to know what it's for?'

She considered me for a moment. 'Which one of them is your husband?' she asked. 'Is it the ailing brute? Worth saving, is he?'

I almost laughed in reply.

'If he's beating you, I could make him sleep a long, long time.'

My mouth slackened and fell a little open. 'No, the herbs are for me.'

She cackled heartily, entertained by my surprise. 'Are you minded to chance your poisoning?'

'I'm minded to have options,' I replied, recommencing my work.

'Ah,' she breathed, a sultry sound that was surprising to hear from the crone's throat. 'Not sure if you be wanting or not?'

'Something like that.'

Gudrun took the bowl from my hands and looked down at me with pity. 'That nasty scar'll be enough to stave off the husband's advances, I'd wager.'

Perhaps that was what I was afraid of. *Would Kjarr spurn me if I turned up with scars?* Men always valued fresh-faced wives, free of illness or injury. No reminders of life's harshness marked upon their youthful faces.

'Will it fade?' I worried.

She pursed her lips as she ground the pestle into the bowl a final time. 'In time,' she answered. 'The gods have marked you now, girl. Though favour you still, they do.'

That last part surprised me. It was not uncommon for healing women to practise *seidr*, the ancient magic, but her manner took me as practical rather than mystical. I glanced over at Eskil. Whatever ailed him and whatever treatment he received, be it worldly or otherwise, he needed. I was not about to argue.

'Make an offering to Eir,' the healer suggested as she scraped out the mortar.

'To Eir?'

'She'll bring you succour from her hill of healing,' she promised. 'Though your face will never be unmarked, she will calm the worst of it.' Gudrun pressed her palm against my scar and muttered some words in a low voice I could not discern. 'In time, you will know. He will welcome you when you have decided.' Her eyes dipped to the Valkyrie pendant around my neck.

She spoke in riddles.

'Who will welcome me?' I asked.

For an answer, she pushed the herbs I'd requested into small linen bags and pressed them into my hand. 'Three days,' she repeated, pushing me out the door. 'Tell your men to return with the silver, then you can have the brute at full health.'

I pushed the leather curtain to one side, stealing a last look at Eskil. 'What will you do to him?' I asked, a little too late.

She wagged her finger. 'Better you not know how it's done, just that it's done right. Worry about the things you need to worry about,' Gudrun uttered, disappearing behind the door cover. 'Go, now. Go to Eir.'

'I will,' I promised.

'And return in three days,' she muttered from behind the shroud. 'With silver,' she added, shouting the words as I walked away.

The men had disappeared. Either too frightened of Gudrun, or too eager to explore what Gnezdovo could offer them. I recalled the wharf-man mentioning the Stinkhorn for lodgings, and made my way there, finding Sven seated alone at a table outside.

'Ale?' he asked, raising a cup to me.

I threw my leg over the bench and sat. 'Just the one. Then we have things to do.'

He flagged down the serving girl and tapped his cup down for a refill. 'We've got rooms out back for the lot of us for the next three nights. Two of the crew will need to stay with the *Bhobain*, but Sihtric said we would take it in turns, and tonight it's Frodi and Björn.'

'And where are they now?' I asked as I tucked away the herbs Gudrun had given me into a leather pouch.

Sven slapped the table and laughed. 'Getting to know the Stinkhorn's ugliest whores, I imagine.'

'Did anyone have a look at the Rusty Hauberk just to compare?'

The serving girl returned with a pitcher and filled two cups for us before slinking away. 'Sure did, especially after Sihtric found out the Stinkhorn is owned by the wharf-man's brother in marriage. He was right, though; this is the better establishment.'

I gulped a mouthful of the ale, bright and flavoured with pine spiciness. 'What's wrong with the other place?'

Sven's eyes widened. 'Full of men like Gunnar,' he mumbled, keeping his voice low as he refilled my horn mug.

'Is that so?'

'And slavers, too. Out the back of the place, they have pens for the poor thralls instead of stables. I'd reckon the horses are kept in better conditions,' he complained, shaking his head. Sven ran his hand through his dusty blonde hair and tucked it behind his ear, showing the edge of his ink markings that ended there. 'It'll be cramped accommodations here. We could only get two rooms, four of us in each. Not sure who is with who yet.'

I shrugged. I'd just spent the last weeks with the lot of them and I didn't mind who I roomed with, as long as it wasn't Gunnar. 'As long as I have somewhere to sleep that isn't rocking, or smelling like river water, I'm content. Anyway, I've got to see the blacksmith,' I began. 'And I promised Gunnar new chains for Odrun. While I'm there, I'll see if the *smedr* can do anything about Skara.' My heart sank at the thought of losing my axe.

'Do you want me to come with you?' he asked, rising from the seat.

I stilled him with my hand. 'This I need to do by myself.'

# Ten

Blacksmithing was dirty, hard, but skilful work. It took many years to learn and much longer to master. A good smith was worth their weight in any metal, and Gnezdovo had a well-renowned *smedr* by the name of Volundr the Norse.

Burly and hunched as blacksmiths often were, Volundr spent his days bent over his creations, toiling away in the heat. Sweat dripped off his bushy eyebrows above eyes of piercing blue, and he set his mouth in a thin line without expression. Tall and broad as any mountain, he protected himself from burns by wearing a long apron of thick leather. His hands, however, bore several scorch marks healed over, but were still pink against his swarthy complexion.

As I presented Skara for his inspection, he took one look and grunted, 'She's done, *Kona*.' He ran his soot-stained thumb along the edge. 'That blade is compromised. You'll need a new one,' he advised, not unkindly as he strode to the wall to take a plain-looking weapon from the display. 'One like this will take naught but a day. You can pay half now and collect tomorrow.'

Volundr motioned for a boy, likely his son by the youth's resemblance to the smith, to keep pumping at the bellows.

'Hurry up,' he rushed the boy gruffly until the coals glowed red and the forge smoked again.

The smell inside the stall was all-consuming. An aroma like rotting eggs wafted through the air, mixing with the metallic scent of iron and scorched wood. It was dark, dusty, and hot. Not somewhere I would want to spend my entire day, especially if I valued my ability to hear anything come evening time.

I bit my lip. Volundr's evaluation was what I'd been afraid of. Parting with Skara was like a knife to the gut, but replacing the gift from my father with a paltry weapon was all the worse. 'I'm looking for something special.'

Volundr shot me a look over his shoulder, brows raised, and a smile that lit up his entire face, changing his features entirely. He took a cloth from the stool and patted it against his forehead, and waved at his son to continue before speaking, 'All right. But something special won't be cheap.' His smile had turned to an outright grin, creases forming at the corners of his eyes. I'd piqued his interest.

I took a step further into his stall. 'I've heard you're good,' I began with flattery, 'skilled with inlay. Men say you can craft an axe blade so sharp it'll cut the wind.'

'It's by the gods' hands that I have such a skill,' he mumbled his humble response. 'And I'll make it so by your silver.'

My hand patted a pouch on my belt. 'You will have it,' I agreed. Skara lay on the levelled tree stump between us. I pushed her towards the smith and explained my hopes for the new design. 'So, you understand what I need?' I asked.

He nodded, gnarled hands taking my weapon into his keeping. 'You won't know her when you return.'

I slumped onto the stool as I counted out some coins. 'How long?' I asked, stacking the silver dirhams on the now bare slab of wood.

Volundr picked up an enormous hammer. 'A week,' he grunted as he smashed it down on the iron he held with tongs.

'I don't have a week to wait.'

He didn't cease his work, just threw a chuckle across the room and said, 'Then you'll need more silver. I'm always busy, but I'd rather spend my time making the greatest of weapons,' he explained as he glanced at my tower of coins. 'Just bring the silver,' he said, voice deep and saying more than the mere words he spoke. His eyes bore into me, and I felt a strong sinking feeling as the realisation came to me.

Not just any silver. I must bring *the* silver I wanted my new axe to be imbued with.

I left the coins where they were, adding more to the top as he said I should. It was half the agreed amount. The total would be a sizeable dent in the funds I'd brought from Aldeigjuborg, but I could manage it thanks to the success of my sail manufacturing and cloth business.

*Three days*, Volundr said it could be done. It was enough to get my new axe, retrieve a hopefully repaired Eskil, and resume our journey to Kyiv. Yet, I still needed to get Egbert parchment, and help Odrun with the plan she refused to explain to me. Much to accomplish in precious little time. If this was the gods toying with me, I wished them well entertained as I danced in time to the music they played. They alone knew if it ended in my demise or victory. And if what Gudrun the Grey had said was true, and the gods favoured me still, perhaps everything would turn out in the end. In the meantime, with Skara absent from my belt, I felt unarmed even though my seax hung around my waist. As I strode back to the Stinkhorn tavern to rue on his words, *just bring the silver*, I understood it had to be significant. It had to be the worthiest of offerings, not just the finest of silver.

I almost heard the gods laughing from Asgard as I realised what they demanded of me.

I had been tasked with fetching food items for the last leg of our journey. Sven had gone, charged with procuring more ale and foodstuff, and hopefully, our gains united would be enough for the crew. There was always fishing, hunting, and foraging along the way, but that would not be certain. Best if we could fill our barrels and not rely on the unfriendly lands to come. From Gnezdovo, we would follow the Dnieper all the way to Kyiv. Though we had made it to the halfway point by distance, the lack of portages meant it would be the faster of the halves. The small rapids to come, however, would keep us ever alert as would the lack of safe harbour, which the further we travelled was less assured. Now that Kyiv had been taken by Grand Prince Oleg, he would begin creating outposts along the river route to keep it secure, but that would take time. It was best to gather supplies from this settlement because we might not have another opportunity.

The marketplace was alive with noise, vendors yelling, goods being unloaded, and animals clamouring from their pens.

'Ship's nails!' a young boy called from behind another blacksmith's stall. He had set up a small shop selling simple, forged pieces like iron eating knives, ear scoops, and tweezers. They weren't anything fancy, but for crews who might be in need and had no time to commission something better, they would do the job.

'I'll take four *dosin* of those,' I said, pointing to the iron nails.

The small boy nodded, his crop of mousy hair uncombed and unruly. He held his hand out for payment, running his thumb over the hack to make sure I had not underpaid.

'Have you seen a tall, broad merchant with sandy locks and bug-eyes wearing a red tunic? He'd be with two thralls, a woman, and a man?' I asked, searching for Gunnar, or rather Odrun and Egbert.

The blacksmith's boy looked around the marketplace. 'What's he selling?'

'Bronze trinkets,' I answered, though I wasn't exactly sure that was the only trade Gunnar engaged in.

'The metal workers are down that way,' he answered, pointing to a street lined with small huts and reeking of smoke. I thanked the boy and scooped up Sihtric's ship's nails into a cloth bag and tied it to my belt.

The crowd thinned before the lane of small shops, and it didn't take me long to find Gunnar. He was haggling with another trader over small ornaments. Odrun and Egbert stood behind him, holding open a small chest full of his wares, as Gunnar tempted the local seller into purchasing his goods.

Gunnar's voice was higher than usual, and I wondered if the other trader could hear the desperation in it as I did. 'Finely made in the metal works of Birka,' he continued, waving his hands for emphasis.

Odrun and Egbert acknowledged me with a small nod before returning their blank stares into the distance. The local merchant tugged at the hem of his neatly woven brown tunic, tied at the waist with a long brown belt that was stamped with an intricate design of knotwork.

He cleared his throat. 'Our metal works make finer stuff than these,' he grumbled, flicking over the bronze figures within the chest.

I looked at the leather scabbard at the merchant's hip, just as delicately etched as his belt. Inside, a richly handled *knifr* was adorned with brass fittings. This was a man of fine taste, that much was evident, and though Gunnar tried, he would not be fooled.

The man wearing the brown tunic proceeded. 'You can see the pouring marks on this pendant,' he scowled, pointing to the protrusion at the back of the piece. 'The workers were not quick enough to trim the joins.'

Gunnar ignored the criticism, scooping up an amber-dotted piece. 'This one has real amber,' he continued, unperturbed. 'Look, see. And, this ring.' He offered the merchant a set stone of orange-brown atop a small ring.

The other man held it aloft, letting the sun's light shine through the cloudy substance. 'Amber, you say?' he asked with an arched eyebrow. He shook his head. 'Looks more like a glass bead to me,' the merchant replied, placing it back into the box the thralls held and shut the lid, finalising their interaction. The man turned on the heel of his well-made boot and left Gunnar with a glower, taking with him the wealth Gunnar had hoped to take advantage of. We watched until the merchant vanished into another metal worker's stall with better offerings than my bug-eyed acquaintance.

I stood back while Gunnar huffed and cursed, all the while Odrun and Egbert remained still and mute.

Gunnar turned to me. His mouth crumpled in anger. 'What do you want?' he growled.

I shifted, right foot to left, before speaking, 'I need Odrun and Egbert.'

'What for?' Gunnar's eyes bulged horribly from their sockets sometimes, and they might have popped right out except he had a strange habit of squinting when he was annoyed, which was almost all the time.

'There's work going down at the tanner's, and he will pay you for it,' I replied, hoping the idea of earning something might soothe his rampant rage.

He grabbed the chest from Odrun and shoved her rudely. 'They're not for sale.'

'I didn't say they were. The tanner needs a couple of hands for three days and we're stranded here for that long, so....' I searched for my next words. 'Why don't you put them to work to make some coin?'

Odrun stared at me with disdain, but Egbert seemed almost relieved to be free of Gunnar, even if that meant he would work in the dangerous pits of the tannery.

Gunnar thought about my proposition before replying with a curt nod. He turned to address the thralls. 'Listen to Signe. Do as you're told,' he warned them. 'And if they die, I want recompense,' he said coldly. 'If you need me, I'll be at the Rusty Hauberk.'

*Of course you will,* I wanted to say, but thought better of it. *He would like it there. He might even fit in with the slavers,* but I just offered a patronising smile.

He huffed, tucking his chest under his arm, and strode off, disturbing the dusty soil as he did.

Odrun was the first to speak. 'I don't want to work at the tanner,' she complained.

I ignored her protest. If this was going to work, they both had to be compliant. 'I assume you know how parchment is made, Egbert?'

The wiry man nodded. 'From calf-skin,' he answered.

'Have you made it before?' I asked, guiding them away from the crowd where we wouldn't be overheard.

He nodded again, now looking eager rather than downtrodden. 'Many times.'

Odrun's breath caught as she followed my plan and, by the twitch at the edge of her mouth, I knew she approved.

'Good,' I said with a nod at Egbert. 'You'll be making it while we are here.'

'How can we be sure it will work?' Odrun whispered, her amber eyes looking towards the ground.

I ignored her question because I couldn't be sure it would work, but didn't want to say as much. So, I focused on what I had planned and set about explaining it. 'You'll both work on the skins for the next three days. I've paid for preparing one unblemished calf-skin, but Egbert will take it to be stripped before the rest is baited. Then you will stretch it too fine and leave it too long in the sun to suit my stated needs. Do you understand?' I asked.

Egbert swallowed hard. 'You want me to ruin it?'

'You'll make a mistake and put some holes in it,' I explained as comprehension dawned on his face. 'The master will punish you, though I've paid him for his silence. He'll still need to make the ruse look convincing.'

Egbert nodded. 'I'll make it crisp and appear repentant when discovered.' He dipped his head and when he looked up, there was a steely resolution to his eye.

'When they tell you to cut it down, only take what you need and scrap the rest. Make sure no one sees you.'

'I will be diligent,' he promised.

The scheme made me sick. 'It will be stealing. If anyone catches you, it could mean death,' I warned, bile rising in my throat. *Why did Odrun have to ask this of me?*

Odrun pinched the skin at her throat, her fingers making their way to the collar of her woollen cape.

Egbert smiled proudly, as if tasked with a heroic deed. Perhaps he was. I was not privy to their wider plans. It was always the devout believers that went into peril blindly thinking their god would keep them safe, so long as they prayed and lived a life free of the joy they called sin.

Egbert's brown eyes twinkled, more alive than I'd ever seen before.

'You understand how dangerous this is, Egbert?' I asked, concerned he'd misheard me.

'Of course,' he replied.

I shrugged. 'All right. Make sure you work hard and show Odrun what to do or she'll be whipped for incompetence. Work for your pay, even if it's going to Gunnar. Remember why you're doing this, even if I don't.'

He gritted his teeth. 'I will,' he promised, taking Odrun by the hand and patting it gently. 'Thank you, Signe. I beseech all the gods for their help, and thank them for sending you to us.'

'All the gods?'

Egbert stood tall and held my gaze. 'I care not which god guides us, so long as we succeed.'



Gnezdovo was a place that Sihtric knew well, even if it made him feel uneasy. A few seasons prior, he had been stranded there for almost a year whilst he waited for a new sail. His original one had torn coming back from trade, and being late into the travelling season, he did not have time to have another made before the weather turned, making the rivers unnavigable.

Sihtric loved being on the water. He thrived on trade, adventure, and exploration. He'd been born in lands abroad to a war-chief father and an enslaved mother and had strong opinions about both stations. As a youth, he'd boarded a merchant's ship and never looked back. Once he had established himself in the spice-trade, he travelled to the uncomfortable outer limits of the river road, and still, he wanted to push further. Sihtric dreamed of sailing unnamed lakes, following water paths that carved foreign lands into unpronounceable kingdoms, and discovering flavours that tingled the tongue and delighted the senses. It was an enthusiasm that I could understand and, in me, he found a friend he did not have to explain his restlessness to wander.

'Have you met with Chestimir's wife?' he asked when we sat down to eat at the Stinkhorn the next evening.

'I have,' I answered through a mouthful of roast pork in mustard sauce. The wharf-man had been right, the tavern keeper's wife made a delicious meal. 'This is great,' I said, spooning another helping into my mouth.

He passed a plate before me on the table. 'Try the parsnips in butter. They slide right down.'

'Mmmm,' I mumbled appreciatively. 'Yes, Chestimir's wife, Milaslava. I met with her this afternoon.'

'Mila, aye. I remember her. She mended my sail enough to get home,' he recalled. 'Are they keen?'

'They have some wool and the fat to coat them. Even the tar to paint if merchants want symbols painted. They just don't have enough of anything,' I explained, spearing a long parsnip with my knife and taking a nibble.

'That's where you come in, *bhana charaid*?'

The knife clattered onto the plate, and I leaned my elbows onto the table. 'I believe so. Björn has secured a constant flow of fleeces from the north using his network. Hilde and Helga will sort those at the workshop in Aldeigjuborg before sending them on to our southern partners.'

Before leaving for Kyiv, I had lived in Aldeigjuborg, the most northern settlement of the Rus' territories. There I had begun my work as a wool merchant, but more recently my women and I had started making ship sails. It was a need we saw that went unmet as merchants coming from the northern trading ports could not purchase new ones or had to wait for a lengthy period for their production.

'You'll send packets down south?' Sihtric asked, pulling me from my fond memories.

'Yes,' I started, picking up the knife again, 'I've agreed with Mila to have regular shipments delivered here. She'll have more than enough to maintain continual production of sails. So much so she will recruit more women to keep up with the demand.'

'Well done,' he commended me.

I took a great mouthful of pork but kept talking. 'They have their first buyer.'

'Let me guess, is it someone commissioning a new ship?' he teased.

'Folcmarr has a light, broad-hulled *knarr* on order with a deep belly for cargo. And, what do you think he has need of?' I asked, though we both knew the answer.

'A sail!' Sihtric put in. 'I saw them down at the shipyard. I'm envious.'

'Mila will use her husband's connections to get further transactions, though I'll make sure word is spread that our products will be available in both Aldeigjuborg and Gnezdovo, and hopefully in Kyiv.'

Sihtric waved the serving girl over for a jug of ale to celebrate. 'All this done from the very goodness of your *wee* heart,' he beamed.

I laughed. 'If you know anyone willing to make those deliveries for me, you'll let me know?'

He watched me for a moment as I poured ale into cups. 'For a fee, *bhana charaid*,' he jested.

Sihtric might journey with me this time, but it wouldn't always be so. He had a house in Aldeigjuborg and preferred to travel as frequently as possible, such was his adventuring soul. Every two years, he took to the rivers on either the Volkhov or Volga routes, and each time he would pass Kyiv, and almost always, Gnezdovo.

'I'm glad Kjarr didnae move back to Aldeigjuborg before his father died. If he had, he might never have met you.' Sihtric opened his mouth again to speak, but stopped. Perhaps he hadn't meant to say as much as he had already. He took a deep swig and added, 'Kjarr picked a canny one.'

As he lifted his cup to toast me, his eyes did not meet mine, and I saw the shadow of dread that passed over them.

# ELEVEN

The final evening in Gnezdovo had arrived, and the sky grew dark and moody. Grey clouds gathered thick, and the air became sticky, threatening of storms to come. Locals brought their washing in, packed their stalls, and prepared for the onslaught. Merchants and travellers alike hoped aloud that it would pass, and we might all resume our journey in the morning.

I'd spent the day as a student to Ahmed, copying letters as he wrote them in the parched soil with a long stick to take my mind off Volundr's progress with my new axe.

'You are a fast learner,' Ahmed congratulated me. 'By the time we reach Kyiv, I believe you will be competent enough to compose a short correspondence.'

'I should write to you when you return to Baghdad,' I suggested, trying again at the shapes that looked like snail shells.

He corrected my mistake, reminding me the curve pointed in the opposite direction. 'It's not prohibited,' he replied.

My mouth curved at one side as I laughed through my nose. 'That almost sounds like a yes, Ahmed,' I teased.

He closed his eyes momentarily and dipped his head. 'My daughters and I would very much like to hear of your journeys.'

We ended the lesson when Ahmed's stomach grumbled, and wanting to avoid the tavern, he left for the only food stall that remained open to sate his hunger while I wandered down to the Volundr's blacksmithing shop. His craftsmanship was unlike anything I'd seen before. Sure, I had seen a *smedr* work metal previously, hammering shapes from glowing iron and steel until they resembled axe heads, spear-shafts, or swords. What Volundr did was more than that. It was art. He'd taken the burgeoning axe head on the first day, splitting the metal in two.

Then wrapped the long piece around a pole the same size as the shaft that would be its handle. Then, he hammered the metal down, shaping it until the edge was fine and the width even around the eye. Volundr worked until the blade was sharp. To watch him was to marvel at his strength and precision. Once pleased with the shape, the smith eased it off the rod and in its place put the wooden grip. Today, Volundr had expertly etched the agreed-upon design and would place the silver he had melted and rolled into rods in the relief. Everything would fit together exactly.

Volundr's son spied me as I sheltered under the awning as a light rain fell. 'He's almost done,' the youth said. For a child not more than twelve summers, his forearms would already rival a full-grown man. He could earn a bit of change from arm wrestling at the tavern, though he might have made his way through the local men and have a reputation for it already.

The boy scooped up an order from a nearby basket. 'Chains as you requested, *Kona*,' he said, handing me the shackles I'd bought on Gunnar's behalf. Just as I had asked, Volundr had made them weak by quenching the hot metal in a way that made it brittle. He'd been paid well for the ruse, which went a long way to save the injury to his reputation.

Volundr continued working, bent low over his craft, tongue protruding between his teeth.

His boy nodded effusively. 'He'll work through the night, even if the lightning comes.'

The sun had gone now, even though night had not yet arrived. Inky clouds clumped together, as the rain thickened. Moisture filled the air so heavily one could almost swim through it, and inside the shop, it was even more stifling.

'Sometimes Pa works himself into a lather, not speaking even to me,' the boy explained. 'Frenzy of the gods, he calls it. It only happens now and then, and only when he's making something like you've requested.'

I saw the determination in the smith. His muscles were tense, jaw set hard, eyes focussing on the tiny details before him. No sound could have roused him. Even if the world were disappearing beneath his feet, he would not have gazed at it. My hand brushed my forearm where Bjarndýr, my armring, usually lay but now was bare.

Volundr's boy looked me over. 'It's silver of good quality, *Kona*. Pa said it will give the piece great power.' His voice was still high, and his face was round to match.

My eyes pricked with tears, but I hid them behind a hand that pretended to sweep away sweat at my brow. 'It was my father's,' I replied.

When Volundr asked me to bring silver, I initially thought he required additional payment. As I thought of that meaningless metal fusing with the remains of Skara, it sat uneasily, and I knew it wasn't what the smith had meant. Our gods demanded tribute not comfortably given. They required sacrifice.

Volundr had taken one look at the armring and nodded before striking the bear heads off. These he melted down to join with my new axe. My father's namesake would be part of the weapon I possessed until the end of my days. Sven tried to stop me, but even he knew the gods were not satisfied with paltry offerings, especially when what we asked of them was so much. So, I'd given half of what was most dear to me to Eir when I prayed as the healer instructed. In the grove, I'd given the goddess one part of the armring my father had worn for many years, and I for years after. On my knees, I called on her to watch over Helga, my good friend, who would soon birth her child in Aldeigjuborg, and protect me as well. As payment, she took into the earth that which I held most sacred, what hurt most to give; Bjarndýr.

The next morning, when I returned to collect the axe, I was stunned. As his son had foretold, Volundr had worked through the night, through the storm, and certainly through a frenzy. He was soaked through, eyes calming from their wild state as he gulped from a pitcher of ale. When he saw me, he hailed me inside his stall to see the new blade that shone slick after his polishing and buffing. Silver inlay sparkled against the duller iron in the knotwork shape of a bear's head where metal met wood. Its mouth was open and snarling at its enemy, who faced the sharp edge of the weapon. The design wove through itself to create the shapes, and around the animal, in delicate contrast, were four small flowers. They were the same as the yellow blooms that had decorated Freyja's sleeping cap. Most of the time, I kept it in the small leather pouch tied to my belt, a reminder of my daughter taken too soon. This weapon represented both my child and my father. As I held the metal to the morning light, I felt tears welling in my eyes. I sniffed them back.

'It's well done,' I managed. My voice was tight as I spoke.

He reached across with his great paw and took it from me. 'A pleasure to make,' he replied as he whipped her through the air to test her speed. 'She'll cleave the wind, as requested. Perfectly balanced. Just keep her clean and oiled.'

'I will,' I promised.

Volundr cradled the axe in his massive hands. 'A voice came last night while I worked,' he began, and I wondered where it would lead. 'Thunder raged through the night, but then it stilled, and a name was spoken.'

'Oh,' I said, not knowing what else to say.

His son had warned me Volundr was likely to become half-crazed through hard work, but I couldn't dismiss his words as nonsense.

'Signe, I hope you haven't decided on a name for her yet.'

I shook my head and fumbled with the pendant around my neck. 'Not yet.'

'It has already named itself Forlog-Enda,' he announced, holding her forth and aloft.

The name meant "the ender of fates, of destiny". My lip quivered as I tested the sound, 'Forlog-Enda.'

'That's what I heard,' he confirmed, releasing the ender of fates into my shaking hands.

'Usually, they're named something like Head-Cleaver, or Skull-Splitter,' I rambled.

Volundr silenced me with a shake of his head. 'The Norns have spoken, and we must listen.'

# TWELVE

When my father gifted me Skara, I felt elated. Never had I owned a weapon, always borrowing or making do with what I found. Though she hadn't been much to look at, Skara had been my rough weapon that did the job she was created to do. With Forlog-Enda's forging, I owned one that others knew at once was of great worth. I had an axe to be proud of.

'Thor's might!' Sven exclaimed as he examined Forlog-Enda for the umpteenth time as we sat at one of the Stinkhorn's tables. 'It's beautiful.' He turned the blade over in his hands, running his thumb over the silver inlay of my bear's head.

'She's the kind of thing a warrior dreams about,' Thorsten agreed though, by his own admission, he was not one of them. 'Or the kind a skald would sing for,' he added as his tentative hand reached forward to stroke the shining metal. 'This is Volundr's work?'

'Who else?' I replied with a nod as Thorsten glanced towards me, a request to hold the axe.

He held her with the reverence of a fellow craftsman. 'Volundr's craft is legendary. I wish I could have seen him work.'

I took Forlog-Enda into my keeping. 'You should have said. I'm sure he would have been glad of the company.'

Sven thumped the shorter man on the back, ruffling his flaming hair. 'You've been too busy with your trade,' he pointed out.

Thorsten rifled through his pack and produced a few combs from it. 'Take a look, Signe. I've made all these from the antlers I purchased in Holmgardr.'

My fingers trailed along the lines he etched into each one, designs swirling into animal heads. 'Fine work, Thorsten,' I congratulated him.

'These are good enough for around here. But when we get to Kyiv, I'll wait for inspiration to come from the forests and animals. Then I'll sell them to the fancy folk within the city,' he explained, his youthful face creasing with excitement. 'None'll be as lofty work as your weapon, though, Signe.'

The men had been gushing over Forlog-Enda all morning. We took it as a welcome reprieve from worrying about Eskil's state. This morning, we would leave with the favourable winds, but first, we had to collect the big man from Gudrun the Grey's hovel on the far western side of Gnezdovo. And they all seemed nervous about it.

Sven shielded his eyes against the sun with his hand, looking towards Gudrun's place. Gnezdovo's inhabitants were busy watering and weeding, tending to their crops and leading animals out to pasture. Further to the west, the outline of Olsha watchtower was just visible as it looked over the river in both directions. I could easily understand why people travelling through here stayed. It was like Aldeigjuborg, but in its ascendancy. The prime position of the settlement, fertile lands, and mix of industry that drew many to its shores made it a profitable location for almost all who lived within. It might have been somewhere I would have chosen, but my fate was not to be a merchant of Gnezdovo, just as I had been in Aldeigjuborg.

Sven interrupted my musings by speaking, his voice too loud in the peaceful quiet. 'Do you think Eskil will be mended by now?'

'Either that or Gudrun will have disappeared. Isn't that how the stories of the *seidr* witches go?' I replied with a wicked grin.

Sven shuddered, recalling the tales we'd repeated as children. 'That woman scares me.'

'Me too,' I admitted. Perhaps that was part of her strategy, to scare people enough that they left her alone. Maybe I should admire her.

Gudrun's home looked no different from the way it had days before. Smoke issued from a small hole in the roof, the leather curtain still drawn against the outside world. Sihtric, Kari, Björn, Gunnar, and Thorsten crowded outside the small house.

'Everyone here?' Sihtric asked, rubbing the back of his neck.

Sven glanced around, counting heads. 'Everybody except Ahmed and Frodi. They were down at the *Bhobain* last I saw.'

'They still are,' Björn confirmed. He'd been there too, but his curiosity over Gudrun's magic had got the better of him and he came along to see if the crone had been successful. 'Someone's gotta watch those thralls,' he continued. 'Odrun's been howling like a starving barn cat since you snapped her back into chains.'

Gunnar's lips quirked. He'd enjoyed every moment of pulling Odrun to the ground, her head between his knees as he closed the manacle around her neck and locked it, threatening her with one last chance to please him before he sold her in the markets of Kyiv. For his part, Egbert had wasted the skins just as I instructed him to do, and he cowed most convincingly whilst apologising for his error. After being punished by the tanner, I congratulated him for the well-managed deceit.

'I know not which god led my hand,' Egbert had whispered, 'but it was the lightning that helped our cause.'

'That'll be Thor,' I murmured back and Egbert's eyes shone for a moment, a shadow of the man he had been before Eskil had renamed him Toki the slave.

Egbert didn't dismiss the attribution of victory to my gods, he didn't mention his own. He grinned broadly. A man buoyed by hope found among the nettles, too long forgotten.

Gunnar stopped complaining when Egbert handed him the payment from the tanner and, as he weighed the bag of vittles in his hands, he was more cheery than I'd ever seen him. His business dealings must have been poor if he delighted in bread, cheese, and mealy apples.

Gunnar's smile had worn off as the crew milled outside Gudrun's hovel. 'I don't want to go in,' he said in a gruff voice that barely covered his discomfort.

Thorsten kicked his shoe through the loose dirt. 'Nor I,' he added.

'Scared of an old crone?' I teased the men, walking towards the doorway and rapping my fist against the wall.

A man's hand brushed aside the leather curtain, and I was surprised to see Eskil standing before me, the colour of his face even and healthy. 'Just saying my goodbyes,' he mumbled, turning into the damp and dark interior.

'Was that him?' I heard Gunnar ask the men behind me, but heard no answer. Only I was close enough to see inside and what I saw there was not what I expected. A young woman with a round and pretty face smiled up at Eskil as he kissed both her cheeks. She pressed her body to his and whispered into his ear. In reply, he stroked her cheek before kissing her fulsomely on the mouth. Eskil bid her farewell and, walking out the door, passed me without so much as a greeting. Our crew waited no longer than it took Eskil to join their ranks and set off down the path, leaving me alone and dumbfounded, standing in the doorway.

The girl walked into the light streaming through the threshold and held out her smooth hand. 'Silver,' she croaked in a voice much older than the years lining her face.

I dropped pieces into her open palm. She counted them and flashed a brilliant smile, straight, uncoloured teeth behind her full lips.

My hand slipped beneath the neckline of my *serkr* and felt for my Valkyrie pendant. 'What did you do to him?' I asked curiously rather than accusingly.

She tilted her fair head, hair unbound like a maid, and fluttered her large round eyes. 'The brute got what he needed to heal and I have what I need to continue in this life,' she answered enigmatically. 'I did not forget about you, girl.' From the darkness, she brought forth a small pot.

I recoiled, fearing her power. A cackle bubbled from her.

'The ointment you require,' she clarified, placing the container in my hand and closing my fingers around it. Her hand held mine, eyes meeting one another's in an uncomfortable lock. 'Eir hears your pleas. She hears and she answers.'

A quick shuffle. Her body lurched forward and held me close, one hand on my lower back, the other pressed firm against the flesh of my stomach. Her voice rasped out of her unwrinkled throat, 'A womb remains barren until it serves the worthy, girl. Only when the Queen of Cities is home will life grow.'

I tried to pull from her embrace, but she was strong.

*What do I care if my womb remains empty?* I wanted to ask, but couldn't make a sound. Even if I could have spoken, it would have been a lie. I knew Freyja had left a void in me that might only be lessened by a child of my own. The witch's words frightened me, sending shivers down my spine as I writhed in her arms.

'Let me go,' I finally managed, voice strangled.

The round-faced girl released me, watching me with half-closed eyes as I staggered back. Her lips parted as she repeated, 'Only when the Queen of Cities is home will life grow.'

What her prophecy meant, I did not know, but I didn't fight the urge to flee. And I ran fast as if chased by her prescient words.

# THIRTEEN

'Not yet,' Odrun hissed at me under low-hanging branches full of glossy green leaves. Her eyes followed as I stooped to gather kindling into my arms. 'I will tell you when it's time.'

I glanced over my shoulder, making sure we were on our own. We often gathered firewood to facilitate these covert conversations. Sometimes Egbert joined us, though, since Eskil's recovery, Egbert found it harder to get away. Today, Odrun and I had to walk quite a distance to find enough fodder to feed our meal-fire.

'You may not have much left,' I warned her. There were only two more days until we arrived in Kyiv and once there, access to both her and Egbert would be more difficult. 'Gunnar swears he will sell you at the slave markets of Kyiv,' I reminded her.

Weeks had passed on the Dnieper as we wound our way towards the newly captured capital of the Rus' territories. Some days we had the company of other vessels, sharing stories and food for a time. Even Ahmed had been in good spirits, I realised his comment about the "shrill and jaunty" nature of our music might have been accurate when I heard Thorsten join another passing merchant in a trilling song of bone flutes. My ears still rung with the high-pitched notes.

The traveller from Baghdad's mood was all the more improved when I began to master entire sentences of his language. I now had enough of the tongue to understand basic phrases and, at times, Ahmed and I spoke Arabic together. Still, I feared, I was little better at it than a babbling youngster. Writing was something else. I loved the way the script curved, the lines, the dots, they almost appeared as pictures. Symbols that conjured words that anyone familiar with the language could read.

'If you write to me when I am returned to Baghdad, you shall not lose your knowledge,' Ahmed said one morning after we concluded yet another discussion of the importance of books.

'Even if it's the same repetitive questions, the same few phrases I've been able to accomplish?' I asked.

'Even then,' he agreed, running his fingers, nails clipped and clean, through his wiry beard. 'My girls would find it entertaining.'

I did not know if it was my tales they would find amusing or my poor attempt at their language. And, as I met Ahmed's eyes, his purposely expressionless face betrayed no hint of meaning. His humour was quiet, never bawdy, and I enjoyed these bouts of quips. Sometimes Ahmed left me ink to practise but never unused parchment, just as I had expected. I was glad I hadn't had to steal from the traveller. Egbert had gathered what they needed from Gnezdovo and, with Ahmed's unattended pot of ink, he penned his mysterious letter. Whether Ahmed ever knew about the deception, he never let on, but he was gone just long enough that Egbert had time to scrawl his words. Once completed, it was my job to keep it safe until a trustworthy messenger could be found. But not before Odrun told me its destination. Her tight-lipped approach to the scheme had me losing patience.

As we collected the last few branches, she tossed her golden-brown tresses and fastened her wadmal cape back around her neck. 'It's all in hand,' she replied when I had asked again for the intended target for the missive.

I drew in a sharp breath. 'Is there anything you would like to tell me?'

Where she got the confidence from, I didn't know, but she hadn't surprised me when she'd advised, 'I wasn't born a slave.' That much was obvious.

Her straight nose pointed upwards as she looked at the sky. 'You're going to buy me from Gunnar,' she announced, breaking a withering arm from a dry tree.

I stared at her, open-mouthed.

'Not these. They're too green,' she mumbled, flinging the twigs into the undergrowth.

'Odrun, you know how I feel about keeping slaves,' I managed when I found my voice.

She shrugged. 'If you ask your husband, I'm sure he will agree.'

'That's not the point. I don't want to own anyone,' I replied, arms heavy with wood.

She picked her way through the leaf litter of the forest-floor. 'If my plan works, you won't have to *own* me for long,' she promised. Her tone changed then, softer and more appealing than before. 'Signe,' she started, looking at me with hurt behind her amber eyes, 'I swear if you do this you will be rewarded.'

'You're demanding too much.' I shook my head and kicked at a rock. We both knew if Gunnar sold her in Kyiv, she would have little chance of success.

'I'm asking you to trust me,' she replied.

'When you won't trust me,' I argued. A bird tweeted above us, voicing its arguments.

She bit her lip and turned her face away. 'I want to,' she began, her voice hitching at the words. 'All will be revealed once the letter is delivered. Once a reply comes, I will tell you all. I promise.' She stooped and grabbed a fat log.

'How long will that take?' I asked, eyes wide as I shook my head.

Odrun grunted under the weight in her arms. 'If all goes to plan, we should have a response by your pagan Jol.'

'Odin's beard. By Jol? Odrun, you're mad!' I exclaimed. *Not mad,* I amended my thoughts, *determined, crazed, desperate. Every one of those descriptions fit.* If the reply wasn't expected until winter, this was a letter set to travel some distance. *What land might that be?* 'Until then, I am to keep you in my household? As what? A servant?'

Her bottom lip jutted out as she shrugged. 'A servant, all right. But I warn you, I'll not be a very good one.'

An exasperated laugh escaped me. 'I expect not! Do you even have any experience with it?'

She glared at me through her fair lashes. Odrun didn't need to answer. Her response was straightforward enough.

'You'll have to at least pretend to try until your reply comes,' I explained as we began walking back to camp. I looked at her next to me, arms full of logs and branches. 'How much will you cost me, I wonder?'

Her hair whipped about her face, and without a free hand to tuck it behind her ear, she made do with her shoulder. 'We would need a place for Egbert, too.' She pushed her long golden locks out of the way.

I swallowed hard. If whatever plan she had was going to work, they both needed to be kept safe. 'If it is possible,' I began, 'I'll bring you both into my household.'

Kjarr would welcome into his house a damaged wife, who was immediately demanding things. I could only hope he was amenable, and that I was not making a monumental mistake by accepting the danger lurking in Odrun's shadow.

Down by the shoreline, I loitered. Everyone else was unpacking what we needed for the last night on dry land before we came into Kyiv. Odrun and I had gathered firewood earlier in the day and now it was time to give thanks to the gods for our journey, for Eskil's recovery, and for a smooth onward path. The men still bickered about the offerings each would take and which were more important. Wanting no part of the tedious argument, I left them to it and wandered towards the still water of the river, trying to catch my reflection on its surface. I had no polished metal to gaze into, no way of seeing how well my scar healed unless I was prepared to trust the laced words of my comrades. They were almost as bad as the placating comments of Sven, who considered such a wound an attribute rather than unsightly.

Someone stepped behind me, shore crunching underfoot. '*Bhana charaid,*' Sihtric mumbled as he eased onto the rocks beside me. 'Still trying to see your scar?' he asked, taking off his shoes to dip his toes into the cool water.

I drew some strands of hair over my eye, attempting to hide the mark. 'It would be better if I could see it myself.'

'It's nae so unsightly,' he replied. 'If you're worried about Kjarr, he will say naught. He'll be so happy you've returned to him, he willnae even notice it.'

'The ointment has done its work then,' I joked, a light laugh to cover my awkwardness.

'As the healer said, it'll always be a *wee* bit pink, but it's nae bad. Pity's luck it's on your face though.' Easy enough for him to say. His own face was unscarred by illness or injury. Fair and handsome as ever, eyes as green as the lichen that grows on tree-bark, russet hair with a healthy shine that combed or tussled appeared well cared for. Both men and women looked at Sihtric and saw his charm. When they looked at me, they saw my scar.

'It's not like I can do anything about it,' I complained, 'but I wish I could forget and pretend it never happened.'

Sihtric gestured behind us, towards the camp. 'That's what most of them do,' he agreed. 'Eskil will make light of that horse's kick, spin the tale so he's some glorious hero. It's what they do. We all bear the marks of our past, *bhana charaid*. It's only a disfigurement if you make it so,' he added softly as he stood and waded into the water until it reached his shins. Sihtric stopped to roll up his trousers.

My fingers traced the line where the damage had rutted the skin, a long line from my eye to my temple. Sven told me it was pale now, not the angry red of infection, nor black and blue from bruises. Just new skin, knitting back together, covering the wounds of war.

'Be careful when we get to Kyiv, *bhana charaid*,' Sihtric warned, auburn hair glimmering under the afternoon sun as he skimmed a stone on the river's surface.

I stood and walked towards my friend, squatting beside him, the hem of my dress soaked in an instant. 'Why, Sihtric?' I asked, throwing my stone, but instead of skipping along the surface, it plonked into the river's depths.

'It's nae like Aldeigjuborg. The court of a grand prince breeds a different sort. People like that do dangerous things when they're close to a throne.'

I rubbed my arms even though the air was warm. 'Not that I have to worry about that,' I replied with a laugh. 'Neither Kjarr nor I would be interested in that sort of power. We wouldn't even want to set foot in a court.' Another rock fell out of my hands. This time I didn't bother throwing it, just dropped it and watched the swirl of rising bubbles as the pebble fell to the sandy bottom.

He took a deep breath before speaking. 'I would tell you something, but I swore not to.'

'Swear what?' I asked, dragging my eyes away from the rippling surface.

Sihtric trudged backwards. 'To tell you naught,' he replied. 'It's an oath that cannae be broken without the gods' displeasure, but I willnae have you go in blind.'

I stared, waiting for him to say more.

'Keep close the people you trust,' he whispered, picking up another flat stone, 'mistrust all those you dinnae ken.'

I said nothing as he cast the rock out again, skipping three times before sinking. 'What are you saying, Sihtric? Is Kjarr in trouble?'

'I cannae say. Promise me, *bhana charaid*. Keep Sven close, you might have need of him. Keep watchful.' He stooped low and gathered up a handful of small stones.

'My eyes will be open,' I swore.

'And watchful,' he added, throwing all the stones into the water at once. So many rained down that, for a moment, the river looked like a bubbling firepot.

I nodded. 'Open and seeing. I promise.'

Then I saw the large rock he held in his hands. Only once the river's fury had calmed did he throw that one too and when he did, a wave formed, racing in to drench us both. 'Dinnae get distracted, *bhana charaid*. Eyes open, always.'

# FOURTEEN

In the cool afternoon, Sihtric led us to a rise away from our camp, past a long-overgrown field devoid of trees, to a small copse where we would make our pleas to the gods. Inside the dark space, stoic faces emerged from the towering trunks. Fine carvings etched into pillars of wood. They might have been any of the gods with two eyes, certainly not the one-eyed god Odin. Each had a strong nose, open mouth, and nothing else to identify them from any other, not that it mattered to us.

'Those who came before us put them here for travellers on their way to and from Kyiv,' Sihtric explained as he parted leafy barricades for the rest of us to step through.

'There is much to thank the gods for,' Thorsten added, producing one of his finely finished bone combs and a wild fowl, dispatched from the clutch of animals we'd caught earlier in the afternoon.

Each of us would lay or kneel before the god's likenesses and give forth our offerings.

Sihtric began. 'With me, I bring these gifts,' he said, loud and clear. At the foot of the effigy, he placed a jar of mead and a handful of salt. 'Upon entering Kyiv, deliver to me a merchant who'll buy all my goods with nae argument. Fill my pouch with coin, the chests with good trade, and my heart with gladness.' Sihtric's hand brushed the salt into the soil while he muttered into the grass, then he lifted himself and moved aside for Eskil, who stumbled onto his knees.

'Urgh, I've got some onions and some leeks,' he started. The allium's dry skin crinkled as it rocked back and forward on the ground, the scent reminding me of the broth that bubbled over Gudrun's hearth.

'A fine gift, Eskil,' Sihtric said, patting the man on the shoulder.

Eskil mussed his tawny hair. 'Two onions,' he corrected himself, pulling the other from his pouch and leaving the vegetables on the ground. Sweat ran from his neck down his back as he spoke. 'Thanks to Eir for healing me. She sent Gudrun the Grey to cure my malady, and my, um, guts, thank you,' he finished.

From behind him, Gunnar covered his laugh with a cough.

Eskil grimaced, but continued. 'I give this in thanks. So that I may find a new bloody lord to serve and ask the gods for an easier onward journey to the Great City,' he added, before making way for Gunnar.

The merchant cleared his throat and doffed his brown cap. 'Great and glorious gods,' he declared, raising his voice so it might be heard by all. From his tone, I wondered if he counted himself amongst the Aesir. 'Blessings may you bestow upon my trade. Send me a buyer with a fat purse and an empty head. May they see Valhalla in my trinket chest,' he wished.

Frodi and Björn sniggered behind their hands, and Gunnar shot them a reproachful glare.

Gunnar threw one of his inferior baubles on the ground before the god, already broken and unsaleable. He turned to the still sneering ship's men. 'Let's see what you're wanting then,' he taunted, curling his lip.

The two seamen approached the effigy together. 'Simple,' Björn began. They coughed once before speaking. 'Ran and Njord, we thank you for guiding us this far. May your blessings be upon us still a while longer,' they finished in unison.

'That's it?' Gunnar demanded.

For a gift, Björn delivered a tooth. 'What?' he scowled at Gunnar. 'Did you think they just fell out?' he asked. 'One for every safe passing of those rapids and portages. Gotta be worth something for the gods to listen, Gunnar,' he chastised, smiling through the additional gap in his grin.

Frodi held a wrapped package. 'Short and sweet, always the same. That way, the gods know what to expect of us,' he answered, laying it down and peeling back the layers. Inside, a bronze brooch with an amber set in the middle.

My mouth fell open. It was a fine ornament, one I would never have expected to fall into Frodi's possession, and it showed the esteem in which they held the will of the gods.

'Who's next?' Frodi asked, looking around.

Thorsten approached, giving thanks for his talent as a bone craftsman. He turned to Sihtric with a frown. 'I already laid my offering,' he worried. A comb made of the antler he purchased in Holmgardr.

'It'll be fine, Thorsten,' Sihtric said, watching the man with his arms folded over his chest, leaning against a trunk.

Thorsten nodded and muttered to himself, touching a hand to the antler comb sitting in the dirt. He picked it up, and with a thin piece of cord, tied it to an outstretched branch, leaving it to dangle in the breeze. 'Pray the gods find my work of good quality. Help me hone my craft in Kyiv. And,' he lowered his voice before he finished, 'send me a woman with fire in her blood to warm my bed.'

His addition garnered roaring approval from our gathered group and, as Thorsten returned to the crew, Eskil thumped him on the back while Frodi messed with his red-blonde hair.

Sven stepped forward next with a jumble of praise for Ran and her beauty, asking to be guided towards a new lord to serve just as Eskil had. He had nothing much to offer, save for his portion of morning bread, which he'd saved for the purpose.

Of course, Odrun, and Ahmed abstained from the ritual not least because they did not share our belief, but because someone needed to remain with the *Bhobain*. Egbert, however, came. Though he made no offering, he stood close to the towering sculpture, eyes wide, mouth parted with wordless wonder.

Once Sven was done, it was my turn. I was sure they expected me to ask for the healing of my face, but I knew that request to be futile though I would not spurn the gods for it. 'Eir, thank you for your healing. And Meili, for your protection on our travels.' I glanced over my shoulder.

Gunnar was bored and was poking the ground with a stick, but most of our group were still paying attention.

I steeled myself with a deep breath. 'Norns, I beseech you! If it is possible to reach you, weavers of fate.'

A sharp intake of breath behind me. No one prayed to the Norns.

'Still your shears on the thread of my life. Where you lead me, I will follow should it be true.'

'You cannot call upon the sisters of fate,' Sven whispered in panic. His eyes were wide as he tugged at the neck of his tunic. 'Do you want to be cursed?'

'Why? Don't tell me not to do something just because someone once told you not to.'

He said nothing in reply.

'Why else would Volundr have said the gods named my axe Forlog-Enda?' I turned back to the figure, standing to tie my offering to the tree; a portion of the metal from my previous axe, Skara. Volundr had made it into a rod, so I might do this now. 'Deliver me to my destiny. Show me the way of the worthy,' I finished, letting go of the iron rod. It spun on its rope, twisting this way and that. By the time I turned around, the men were backing away except Egbert, who glanced at me with a blank face.

Sven shot me a look of disbelief as he shook his head.

'If you don't ask, you'll never know,' I muttered to myself.

'What was that?' Egbert asked as he walked next to me. We were now far behind the others. They'd cleared the field and must have scampered back to the safety of their campfire, sure to ward off the bad luck they thought I'd called upon myself.

'They think I'm crazy for praying to the Norns,' I answered him.

'You don't usually pray to them?' He looked at me with his intense mud-brown eyes, full of genuine interest. 'Why?'

'I don't actually know why,' I replied truthfully. 'Some people think our fate to be fixed, that it's not possible to change. To request it of the Norns is to attempt to move the inevitable.'

He nodded thoughtfully. 'You don't believe that?'

'How could I?' I shook my head. 'If the Norns are so offended by my asking, they will make it known. I suppose that's what they're afraid of.' My hand waved toward our camp and we slowed our stride.

Egbert struggled in the long grass, lifting his overlong tunic. 'Are they afraid of Eir?' he questioned further. 'I heard both you and Eskil praying to her. That's your goddess of health and healing, isn't it?'

I chewed on my bottom lip and narrowed my eyes. 'Mm-hmm,' I agreed.

'And Thor is the god of war?'

'Not exactly,' I tried to explain, but Egbert had already gone on.

'Thunder and storms,' he corrected himself. 'His father is Odin, and his mother is…' he paused, searching for the name.

I rubbed my unscarred temple. 'Jord.'

Egbert leapt over a fallen log and looked back. 'The earth goddess?'

'More or less,' I agreed as I sped up to match his pace.

'You have a god for just about everything,' he replied breathlessly, his dark hair falling into his eyes. He brushed it back.

'What I've never understood about Christians is how they expect one god to be responsible for so much,' I detailed as we started the decline. I scratched my scar. *Itchy wounds were healing wounds*, or so they said.

He pinched the point of his chin between forefinger and thumb. 'How do you remember them all?'

I blinked. 'How do you remember the names of the trees, the flowers, the seasons? Do they not all have names? Yet, you remember this with ease,' I explained, pulling a small yellow flower from her stalk as we passed through more long grass.

He nodded sagely. 'Well said,' he agreed. 'I would learn them all in time.' His face was still a little rounded, but there was a powerful jaw there hidden beneath. Now, that jaw set as he looked ahead.

'You wish to know our gods?' I asked cautiously. 'Why? Are you making notes for Odrun's grand scheme?'

His head drew back, and his eyebrows raised. 'Your gods have brought us much luck on the riverway and they should be honoured.'

I couldn't tell if he was lying, but something about the wiry man told me he wasn't in the habit of telling lies. 'What of your own god?' I wondered.

He snorted then, open derision as he turned his palms towards the sky. 'God? Sometimes I think he forsook me on the banks of the Meuse.'

I stopped him with my hand and directed him to sit with me on the hill. We were too close to the camp to continue our discussion unless we rested for a while. 'Is that where you're from? This Meuse place?'

He sat beside me and tore at a clump of leaves that protruded from the earth, splitting their lengths one by one. 'It's a river. I was raised in Aldeneik, given into the church as a child.'

'After your parents died?' I searched for meaning in his expression.

He looked at the ground, discarding the fragments of green into the straw-coloured overgrowth, and shook his head. 'At two summers old, they gave me to God for the riches they had received in their lives,' he seethed, and his shoulders stiffened.

'I take it you did not enjoy the experience?'

'You could say that,' he agreed, meeting my curious stare. 'I was sent to a monastery belonging to the Benedictines.'

I stared blankly at him and tilted my head. The word meant nothing to me.

'The Black Monks,' he clarified, as if it made more sense, 'that's what they call themselves.'

My lips twisted as my mind teamed with questions. 'You're not a priest, then?' Not that I had the barest notion of what difference there was between a monk and a priest if there was one.

'A priest? No!' he gasped. 'I'm what they called a lay brother. Nothing. Someone they could boss around, not much more than a slave except in the monastery there was at least the pretence of freedom. Oh, and a garden. I miss the garden.' His eyes glazed over as he looked into the distance, no doubt recalling his time spent there.

'Odrun has asked me to take you into my household when we arrive in Kyiv,' I informed him.

He was jolted from his memories. 'Did she?' he responded and surprised me by grinning.

'Unless you would prefer to continue serving Eskil?'

'I'm no soldier's man. I know nothing about weapons, women, or war and no desire to learn.' He dropped the last of the weeds into the grass.

'What would I do with you if you served me?' I wondered, more for my benefit than his own. I needed something to offer to Kjarr in exchange for the wealth he'd pay for the slaves.

Egbert chuckled to himself, giddy with excitement. 'I can write, prepare parchment, and…' he lowered his voice, though we could not be overheard, 'I am observant. Years cloistered and told to hush will allow you to hear the words that go unspoken.' His eyes were suddenly full of purpose.

'That would come in handy,' I agreed as I pulled him to his feet and started in the camp's direction. Not far now, and the men would be cooking dinner.

Egbert walked by my side in silence as the burning question formed on my lips, 'What is she to you?'

'Who?' Egbert asked, his usually smooth brow furrowed. 'I assume you mean Odrun?' His hand brushed my forearm briefly. 'I would tell you, but she…'

'Toki!' Eskil called. His foot was buried in the ground while Gunnar cackled at the prank beside the roaring meal-fire. 'Come and pull me out, boy.'

Egbert swallowed a laugh as he looked over the scene, and before he scuttled off to rescue his master, mumbled over his shoulder, 'When we have our answer, you shall have yours.'

# PART TWO

## KYIV

# FIFTEEN

## 883 CE KYIV

I stared at Kjarr's ship in the harbour. *Freedom*, he called it. Lacking the usual beast names men chose, Kjarr's was named for that which he treasured most. Its prow was naked as it bobbed in the crowded water, sitting, as it must have, without journeying these many months.

A man stood before me, clearing his throat to attract my attention. 'I'm sorry,' he began, shaking his head in reply to my earlier protest. 'There is no time.' It was clear by the clothing he wore he was a court messenger. His dark brown pants billowed beneath a tunic of cream belted around the waist, and split from the belt to the knee, where its length fell open. A tablet woven belt in Kyiv's colours of yellow, brown, and red gave his garment shape. The excess length of which draped almost to his shins. Over his left shoulder was a cape of red, fastened with a broach bearing an insignia of a sloping bident. I thought the man was young, with his youthful face and beard clipped short. But he squinted so much that it wrinkled his face, so he looked much older.

I didn't have to ask who sent him. He'd announced it multiple times already. 'The Knyaz demands your attendance immediately,' he repeated, his tone insistent, but there was a softening in his eyes that held some sympathy.

'Is this the way things are here? I'm to be summoned without the hospitality of respite?' I complained ignominiously from the *Bhobain*.

Sihtric bristled on my behalf. He had barely stepped foot over the gunwale before the man had set on us. 'Lad, we've just arrived,' he objected.

After sailing into Kyiv's harbour, the messenger was already waiting on the platform, waving us into position and helping to tether the mooring lines. I had thought it a welcoming party that would usher our crew to food and water. A bath was what I had hoped for. It was *Laugardagr*, the bathing day when one would smell fresh and step into clean linens. Yet, I would greet the greatest man of the land travel weary.

Sihtric exhaled. 'Is there nae time enough to bathe and change?'

The rest of the *Bhobain's* crew behind me was just as agitated. No doubt Gunnar and Thorsten would want to head to the market. Frodi, Eskil, and Björn would go to the tavern, and Ahmed would likely plan for his onward journey over land. But all would desire to wash and fill their bellies with something warm.

'For you, yes,' the messenger replied, pointing to Sihtric, 'but Lady Signe must come now.'

'At least he calls you "lady",' Sven interjected from somewhere behind me. 'Doesn't a lady need time to dress?' he pointed out.

The messenger man was less than impressed by my friend's attempted interjection. He took a deep breath, swallowing his annoyance. 'You are welcome to go to the bathhouse. However, Lady Signe must come with me presently.' He turned to address me. 'We have been expecting you for some time, Lady Signe. When we heard of the problems in Aldeigjuborg and the subsequent Battle of the Abandoned Paragon, your husband was concerned.'

'All this because you beseeched the Norns,' Sven mumbled. 'I told you it would come back to bite you.'

'I think the Norns would do more than deny me a bath if I'd displeased them,' I responded.

Sven pushed his way to the front of the ship and glowered at the man. 'Who are you anyway?'

The rest of our crew had given up on the argument and began unloading the *Bhobain* onto the platform. I jumped out of the path as Eskil rolled a barrel up the walkway.

'I'm Runolf, messenger to Knyaz Oleg. Of course, many still call him the Grand Prince,' he replied, blinking slowly beneath his brown cap. 'He was most eager to meet you as soon as you arrived,' Runolf spoke more softly now, pulling on the edge of his cap.

I pursed my lips. 'And where is my husband?' I asked, no longer attempting civility.

'Awaiting you in the Great Hall. He was attending Knyaz Oleg,' he answered.

Sven hefted a chest over the side of the ship into Sihtric's waiting arms. 'Why didn't he come to collect his wife, then?'

Sihtric hushed him with a breathy reply, 'He's unlikely able to.'

I rounded on Sihtric and glared.

Sihtric opened his mouth but thought better of it.

'Still keeping me blind to whatever is going on? Well, we're here now and I'll be finding out soon enough,' I seethed.

Sihtric's auburn hair shone as he stared at the ground, shuffling his toggle-shoed feet beneath him. 'Aye, *bhana charaid,*' he muttered, and I sensed he would shortly be relieved of the burden he carried. Perhaps then he would speak more freely.

It was all too much; I felt like the condemned being led to the dispatcher's blade, and everyone else was content to watch. But what could they do? When royalty summoned you, one had to obey. *I had imagined my arrival in Kyiv rather differently,* I thought as the red-caped messenger coughed dryly.

'Lady Signe, will you come?'

'It seems I don't have a choice,' I said. 'Does the Grand Prince not care for his guests? Is that how it is here?' I asked, still rankled by the demands, but not expecting him to answer my question, and he didn't. 'May I bring someone with me?'

'I'll gladly go,' Sven offered. 'If only to see this man and the court finery.'

Runolf shook his head. 'You may choose to bring your men with you, but they are not invited to attend Knyaz Oleg. They are, however, welcome to Kyiv.' He bowed a little, and it was clear any attempt to resist the process was futile.

Sihtric squeezed my forearm gently. 'Do you want me to follow?' he asked.

'Don't bother,' I replied curtly. 'If I may leave whatever *it* is I am now walking into, I will find you all later.' I didn't even trouble myself to look back at Sven. He was likely standing just as dumbfounded as the rest of them.

The only one who looked on with eagle-eyed interest was Odrun. She brushed my arm as I readied to depart. 'You'll remember?' She reminded me of my promise to bring her into my household.

I nodded and tightened my belt.

'Please follow me,' Runolf replied courteously enough as he swept people from the path he burned towards the walled town.

In his wake, I walked, picking specks from my clothing to appear more presentable. It was an absurd task, given the circumstances. Runolf's pace was swift, his long legs carrying him forth as he divided tradesmen and townsfolk with a wave of his hand. I had scant time to look up at the towering ramparts as we passed through with a brief nod to the sentry on the gate. It was all a blur of wooden structures, crisp white headcloths, and snugly worn caps until we stopped at a set of heavy doors that must have been the entry to the Great Hall. My breath was ragged and my heart was pounding as Runolf turned and met my eye.

'Please, wait here,' he mumbled, his breathing even and unaffected as he disappeared within.

Left alone, I studied the ornate carvings that surrounded the doors. Dual posts arched to meet at the top, framed the opening. The one-eyed god Odin sat at the apex, looking down on the waves that raged around him. On their foaming crests, great warships rode the storm, men aboard their deep bellies with mouths open as they called to Ran and her daughters for protection. Detailed chains of knotwork decorated the panels surrounding the posts and doors. They looped and encircled animals, plants, and wings detached from their hosts. And, as I stood back, I gazed upon the final picture. Well above Odin, the animals, and the waves sat a bident, the same as the insignia Runolf wore on his cloak pin. Tablet woven bands around the edge and etched right into the wood made it stand out from the other depictions. Whilst Odin was worshipped here, it was clear the Rus' ruled, and they wanted all to know it.

It felt like an aeon examining the extraordinary craftsmanship of those wood carvings, waiting for the great doors to be opened and draw me in.

Eventually, they creaked open, and a guard stood aside. He did not gesture, he just stood still, expecting me to know it was time to go in.

My palms were sweating as I stepped through that dark doorway. The shadows seemed to pour out as my eyes adjusted to the dim light. I could see the people within peering at me like some fascinating rarity.

The hall was lit by braziers, and lamps ensconced upon the wall. Its central beams were as richly carved as the main door, tableaus of battles, and the tales of our gods. Men and women lined the length of the building, so many gathered in one place. Half were now turning to the front. Others watched my progress down the aisle that lay clear between the entrance and the raised platform at the front, on which a man was seated in a high-backed chair. Noble men preened proudly in fine breaches and tunics trimmed with expensive fabrics. Their wives turned their piercing gazes on me. The new arrival. Upon the women's heads, delicately woven cloth covered their hair, temples ornamented with bronze, silver, and gold rings of varying ostentatiousness. Their chests were adorned with beads of every colour, whilst their husband's arms glittered with rows of armrings. These were the elite and, it seemed, my first meeting with the ruler of the Rus' territories was today's entertainment.

I pulled at my travelling garment self-consciously, wishing I'd had time to change into my garnet-coloured dress cut elegantly with long sleeves. It was one of the best pieces I had, the ideal thing to wear to greet royalty.

From the whispers behind their hands, I knew this crowd was the judgemental type and my current attire was doing nothing to help my cause. My mother would have loved this display and thrived off the pettiness and attention.

And then I saw him.

Kjarr was standing before the dais, his green eyes pools of concern as he watched me approach. His mouth, usually occupied with a bright and thoughtful smile, was a tight line, and the bulge at his throat swelled as he swallowed hard. I looked at him, but he said nothing. I suppose it would have been improper to do so. Even I, who knew so little about the etiquette of the court, knew that.

My hand crept to my temple, making sure my hair still hid my scar. I tried to channel pride, holding my head high, no longer watching the richly dressed people around me. If I was going to be presented to the Grand Prince in this manner, I would wrest control with confidence.

Kjarr's hand flicked as I drew nearer, willing me to come and take it. His amiable nature seemed changed, clipped by duty, and, although he stood tall, his posture was stiff and his jaw was clenched. My hand clasped his as we walked the irrevocable steps to the high seat. I swept a glance along my well-dressed husband. His clothes were grander than the comfortable breeches and long tunics he had favoured in the north. I breathed in his scent of amber and moss, still the same, but the silk at his collar and cuffs gave me pause. It wasn't until he knelt and threw his cloak over his shoulder that I saw the garment was made entirely of crimson and gold silk.

I spluttered, coughing, and choking on my shock.

The handsome, fair-haired man on the dais looked down with amusement.

'Apologies, Grand Prince. My wife needs a moment,' Kjarr spoke with a deferential bow and turned away. 'Are you all right?' he whispered.

The Grand Prince summoned someone from the shadows. 'A drink,' he commanded.

I wanted to ask Kjarr what in Midgard was going on because I had a thousand questions on my lips but scarce opportunity to speak them. A servant brought a drink in a delicate-looking glass sitting on a platter. Before I could say anything, Kjarr lifted it and pressed it into my shaking hand. Even as I took the vessel in my fingertips, I could not stop the tremor. It was made all the worse by imagining what would happen if I dropped it.

The Grand Prince addressed me in a sonorous voice, 'So, this is the great Signe of Aldeigjuborg.'

Kjarr inclined his head, and I mimicked the gesture before placing the finished glass back on the platter.

'I hear you were involved in the Battle of the Abandoned Paragon,' he stated. 'Is it true?' He grasped the arm of his chair and sat forward, brow furrowed.

I hesitated.

Kjarr glanced sideways and nodded that I should answer. He obviously knew the protocol here.

'It is…,' I replied in a strangled voice before clearing my throat. 'Grand Prince,' I added, as I thought I should. 'I bear the wounds to prove it.'

Kjarr scanned my face. With my scar on the opposite side, he could not see it. For the time being, his imagination would have to fill in the gaps.

The Grand Prince nodded thoughtfully before gesturing again to the shadows behind his chair. 'A veritable Valkyrie,' he beamed. 'You shall receive gifts for your service.'

I stroked the outline of my Valkyrie pendant beneath the neckline of my dress as the man who had earlier brought my drink emerged with yet another plate. This time, an armring of silver sat atop the platter, and he presented it with a downturned nod. In the lamplight, the jewellery shone, as magnificent as any other. No nodes of animal heads, just simple round balls of burnished metal. I felt a pang for the distinct beauty of Bjarndýr, melted down, gone forever.

'Thank you, Grand Prince,' I replied, tucking the gift into my pouch that contained Freyja's sleeping cap, never far from my side. I ran my fingers over the fabric as another jolt of discomfort flashed through my chest. *That was a conversation I needed to have soon enough.*

The Grand Prince waved his plate bearer back to the periphery with his broad hand, and his narrowed eyes fell on me. 'When my cousin first informed me he had married without my consent, I confess, I was confused why he chose a woman with no ties to any noble families.' He kept his voice low, the entire hall leaned in to hear. He drummed his long fingers on his knees. 'I see he has chosen a woman who would stand up for our people. Someone who fights our enemies with honour. I would expect no less from your wife, Cousin,' he finished with a laugh, light and contagious.

*Had the Grand Prince called him cousin?*

My head was spinning. I didn't have time to fall, not now.

Kjarr's grip on my hand tightened as he covered for my surprise. 'Married with the gods as witnesses.'

The Grand Prince blinked. His nostrils flared; there one moment, gone the next. 'Not that we would want to undo it now that you already have a daughter together.'

Kjarr blinked a heartbeat too long. 'Yes, Grand Prince. A daughter named Freyja,' he replied, voice steady.

The conversation was almost too heavy to bear. *It wasn't the place to tell Kjarr of Freyja's death;* I reminded myself. But I could not let it continue.

*Oh, why had I not sent a message about this to Kjarr during the winter?* This whole thing was too much. I felt mute, unable to speak. *Cousin, Grand Prince, Freyja.* All the words spun around in me and jumbled until there was no meaning. Just a threat to strangle me.

Kjarr and Oleg continued their exchange until the Grand Prince's gaze set on me again, delving deeper than was comfortable. 'Is she with her nursemaid?' he asked.

'Uh… no, Grand Prince,' I managed in a thin voice. 'She is not here.' I could say no more, not in a room full of strangers.

Kjarr changed his grip on my hand, threading his fingers through mine and rubbing his thumb against the back of my hand. 'It is a long journey for one so young, Grand Prince. No doubt she will join us when she is able.'

My heart sank. But I lifted my chin and I set my face in a resolute manner that brokered no tears to fall.

Grand Prince Oleg watched me with a curious squint.

*Was he trying to take my measure? To read my thoughts? Were there men of such abilities?*

Whatever it was, he decided he had seen enough. 'I shall not detain you any longer, Lady Signe,' he spoke as he ran his hand through his hair, just like Kjarr often did when thinking. 'I expect you are weary, but I do hope you'll excuse my curiosity.' He smiled, the veil of composure slipping for a moment before he straightened up. 'We should talk more of the battle. I have heard much, but would value your retelling, for I sense you are not wont to embellish, Lady Signe. For now, rest and enjoy your reunion with Boyar Hrolfsson.'

'Grand Prince,' Kjarr mumbled as he bowed, face blank against the stares of the court.

I followed, bowing low before we both backed away, excused from the following court business. Outside, Kjarr led me to a courtyard where we were far from the prying eyes of townsfolk.

'From here we can access my lodgings,' Kjarr began, taking me by the hand. His features lit up once we passed through the door, smiling into the warm sunlight. 'Why didn't you send word you were leaving Freyja behind?' Kjarr asked, disappointment lacing his voice. 'I was looking forward to seeing how much she has grown. Is she speaking many words?' he wondered without stopping for breath. 'I have so many…'

The shock that had stupefied me gave way to anger. 'Why didn't I tell you?' I demanded, shaking my palm out of his grip. 'Tell me this, Kjarr, why didn't you tell me your cousin is the Grand Prince? What exactly is a boyar?'

This was why Sihtric had warned me. *Bastard!* I cursed inwardly. *He knew all along.*

Kjarr assumed a defensive stance, arms crossed over his chest, and leaned away from me. 'It never seemed relevant until Oleg planned to take Kyiv,' he said. 'By then, I realised this was something that I needed to tell you in person, and I was too late.'

That was reasoning I couldn't fault.

'When I returned to Aldeigjuborg from Holmgardr, I wanted to tell you everything. Even then, I hoped once Oleg had captured the territory, he would let me go back home and things would return to how they were,' he explained, unfolding his arms.

I paced a square around him. 'But they didn't.'

He frowned. 'Would you have married me if you knew?' There was a hint of his playful smile behind his downturned mouth.

I stopped to glare at him. 'Are you telling me this entire time you hid this from me? When you said you wanted me to be the one to decide, were they just words?' There was no masking the hurt in my voice.

'None of this is what I wanted,' he replied, reaching for my hand as I continued to pace. I snatched it away. 'I was truthful when I said you had to be the one to decide whether you wanted to marry me. All of this was far from my mind then,' he groaned, shaking his head. 'This court was never one I wished to be a part of. I was like you; wanting to live a life free of these sorts of constraints. But Oleg is my family, and he has called on my oath. I am no oath-breaker, to do so would be worse than death.'

He could not break what he had sworn without angering the gods. This I knew and respected.

It felt like I was back on the boat. The world tilted, and I stumbled, grabbing for the fenced side of an animal pen. 'Why did you force Sihtric to be silent?'

The poor man had been biting his tongue since the first day he met me. Our entire friendship was created in the spaces between his secrets and what he could tell me.

'Well, he's been good at hiding the truth before,' Kjarr mumbled in response.

'Sihtric can keep confidence well enough,' I agreed.

'I thought he might tell you something.' Kjarr stroked his jaw, running his hand through the stubble there.

'The only thing he told me is that you had little choice in the matter. He's warned me on a few things, but he is ever the stoic friend to you, not that you deserve it,' I raged. 'I thought better of you, Kjarr. Better than this.'

'Astrid,' he whispered, reaching for me.

I flinched away from his touch.

'I'm sorry. Please believe me when I say I never looked for this. I've tried my best to avoid Oleg's court for years. I left as soon as I could to live in Aldeigjuborg. Honestly, I never thought it would come to this.'

I stared at a part of the railing. There was a nail missing and my eyes bore into that hole as if I would fill it with iron, willed from my mind as I let the wave of anger wash over me. There was nothing to be gained from fighting about this now. Kjarr could not end his kinship with Oleg any more than I could change the past, and there were things I had kept from my husband, too. The throbbing in my head subsided. My eyes were clear now as I glanced at Kjarr's sorry green eyes watching me.

'You're disappointed, I know. But, I am happy you've come. There is no one else in the world I would rather have by my side and, if I'm being honest, I'm in sore need of someone who'll be truthful with me.'

*A court of vipers.* No wonder Kjarr had worried about telling me.

'It's been a long journey. Not one wholly unenjoyable,' I conceded.

He smiled a half-roguish grin. 'A true adventure, huh? Still keen to keep going?'

I cocked my head to one side. 'To Miklagard?'

Kjarr nodded. 'Of course. I remember you talking about it.'

I took a step towards him. 'As I've just arrived in Kyiv, I suppose I'll stay awhile.'

'Did you see my ship when you arrived?'

I chuckled, thinking of her mooring ropes tied to the poles, not going anywhere. 'Looks like your *Freedom* isn't so free at the moment.'

Kjarr's mouth formed a thin line and nodded. 'She's Oleg's now. Part of his fleet. But I don't want to think about that. I'm just happy you're here.' He edged closer, slipping my hand into his. 'You don't look changed at all,' he whispered. In a quick motion, he pulled me close, sweeping my hair from my temple to see my scar. 'A recent addition.'

I tried to move away, but he held fast, tracing a light finger along the rift in my skin.

'You should have seen it when we left Aldeigjuborg. It was black and blue.'

Kjarr planted a gentle kiss on my scar. 'Hardly noticeable,' he mumbled against it.

The tension in my body melted, my shoulders relaxed, and my breathing deepened. 'I missed you,' I admitted, looking up into his deep green stare. 'But, I need time to...'

'Decide if you'll stay with me?' There was more than a hint of concern in his voice, though I couldn't see his face as he squeezed me tight against his chest.

'Don't worry. I'm not about to divorce you because of your position. I just need time to think about it,' I explained as I pushed away.

He gave a small, relieved chuckle. 'Ah. I see. When you say "think" you really mean that you want to go to the practice yard and hit something with your axe?'

*Attack someone else before I let my anger get the better of me?* 'You know me well, Husband,' I answered, giving him a playful shove.

'Do what you need to. I'll be waiting. You can take as much time as you need... urgh,' he groaned, running his hand through his hair as his head dropped.

'What is it?'

Kjarr rubbed the base of his neck. 'Oleg has planned a feast tonight.'

'And, I'll be expected to be at my husband's side to play the role of a dutiful wife?'

'Just so,' Kjarr agreed.

He took my moment of softening to reach for me again, pulling me in close and tucking my head beneath his chin. 'I'm sorry, Astrid. I wish I had told you sooner.'

'You should have,' I concurred. 'Now that I am here, there is something I need to ask of you.' If I was going to be at Kjarr's side, as a boyar's wife, whatever that was, I would need people I trusted. Though I might not yet fully comprehend Odrun's plans, she needed me and that might just be enough to make her trustworthy. Egbert, I held in confidence. There was something about the monk that made me like him, besides his obvious value as a scribe.

'Hmm?' he mumbled, intrigue in his tone.

'There are two thralls I wish to bring into our household, if we have room for them.'

'Thralls?' He repeated the word. 'You always hated the idea.'

I grimaced. 'I still do. You'll have to trust there is a reason.'

He stroked the edge of his jaw, looking down at me with unwavering eye contact. 'How much are they going to cost me?'

'A lot I imagine. I suppose one will prove a poor servant, but I need her. The other, well, he can write.'

He chuckled heartily. 'You've found a rune man?' he inquired.

'Not runes. Latin.'

'Huh,' he mumbled, head bobbing as he thought of Egbert's many uses.

'Is that a yes?' I asked.

He nodded. 'Fine. A man with writing skills could be rather useful for us both, and this woman, whoever she is, shall be welcome. Have Runolf bring them to our rooms. He'll know how to get there.' He brought me back into his embrace. 'Gods! How I've missed you and your bold schemes.' He kissed the top of my head and breathed me in. 'I smell the river on you.'

'And every place in between,' I added apologetically. Washing in the lake had been fine, but nothing did the job quite like a good scrub at the bathhouse. I needed to steam the journey from my pores.

He sniffed again. 'It's not that bad.'

'There is one other thing,' I began, sinking my fingers into the folds of his silken cape, cool against my grasp. 'I have a letter to send, but it needs to go with someone you trust completely.'

'Who do you want to reach?' he asked, pulling back.

*How could I explain?*

'For now, I cannot say.' In fact, I did not know the letter's destination. 'Have the man brought to my rooms where I can speak with him privately.' From there, Odrun would have her opportunity.

'Are you sure this is a good idea?' he wondered, tilting his head to one side.

I laughed through my nose. 'Oh, I'm almost certain it's not, but I am sure it's the right thing to do.'

'And when have we ever done things the way they are supposed to be done?' He repeated the phrase he so often did when we embarked on something unknown. 'The practice yard is down that way,' he said, pointing across the courtyard. 'No doubt the rest of the crew will be with the guards trying to figure out lodgings. I'll send someone to fetch you before the sun sets. You'll need time to get ready for the feast; court gowns and fancy things, you know? Don't say I haven't warned you this time,' he added with a wink.

I glowered at him playfully. 'Are there *any* advantages to being a cousin to the Grand Prince?' I teased.

Kjarr laughed and squeezed me tighter. 'Just wait, tonight you will see.'

# SIXTEEN

'He's what?' Sven asked, his mouth agape.

I took the moment of distraction to launch my attack.

'Hey!' He stepped back and blocked with his shield as he parried my rather aggressive back-handed swing. 'How could I pay attention when you come in saying things like that?'

My axe bit into his shield, and I tore it away. 'How do you think I felt?' I seethed, baring my teeth. 'A cousin. Can you believe it?'

'Cousin,' Sven repeated, trying to set me off balance with a thrust of his shoulder. He was a formidable foe when armed with a bow and arrow, but excelled in hand-to-hand combat. Sven launched forward, hand out to grab my arm, but I was faster. A sidestep outmanoeuvred him before he could land the hit.

'What does that make Kjarr?' Sven asked breathlessly.

I jabbed his unprotected middle with the toe of Forlog-Enda. He yielded after suspiciously little time, and I suspected he was tired. A raised hand ceased the fight while I doubled over to catch my breath.

'I'm still trying to figure that out,' I responded, walking over to the bench to get a cloth to mop the sweat from my face.

Guards milled about on the periphery, waiting for their turn with other opponents.

'Ooof, not sure I can compete with that,' Sven complained as he sheathed his weapon. His blonde hair was slick with sweat as he pushed it out of his face.

I shot him an unamused glare. 'Lucky there is no competition,' I answered dryly, throwing another cloth at Sven's head.

He deftly snatched it from the air.

'Pity the seer in Uppsala never mentioned this. It would have been nice to be forewarned,' I complained.

'You mean she didn't tell you of a marriage to a man so close to the throne?' Sven laughed.

All those years before, the *völva* had seen me on the hill and told me my future; the betrayals, life lost, fresh paths to follow. Her premonitions were as clear as the mud of the practice yard.

I shook my head and plonked my backside onto the bench.

'Does it?' he asked.

The cloth was dripping wet now, so I threw it in the wash bucket. 'Does it what?'

Sven sank into the seat next to me. 'Make him close to the throne?'

'Honestly, I don't know. Kjarr and I have not been able to discuss that yet. We didn't talk about anything more than buying Odrun and Egbert for our household. There was enough time to tell him how mad I was with him, though,' I grumbled and chewed on the inside of my lip.

'Did he shed a tear over Freyja's passing?' Sven wondered, stopping to stare at me. 'Or when you told him about your illness?'

I shifted uncomfortably in my place. 'I've not had the chance to tell him.'

'Still keeping secrets?' he teased, sending an elbow towards my ribs.

'Stop it.'

'You have to tell him,' Sven reminded me.

'I know and I will,' I agreed as I pulled on the sleeve hem. 'You should have seen it in there. So many people in ridiculous clothing, thinking they are so important. How can any good come of this?'

Sven chortled with his head tossed back. 'Really? You're going to ask how being the wife of Oleg's cousin might be beneficial?' He jabbed me in the side again, this time harder. 'Think of your business. You don't need an introduction; you are the family of the ruler!' he scoffed. 'Pity the fools like us who lodge in the halls where we can find a bed.'

'Do you want to serve Kjarr?'

'Gods no!' he roared. 'Oleg, maybe,' he considered. 'What about this armring the Grand Prince gave you? Does that mean you're sworn? Did you give your oath?'

'It's no longer mine to give,' I replied. 'My husband is sworn to him and that makes me bound. It is assumed, but he has valued me nonetheless,' I answered, kicking the dirt.

'What do you make of him?' Sven asked. He took a swig from a waterskin and handed it to me.

'Oleg?' I downed the remains and passed back the empty drinking vessel.

He nodded.

'I've not made up my mind. He seems conscious of the weight of his crown, and curious, but other than that; I don't know if he is worthy of my oath, or your service.'

'Hmm, perhaps Oleg will receive it. But even then, I have yet to hear Sihtric's plan for our onward journey. If we overwinter here, I'll need to find something to do. I suppose I'll become his man then.'

'If we overwinter?'

He nodded again. 'Some men here have told me there is strife with the neighbouring tribes. Kyiv might need more warriors soon,' he mentioned, stretching his legs out long.

'And here I was thinking we might have peace for a time,' I retorted, but even I did not expect any order would be lasting.

Sven laughed at my comment. 'Peace!' he said scornfully. 'What would I do if these lands were calm? Be a farmer. I could, I guess. Sihtric would turn me into a craftsman to make his prow-beast. That might keep me busy enough. Perhaps I will find work with the shipyard if Oleg doesn't need me. It all depends on Sihtric's plan. He's the man with the ship, after all.'

I nodded. 'Where is Sihtric?'

Sven waved his hand towards the town. 'Off doing business with his man, Kari.'

'Hmm,' I mumbled. 'And the rest of them at the tavern, I suppose?'

'That's where they said they were going. Eskil and Gunnar are probably gone to spend the funds you gave them,' Sven explained.

'I thought Gunnar would protest when I offered to buy Odrun, but he was suspiciously eager to sell her after insisting he would take her to market.'

'He might have just grown tired of her,' Sven suggested. 'Eskil wanted money, and now that we don't need to do any ship lifting, he has little need for a thrall.'

'How much did you end up paying for Odrun?' Sven asked.

'Way too much. I hope it'll all be worth it.'

Sven nodded his head to the left as I felt someone watching. 'Looks like an official has come to fetch you.'

'This time I know where I'm going.'

'Find me on the low tables, Lady Signe,' Sven replied mockingly, bowing, and sweeping his hand along the ground.

I squeezed him hard on the shoulder, digging in my fingers. He winced. 'Oh, don't worry. I'll see you there and make sure I send you all the beets.'

'Urgh, disgusting,' he groaned, 'I hate them!'

A malicious smile curved my lips. 'I know. I'll make sure there's no meat for you,' I went on. 'While I'm feasting on the juiciest cuts, you'll be nibbling roots. All I must do is play the dutiful wife.'

Sven scoffed. 'Is it too much if I wish he chokes on a piece of meat?'

'Don't be like that,' I demanded, standing to leave. 'You two might like each other if you gave it a chance.'

Sven jeered. 'Never!'

'Have Odrun and Egbert already been taken to my rooms?' I asked the messenger standing outside the yard.

He nodded, but said nothing.

I turned back to Sven. 'Promise me you'll not stir up any trouble tonight?'

He grinned and leaned back in his seat with his arms behind his head. 'I'll give you tonight, *minn Svanr*. Then I'll be back to myself.'

# SEVENTEEN

Kjarr and I stood at the entrance to the Great Hall. The court announcer held us back as he bellowed at the people within. 'Knyaz Oleg,' Runolf began as he addressed the Grand Prince. 'May I present Boyar Kjarr Hrolfsson and his wife, Signe,' he finished, bowing low as we passed him, hands clasped tight.

The length of my skirts gently dragged along the freshly laid rushes on the hall's floor. Their sweet scent was strong, but by the end of the night that would be replaced by the overwhelming odour of anything that fell upon them; ale, fat-glistening pieces of meat that hounds would sniff out, and worse, the excesses of drink when men heaved their guts out.

I felt like a hard-struck thumb in a timber yard as the court watched me. Unlike before, when I was roughly dressed and in sore need of a bath, they now gaped at the finery. Kjarr and I made a handsome pair, wearing identical fabrics of the most brilliant reds and blues; colours reserved for only the most senior of the boyars. Kjarr's tunic was silk from the waist to the hem, and at the collar and cuffs. His trousers were bright blue and billowing in the southern style. Leg wraps of vermillion were wound around his calves, matching his cloak, which was fastened with a silver brooch bearing the insignia of Oleg's bident.

Kjarr swept into a graceful bow, now gripping my hand by the fingertips.

Next to him, I sank deeper, but far less elegantly, and lowered my gaze. Temple rings jangled by my ears and draped forward into view. They were huge silver things, and I wondered how anyone could wear them all day without wanting to tear them off for their impracticality. The women of Kyiv, and many neighbouring Slavic tribes, wore them attached to bands around their heads. Mine were slotted into loops on my headband of red silk that surrounded my head like a crown of fabric. Rings would be changed depending on need if the woman owned many pairs, and the band itself could be worn without the adornment of large swirls of precious metal. Though Kjarr advised me, women in Kyiv displayed their temple rings as often as they could. They spared no occasion.

As I stood, I straightened my vibrant red gown the colour of berries in the Jol time snow. Just like Kjarr's garment, a broad hem of matching silk also trimmed mine. The pattern had amazed me, its swirling gold flourishes in repeating patterns set in the shade just the same as the linen the rest of the dress was made from. Silk appeared at both the neck of my gown and the cuffs of my wide sleeves flowing over my wrists. An underdress of blue was visible under my sleeve's opening as I moved my arms, but otherwise, the beauty of the woad-blue garment was mine alone to enjoy. The exquisite weave of the linen against my skin was only achieved by a woman who was a master spinner and expert on the loom. Kjarr had told me her name was Mirca, and I would meet with her to discuss my plans for expanding my network of sail and clothing production. But tonight was about establishing my presence in the Grand Prince's hall. It was a matter of family, not of business.

The ruler gazed down from his raised platform as he greeted us, 'You are most welcome at my table, Cousins,' he spoke, waving us towards his high table.

Two vacant seats remained on his left, while the Grand Prince stood before a group of warriors, dressed in their best, metal gleaming in the low light. There stood Eskil, Sven, and, to my surprise, Sihtric. It seemed they wasted no time in swearing oaths, for they already wore new arm rings. No doubt, they too, had regaled the Grand Prince with their version of the Battle of the Abandoned Paragon.

'Does this mean we are staying?' I whispered the question to Kjarr.

'Sihtric agreed the crew will remain here through the winter,' he answered just as quietly.

I had thought we would stay for a time, a few weeks, a month perhaps, but through the entire winter would mean we would have to wait for the ice to thaw before leaving. We would be in Kyiv far longer than I'd expected. I opened my mouth to protest, but Kjarr strode forward to grasp his friend by the forearm. I glanced at Sven, but he was deep in conversation and had not turned towards us.

'My dear Sihtric,' Kjarr beamed in welcome. 'Thank you for taking such good care of my wife.'

Sihtric peered at me with an apologetic tilt of the head.

'All is forgiven,' I said before he could say a word. 'I hope now you can speak without holding your tongue.'

He exhaled. 'It's a relief, *bhana charaid*,' Sihtric acknowledged. 'You're bonnie!' he added, taking my right hand out to inspect the dress. 'You had a good measure of her to get such a fine fit,' Sihtric congratulated Kjarr.

'Her image has been burned into my mind,' Kjarr replied, perhaps a little too crudely.

Sven didn't miss it and breathed a snort. Sihtric braced his arm, and I felt Sven's eyes boring into my profile. Colour rose in my cheeks, but I refused to confront him when all I got from him was derision and no merrymaking.

'Have you been well looked after?' Kjarr was asking Sihtric. 'Do you have rooms?'

Sihtric nodded. 'Yes, dinnae fash yourself about us, Kjarr. Back in the grand side of things?'

Kjarr ran his hand through his hair. 'You know, I tried to stay away. When I am given leave, I will find you and we can talk more,' he promised as they shook arms again before separating.

'Come. There is someone I wish you to meet,' Kjarr said, pulling me towards the raised table.

We walked ahead of the rows where I knew the rest of our crew was seated. Even Ahmed had accepted the Grand Prince's invitation to the feast. I glanced over my shoulder and saw Sven still watching me. He had promised to be on his best behaviour tonight and I hoped he would keep to it, though from the murderous glares he kept throwing at Kjarr's back, I wondered if he could.

A few quick strides and I was again curtseying to the high table before taking my seat. The second attempt at the gesture was far more successful than my first, and Kjarr smiled encouragingly as he stood aside to let me sit. On my right, Kjarr assumed his position next to

Oleg, and to my left, a young girl who was staring out on the crowd with eyes round as soapstone platters.

It took a moment to register Kjarr's proximity to Oleg, seated directly next to him. 'What exactly is your relation to the Grand Prince?' I whispered as a court thrall filled our cups with mead.

Oleg had no wife, or else she might have been the one to honour those seated with her husband. In that role, the prettiest of thralls took up ewers and poured the contents into horn cups.

'Hmm?' Kjarr mumbled, turning towards me, and placing his palm on my knee under the table. 'My mother was the twin sister to Oleg's own,' he replied at a barely perceptible level, as his hand moved from my leg.

'Sisters,' I repeated. So close to one another. Much closer than I was comfortable.

Kjarr laughed to himself. 'Only two summers separate us in age. We were like brothers when we were young and our mothers were still alive,' Kjarr explained as we sipped.

*Almost brothers,* I saved that thought away to worry about later as Kjarr turned back to his discussion with Grand Prince Oleg.

I stared at the carved central pillars holding up the roof. Each stood as tall as two men and as wide as the burliest of Oleg's warriors. Even Eskil could hide behind one without being seen, and perhaps that's what people used them for. I could see a couple whispering to each other, only one of them visible from this distance. It almost looked like the man was talking to himself until his friend laughed and leaned forward into view. Shields of many colours hung from the walls, alongside skins, tapestries, and lamps. Between it all, thralls rushed back and forth, filling cups from ale and mead jugs.

Benches lined the length of the room, with patrons hip to hip on each trestle. Plates of glistening meat, roasted vegetables, or stewed barley were clattered onto tables slower than the crowd could clear their plates. Almost all were watching the slaves, ready to scoop up a tasty morsel before the platters were even set down. That wasn't a problem at the high table, where, I had to remind myself, manners were expected.

Kjarr served me juicy slabs of bacon and ladled some barley and root vegetable stew laced with nutmeg from a soapstone serving dish.

'I like your hair,' sang the sweet voice beside me, and I turned to see the round-faced beauty smiling at me. She was serving herself from the same bowl Kjarr had just used.

'Thank you,' I replied. Unlike other married women, I wore my hair uncovered, my only rebellion against the rigid dress requirements of the court. Beneath my headband of silk and temple rings, Odrun had coiled my hair into a series of elaborate braids, slotting tubular ribbons of silver among my tresses. It all shone in the hall's firelight. Though Odrun had professed herself a poor servant, she turned out to be an exemplary hair weaver.

I shovelled a spoonful of barley into my mouth. 'Mmm,' I grumbled, chewing the delicious creation.

'Signe,' Kjarr spoke to both of us now and I turned with a full mouth. 'This is Ellisif Heilagrsdottir.'

I swallowed and smiled with a nod towards the girl.

Ellisif also wore her hair uncovered, her golden locks streaming down her back.

Kjarr leaned in to offer further explanation. 'Ellisif is the daughter of one of the most senior members of the druzhina.'

'Druzhina?' I asked, stumbling over the words. It felt like the barley was lodged in my throat and I took a gulp from my horn mug.

'That's the group of men who fight for the Grand Prince. My father was recently appointed as Hersir of Kyiv,' Ellisif explained. 'But I'm sure you know, Signe, it's not always the men you have to worry about. Take my mother, for example. She'll know what you ate to break your fast before you've even uttered a single word,' she rattled off quicker than I could comprehend. 'There she is,' Ellisif pointed her slender finger towards a woman coming into the hall.

I sliced into a cut of bacon and tasted its smoky flavour. The cook was good, some boiled the meat until it was tough and the fat chewy, but this was succulent.

'Knyaz Oleg,' the court announcer bellowed above the din, and I looked up. 'Hersir Heilagr and his wife Estrid.'

'Of course, the Grand Prince knows who all these people are. It seems an awful waste of time, but they only announce the upper ones, you know? No point mentioning everyone on the low tables; we'd be here all night,' she babbled, spearing a chunk of cabbage on her eating knife. 'Though for you, it's good to learn all their names,' she spoke through a half-chewed mouthful as she gestured towards the door.

Ellisif's mother, Estrid, was a diminutive thing, with a pouty mouth and a sloping nose that looked too big for her face. She held tight to her husband, the enormous Heilagr, who towered above her. His belly bulged against his tightly fastened leather belt, straining the weave of his embroidered linen shirt as his squinty eyes darted around the hall. It was a wonder that these two had produced such a beauty as Ellisif.

'That's your father?' I confirmed, gesturing towards the man with an arched eyebrow.

Her nostrils flared mildly, and she nodded. 'More bacon?' she offered, dragging another slab of the deliciously pink meat from the platter.

'If you wouldn't mind,' I agreed, as she plonked it down before me. She took a bit for herself and sliced it into chunks, then chewed on each piece while her eyes roved around the hall. This habit she might have inherited from her father, as he continued to do the same. I watched with serious concern for his clothing as his barrel chest and considerably muscled arms fought the seams of his tunic. Heilagr bowed once more, he and Estrid finding space at the table below. Heilagr's tunic was safe for now, but he needed a new one.

'Does your mother not spin and weave?' I asked Ellisif.

She lowered her eating knife and laughed. 'She is almost as loath to do that as she is to bend the knee,' Ellisif informed me and, from the pinched expression her mother bore as if she'd been forced to smell the midden, I believed her. 'You would be surprised to learn my mother is a textile merchant of some fame.'

'I would,' I agreed.

'She doesn't do the work herself. That she leaves to others. Though I agree my father needs a new tunic,' she murmured, and we both laughed.

The sound rippled along the tables. Heilagr and Estrid turned to the dais, saw their daughter there and, behind the veneer of a smile, almost snarled.

Two men of fair colouring and identical mannerisms sauntered into the hall unannounced.

It was clear from the way they preened themselves, between the long benches, that they already held themselves in high regard, even though they did not yet hold their parents' high-status in their own right.

'Who are they?' I asked, leaning in to speak more closely with Ellisif.

She looked up. 'Those are my brothers,' she responded, tossing her untethered hair over her shoulder. 'Helgi and Harald,' she added, 'and utterly troublesome.'

I speared a leek with my knife. 'Why are they allowed to come to court, then?'

Ellisif freely cackled and grasped my wrist as she threw her head back. 'Oh, Signe. You're a delight. They come to serve, of course, but their blood is as hot as all young men. Helgi and Harald grow bored if they're not fighting, so they put that to the Knyaz's use.'

'If they're your family, why didn't you enter with them?' I asked her and hoped it wasn't impolite.

'It almost sounds like you don't believe we are related,' she replied, her tone serious for a moment. Ellisif nibbled on a parsnip and continued, 'My nursemaid brought me.'

'Nursemaid?' I asked, turning to her. She didn't appear to be a child. A young woman, no doubt, but not one in need of such care.

She giggled. 'Licinia has been with me since she was a girl herself, and I, a babe in arms. She tries to keep me out of trouble while I'm sitting around waiting for my parents to find me a husband. Otherwise, they don't concern themselves with me,' she explained, dissecting a lump of bacon.

'I know what that feels like,' I replied, thinking about how my mother had threatened me with marriage every time I stepped out of line.

'Any day now,' she added, leaning across the table to see down the hall. 'And then I'll be someone else's problem.'

I watched Ellisif as she observed the room, mind working hard to note all that happened. She looked so young, and then a thought struck me. 'Has anyone ever told you that you look like one of those godly cherubs?'

'What's a cherub?' she asked, her plump cheeks flushing pink.

'Angel babies created by the Christian God. That's what Father Niall told me. But I wasn't very good at listening to his boring stories,' I tried to explain. 'He showed me a picture of one in his enormous book full of colours. His Biblio.' I tried to remember the word, but it didn't sound quite right.

Ellisif reached forward to spear another chunk of cabbage. Her sleeve dipped into the stew, absorbing the liquid. 'Oh, no! Mother will be mad,' she lamented, gripping the cuff and, for a moment, I thought she meant to lick it clean. She released her sleeve, dabbing it on the fabric of the table. 'Maybe Licinia will be able to remove the stain,' she mumbled and turned back to me. 'Are you talking about the Christ?'

'I think so,' I replied uncertainly. 'Don't you have Christians here?'

'If we do, they don't go around announcing themselves. Sure, we've had a few envoys from Miklagard, but nothing serious.'

'So, no one is interested in the baby god?' I asked.

She touched my arm lightly and giggled. 'Not if he is indeed a child god.' Ellisif shrugged. 'Not when they had Thor or Odin, or Frigg, or Baldr…. Or.'

'Loki,' we said in unison and laughed.

'No, you won't find a church here. The tribes on our fringes worship their own gods and our Knyaz follows the Old Gods, just as it should be.' She glanced at the ruler, who was engaged in animated conversation with my husband.

'Interesting,' I mused, gazing out at the people in the hall. Some on the lower table were stuffing their mouths, filling their plates, and clashing cups together in joyous feasting. Others were standing and speaking in the dark corners of the room.

'Look how they wriggle about the other high ones, like maggots on rotting meat,' she whispered, eyes wide with disgust as she watched her parents speaking, lips to one another's ear.

Her comment took me off guard. 'That's quite a revolting image.'

'It is, isn't it?' she replied, sitting back in her chair, arms folded against her deep blue dress which was trimmed with dainty borders of silk in contrasting colours. She tilted her golden head towards me and arched a fair eyebrow. 'They're always whispering away. Oh, why can't they be more likeable people?'

'We cannot choose who we are born to,' I commiserated. My mother had her plans, but I imagined a whole family of vipers was infinitely worse.

Kjarr leaned away from his conversation with the Grand Prince. 'I thought you'd like Ellisif. I asked Oleg to seat you together tonight. It might be nice to make a friend.'

'An unmarried girl?'

Kjarr chuckled, unperturbed by my protest. 'When has that ever worried you? And, besides, she reminded me of Helga, who I assume you are missing.'

My mouth opened in surprise. 'Helga was sweet.'

'And mischievous,' Kjarr added, his mouth curling into a grin.

He wasn't wrong.

'And probably giving birth to her child now,' I said.

'So soon?' he marvelled. This was all new information to Kjarr. Last he heard, Helga and Mikel were married, blissful in the early days of their union.

'A shock to Mikel, but a delight to his wife,' I explained, though I was ever aware of how little Kjarr knew of my life this last year. The longing to be by my friend's side was painful. I missed her more than I had realised. Perhaps I needed a friend.

'If Ellisif is talking about her family, then don't expect her to be agreeable. She might seem brash at first, but I promise you, she is a sweet girl. As honest as you'll find in this place. That's something you value highly if I remember right,' he pointed out.

'Next time I'm in need of friends. Perhaps you might not seek them in the nursery?' I said, a little too unkindly, and instantly I regretted it.

Kjarr's mouth turned down. 'It was through her maid Licinia that I discovered Ellisif. For months I've been learning the language of Miklagard from Licinia, and Ellisif has proved to be my equal as a pupil. I was hoping you would join us in learning it. As yet, I am far from proficient and if I recall correctly, you have a particular talent for learning.'

I gritted my teeth. 'I'm sorry. That was unfair of me, especially when I should thank you.'

He squeezed my hand. 'I know this is a lot to take in, but give her a chance.'

I turned back to Ellisif, who was staring out at the crowd with a bored expression. 'Ellisif?' I spoke, shaking her from her apathy.

She blinked quickly. 'Uh? Yes? Sorry, I was staring at old Boyar Odholf down there trying to chew through the gristle with only six teeth in the front.'

I followed her hand as she gestured to a man of at least fifty winters with greying hair. Not so old, I thought, but his stooping shoulders and lined face betrayed the years spent on horseback staring into the distant sun, scanning the land for enemies.

'It's a wonder sometimes he commands such respect, but he is a favourite,' she said with a shrug.

'What do you like to do for fun?' I asked her.

She smirked, 'Riding in the forest. But Licinia never lets me go very far, or very fast. I'm a rather excellent horsewoman, though,' she replied. 'Can you ride?'

'Not well, I'm afraid.'

Some sweets had been brought out. Hazelnut patties and skyr with berries. I reached across and grabbed a fat cake and dipped it in the sour milk cheese.

'I could teach you,' she offered, clapping her hands together.

The sound startled Kjarr and Oleg from their conversation and they both looked towards Ellisif, who blushed at the attention, and I ducked behind my hands to hide my overfull mouth. She bit her bottom lip as she bowed her head. 'You'll be enviable in no time,' she whispered. When we were unnoticed again, she plucked one of the hazelnut patties from the platters and nibbled on the edge.

'The senior boyars and their wives often ride in the mornings,' Kjarr whispered over my shoulder. 'Perhaps Ellisif could join us sometime.'

Ellisif set the cookie down and grinned. 'Oh! I would love that.'

'I warn you; I don't know the first thing about riding,' I confessed after I swallowed. 'Which way do I sit on a horse?' I asked, pretending I knew nothing.

Kjarr squeezed my knee under the table.

'Stay away from its rear end,' Ellisif replied knowledgeably, 'unless you want a good kick and never let one bite you. When I was little, my horse chomped my arm and left me with a nasty bruise that took the longest time to heal. It was so unsightly my mother wouldn't even look at me.'

'I suppose that advice is as good here as it is in the stable yard,' I said to myself.

Ellisif laughed melodically, then seriousness darkened her face. 'But I hear there is trouble in the forests with the Drevlians. For the moment, they refuse to submit to the Grand Prince's protection.'

I pursed my lips, and my eyebrows rose. 'You mean they won't pay his taxes?'

'It's the same thing. Money for protection. Protection for money. But it gets worse because they've been spotted lurking in the trees, waiting for merchants to rob,' she explained. 'I don't think there are the same issues with the Polianians, though they seem keen enough to focus on their farming in the fields. Which suits us here.'

'You trade with them?'

Ellisif chewed on a bit of remaining gristle that must have been cold by now. 'Not me. But I've heard my mother speak of it often enough. They've been trying to set up something in the wool trade for a while with no success because there is another woman in town who receives fleece from the north, or something like that,' she rattled off.

I guessed she was speaking about my trading partner in Kyiv that Kjarr had organised to facilitate my endeavour into sail manufacturing. Ellisif would find that out in time, but I was sure I did not want her mother Estrid as a rival. I made a note to discuss that with Kjarr when I had the chance.

'So, yes, Oleg's men do trade with the Polianians,' Ellisif began again. 'Their honey is quite good. Though they're not the ones we have to look out for if we go riding in the forest.'

'That would be the Drevlians?' I confirmed.

'Mm-hmm,' she agreed. 'Or the Severians, because they're presently aligned with the Khazars.'

'I think I've encountered some of those Khazars before,' I responded.

It would be too soon if I ever saw them again. Their scale-like armour was singed into my memories, their plumed helmets still moved in my nightmares.

'You have?' she asked, as she set her elbows on the table and leaned towards me, eager for the story to be told.

I ignored her questioning stare. That story was for another time. 'With so many warriors accompanying us on a ride, would you feel in danger, Ellisif?'

She shook her head, tendrils of light honey curling down her back. 'Being so close to the Knyaz, how could I?' She nestled her cheek against her shoulder as she glanced at the ruler and smiled to herself.

'I told you she might be a good friend to you,' Kjarr mumbled into my hair. 'She talks a lot about nothing in particular, but her family has ignored her for so long that she is often privy to important conversations without regard.'

'Hmm,' I responded, leaning back in the chair.

'It's late, Wife. Shall we retire?' Kjarr requested. His voice was hardly above a purr.

'Would Oleg mind?' I wondered.

Kjarr nuzzled my neck. The whiff of breath spiked with drink was unmistakable. 'He has given us leave.'

'What about Ellisif?' I asked.

But as I spoke, her nurse, Licinia, came to take her away before the night got too late. 'Goodnight,' Ellisif said in farewell. 'I'll look forward to our ride together, Lady Signe.'

As I took Kjarr's hand, I waved her goodbye.

'I'm eager to show you the comfort of our lodgings,' he whispered, kissing my palm, and leading me out of the hall.

If anyone watched us leave, I did not know, for I was too distracted.

# Eighteen

Kjarr led me through the heavy curtain separating the receiving room to our secluded sleeping place. Our rooms were spacious, more like our own small hall, with alcoves lining the wall where our servants would sleep. Behind a carved divider shielded by the drapery, a pallet bed covered with inviting furs and sheets waited. The space was warm, lit by the soft glow of ornate braziers that wafted smoke and the scent of chestnut-wood.

We stopped before the fire. Kjarr searched my face with a hungered intensity. 'What do you think of it?' he asked. 'It's grander than our tastes, but Oleg insisted.'

'I wouldn't have said grand. Lavish is the word I would use,' I offered. 'The bed looks…comfortable,' I added. Sleep would be welcome after such a long journey and an eventful first day in Kyiv, and suddenly, I was exhausted. I wanted to crawl into its warmth and discover if the mattress was made of feathers instead of straw.

'Astrid,' Kjarr called, holding his hand out. 'I want to show you something.'

I followed him to the wall where a long table bore many chests. 'During our time apart, every time I missed you terribly, I would have something made for you,' he explained.

By the number of items, I judged he missed me greatly. Garments of various colours were draped over the benches and whatever was inside those chests I had yet to discover.

'More dresses?' I asked with a laugh as I motioned to the clothes.

He ran his fingers over my forearm. 'Apparently, simple dresses are insufficient for the Kyiv court. But that one,' he said, pointing at the one I wore, 'is my favourite. It looks just as I hoped it did. As I imagined.' His hand travelled up my arm, sliding along my back, and as he did, he pulled me to his chest.

'And do you have matching tunics for all of them?' I asked in jest.

He lowered his head and pressed his mouth to mine with a heated kiss. 'More or less,' he mumbled against my lips. His fingers tugged at my gown. 'It seems the done thing to match one's wife.'

I drew back. 'And not for the wife to match her husband?' I wondered as I broke from his embrace to run my hand along the bands of silk on each dress.

He followed, wrapping his arm around my waist. 'I had most of your garments made first, and then knew I wanted the same,' he said as I continued perusing the fine finishing of each dress.

My hand paused on the silky trim of another sleeve.

'Fabric purchased from the merchants of Miklagard,' he instructed, 'on whose streets you will one day also walk.'

I leaned against him. 'With you?'

He released me. 'I would hope so,' he mused, his face turning pensive as he considered his next words. 'I believe Oleg will name me envoy soon enough. He needs a man he trusts to represent his interests, but the unrest here may delay that journey.'

I gaped at him.

'Speechless?' he asked. 'That's not like you.' He kissed my cheek, then my ear, before his lips travelled to my neck. 'You wondered if there were any benefits to being Oleg's cousin.' Kjarr looked down at me with dark eyes as I pulled away.

'Is it worth the cost?' I questioned. In one night, even I could see the dangers that came from being so close to the throne.

He shrugged carelessly. 'I have all I need now that you are back in my arms.' He gathered me into him. 'And I enjoy heaping lavish trinkets upon you. Just wait until you see what is in those chests there.'

Kjarr raced to a small box with its closed lid and opened it. 'Beads!' he crowed, 'a golden torc.' He held forth the neck ring for me to inspect. 'As many temple rings as you could ever want. I used the process to keep me busy, not that I haven't been busy enough.' Kjarr stopped before the last chest.

'What's in that?' I probed, joining him by the boxes.

He patted the lid. 'It was laid out earlier, but I asked your thrall Odrun to pack it away before you came up. I wasn't sure how you would react. Whether you wanted to wait.'

'Wait until what?' I questioned, pushing him aside playfully.

Kjarr put his hands on either side of my face and kissed me.

'What's in the box?' I demanded when our lips parted. 'Show me.' My hands fumbled with the opening, and I peered inside. Tiny dresses, miniatures of my own to match Kjarr's tunics. Little deerskin slippers for a child's feet. A cloth doll with spun wool hair, cheeks coloured, and features embroidered with delicate care. Carved animal figures for minute fingers to give life to, making them move through long grass and growl at their friends. Linen underclothes, and a simple sleeping cap embellished with small flowers.

Kjarr looked down and frowned. 'Astrid. I didn't know she wouldn't be with you,' he mumbled a little too late.

My throat constricted. I closed my eyes as I tried to dam the tears that flooded behind my eyelids. The heart inside my chest pounded too fast, and I lost my breath. I was dizzy, and this time it had nothing to do with the weeks I'd spent on a ship. The ground was rushing up to meet me.

Kjarr caught me under my arms. 'She must miss you just as much.' He closed the lid of the miniature trunk.

'No,' I managed, sliding my hand into the chest to retrieve the sleeping cap. It was almost identical to the one I always carried, except the flowers were light pink instead of yellow.

Kjarr looked at me with a wrinkled brow. 'No?'

'Freyja cannot come to Kyiv.'

Kjarr sat beside me on the floor, taking the small garment into his hands. He pulled me against him, my head on his chest, arms wrapped tight around me in a protective embrace. 'What happened?' he asked. I felt him swallow hard as he waited for my response.

'Neflaug,' I moaned, the terror of that night flooding back. I buried my face in his shoulder, the smell of him a comfort in my grief.

'Will that woman ever leave you alone?' he growled.

My previous master had been a stubborn thorn in my side since her ousting from the guild, but she would bother me no longer. Not in life, anyway. 'She is dead.'

'I can't say that I mourn her,' Kjarr replied. 'What does that have to do with our daughter?'

I twisted where I sat to look at him. 'After you left Aldeigjuborg and the snow came and the river froze, Neflaug stole Freyja from her bed, and together, they fell through the ice. One was saved, but it was not our girl.'

His lip quivered as he listened. 'Freyja is gone?'

I nodded, pressing my face to his chest. 'She was never found, though a cap just like this one washed up in the reeds after the thaw.'

He said nothing, but his breathing grew ragged as he clung to me. He sobbed.

My head against his steady beating heart calmed me, a stable influence in a world that thrummed around me like pulsing water. It felt like I was back on the *Bhobain* and that brought me some comfort.

After some time, he clutched the hat and kissed me on the forehead. 'What became of Neflaug for her crimes?'

'Declared a *skogarmaor* by the Lawspeaker,' I replied, able to speak free of tears now. 'She crept away to a small hut off the estuary and there she died.'

'By your hand?' he asked.

I pursed my lips and inhaled. 'I wanted revenge. And, in a manner of speaking, her demise was by my hand but not as intended.'

'Not by Skara, then?'

I turned to face him, both of us sitting on the floor cross-legged, now knee to knee. 'Skara is no more.' That loss was still present, but none so raw as losing my daughter.

'Neflaug deserved your revenge. I would have avenged Freyja had I known,' he swore. Kjarr's eyes were shadowed.

'This wasn't something I could send in a message.'

He reached out his hand and left it on my knee, stroking it gently. 'I understand. It seems I've missed far more than I ought to have in my absence.' He rocked forward to kneeling and drew my face up to his. I felt his eyes pass over my scar. 'Tell me everything.'

So, I did. Kjarr sat without speaking mostly. He angered over Freyja's death, solemnly shook his head when I recalled Neflaug dying from the unclean water I pulled up from the stagnant well. Kjarr listened with horror as I detailed the weeks I lay in bed, sweating, and fevering from the same illness that had claimed Neflaug's life. He heard of the long weeks it took me to rebuild my strength and the message he never received about it. Then of the unrest that plagued Aldeigjuborg when the rebels tried to invade the town and later made their stand at the Abandoned Paragon. And, just when he thought the worst was over, he watched me pace around the room, describing how close we came to losing Eskil to the armies of Itil, and the journey that took my last reserves of energy. By the end, I was drained, my tears were spent, and my mouth felt dry.

'And all the time we journeyed to Kyiv, I was worried that this,' I said, motioning to the healed wound at my temple, 'would displease you.'

'Really?' He frowned.

'That you would love me despite it.'

'Despite? No. Because of it.' He leaned down and planted a kiss along the rift. 'You are so strong, Astrid. You had cause to question my love for you, and for that, I'm sorry. I will never allow such a thing to happen again.'

Kjarr offered his hand as he pulled me to my feet. He helped me out of my fine dress, hanging it over a beam to air overnight.

I took his hand. 'We can still mourn her and want more,' I said, reaching with my free hand to stroke his bearded cheek. 'I've often found myself wanting to fill the loss with another.'

His hesitation was stilled when I slipped my palm behind his head, dragging his mouth upon mine.

He kissed me hard in response and I surrendered to whatever thread those sisters of fate now wove for us.

# NINETEEN

'Does it go here?' I asked Kjarr playfully as I slipped my foot into the stirrup.

He squeezed my booted toes between his fingers. 'You know, I could have you sit in front of me if you're planning to fall off,' he threatened as he hoisted me upwards.

I eased myself onto the mare's back. 'You wouldn't,' I replied with a glare, and slotted my left foot into the remaining stirrup. 'Promise to keep my feet where they should be, and my backside firmly planted,' I vowed.

'Embla is a good horse,' he agreed, stroking the mare's mane. 'She won't throw you unless you try to kick her on while she's drinking.'

'I would never,' I replied, tickling the horse's poll. She flicked her ears back. 'If you need a drink, old girl, you take it.'

He chuckled to himself as he checked the buckles on my stirrup straps. 'They look the right length now.' Kjarr patted Embla's muzzle as she pushed against his hand, searching for food.

Kjarr's tawny mare, hands higher than Embla, pawed at the loose soil while she waited for her rider. He hauled himself onto the blanket, straightening it out beneath him before adjusting his reins. 'We're just waiting on the others now,' he informed me, nodding toward the stalls.

Ellisif trotted out of the stables on a dappled grey, looking like the picture of controlled horsemanship. 'Good morning,' she beamed, a radiant smile across her face. Golden hair streamed down the back of her pale blue gown in loose braids that bounced along as she rode towards us. 'I hope we go to the ponds. Licinia never lets me go that way!'

Kjarr winked at me. 'I'm sure Signe will also want to see them. Is Licinia coming too?' he asked.

Ellisif shook her head. 'She has a stomach-ache and has taken to her pallet. Besides, Signe is here, so I shouldn't get into any trouble.' By the glint in Ellisif's cornflower blue eyes, mischief was exactly what she was pursuing.

'I'd like to see these ponds,' I agreed without knowing what I was consenting to. 'Is it just the three of us?'

There was a crunching noise from the byre as the Grand Prince rode into the yard on his shining black mount. He halted and his horse paced back and forth, nickering joyfully.

'Grand Prince,' Kjarr howled between laughs. 'Are we not going for a gentle ride in the forest? Do you need your warhorse for that?'

Oleg cackled in response. 'Cousin, you are squinting. Perhaps your old man's eyes cannot see that this is not my charge, Magni,' he replied. 'I've left him stabled as I do not need to fight today, at least I hope not.' He bristled, as he no doubt considered the threat that the Drevlians held just northwest of Kyiv.

'Old man's eyes,' Kjarr grumbled. 'I'm two years your junior.'

Oleg patted the horse's mane, ignoring Kjarr's rebuttal. 'Sindri is a good, calm mare if ever there was one. I can't believe you cannot see the difference, Cousin.'

'They're both big and they're both black,' Kjarr replied, shrugging with indifference. It was good to see Kjarr so relaxed with his kin, in stark contrast to his rigidity at court functions.

The Grand Prince greeted me with a nod before turning his surprised gaze to Ellisif. 'Are you to join us as well…' He paused, searching for her name.

'Ellisif Heilagrsdottir,' Kjarr added for him.

'Ahh.' Oleg made the noise as he realised who her family was.

Ellisif opened her mouth to speak, but no words escaped.

'I invited her,' Kjarr chimed in, 'as a companion for Signe. Ellisif knows the local customs which interests my wife. Do you agree she may come?'

'Fine,' Oleg answered as he turned his horse towards the gates. 'Your wife will need someone to ride with her while we race each other,' he called, spurring Sindri forward. 'Yah!' Oleg sped out of sight with Kjarr and Ellisif not far behind, and me doing my best to keep up.

Outside the city walls, pace kept time with the horse's stride. It was early; the farmers were rubbing sleep from their eyes and stepping into the fields as their wives set broth to boil on hearth fires. Dew beaded on small leaves as we followed the well-worn path towards the forest where fresh air, devoid of the stench of close living, filled my nostrils and tufts of white clouds drifted in the blue sky with no threat of rain. It was the release I had desired since arriving in the stifling court. Instead of tall fortifications, gigantic oaks as old as the gods towered above our heads in every direction as we trotted along the trail. Each trunk, thick as the belly of a man overfond of ale, each so tall it could scrape the blue hue from the fabric of sky above. Scrub critters scattered as our mounts clipped their hooves on the undergrowth, careful not to become snagged on gnarled roots. Streams of sunlight peered through crowns of leaves, illuminating the rich green woodland beneath.

The calm of the forest reminded me of my time on the river. Those days seemed a faraway memory since my arrival in Kyiv. When our backs were sore from rowing, but laughter rang often, and even if the crew had disagreements, no one was baying for blood. Maybe Gunnar was. A cunning one that, as soon as we arrived in the city, he had disappeared into the fold of boyars. No doubt serving one of their numbers and his own interests. Sometimes I saw him loitering in the Great Hall but had no cause to speak with him, and nothing to say if I had. He had slotted back into life as if he'd never been gone.

Sihtric was busy with his spice trade, running a small stall at Kyiv's markets and servicing every noble household in need of his products. Eskil was a sworn *huskarl* to Oleg, as was Sven and he practised at bow and arrow so often I scarcely saw either man unless I went to the practice yard.

As my thoughts wandered, so had I lagged. I spurred Embla on with a kick of my heel, and she lengthened her step, catching the trio before too long. From above, there was a piercing shriek as an eagle took flight, circling while it looked for prey.

'That one likes to eat snakes,' Ellisif announced as we pulled up to watch the eagle soaring high. 'I once saw one just like it, with a serpent dangling out of its mouth.' She squinted towards the sun, shielding her eyes with her hand as she watched the bird drifting in the sky.

'Is that so?' Oleg asked, watching with raised eyebrows. 'How can you be sure it had not bitten the bird, and the eagle was trying to fly away?'

Ellisif looked directly at the Grand Prince. 'The snake was quite dead, Knyaz. And besides, I've also seen snakes pecked through.'

'Hmm,' he answered as the eagle disappeared into the tree cover. 'A fearsome foe.'

'Yes, Knyaz,' Ellisif agreed. 'Some of them like to hunt the strangest things.'

Oleg leaned forward and patted his mare's neck. 'I'm usually looking for a bigger quarry.' He sat upright. 'But not today. We will do no hunting.' His hand rested on the hilt of his weapon, narrowed eyes on Ellisif before he took up his reins and set off once more through the trees. We followed.

It was easy to maintain silence in the calm space of the forest. Beneath soaring trees, we rode all morning. Kjarr and Oleg rushed through the woodland, racing, and whooping loudly, and I marvelled at Kjarr's ease on horseback. It was something we had never discussed before; it made me wonder what else I had yet to learn about my husband. My awkwardness on horseback had given way to the discomfort of an aching backside, a pain the others seemed oblivious to. Embla was a good horse, sure and steady, and though my directions were lacking, she was content enough to follow along after the group.

Ellisif slowed her horse's stride and circled around to ride beside me. 'They're up ahead,' she muttered.

'The ponds?' I asked.

She nodded. 'We should be close now. You know, the people of the forest and field believe their world is ruled from both the sky and their underworld,' she explained. 'Perun's dominion is there,' Ellisif said, pointing skyward, 'and Weles rules from below.' She motioned to the ground.

'They have only two gods?' I questioned. I was always interested to hear of other beliefs.

She shook her head. 'No, but I can't remember all their names. It's hard enough to recall all the Aesir and Vanir, isn't it? Licinia told me they live their life by some kind of balance between these two big gods,' she continued. 'Always a struggle between the good and the bad within everything; themselves, the land, the skies, the water.'

'It seems tiresome to be worrying about good and evil constantly, and not too dissimilar to the Christian idea of God and the Devil,' I responded.

Ellisif cocked her head. 'You know a lot about this faith?'

'I knew a rather motivated priest in Aldeigjuborg, who harboured hopes of my conversion. Little did he know my questions were borne from curiosity alone,' I replied with a laugh.

She smiled at that and nodded, as if she, too, understood my compulsion for learning.

'From here we walk,' Kjarr called back over his shoulder as he dismounted.

The men helped us from our horses, leaving them to graze and guzzle water from a small stream where we tied them. Ellisif held onto my arm, her other hand clutching her skirts so they didn't trail along in the mud.

'These pools are sacred to the Polianians,' she whispered, running her hands over the long reeds that grew near the shallows.

Oleg was already loosening his garments, ready to disrobe as a small herd of swans drifted on the surface.

Ellisif turned away, blushing deeply. 'They shouldn't do that,' she started. 'It could cause a lot of trouble.'

'Because of some swimming?' I asked, 'or because they're half, oof, almost entirely naked?'

They had stripped off their tunics and begun tugging at their trousers. They meant to wade into the water bare.

'No, but the spirits will curse the Knyaz if he enters these sacred waters,' Ellisif worried.

Superstition or not, bad fortune was something to avoid, especially if Oleg had hopes of ruling over the people who held the waterway sacrosanct. I raced forward before the Grand Prince was out of his trousers and pulled on Kjarr's arm, mumbling what Ellisif had told me into his ear. Kjarr fumbled his pants back on and grabbed Oleg, explaining the situation. After the Grand Prince had dressed himself, he trudged back, staring intently at young Ellisif, who had kept her gaze lowered.

'You can look at me now. I'm dressed,' he began. 'I'm sorry to have upset you. When I'm outside the city walls, I can forget myself, and who is around me. I apologise.'

He tried to catch Ellisif's eye, but she was still looking at the ground as she mumbled, 'No need.'

Oleg touched a finger to Ellisif's chin and raised her face. 'Boyar Hrolfsson told me you have some knowledge of these pools?'

'They say a water god inhabits here and to disturb her is to bring a dreadful fate,' she explained as Oleg's hand fell to his side.

The corner of his mouth crooked, and, for a moment, I thought he would laugh. 'We don't want to anger any spirits today, whether or not we worship them. I have no desire to disrespect the beliefs of our allies.' He prowled the edge of the water. 'What then, should we do with these pools?' he asked, directing the question at Ellisif.

She seemed shocked to have been considered. 'Observe them, Knyaz. See how the swans drift along? If you are quiet and watch close enough, sometimes you'll see a little shrew that walks on water to eat the small fish.' She motioned with her dainty hand and mimicked the small creature's walking.

I eyed her curiously. 'You said you hadn't been to the pools before.'

'I never said that,' she replied, blinking rapidly. 'I said Licinia never lets me go.'

'Hmmm,' Oleg mused as Ellisif parted the reeds by the pond. 'It's fortunate you've come with us today or else I may have cursed my entire reign,' he responded, and I couldn't quite tell if he was joking.

'You mean your protection of Igor's reign,' Kjarr put in and was greeted with a bristling grunt from his cousin.

Ellisif squealed with delight and pointed to something out of view. Oleg followed and squatted down by her where they stayed, side by side, whispering over something they found.

Kjarr stood back, face blank and staring into the distance.

I wrinkled my brow. 'Should we join them?'

He blinked and shook his head. 'This feels like something we shouldn't interrupt. Oleg rarely has such freedoms. I haven't seen him so unburdened since we lived in Holmgardr and would go exploring with his sister, Alfvind.'

'Even if he is the Grand Prince, I shouldn't leave Ellisif alone with Oleg. I'm supposed to be her safeguard.'

'We won't go far,' he agreed. 'The ground here is dry enough to put out the blanket,' Kjarr suggested, and we grabbed the provisions from the pack on the horses and set up a place to eat.

I sat watchful for a while, straining my ears for any sound that might have given away Ellisif's discomfort. But nothing came, save for laughing and constant chatter. Kjarr tried to distract me with stories of his trade adventures and I laid back and listened with eyes closed to the melody of his voice. Kjarr described his journey to Miklagard the year prior, of the sounds and smells of the golden city.

'There is this fruit of green leathery skin,' he began, 'and inside a flesh of pink and white that tastes of berries and… you've tasted a date before?'

'Mm-hmm,' I agreed. My previous mentor, Eryk, who had taught me languages and business, had given me some a long time before. I recalled their sweet savour.

'The taste is a bit like a date and a berry mixed, but the texture is crunchy inside because of the many small seeds. You will seek it out when you go,' he mumbled, sitting beside me. 'For now,' he said, parting my lips with his finger, 'you'll have to content yourself with chewy, stale apples.' Kjarr slid a small slither of dried apple between my teeth and though the flavour was sweet, it did not compare to the fruit he had described.

When Ellisif returned, her arm was draped over Oleg's as they walked stride for stride, continuing their conversation in low voices, glancing at one another with broad smiles. It wasn't until they were almost upon the blanket that they noticed us.

'We saw one,' Oleg declared, 'a little rat-like thing nibbling on fish guts.'

Kjarr made a face. 'Fascinating,' he replied, offering some bread to his cousin.

In his excitement, Oleg was impervious to Kjarr's comment but accepted the food.

'Who's hungry?' I asked. The sun was reaching the midday mark by now, and my stomach rumbled. 'Odrun packed us some bread, cheese, and apples.'

As we feasted, the clearing was full of sunshine and a colourful smattering of primrose flowers. Food went down easily after a morning of riding, and after eating, both Kjarr, and Oleg reclined on their elbows sipping from a skin of ale.

Oleg sighed. 'Trees don't make demands of me.'

Kjarr looked at me and shrugged.

'Here, people aren't asking me for things. They aren't watching my every move,' he complained, rubbing his forehead with one hand.

Ellisif caught my eye and raised a fair eyebrow. We both thought to excuse ourselves, but Oleg made no gesture to dismiss us, so we sat quietly. Ellisif produced a small cloth bag. Inside was a band half-woven, tiny tablets dangling off each strand of wool.

'Did you bring work with you?' I asked.

She shushed me, holding a finger to her lips and threw her head towards the men's conversation.

'They refer to me as a knyaz now,' Oleg was saying, 'even some tribes accept that. But I need to be khagan as well. A king the Khazars can also acknowledge. On par with their own ruler… until then, there is no respect. They will think me a lesser ruler,' he continued, tearing the petals off a small pink bloom he had ripped from the forest-floor.

'Do they?' Kjarr asked.

'They won't think of me like that when I assert dominance,' Oleg answered with a curt laugh. He tossed the petalless stem into the bushes.

Kjarr sat up, massaging his elbow. 'Is that what you want?'

Oleg reached for another flower to destroy. 'Before Rurik died, he had dreams of empire.' Rurik was Oleg's brother by marriage, I remembered, and father to Igor, who was just a child. Oleg ruled in his name after he rescued Igor from Kyiv the year before.

'In order to do that, I must send envoys to the other powers. I should meet Frankia and Miklagard on equal terms. And, if they cannot perceive me as equal, I will need eyes and ears to bring me information on how that may be achieved.'

'They still doubt you because of Igor?' Kjarr pressed, green eyes focused on Oleg's cool blue stare.

He shook his head. 'They know a child cannot rule! This is not some land where the son of a king takes the throne because of his blood!' Oleg was on the verge of anger. 'Never! Might rules, as always,' he roared, throwing the limp blossom on the grass. 'Igor is not yet old enough. One day, he will be, and I must ensure the kingdom he inherits will be strong. That was Rurik's dream, and the wish of my sister, Alfvind.'

'And he will,' Kjarr consoled him.

There were flowers all around us. I plucked dozens and started weaving them together in a long chain, keeping my hands busy, so I was free to listen but was not tempted to look.

'People have such short memories, don't they? It's accurate enough that Rurik was invited to rule, but it was because his much older brother lay dying, and he was a warlord who would protect them. His family had ruled here for generations before he sailed with my sister and me. He was hardly the first. This land was hard-won, each settlement a victory in establishing a new empire. Rurik was the one to capture Holmgardr and build the fortress there and so began the Rurikids.'

'He will feast with the *einherjar* in Valhalla, and when you meet him there, he will love you for your service to him,' Kjarr said. 'We need to do something about the Drevlians before you let the Valkyries take you, though.'

Oleg laughed and stuffed his mouth with bread. 'Not yet, Cousin. We will not begin our campaign until winter, then we will hit them with our full power. Unless, of course, they submit first.' He tore a chunk off his bread and tossed it into his open mouth.

Kjarr scrunched his face. 'So, you'll send the tax collectors first and see who comes back?' he asked.

'With money and tribute, Cousin. You sound like I'm sending these men off to their deaths.'

Kjarr looked over and saw the length of yellow primroses I had knitted together. He took them in his hand and showed the Grand Prince. 'Do you remember when your sister would return from the forest with chains of flowers like these and try to make us wear them?' Kjarr asked, chuckling.

'I do.' Oleg smiled, taking my creation into his palm. 'Do you think she would have approved of my raising Igor?'

'She never wanted Haskold and Dir to have anything to do with him.'

'The bastards,' Oleg spat. 'When I heard they'd taken the boy, I wanted to boil them alive in a vat of hot oil. Igor was the last tie I had to my sister, to Rurik. He's just a small boy, and they thought they could rule through him, but it is I who must keep Igor safe until he is old and wise enough to exercise that power.'

'You did the right thing,' Kjarr replied.

Oleg leaned back again, gazing up at the bright blue sky. 'He'll need a good wife beside him when he is ready to marry.'

'Pity Ellisif is a woman grown. She'd make a fine match for Igor. A powerful family to protect him, but she is too old to wait and the age difference between them is too great,' Kjarr stated.

'No younger sister?' Oleg asked.

Kjarr shook his head.

Oleg watched the young woman for a moment as she weaved her band, pretending not to listen to their conversation. 'She should be married by now. Most women are at fifteen,' he said. 'What is her family waiting for?'

Kjarr sliced a section of apple with his knife. 'Don't they need to seek your approval for any match?'

Oleg nodded slowly. 'I suppose I have been busy this last year, but I will consider it. Her marriage should be to someone on the rise.'

Ellisif shifted on the ground and beckoned me to walk with her away from the men as she packed up her weaving.

'Are you all right?' I asked, catching up with her quick strides.

'Oh, people are always talking about my marriage,' she answered. 'It doesn't mean it's going to happen soon. And my father will keep me until he can trade me for a good connection,' she explained.

I must have made a face because she laughed and threw her hands up.

'It's my duty to marry. I know that and it worries me not.'

'Don't you want a say in it?' I asked.

She shrugged. 'What do I know of men? I'd rather my father chose for me. He sees them at drink, at war, at dinner. The only time I'd get to see the man I'm to marry before the event would be serving him at a feast. How am I to judge him then? By his looks? By his voice? Or his gifts?'

'Isn't that how a man considers a woman for a wife?' I asked in retort.

She cocked her head and smiled. 'A comely face smooths the process, but we marry for our families. Well, most do. Boyar Hrolfsson didn't, I take it?'

I shook my head. 'I'm a merchant. No family to speak of and no money, except that which I've earned.'

'No alliances?' she added with interest, the tone of her voice raising. 'Perhaps that's what makes you so attractive. You have no ambition.'

My eyes bulged. I couldn't hide my surprise at her words.

She patted my shoulder with her hand. 'Oh, I'm sure you're a fine businesswoman, but you have no designs on the throne. I'm sorry if I spoke out of turn.' Ellisif looked at me with her round eyes full of apology.

I grasped her arm and slotted it through mine as we walked just out of earshot of the men. 'You're right. I don't want to further our family in Kyiv. Our only ambitions are adventure.'

'Adventure?' she asked, stepping over stones and oak roots near a wide trunk.

'Exploration down the trading routes. Into far-off lands,' I replied.

'Signe? Ellisif?' Kjarr's voice called from between the oak trunks.

'We're coming now,' I called. We travelled back the way we came, retrieving our horses from the stream, well-watered and fed. Oleg and Kjarr helped us onto our horses and, despite the discomfort of being on horseback, I was glad I didn't have to walk to the city, as it would have taken all day.

'On the way back, we should try a canter,' she suggested once we were all mounted.

I'd gone no faster than a trot, only on a wagon or a ship had I travelled faster than on foot and to ride on horseback at speed was a novel sensation altogether.

'You must squeeze with your thighs if you don't want to fall off,' Ellisif advised.

So, I squeezed with all my might, pushing my legs against Embla's body. With my hair unbound and catching in the breeze, it felt like fast freedom. I wanted to spread my arms out and fly.

'You must hold the reins,' Ellisif called as she pulled up alongside me. 'Don't let go.' She forced my hands back onto the strips of leather.

The temptation was too grand. I flapped like a bird despite her warning. 'But the horse knows what to do.'

'You are her master,' Ellisif chastised me as she took my reins to slow Embla. She tickled the mare under the ear once we stopped. 'It is your task to direct her.'

Oleg looked over his shoulder towards us, and Ellisif blushed. 'Isn't that so, Knyaz?' she asked, looking at him for approval.

'I would have to disagree, in part,' Oleg began, and Ellisif's cheeks grew redder.

'At first, you will need to tell her everything,' he spoke, pushing between our horses, 'but in time you will know each other so well that a small touch will suffice.' He ran his hand along Ellisif's reins. 'Then, without a word, she will know. Both Magni and Sindri have been with me so long I barely need to direct them to anything.'

'Yes, Knyaz,' Ellisif agreed as he handed the leather straps back into her hands.

'Signe is still learning,' Kjarr interjected, trying to save Ellisif's pride.

'I'm sure old Embla does not know what I want,' I tried to explain. 'Ellisif's a far better rider than I could ever hope to be. I should listen,' I replied. 'Right now, I feel like I'm just sitting here letting her do all the hard work.' I offered Ellisif an apologetic smile.

Everyone laughed at that, and Ellisif's cheerful demeanour soon returned.

We pulled into the stable yard where Oleg and Kjarr slipped from their horse's backs. Kjarr paused by my leg as Oleg went to Ellisif, where he eased her shoes from their stirrups and helped her down.

'Thank you, Knyaz,' she whispered, sweeping the ground in a low curtsey as he stood above her.

Licinia, Ellisif's maid, was waiting in the yard and she rushed forward. 'Come,' she nipped, bowing even lower than Ellisif had when she saw the Grand Prince. 'Knyaz,' she mumbled as she closed her dark-lashed eyelids. I saw little more than her cloth-covered dark hair as she swept her young charge from our company.

'You should ride with us again, Ellisif,' Oleg called, patting Sindri's neck. 'You might show us more of the creatures of the forest.'

I slid down from Embla into Kjarr's arms, and he whispered, 'I don't know what we've started, but I hope it doesn't end up scalding us.'

# TWENTY

'Another feast?' Odrun asked as she dressed my hair later that evening.

I had come home and slept, too exhausted from my forest ride to keep my eyes open for another moment.

'Not this time,' I replied, as Odrun's fingers weaved my hair into lovely braids. 'It's a private meal between cousins. Kjarr wants me by his side.'

She nodded, a pin between her teeth as she forced another into my thick plait. Odrun picked up a bottle from the table before me and unstoppered it. The room filled with the heady scent of warm spice as she allowed a couple of drops to fall into her hands. She rubbed them together briefly, then smoothed them over my braids, and ran the residue across my collarbones with a practised touch.

'Lady Signe,' a stoic voice from the corner of the room addressed me.

I turned to see Egbert enter. 'You needn't call me that,' I scolded him. 'Signe is fine.'

Odrun steadied my shoulders, making me sit straight once more. She set about tucking in any straggling pieces of hair back into the style with a shake of her head, her lips pursed in concentration.

'If I were to call you by your name, I would appear too familiar,' he responded, his dark brows furrowed and his forehead creased. The clothing he wore was so dark that he almost seemed to be a shadow as he moved about the room. He was so light on his feet that had I not known he was there, I might have been startled to see him.

'Any word from the messenger?' I asked without looking towards him again. 'Are you sure this man is trustworthy?'

Egbert came to stand beside us. He was much changed since I'd taken him from Eskil's service. No longer was he intimidated by the presence of others. He stood taller, more confident of himself. Though there was always a strength about him, he was stronger in body and mind. His health, too, had improved. His once lank-hanging hair had become a volume of loose curls. Dull skin was now clear and smooth. Egbert's skill in writing was valued so highly in my household that Kjarr had gifted him a bronze cloak pin for his work. I studied the piece as he nodded.

'I believe the man is trustworthy. Yes,' Egbert answered.

Odrun scrutinised her efforts, standing back with her hands on her hips, looking down at my hair. She slotted in a last pin before turning to Egbert. 'We need to be sure. Your beliefs are not enough.'

He twisted his mouth and glanced down. 'I understand well how important this letter is.'

'That you will not share the contents of,' I complained, moving in my seat to see them both.

Odrun looked down with a scowl. She was sick of my asking and had made it known. Egbert moved away. 'Soon, Lady Signe. We will have our response.'

I breathed in sharply, 'So, you have sent it?'

For an answer, he nodded as he disappeared behind the partition to the hall where he slept and kept his meagre belongings.

I felt Odrun's hand clutch my shoulder and a small gasp escaped her lips.

The scent was strong in the room and mingled with the heat of the brazier; I thought she might faint.

'Sit down,' I said, offering her the seat I sat on. 'All will be fine,' I tried to comfort her, but without knowing what was going on, that was hard to do. 'I'll get you a drink.' I moved to the small table that held a jug and cups and poured one out for her.

'What if?' she started, but stopped herself before she gave anymore away. Her hands pulled at the wadmal cape she always wore around her neck, its edge frayed and discoloured.

'You know, if you had me in your confidence, it might ease the burden,' I suggested as I pressed the cup into her hand.

She took a sip of the bitter ale and swallowed hard.

Egbert called back from the small hall, 'She has been a good friend to you.'

'How can my master be my friend?' she yelled back at Egbert's voice in the other room.

'I would release you,' I began, 'but you have prohibited me.' I reached my hand to hers. 'Let me free you as I have Egbert.'

At first, even Egbert had refused, thinking that to be free he must also return home, something he vehemently wanted to avoid. So, after a brief hesitation, I told him he could remain in my service if he desired so. In the end, he agreed and both Kjarr and I were glad to have a scribe in our employ. He now wore the simple knife I had gifted him, the mark of the freeman, upon his belt with great pride. It was only Odrun who could not be convinced.

'For this to be successful, I must not be free,' she repeated the same explanation she always did when the subject was broached.

I sat on the edge of my fur-covered bed to slip on my doeskin shoes. 'Very well, Odrun. If you change your mind, you need only say so. But I wish you would tell me something about this scheme, especially if it presents danger to anyone under this roof.'

Having righted herself, she nodded and stood up. 'I will tell you only this: The messenger is the one Oleg is sending with the Envoy to Frankia.'

I looked at Egbert for an explanation as he rounded the partition, entering the room again like the shadow he was. 'West or East?' I asked, looking down as I fastened the cords on my slippers.

'I will say nothing more,' she responded.

A grumble almost slipped from my mouth, but she had told me more on this night than she had in the weeks before, so I held my tongue.

Egbert leaned against the carved wall and laughed. 'I'm shocked you've given away that much,' he added lightly, a half-smile at his friend.

I looked at Egbert, unimpressed. 'I can't say I find that trifle very enlightening.'

Odrun ushered me back into my seat before the table, so she could finish dressing me for the night. 'You might make sense of it in the end,' she said.

Egbert edged closer, taking a seat by the small table that contained the ewer and cups. He poured an ale out for himself. 'Have you found a suitable location for the warehouse yet?' he asked, getting his ink and parchment out to make notes.

'In fact, I have,' I replied. 'There is a building overlooking the docks that is big enough. Mirca thinks it to be our best option. Her women have already begun working on cloth for two sails besides the more delicate fabrics the ladies of Kyiv require.'

'A formidable woman,' Egbert commented. 'I'm glad she is with you and not against you.'

'Only if she hated money would she be against Signe. A senior boyar's wife, so close to the throne, it wouldn't make sense to shun her,' Odrun declared.

I'd already had several meetings with Mirca. She was a local, unlike me, but what she lacked for status, my new position leant us. What she had was a plethora of skilled ladies who needed work, women who spun long and fine thread, and were like goddesses at the loom but had little money to finance such an operation. Together, we would accomplish it.

Odrun crossed the room and retrieved a length of beads Kjarr had recently given me. She looped them around my neck and fussed with them until they lay pleasingly, careful not to entangle them with my golden neck ring.

'We have Kjarr to thank for that. Mirca was agreeable before we arrived and after meeting her, well, she makes me think of an old friend,' I explained. Mirca was as resolute as Hilde, my greatest support in Aldeigjuborg, and as forthright as her daughter Helga, one of my best friends.

'That reminds me,' I began. 'I will need to send a message to Aldeigjuborg,' I continued, inclining my head to Egbert.

'You said there is a priest by the name of Niall who might receive comprehensive correspondence and relay it to Helga?' he asked.

'He would,' I agreed. 'Helga will have given birth by now and I would like to send gifts.'

'Then I will begin by writing to him. It would give me a chance to keep my written Latin in good use,' Egbert advised with a proud smile.

I held my hand out to count the remaining tasks on my fingers. 'We also need to finalise the shipments coming from the north next season. Deliveries will cease when the frost comes and it will feel like an eternity before we get anything new unless we trade with the Polianians.'

'Or unless you decide to forgo ships and turn to sleds,' Egbert suggested, but I couldn't tell by his tone if he was making a jest.

'Are we so desperate for wool that we need to?' I asked, turning to look at Egbert as he smudged out a mistake in his writing.

He looked up. 'I will make enquiries with the farms and see if we can secure the next shearing. It should be the last before their flocks grow their winter fleeces,' he explained, making scribbles on the parchment before him. The scratching ceased, and he touched the tip of his feather quill to his tongue. There the ink stained his mouth. 'Urgh,' he groaned, sticking his tongue out before he dipped the tip back into the dark pot.

'Ask Mirca. She'll know who to start with,' I suggested.

Odrun draped a silk headband of brilliant blue around my head and secured it with more pins. Quiet as a mouse, she slid a coiled temple ring through the loops of fabric on the band on each side. She sniffed, and I caught her hand with mine.

'All will be well, Odrun. I will keep you safe,' I promised as Egbert excused himself, packing up his writing tools, and leaving the room.

She looked down at me through welling tears.

'If whatever message you have sent is not well received, you will be freed, and you can live a life of your choosing. Should you want to stay with me, you are welcome, and if you wish to go, I will not stop you,' I swore, releasing her palm.

'Thank you,' she breathed as tears streamed down her beautiful face. Her amber eyes twinkled in the dim light of the brazier, and she laughed through her sorrow. 'I will say this, Signe. Though I hate the work and make a poor servant, I'd rather be here in your rooms instead of serving at feasts. By the end of the night, I've always got sore feet, a man trying to direct me into his bed, and a very hungry stomach,' she said.

I looked at her with concern. 'If I find anyone trying to take you to bed, they'll have to answer to Oleg. He has promised you will remain unhindered.'

She blinked at me and cleared her throat. 'What I'm trying to say is: If I have to serve someone, I'm glad it's you.'

# TWENTY-ONE

Warmth waned as the cooler season warned of its approach. There was a chill in the air and I wrapped my warm woollen cloak over my shoulders, careful not to obscure the band of gold I wore around my neck. Though I disliked such a blatant display, Kjarr felt it was important I looked the part of a boyar's wife. Seldom did I leave my small hall without donning a fine gown of vibrant colour, decorated with various beads, brooches, gold jewellery, and a flash of silk. The only reprieve from the pageantry came from a visit to the practice yard. There, I relished in the simple clothing that allowed for effortless movement.

Today, adorned as I was, the practice yard was not what I sought. People nodded in acknowledgement as I walked down the well-trodden path of the city. Joiners heaved great planks into position as new buildings, wood bright and unblemished, sprang up from the ground. Their apprentices ran to their master's sides, handing them tools to secure each piece in place. Hammering sounded over the vendors this market day. I wandered on, leather tarpaulins in view, stretched over small stalls erected by merchants both itinerant and local. Beneath the roofs, women chopped vegetables for stews at the brewing houses, their rumps squashed together on a long bench as they chatted merrily over their work. A younger woman, cheeks flushed with exertion, scooped the root chunks into a vat, bubbling away as she stirred it with a massive wooden paddle. To the market-goers, she called to come for a taste.

Enormous baskets of fruit and vegetables lined the path, stuffed with apples, plums, and an array of colourful produce, which sweetened the air pleasingly. Small casks of salt were on offer at an excessive price, and I thought Sihtric had been right in procuring so much to bring here, so he might make a large sum from its sale. At the animal trader, fouls in twig cages stacked high threatened to tumble as the birds within flapped their wings. The merchant ran out to steady the tower as a cockerel crowed and saved it from toppling just in time.

Passing the purveyors of foodstuff, I gazed upon the tables of bronze ware, trinkets, and goblets, each made by a craftsman's hand. Then I passed more exotic offerings which would usually catch my eye, but I searched for someone in particular. Soapstone sellers held forth dainty dishes, while many a merchant took out their small brass scales to set silver hack against their weights, being sure not to be swindled out of the smallest measure. Haggling buyers waved their hands before clasping palms with the traders once they'd decided on payment. Animals were led through the square as people gathered in groups to discuss the day's purchases. Maids with woven baskets on their hips, doing their lady's shopping, gossiped about boyar's wives while out on the guise of ticking off their lists. All the while, stall-holders cried out to one and all.

'Come and view the latest amber,' a merchant with a springy black beard called from his booth. The hat he wore was tall and his rust-coloured trousers surprisingly straight. 'Honey-coloured amber for your wife! Adorn her neck, her wrists, and fingers!' he shouted above the din. The black-bearded man held the rock to the light, attracting some of the young women's attention, and gestured for them to approach.

'Modern styles,' cried another salesman even louder than the amber merchant, while producing trinkets from a box in his arms. He was much shorter than the dark bearded man, with fair hair and a paunch over his belt. A long necklace rattled in front of me as I passed. 'Be the first in Kyiv to wear such a thing.'

Gunnar, too, was offering his baubles for sale but his scowling face put people off and none approached his stall. I moved to one side to avoid him, but walked straight into a portly man with a long, twisted grey beard holding a soapstone dish.

'Your neighbour will envy your table if you have these pieces. Round or square, every piece finished to the most perfect quality. Your feasts shall be all the sweeter!'

There were many ladies gathered at his stall, so it was easy for me to back away without being noticed. The soapstone seller rubbed his hands together in anticipation. He set to work, converting the women's curiosity into purchases. The atmosphere of a bustling marketplace was always one I enjoyed. It had been at the Aldeigjuborg markets where I met Kjarr for the first time, all those years ago. When I had arrived, my days were spent working in the warehouse, except for when Neflaug tasked me with attending the market to inspect wool and gather information. Those afternoons were my favourite, rare freedom from the drudgery of spinning.

But today, my purpose was not soapstone dishes, or trinkets, nor even a midday meal. I came seeking a friend, and I found his booth set up before the sheep byre, now vacant of its woolly occupants.

'I dinnae see you down this way, *bhana charaid*,' Sihtric said, beckoning me forward. 'But I suppose you've been busy with everything or you would have been enjoying market day like the rest of the townsfolk?'

I offered an apologetic smile. 'It's not because I don't want to be here,' I replied. 'You know how much I enjoy the markets.'

He nodded, his auburn hair bright in the morning sun. 'Aye. So, have you come for my products, my good looks, or my friendly advice?' he asked, chuckling to himself.

I looked at the canisters, baskets, and pots on his table. 'I've come for some clove if you have any,' I requested, lifting the lid on a small clay pot.

'You could have sent Odrun down to order and I'd happily bring it,' he responded, taking the tops of several containers to check their contents.

I plucked a cover from something spicy and warm, but the name was unknown to me. 'It's more fun to wander out of the hall. How else would I get the town gossip?' I asked with a wry smile.

'Aye,' he agreed, 'and what have you heard?' Sihtric replaced the lid on some mustard seeds, rattling them around in their pot like beads in a box before setting them back down.

'That you've taken a woman,' I murmured, watching for his reaction.

His lips moved about without opening, eyes still focused on the pot he'd placed on the table. Sihtric's hands drifted over the container lids, tapping their small handles with the tips of his fingers. 'Have I now?' he asked, allowing his moss-green eyes to meet mine. His bell-adorned hand shot to his chest in pretend injury.

This, then, was no surprise to him. He had heard the rumour.

Sihtric stood close to me, leaning on the table. 'Better they speak of a lover than call me a *fluthfloggi*,' he whispered.

In my shock, I looked over my shoulder to make sure we remained unheard. 'You shouldn't say that here,' I warned, grabbing his arm. Open ears were everywhere, waiting for a tasty morsel to sell to gossip merchants. A man being labelled as someone who shunned marriage was assumed to abhor lying with a woman. That made him dishonourable and unmanly. No matter my love for Sihtric, if he was called a *fluthfloggi*, some would consider him unfit for our society, cast out, unable to trade and live with our people.

Sihtric looked away, pushing the sleeves of his tunic up over his forearms. 'People already spoke as much when I walked in with my jangles and colours,' he explained. 'Being unmarried at my age is nae a good look to these sorts,' he complained.

'You intend to marry her?' I inquired, eyebrows raised.

'Och!' he exclaimed. 'Nae chance of that. The woman is content to have my patronage, and I am protected by the ruse.'

I resumed my perusing of his goods, sniffing powders and seeds. 'Who is she?' I asked, looking over the top of a large box of salt flakes.

Sihtric took a deep breath. 'Oleg offered me a line of women to choose from,' he began, pulling at the edge of his tunic. 'It was only right I took the most *braw* of the lot.'

'Of course,' I agreed. To choose the most beautiful was to have what other men wanted, to dispel the talk about him. Sihtric had made the wise decision. 'Do I know her?'

He nodded. 'She was Ellisif's nursemaid, but since the girl has moved on, Oleg tried to find other uses for Licinia.'

I had met Licinia when she'd begun our instruction of the language of Miklagard. Aside from her dark hair and accented voice, she could have had twenty summers, or, just as likely, thirty. That explained why we had a man continuing our language lessons. Licinia was allocated elsewhere.

'So, Licinia is a slave?' I asked.

He grimaced. 'I wasnae keen on a bed thrall. As you ken, Kari wouldnae like it at all, but I have paid no coin for her, and she doesnae warm my furs neither.' Sihtric turned to scoop a spoonful of cloves into a cloth bag. 'There you are,' he said, handing it to me.

'Thank you. Pity for her,' I commented. 'I'm sure she would much rather be free.'

Sihtric scrunched his nose, and I saw the rise and fall of his shoulders as he breathed. 'For some, that's nae likely.'

'You're positive she will keep your secret?'

He shrugged. 'I allow her all the comforts I can. Make nae demands of her.' Sihtric seemed content enough with the arrangement. 'And how does your business go?' he asked. A passing merchant waved to Sihtric. He returned the gesture with a radiant grin.

'We've recruited women to spin, weave, and dye. Our warehouse is busy with furniture building. Four looms are complete. All we need is the last shipment from Aldeigjuborg, which is expected before Winter Nights,' I detailed. 'It might just work out.'

'Well, of course it will. Why would you be doubting it?' Sihtric questioned. He placed his hand over the small bag of cloves in my palm.

I furrowed my brow. 'After so many bad things, I was beginning to think that the old witch, Gudrun, had cursed me.'

'Och! Dinnae say such a thing, *bhana charaid*,' he chastised me, making a quick gesture with his hand to ward off evil spirits. 'The gods love you.' He gathered me up into his embrace and squeezed me. After all that time in Aldeigjuborg and on the river, Sihtric knew me so well. Just like me, he, too, displayed his feelings on his face.

'I hope you're right,' I mumbled against the folds of his clothing.

Sihtric released me and patted me on the shoulder. 'So, Estrid wasnae keen on working with you, then, if you're only working with Mirca?' he asked.

Ellisif's mother, Estrid, was the other dominant textile business in town. At first, I had thought to work with her, and grow both of our enterprises into one, but she had shot an arrow through that hope faster than I could hoist a sail.

'Not at all. Estrid is a woman who does everything her own way. Working with me would be beneath her,' I explained.

'She said that?' Sihtric asked, mouth agape and eyebrows raised. 'As a wife to a warrior, it is she that's beneath you, *bhana charaid*, and I hope you told her as much.'

'Estrid didn't speak to me at all. It was her servant, and she likely said it a good deal more politely than Estrid would have. Mirca and

Estrid do not get along, as Estrid believes there is nothing to be gained from associating with *local women*.'

'Different rungs on the social steps. Next time Estrid's woman comes down for some liquorice root, I should sell her twigs for double the price! That *gyte* ol' *cuddie*,' he cursed. His face became a mottled red and when he turned to look at me, I saw the mischief that sparkled in his eyes. His offer was not a threat, it was a promise.

'Sihtric!' I hissed, shaking my head. 'You can't do that! If word got around that you would do such a thing, you'd lose the business of many more.'

'Och! I could imagine Estrid's reaction when it was suggested she work with you and Mirca.' He laughed as he imitated the woman's pinched face and shocked expression. Sihtric didn't do a terrible impression.

I let him have his fun before continuing. 'For now, it's Mirca and I, which seems to work well enough. Pity Estrid didn't join us, but I was not about to force the matter.'

'Doesnae seem much of a loss to you, the greatest textile merchant in Aldeigjuborg, Gnezdovo, and now Kyiv,' Sihtric replied.

'And don't forget the largest network of sails along the river road,' I added.

Sihtric leaned on the table again, staring out at the passing market-goers. 'You've an enviable mind, *bhana charaid*.'

'I feel like myself when I'm out here or running my business. Sometimes, being in there…' I pointed back to the elevated halls. 'I don't quite feel like me.' All the fancy clothes, restricting jewellery, and titles weren't something I enjoyed. 'But there is always the practice yard for me to take my frustration out on,' I joked.

He nodded. 'I ken how you feel. Will you be searching for Sven, then?'

'Perhaps,' I answered, feigning disinterest by resuming my inspection of the spice-lined table. 'I'm also trying to locate a wise woman of herbs, but it wouldn't hurt to pay Sven a small visit,' I agreed. He had been long neglected since our arrival in Kyiv. Aside from our occasional encounter when practising weapons, and glances across the dark hall at feasts, we had barely spoken.

Sihtric looked at me, tilting his head to one side. 'You dinnae have a court healer?' he asked.

I motioned for a scoop of salt flakes, and he wrapped it in a waxed wrapper and placed it on the table. Then I picked it up and secured it in my leather pouch.

'I can't help thinking that if I used her, every word I said would be around the court faster than I could change my clothes.'

'Aye,' Sihtric agreed. 'You're likely right. I'm afraid I'm nae help there. I dinnae ken any of repute, but if you're looking for Sven, he'll be down at the shipyard at this time of day,' he informed me. 'In between his duties as the Grand Prince's sworn man, practising with bow or sword, and his carving of my new prow-beast, he has time for little else. Eskil tells me Sven's already distinguished himself among the men and the Grand Prince had honoured him with more silver,' Sihtric continued.

'I'm glad he's found someone to serve,' was all that I said.

I thanked Sihtric for the cloves and the information, and made my way to the shipyard situated in a protected cove, above which was a rocky bluff. The clang of a hammer on ship's nails rang clear, and the dull scrape of tools against wood as men cleaned hulls pulled out of the water. There was a distinct aroma of a shipyard; tar and burning hair assaulted my nostrils, the combination of which was used to fill gaps in the planks to make them watertight. With the days of sailing nearing their end, crews could not guarantee getting much further along the river and, not wanting to chance being stranded, they would rather pull in for repairs and maintenance. Colder weather meant the harbour was full of ships, their owners overwintering in the newest settlement of the Rus'. There was lots of work for any man willing to labour hard through the frost. This was where both Frodi and Björn would earn their winter keep.

Sure enough, Sven was sitting on a crop of rocks, whittling at the wood in his hands, his pack on the ground by his feet.

He heard me before I sat beside him on the rock. 'You never were any good at sneaking up, *minn Svanr*,' he mumbled with a smile without looking up. The breeze tousled his fair hair and his tunic lay open at the chest while I drew my cloak around me tighter against the chill.

'I remember you telling me that once or twice before,' I replied. The rock underneath me was cold and smooth, but my fine gown made it awkward to sit in, so it was difficult to get comfortable. I shivered against the brisk air.

'Fancy fabrics are not so good for keeping the chill off, eh?' he asked, and I did not miss the slight in his words. 'What brings such a grand lady down to see the common people?' Sven still had not looked up, and I knew he did so on purpose.

I shoved him with my elbow and took him by the chin to turn his face to mine. 'I would see more of you,' I replied. 'With the wool trade, with court, Odrun, and everything else, sometimes I feel like I am smothered,' I confessed, releasing him.

Sven did not turn away this time. 'It is not what I expected when I agreed to come with you.'

There was a pang in my chest. 'Do you regret it?'

Sven put his work down on the lush grass and held my stare. 'I swore to be by your side, even if that is sometimes an arduous task.' He pulled a cap over his ears, pink from the cold, and drew his cloak out of his pack.

'Sihtric doesn't like it here either,' I replied. 'Seems no one does.'

'Gunnar likes it well enough,' Sven answered, 'though I don't know if that's an endorsement at all.'

We shared an uneasy laugh. Sven stopped, his face serious once more. 'I'm surprised Kjarr is letting you out of his sights.'

'Jealous?' I teased.

He gave me a sidelong glance but said nothing.

'You two are yet to meet,' I pointed out, offering a small smile.

'Nor have we come to blows,' he responded.

I gritted my teeth.

'He is possessive at the high table, always with his hands on you,' Sven began with a growl. 'Holds out his cup to you as if you were his thrall, and covers you in all these fancies so that no one can see the real you beneath it.'

He held his hand out to the golden torc around my neck, but his fingers dipped lower, under the neckline of my dress, searching. My heart raced as I realised what he was looking for. 'You no longer wear your Valkyrie.'

I had taken it off soon after arriving. With so many adornments, it would become twisted together with the chains and beads I often wore. 'I keep it safe and treasure it still, Sven.'

There was more hurt in his eyes than I'd ever seen. He glanced away. 'Does Kjarr realise what he has?'

'And you would tell him if he didn't?' I demanded.

When Sven didn't reply, I picked up his carving from the long grass. 'You're making a boat?' I asked, looking at its broad hull. In my hands, it felt perfectly weighted. 'Does it float?'

'I hope so,' he responded. 'I'll take it up to Sihtric's room and test it in a tub before we try it on the lake. He'll want to see it,' he added, staring over the water.

Sven shook his head, clearly wanting to say more, but thinking better of it. From his palm, he plucked out a small splinter and tossed it into the wind.

'You need to be careful, Astrid. This court is full of powerful people playing dangerous games, and you are far too close to the flame to leave this place unburned,' he explained. 'Kjarr does not see what I see.'

'Well, it's clear you've been watching!'

'Everyone watches you. Sometimes you just don't notice. I hope your husband knows how to protect you.'

'I...' I began.

'Don't say that you don't need protection,' he warned. 'Astrid, I hear all the things you cannot say to me or him.' Sven started putting away his things into his leather pack.

'And, sometimes, I think, you hear things that don't even run through my mind,' I responded with anger, shivering down inside my cloak.

Though the wind had risen, and afternoon approached, I wasn't sure if it was Sven's words or the bite of the cold that went to my very core.

# TWENTY-TWO

Ellisif and I filled cups on the small table next to the Grand Prince, who was engaged in a heated game of Hnefatafl with my husband. A few men, including Ellisif's brothers Harald and Helgi, and one of Oleg's most trusted advisors, Boyar Sveineld Sveineldsson or Sveineld the Younger, as most people called him, sat drinking on the sidelines. They watched the Grand Prince's every motion as he attacked Kjarr's king.

'That's a good move!' a tall, good-looking warrior congratulated Oleg as he raised his cup to salute him. Those beside him echoed the praise.

Grand Prince Oleg waved their words away. 'Boyar Hrolfsson is a tough opponent. I need to think.' He stroked his chin while considering his next move.

Ellisif bent over Oleg's shoulder, holding the jug in her hands to refill his cup.

'Would you bring me luck, sweet Ellisif?' he asked, looking up at her flushed face.

'The gods favour you without my intercession, Knyaz,' she answered, sweeping low to bow.

But he persisted, 'Endow this piece with your goodness so I might best Boyar Hrolfsson.' He held a small carved playing piece forward.

Ellisif lowered her head, pressing her lips to it as Oleg watched on with hungry eyes.

'I thank you,' he replied once he mastered himself. 'Would you fill Hrolfsson's cup also?'

That was my job, the reason I was here; to serve my husband. But the shock of Oleg's blatant pursuit of Ellisif had me rooted to the spot. It seemed the same effect had overcome Ellisif, for she moved neither.

Someone took the ewer from my hands, and a swirl of skirts passed me on their way to complete my duties.

'I will do it, Grand Prince,' came the small voice of Alfrunr, Oleg's niece, sister to Igor and a beauty though she did all to hide herself. Her hair, the colour of deep honey, went unbound, as did most maids. Though her blue eyes were downcast, all could see her fine pointed chin, smooth brow, and small nose as she hovered over my husband's cup, amber mead pouring from its spout.

The young men on the benches watched her, eyes roving over her uncovered wrists and face. Alfrunr, yet unwed, would not be a wife to any of them. As the only living daughter of the previous ruler Rurik, she was reserved for the highest of unions. Yet, they could dream.

Alfrunr and Ellisif, their duties now complete, excused themselves to the shadows, lit by the soft light of braziers. Ellisif's cheeks were red by the time she lifted her sewing from the basket she'd left on the bench.

'Ellisif?' I whispered, sitting next to her. 'Are you all right?'

She didn't look up as she wove her sharp needle through the collar of a linen tunic. Her mouth curved into a smile, and I left her to her thoughts.

It was Alfrunr who broke our silence. 'I'm sorry it's me tonight,' she began, her voice hardly a whisper. 'Inga would normally serve her brother, but she has taken ill. My uncle commands me to show my face at court, though I'd prefer to be with Igor in the nursery,' she told me.

I looked across the room where Sveineld, Inga's brother, sat. He was watching Oleg's game with his unusual steel-grey eyes, his heavy brow furrowed, a deep line cutting through his forehead, though he was about my age. Sveineld wasn't boastful, as many men were. He had a quiet assurance that was not dissimilar to Kjarr's, and it made me think of him as a good man. It was likely why Oleg relied on him. He was the complete opposite of his sister, who was often proud and bold. A childhood friend of Ellisif's, and of a similar age, Inga often served her family at the feast table and when her brother privately dined with the Grand Prince.

'Do you have mending to do?' Alfrunr asked, and I realised I'd been staring at Sveineld.

I shook my head. I'd always hated embroidery and was never any good at it, but Kjarr had advised I should at least maintain the pretence of sewing if I wanted to attend these late night gatherings. So, I took in hand a small scrap of linen and threaded a needle with colourful thread and pretended to fashion a simple outline of vine and leaf.

Beyond Oleg's private room, the Great Hall was growing quiet. Those of his men not invited to tonight's gathering were bedding down on benches and soon snoring would replace their chattering.

Oleg stood. The suddenness of the movement startled me and the needle pricked my finger. I brought it to my mouth to bite the hurt, and I watched as the Grand Prince stepped back from his playing board. The men on the bench leaned forward and Oleg glanced at them. Kjarr had arranged his pieces in a semicircle surrounding the Grand Prince's defenders and his king within.

Sveineld offered advice from his vantage, to which Oleg laughed in response.

The Grand Prince stood a head above most men, so tall he often stooped to converse with his boyars, but he would always straighten himself. To lower himself might be seen as defective and Oleg was ever conscious of being watched. And, as I grew to know and understand Oleg, I found he was keenly aware of the dangerous games his courtiers played.

'You just have to move that piece there,' Harald, Ellisif's eldest brother, began, stepping towards the table. His strong nose in profile sniffed once, and he cuffed his wrist to it as he mumbled.

'What was that?' Kjarr asked, turning to the man.

He shook his head, but conceded, 'The movement I was going to suggest won't work, Boyar Hrolfsson. Apologies, Knyaz,' he stammered as he sat down.

Oleg sent a sideways glance at Harald and pulled at the silk edge of his tunic. 'You won't best me, Hrolfsson,' Oleg promised.

Harald looked away, returning to his conversation with Sveineld and the other men.

Kjarr made his move and leaned back in his chair, relaxed in his royal cousin's company. 'I wouldn't dream of it,' he responded.

My eyes trailed to Oleg as my needle moved aimlessly through the fabric. His icy-blue stare studied the markers on the board before he walked a few steps forward to advance his attacker.

'Ow,' I exclaimed as I pricked my finger again.

Ellisif and Alfrunr laughed, knowing I was far too distracted to stay on task. 'The art of appearing disinterested while listening is a skill you need to develop,' Ellisif chided. 'Alfrunr and I've had long years at those lessons and…' she paused, her cheeks flushed crimson once more, and I noticed she had caught Oleg's glance in her direction.

'But you are yet to learn how to hide your desires,' I responded. 'That's something I'm not very good at either.'

Ellisif lowered her fair lashes and looked up at me with her round blue eyes. 'He looks at me like he never did before,' she admitted. 'Harald and Helgi,' she said, referring to her brothers, 'are here to make sure he keeps looking at me.'

'Your parents encourage the attention?' I asked as I sucked the end of my bleeding thumb.

Alfrunr stayed silent, head bent over her work.

'And you? Do you welcome it?' I continued.

'He is very handsome,' Ellisif began, placing her embroidery on her lap and lowering her voice. 'Fair-skinned, but his arms are swarthy from all the forest riding. When he walks past me, I smell it upon him; sweet plums, the scent of his horse, and the earth. And,' she said, leaning closer, 'when we are alone he bids me to call him Helgi, the name his mother gave him, though it feels a little strange as it's also my brother's.' She was breathless. Her hand moved to the base of her neck.

'How often are you alone?' I questioned her and could not hide the shock in my voice.

Her entire face was red as a madder root. 'Not by ourselves,' she confessed. 'Someone is always there on the fringes. But I would be alone with him,' she added brazenly. Her eyes were wide as she breathed in a shuddering breath.

'Odin's beard!' I exclaimed, reaching for a cup of ale and downing it. 'Your family allows this?' I worried that any impropriety would compromise her future happiness. If Ellisif became Oleg's woman, she would have little chance of making a grand marriage later. I couldn't believe her parents would put their young daughter in such a position unless they harboured hopes of something more.

She laughed at my gaping mouth. 'They desire it. Any family with an unwed daughter would push her before Oleg.'

'But not into his bed,' I pointed out. 'They jostle their daughters for marriage.'

'Licinia says he would never take me for his wife, but I see the way he looks at me. You witnessed him call me to bless his tokens. It was as if he bade me to kiss him,' she whispered furiously.

I hadn't the heart to tell her it was her body he wanted, not their union, but that I did not know for sure.

'Anyway,' Ellisif continued, 'Licinia isn't chasing me around anymore now that she has a man of her own, and I have the heart of the Knyaz.'

I pinched the bridge of my nose. A pair of slippered feet appeared through the partition, accompanied by a matronly attendant close behind.

'You'll all be in trouble if anyone finds out you've been serving the men without a chaperone,' Inga scolded as she strode towards us.

'Signe is here,' Alfrunr chimed in, looking up from her needlework.

Apparently, Inga thought my presence was insufficient protection, though she said nothing in reply to Alfrunr's objection.

'I thought you were sick,' Ellisif asked, pursing her lips as she returned to her sewing.

Inga shook out her golden hair and flung a glance across the room. 'I was, but then I heard your brother was going to be here and I didn't want to miss the chance to see him.' The edge of her lip hitched into a smirk as she put down the silver platter she carried. 'This time next year Harald and I will wed and I want my morning gift to be valuable.'

The bowls on the platter rattled.

Ellisif reached over and plucked a lid off one. 'Oooh! Hazelnuts.'

Alfrunr leaned forward. 'And cranberries.'

'And, news,' Inga announced as she chose a seat between Alfrunr and Ellisif. Her maid stood by the brazier, where the light was best for her to spin. 'Sveineld tells me he is to be named Posadnik of Pleskov this coming winter. But it's a secret for now,' Inga continued.

'Is he pleased?' Ellisif questioned, as the men began discussing politics.

I strained to listen, but all I gleaned was something about a Khazar dignitary and their plans to tax the Drevlians once they'd achieved an alliance.

'It's an influential position, especially for someone so young,' Ellisif continued.

Though Sveineld was eight years older than his sister, Inga, he had served Oleg since his youth and had proven his worth in battle and loyalty. It had been Sveineld that brought Oleg the news of Haskold and Dir's capture of Igor, actions that merited such an appointment as Posadnik, to rule in the Grand Prince's name. Pleskov was far away, located to the south-west of Holmgardr and established to collect taxation from the Krivichs and Ilmen Slavs who had recently aligned with Rus'. Any man sent there would have to be motivated, and more than that, trusted by the Grand Prince.

Inga had taken up her needle as well, puncturing the fabric with bright thread as she did her work. 'He would have preferred something just north of Kyiv, but Posadnik of Pleskov would suit him. Still, without a wife, he might end up marrying a local,' she added, tittering away as her needle poked tiny holes in the linen.

'Shh,' Ellisif hushed us as Harald raised his voice.

Inga looked towards her betrothed, chin turned down and head tilted to one side.

'Isn't it time you found a wife, Knyaz?' Harald suggested, raising his cup towards the women who waited to serve. 'A nice northern girl?'

Inga needed no encouragement. She gracefully grasped the handle of the ewer and went to serve Ellisif's brother. Harald held the cup still as she poured and when she was finished, he brushed his finger along her wrist as if by accident. Inga returned to her sewing with a contented grin.

'Or a tribal princess?' Sveineld recommended.

Inga chuckled. 'See, I told you he likes the foreign ones,' she whispered behind her hands.

'What benefit would there be in marrying a princess of a small tribe akin to the Polianians?' Kjarr added with a sympathetic look towards Oleg now flaring his nostrils, though his face was glaring into his mug.

'Not a Polianian princess. They rule little more than an open field. That's like every farmer in Svealand calling himself a king!' Sveineld replied. 'Maybe if the Knyaz were to marry a highborn lady from the Drevlians, it might smooth over their reluctance to surrender.'

'Even the Drevlians would be a match too low for our Grand Prince,' Kjarr added, rankled by the direction of the conversation.

'You're right,' agreed the round-faced Helgi, younger of Ellisif's two older brothers. 'We should aim higher. The Khazar ruler has many daughters. A few of them are quite the beauties, reports say. We could send an envoy there to find you the best one.'

Kjarr grimaced, and Sveineld scoffed. 'You need an education in the powers of this region, Helgi,' Sveineld warned. 'The Khagan's daughters are born of many women and do not have the same status as our girls born to ruling fathers. She would be nothing more than a baseborn daughter and therefore not suitable.'

'You both need to drink less and think more,' Oleg chastised, pushing the Hnefatafl pieces over one by one. 'The Khazar ruler died, leaving his son to assume the role. So, if we were considering a match, we would do better to offer a bride instead of a groom.'

'What's the name of the son?' Kjarr asked, more for the benefit of those who observed than himself. I knew he spoke on these matters with the Grand Prince often and knew just as well as his cousin.

'Tarkhan,' the Grand Prince replied, rubbing his forehead as he listened to the diatribe.

'A Rus' princess for the hand of Khagan Tarkhan might be appropriate, but the wife of Grand Prince Oleg must be someone worthy of the title,' Harald ruminated. 'Do you have any natural children?' he asked a little too boldly.

'No, he doesn't,' Kjarr answered for Oleg.

'But his niece, Alfrunr, is of marriageable age,' Helgi piped up, excited to have remembered this kernel of information. 'She could be the peace cow between the Khazars and ourselves. Princess Alfrunr is comely now that she has grown a bit.'

Alfrunr's needle stilled, her shoulders slumped as she tried to will herself into the shadows. Inga's hand held tight to Alfrunr's palm as the men continued to speak as if she was not there.

'She's fourteen,' Oleg objected.

'Come now,' the stout maid whispered to Alfrunr as she took her by the arm. 'It's late, you two should go to bed,' she instructed, leading both Inga and Alfrunr to the edge of the hall. Alfrunr left willingly, but Inga desperately wanted to remain and kept turning back towards the men as she was dragged away.

'That's old enough to wed,' Harald continued, 'and it would bring peace.'

'We don't know what it would bring,' Kjarr responded, slamming his fist down on the table. Kjarr was never quick to anger, but tonight his patience had worn thin and the love he had for his cousin and his family made it difficult to hear such suggestions.

Oleg sat back, massaging his brow. 'Out!' he yelled. 'All of you, go!' Harald and Helgi were the first to stand, looking at their sister as they hurried for the alcoves of the Great Hall. Sveineld shook his head, but left all the same.

'I won't be their spy,' Ellisif said once they had gone. 'That's what they want. In the places they may not go, they want me to report all I hear.' She folded up her work and placed it in her small basket.

'See how they plot my marriage?' Oleg spoke to Kjarr when they were alone. Ellisif and I were still in the shadows.

'Old Odholf would give me better advice, but Aslaug already took him to her bed,' he complained. A loud groan followed. 'Do you hear them scheme? Every boyar with a marriageable daughter would put her in my bed in hopes of me taking a wife to his advantage.'

'It is your duty to marry, Cousin,' Kjarr replied.

'Is it?' he threw back, a fair eyebrow arched. 'It is my duty to keep Igor alive, to preserve his territory and keep it strong. My sister demanded it of me on her deathbed.' Oleg kicked back the chair and stood. 'Gods, why was Alfvind taken so young? She would not have tolerated the talk of her daughter in such a manner. "Comely"? Alfrunr is a child still!' he raged.

Kjarr slid another cup of mead across to the ruler. 'Alfrunr may have been young when her mother died, but she is grown now and could be a weaver of peace. Cousin, how old was your sister when she wed?'

Oleg hesitated. 'Fourteen,' he responded, frowning.

'And she was happy with Rurik,' Kjarr said, trying to cajole the Grand Prince as far as considering it.

'But she wasn't sent off to a foreign prince who didn't speak her language, with customs and beliefs so different she would be an outsider the rest of her life. Such a fate the Norns never wove!' Oleg lamented.

'Alfvind came over the sea with Rurik. She did not know what she was coming to, and the gods protected her still,' Kjarr continued.

He refilled the Grand Prince's empty cup from the jug on the table. It should have been my job, but I didn't want to interrupt them and neither called us forth.

'They only protected Alfvind long enough for her to give Rurik an heir,' Oleg countered.

Kjarr grasped Oleg's shoulder as he resumed his seat. 'Childbed is the war-field of women. Some live to continue fighting, and some fall.'

Oleg nodded at the comment. 'She would have known what to do.'

Kjarr took a sip before continuing, 'No one is saying Alfrunr must be married now. It is almost winter and we would not look for a marriage until spring comes. But think about it. She will need a husband one day soon and we need to ensure it furthers her brother's expanding empire, not hinder it.'

Oleg nodded and drained his cup. 'You are right, Cousin. I'm sure Rurik would have agreed with that counsel. He was insistent that my rule should not riven the Rus' and I'm doing my best, but I cannot help believing the gods do not want me to marry. It would only cause strife. Factions would appear and…'

'They already exist,' Kjarr interjected.

'I know that,' Oleg replied curtly. 'Any woman I married would have to know her children by me would not inherit. It is Igor who will rule after me.'

'Mmm,' Kjarr agreed, stroking his chin.

Oleg leaned forward, facing his cousin with determination. 'Do you agree I should marry a Slav princess?'

Ellisif, beside me, swallowed hard and reached in the darkness for my hand.

Kjarr shook his head. 'I do not. It makes no sense.' He hesitated before proceeding. 'Grand Prince. Ellisif and Signe are still here waiting for us. Should we excuse them to bed, so we may continue this conversation more privately?'

'Huh? Oh. No. I'm done thinking about this,' he responded, waving his hand through the air as if to dispel the thought. 'Ellisif?' he called to her. 'Is there someone coming to take you to your rooms?'

'No one, Knyaz,' she lied. I knew Inga's attendant would return to fetch Ellisif once Inga and Alfrunr were calmed and in bed.

'I will walk you to your rooms, then,' Oleg announced, standing from the chair and holding his hand out to her. She stepped forward and gladly took it.

'Should we let them go alone?' I asked Kjarr, coming to stand by him.

'We can hardly impose our presence on him, besides all he is doing is returning Ellisif to her parents,' Kjarr replied.

'I'm not sure,' I hesitated.

'Oleg isn't one to do anything rashly. But he has a weakness for… love,' Kjarr finished, taking my arm and following behind his cousin. 'We will walk with you,' he declared, not caring for the consequences.

Oleg's smile widened.

I was sure he had heard Kjarr's comment and found his cousin's concern entertaining.

'As you wish. Though even you cannot stop the will of the gods, nor still the weaving hands of the Norns, if that was your intention.'

# TWENTY-THREE

Familiar sounds surrounded me like a comforting embrace; women's chatter, the gentle hum of wool feeding through spindle notches, and the rhythmic clacking of shuttles moving back and forth on the loom. It was another busy day in the Kyiv warehouse, and Mirca made it all the easier with her keen eye for detail and her ability to clip issues before they got out of hand.

'We will have both sails they ordered come the thaw,' she replied authoritatively to a persistent messenger from the shipyard. He loitered on the threshold, not welcome inside with his muddy shoes and clothing that smelled of tar and sheep's fat. He must have been weatherproofing down at the yard, for the odour was hanging from him like a child at their mother's legs.

Mirca stood, arms akimbo, jutting her pointed chin up and looking upon the messenger with her sharp dark eyes.

The boy mumbled as he shuffled his mud-shod shoes in the dirt.

Mirca huffed before responding, 'Yes. I told you so last week. You do not need to keep checking on the progress,' she roared, shooing the boy from the door, but he would not budge. 'When Lady Signe and I say something will be done, your master may trust our word,' Mirca promised.

Finally satisfied, or perhaps accepting defeat, the boy nodded and scurried away, leaving Mirca to turn on her heel and resume her inspection of a length of fabric coming off the standing loom. Branka, with her dark hair braided and covered, tipped her head towards Mirca as she received instructions to adjust the tension on the shuttle.

Then Mirca turned to me, 'That's the third inquiry we've had today,' she complained as I came to her side, slotting my spindle into my belt.

'I'm beginning to think someone is spreading rumours we are untrust-worthy.' Her broad brow furrowed with concern.

'Undoubtedly,' I replied, running my hand along the selvedge of the loom-woven fabric before Branka. 'If I have learned anything in business, it's that there is always someone wanting to bring you down.'

The girl had the sense to know the conversation was not for her ears, and didn't look up, but continued her work with the accuracy and speed for which she was employed.

'This is always the way,' Mirca agreed as we walked through the open doors of the warehouse that overlooked the shipyard, away from the rest of Kyiv.

We were high enough above the shipyard that the smells did not carry but close enough to see boats sail by and wave to the men as they passed on their way to work, many of whom were married to the women who worked within my weaving shed. The sun was high, and though it glowed, it provided scarce warmth. Both Mirca and I were dressed warmly, hugging our cloaks around our shoulders as we walked towards the hanging pot over the outside fire that contained our simmering lunchtime broth. Delicious aromas wafted on the breeze. Next to the soup, piled high on a trestle table, were rounds of fresh bread waiting to be eaten. A few more months and it would be too cold to cook and eat outside, but for now, we could still enjoy this simple pleasure.

'There is always going to be some competition when businesses vie for the same patrons,' I began. 'They don't make sails, so the animosity cannot be long-lasting. She's just trying to scare us, so we don't steal her customers.'

We both knew Estrid was likely the one spreading discord. She ran a lucrative textile business, supplying most of the wealthy ladies in Kyiv with fine linens and wools to sew their fancy garments. Her business was small, and largely run by others with Estrid's funding. Though Mirca had also been in business for many years, her enterprise had never been big enough to make Estrid feel like her toes were being stepped on. And, besides, Mirca had always supplied fabrics to the lower rungs of the society, never had she aspired to reach any higher than her class and Estrid would not have deigned to service anyone she thought was beneath her. I did not have the same concerns. Mirca was an astute woman, and I valued that far more than an ennobled person who felt she was above everyone else. I did fear, however, that though my title lent status to our operation, it also sparked an envy that could catch fire if Estrid wanted to fan the flames.

'What do you think we should do?' Mirca asked as she leaned against the outer wall of the warehouse.

'Nothing,' I responded.

Mirca glanced at me and opened her mouth. She twisted her full lips and bit at the inside of the lower one.

'We do nothing, Mirca. Just keep doing what we have been doing and let our work speak for itself.'

Cold and hungry, I scooped some broth into a cup for each of us and sipped from mine. 'I've been in this position before and nothing good comes from stirring the waters. Soon enough, Estrid will talk herself into a hole and people will stop believing her lies.'

Mirca nodded, but seemed unconvinced. 'I've known Estrid for a long time,' she replied. 'She's not a woman to leave things alone and I'm worried she will only take this further. This is nothing but a game to her and she has both reputation and wealth on her side.'

Mirca was an intelligent woman, and I always listened to her counsel. After all, she had lived near Kyiv her entire life and she knew much better than I the machinations of the place. 'What would you do?' I asked.

She ruminated while she drank her broth. 'I agree we should appear to do nothing, but we need someone inside Estrid's household to make sure she isn't scheming at something more dangerous.' The wind whipped foul and almost tore Mirca's head covering away. She tightened the cloth at the back of her head and tucked away the small tendrils of her reddish-brown hair that had escaped.

'Is she capable of such a thing?' I asked.

Mirca shrugged. 'She never has before, though where there is power, there will be problems.'

I knew that well enough, and when I had previously underestimated others, it had ended in horror. Before, I'd ignored Neflaug's threats, thinking them just words without actions, but that had resulted in my daughter's death. There was no way that I would make the same mistake again. 'I'll ask Odrun to speak with Estrid's thralls,' I responded resolutely.

'Discreetly,' Mirca added.

'Of course,' I agreed.

She nodded and wrapped her hands around her warm cup. 'You trust this woman to keep whatever she discovers to herself?' Mirca looked at me with her deep brown eyes, always full of caring even when they seemed to pierce right through a person. 'It is not only us that would depend on her.'

'Odrun will not speak to anyone else,' I promised. She had kept secrets, even when revealing them might have been to her benefit, so I trusted Odrun to find out what we needed without divulging it to others.

'All right,' Mirca agreed. 'For now, we do as we are, and this Odrun will make enquiries.'

We shared an uneasy glance, and set our cups down on the small table. 'The road is never unrutted, is it?' I complained.

Mirca laughed, throaty and infectious. 'Never,' she admitted, her face lit up as her usually downturned lips lifted into a smile.

'Perhaps I should make an offering to Njord for good business and wealth,' I suggested, looking towards the shipyard, hoping to see Sven down below, but he wasn't there. He was probably on duty somewhere about the walls. It had been more than a week since I'd seen him last. Even then, it was just a glimpse as he returned from working on the *Bhobain* with Frodi and Björn, who had decided to stay on through the winter. I shook him from my mind and turned to Mirca. 'Something tells me we will need a little help to get Estrid off our backs.'

'And I shall pray to Perun,' Mirca added. 'We can never have too many gods on our side.'

She was ever practical, and I couldn't fault her reasoning. Be them my gods or hers, whichever would listen would render welcome assistance.

'Thank you, Mirca,' I said, squeezing her warmed hand with my cold fingertips. 'We are fortunate to have found each other.'

She wandered back inside, where she opened a box containing various sized loom weights and set about helping another woman tie them to the ends of each cord. I watched them balancing the discs perfectly, stretching lengths of spun wool, and preparing the frame for the next sail panel. I was so absorbed in my observation that I was startled to feel the brush of a fingertip along the base of my neck.

'Lost in your daydreams again?' Kjarr teased. His smile was wide, his green eyes alive with mischief under the tuft ash brown hair that stuck out from his cap. 'If you were thinking of me, you needn't dream any longer.'

A laugh escaped my throat. Kjarr was playful when away from the confines of Oleg's court. My husband planted a kiss on my lips as he pulled me into his arms. I lay my head against his chest.

'I was wondering if you wanted to take the midday meal with me?' he asked.

'Not today. There is too much work to be done, but you're welcome to join us for fresh bread and broth. Branka's sister brought a basket of her cheese for the ladies to share, straight from her mother's farm in the north.'

He wrinkled his nose and looked down at me.

'What is it?' I urged. 'Not keen on cheese and broth for your meal? Or have you been spoiled by all the rich food of court that your poor stomach could not manage this simple fare?' I teased, poking his firm middle.

He shook his head and smiled. 'It's so good to see you happy in your work,' he responded, tucking a strand of hair behind my ear, his thumb brushing my ever-fading scar. 'For too long, you've been a trapped bear in a cage. I'm not sure the court life suits you.'

'Nor you,' I replied. We had both been unenthusiastic about staying in Kyiv through the winter, but Kjarr was needed by his cousin, and I had been away from Kjarr's side long enough. It was a sacrifice we decided to make.

'Out here,' he said, looking up at the warehouse, 'you seem free. Here you are yourself.' He lay a gentle kiss on my temple.

*Almost myself,* I thought. I was still using the name Signe, not my real name, Astrid. 'It's not without its worries,' I mumbled.

He stepped back and raised my face with his hand. 'Is there something wrong?'

For a moment I considered telling him about my concerns regarding Estrid, but Kjarr had so much to deal with I did not want to heap anything further onto his plate. 'It's not anything you need to worry about,' I replied.

'Business woes?' he asked.

I nodded my head. 'Solved easily enough,' I responded, trying to sound unfazed. 'Working with Mirca is like hearing the best-told stories from a famous skald. She knows every beat, each word committed to a memory infallible, and her rhythm is easy to follow.'

He squeezed me tight. 'I knew you would like each other. You've brought together the most experienced weavers.'

'You seem surprised.'

He kissed me tenderly and laughed against my lips. 'I wasn't sure how much you would enjoy managing the hall of a cousin to the Grand Prince, but you've proven I had no cause to worry. Egbert, frankly, is an unsurpassable appointment and worth everything I've paid for him. He learns with ease. His grasp of languages is impressive. Did you say he was a Christian?' Kjarr questioned.

'He was a monk where he came from,' I explained as I smiled at the praise Kjarr had heaped on me.

'I don't think he will be for much longer. He has been listing the names of all our gods and their roles,' Kjarr went on. 'He's asked to come to the *blót*, and for an amulet, though I'm not sure what he plans to do with it.'

'I hope you didn't deny him,' I said, stepping back to see Kjarr's face.

Kjarr shook his head. 'No. I've already commissioned his harp amulet. Egbert wishes to take Bragi as his god.'

'And dedicate himself to the god of storytelling and wisdom? That seems fitting,' I responded with a grin. 'We will see if it is anything more than curiosity, or if he wishes to take our gods as his own,' I replied.

Kjarr grasped my hand. 'He is a valuable addition to our house and I'm glad you freed him.'

'Egbert is a good man,' I added.

'And devoted to you,' Kjarr responded. There was no insinuation behind the comment, just an understanding of the trust Egbert placed in me when he chose to serve as my scribe. 'I wish we had three more like him.'

'There would be no business issues, and keeping Ellisif out of trouble would be...' I began.

But Kjarr cut in, 'I fear we may have failed there. Oleg and Ellisif spend most of their mornings riding together.'

'Even with the reports of the Drevlians marauding through the forest?'

He nodded. 'They ride alone, just the two of them.'

The wind whipped my hair around and I struggled to tie it back under my hair wrap. 'Is it such a bad thing if they find love?' I wondered.

Kjarr scratched at his chin. 'Marriage is one thing for royalty, love is another altogether and the two rarely align. We have been fortunate in that,' he said, reaching for my hand.

'Only because you tricked me into marrying you,' I teased, taking his hand in mine.

He kissed my palm. 'I hope you've forgiven me.'

I nodded readily, though the reason for our handfasting may have changed, our care for one another had only deepened.

'Oleg isn't free to marry like that, nor is he free to love openly. He is meant to make a match that would benefit his people. If he marries Ellisif, it would raise the wrong sort of family,' Kjarr explained. 'Should Ellisif bear a child, her family would want it acknowledged as the heir, in direct opposition to the oaths Oleg swore to Rurik not so long ago.'

'But you said she'd make a good match for Igor.'

'Because her family would fight for him if they wed. If Ellisif were to have Oleg's child, they would want that child to take the throne not Igor.'

'It would mean war?' I asked, thinking of all the battles fought over this same thing.

He nodded. 'A big, bloody, meaningless war that could have been avoided if people thought with their heads instead of their…' He stopped before he said any more. 'I have some good news, though,' he said as he rifled through the small pack he carried. 'A message from Aldeigjuborg that came this morning after you'd left. Egbert had it with him, but thought you might like to see it as soon as possible,' he explained, pulling me to sit on the grass. We leaned our backs against the warehouse wall and faced the river.

Kjarr handed the letter to me. I opened it carefully, seeing it was written in Father Niall's hand, responding to the message Egbert had sent earlier in the season. In the margins, Egbert had made further notes.

'What does it say?' Kjarr asked, craning to inspect the writing.

'Nothing exciting,' I replied, folding it and laying it aside. 'The last packages of wool have arrived, and they expect the weather to turn bad shortly. Business has been going well there and Helga reports they have three new orders for sails,' I finished.

'Three? Well done,' he congratulated me and leaned over to plant a kiss on my cheek as I smiled contentedly.

'There is more,' I began, picking up the letter again and running my finger down the page where Egbert had translated sections from Latin into the runes I understood. 'Hemingr has appointed Laslo as Hersir of Aldeigjuborg and he might even become the new posadnik if Aldeigjuborg becomes a tax collection point.'

Kjarr crossed one foot over the other, his legs stretched out long. 'I think Oleg is undecided if he will send someone from Holmgardr to collect from the northern provinces or add Aldeigjuborg to the list,' he detailed. 'Being appointed to posadnik would be quite the elevation from a country boy.'

I nodded. 'He's worked hard, is well versed in the region's policies, and he would be a good posadnik.' Laslo had proven himself during the Battle of the Abandoned Paragon. Born of its native people, he was familiar with the tribes, their culture, and the conflict that accompanied it. Though his beginnings were humble, his intellect was that of a learned man with little hunger for the ways of war.

'What else?' Kjarr prompted. 'I'm impressed you can read that all.'

I laughed. 'Egbert left these markings so I would understand the contents. I have some ability, but not nearly as good as him.'

Kjarr cackled and nudged my thigh with his. 'I don't doubt that you'll be able to do so one day. Go on, what does the rest say?'

'Let me see,' I said, letting my finger dwell on the rest of Egbert's margin notes. 'Oh! Hilde has married David.'

'Helga's mother married the farmer next door? Gods!' Kjarr exclaimed.

'She swore she'd never marry again after Andrei died, but her land abuts with David's and she needs someone to farm it,' I explained.

'Practical, but not very passionate,' Kjarr retorted, trying to take my hand again, but I shook him off.

'I've saved the best for last,' I began and took a deep breath as I felt my heart beating faster. 'News of Helga's labours.'

'Safe, I take it by the enormous grin on your face?' he asked. 'Tell me. Is it a boy or a girl?'

I laughed. 'One of each.'

'Gods!' he exclaimed again, removing his cap and fanning his face with it. 'Twins? She said she thought there were two.'

'She did,' I agreed. 'It was a difficult birth and Helga was in bed recovering for weeks, but she is well now.'

'Frigg be praised,' Kjarr blurted with joy. 'She'll be busy. Imagine if we had two at once.'

'I'd rather not,' I replied. 'One at a time would be hard enough.'

Helga's dream had come true, a child of her own. In all the time I had known her, she had wanted nothing more than to be a mother. Silently, I cursed myself for not being there, but knew I was working towards a better future for us all, including her two newest additions.

'What did Helga name the children?' he asked, squeezing my knee and jolting me from my daydreaming.

'She named the girl Asta,' I informed him.

'Wouldn't be honouring you, would it? So, you told Helga your real name before you left.'

'I did, but only after she said that she intended to name her girl for me. I didn't want another Signe running around that was misusing the name.'

He laughed at that. 'Asta,' he spoke the name again. 'It's pretty. Not as nice as Astrid.' Kjarr nuzzled against my neck and left a kiss there.

'Of course not,' I replied, pushing him away so I could finish relaying the missive.

'And the boy?' he asked.

'Karl. That's what the message said,' I explained, re-examining the parchment.

'Karl? Not Mikel? I would have thought they'd name the firstborn boy Mikel,' Kjarr wondered. 'Strange name for a boy.'

I chewed on my bottom lip. 'Perhaps she wants all to know he is free, destined for a greater life than one in Aldeigjuborg? And, I seem to recall Mikel's father may have had the same name.'

'A good enough reason,' Kjarr agreed. 'I suppose they'll have more children and one of them will be named for their father.'

'Helga once said to me she wanted to have more children than her mother, though this experience may have quenched the desire,' I replied, remembering a younger Helga gushing over mothering such a large brood. 'That would mean ten children, at the least.'

Kjarr whistled a descending note. 'I would be happy with one.'

'I know you would,' I responded, and snuggled up next to him, his warmth sheltering me from the chill in the wind.

He tucked my head under his chin, pulling me closer. I heard the steady beat of his heart, so loud I almost didn't hear when he said, 'Oleg all but demands it of me.'

# TWENTY-FOUR

That night, I dreamed of my father.

He was as he always had been, with his dark blue eyes framed by a low brow, his mouth unsmiling unless humoured by others but had a ready grin reserved for me. It was I who had changed. No longer was I a girl of fifteen summers, as I had been when he left and never returned. I was a woman grown of twenty-two. A wife who'd been twice married, a mother to a child now gone, and a daughter without parents.

My father looked at me, shaking his head. The movement caused his beard beads to jangle pleasantly, though the look in his eye was anything but welcoming. 'Why are you here?' he asked me in a voice full of disappointment.

'Here?' I responded, looking around because I was not sure where *here* was.

By the high wooden palisade and overwhelming construction occurring in the place, I guessed I was still in Kyiv. A place my father had never seen.

'Why are you here?' he repeated. 'You were on your way to Miklagard last time we spoke.'

'Last time we spoke, I was feverish and the only place I was headed was to Helheim,' I responded.

We were standing in the middle of an animal yard, horse byres and small pens around us. Every stall was empty. Not a single person passed by. In the distance, I could see the Great Hall and the many larger buildings that surrounded it. There was no smoke wafting into the air, no smell of fire on the breeze. It was as if he and I were the only two left to walk the land.

'Still, this is not Miklagard,' he said, gesturing to the filthy spaces devoid of their usual inhabitants. 'How did this happen?'

'I came to my husband,' I explained. 'He is cousin to the Grand Prince, and we cannot leave until winter has come and gone.' It was strange to explain this to my father, who, even in my dream state I knew, walked Midgard no longer.

He frowned, his eyes narrowing. 'And then what?'

'Then I will resume the journey and go to Miklagard.'

'It's not enough,' he said suddenly, a violent outburst that filled the space with explosive sound. 'IT IS NOT ENOUGH!' His voice ricocheted between walls, causing the world to shake around me.

A deafening crack sounded beneath my feet, rumbling the soil. It shook, loose rocks tumbling in one direction until the ground cleaved in two and opened into a void.

I crouched low to stop myself from falling into the yawning gap.

Something unfriendly called me to look within, but a compulsion just as strong warned me to avert my gaze. As fast as it had begun, the earth's quivering ceased. When I looked back to where my father stood moments before, there Gudrun the Grey towered over me.

She looked down at me and scowled. Old once more, wrinkled, and grey as she spoke, 'It is not enough, girl. Only when the Queen of Cities is home will life grow.' Gudrun cocked her head with a hideous snap of broken bone, her head now at an unnatural angle. 'Only when the Queen of Cities is home will life grow.'

I recalled Kjarr's wish that day that we should have a child and felt the sorrow well within me. 'You have cursed my womb to be barren until I do as you have foretold,' I cried. The wind howled, and the sky swirled above me in an inky mess. 'What would you have me do to rid myself of it?'

'Tut, tut,' she clicked as she shook her head. Her gnarled hands reached towards me, wrapping around my throat. 'Drip, drip,' she croaked, 'blood on your hands, and his.' Gudrun's fingers were slick with blood. 'Not worth the price,' she growled, removing her hands from my neck and shaking them towards the dark sky as if she beckoned the gods to stand witness. 'The shadows that stalk here will take you. Not where you should be,' she warned. Gudrun's eyes widened as she stared into me.

I felt her power reach inside and start to pull with immense strength. I fought the tug with everything I had. It stopped, just as sure as if she'd snipped it with a pair of sharp shears.

Her image flickered. She was a flame winking out. She blurred, her haggard face transforming into my father's.

'It is not enough,' he persisted, nose scrunched, brow low.

'Only when…' Gudrun's voice rang out, trying to cover the sound of my father's words.

'Only when the Queen of Cities is home,' their voices echoed together as one smudged into the other and they continued to fight for presence.

'Not enough,' my father's voice boomed.

Gudrun screamed shrilly, 'Queen of Cities…only then will life grow,'

I jolted awake, sweat dripping from my brow, my body covered with gooseflesh. Kjarr stirred beside me.

'Astrid?' his groggy voice mumbled as his arms searched for me beneath the furs.

'It was just a nightmare,' I replied in a strangled voice, and I hoped, with all my heart, that a bad dream was all it was.

# TWENTY-FIVE

Before the frost-laden mornings arrived in earnest, Grand Prince Oleg sent one of his most trusted advisors to the court of Prince Mal, leader of the Drevlians, at his capital of Iskorosten. Boyar Oddrsson had been gone a week and was expected to return that evening.

To mark the occasion, Oleg declared a feast to honour the Boyar, who had also advised the late Rurik. We hoped to hear of Prince Mal's willingness to discuss an alliance, while Oleg and his tight circle looked forward to the tribute that would fill their treasure chests.

Outside, the land was changing. The bounty of spring was passing. The vibrant shades of green yielded to the sunset tones of amber, brown, and rich red as trees dropped their leaves and flowers drooped on their stalks. Animals huddled together in their pens or, if in the field, against rocks or under great boughs for protection against the inclement weather. Inside, women layered their dresses and wrapped themselves in sumptuous cloaks trimmed with furs of fox, wolf, or marten. All gathered near the braziers or cooking flame in the evening, though the days were still warm enough to work outside in the dwindling sunshine. The water road flowed slower than before, telling all that soon it would stop and freeze over. Then, the only way to travel would be overland in thick snow and howling winds. None of this would dampen Oleg's joyous mood.

On our morning ride, he gazed up at the pale sky and declared the gods were smiling upon us. And, that night at the feast, he commanded music and lively dancing for all in the hall even before the food had been served. Hearing the high notes of the flute, accompanied by a lyre, pipes, and drum, I almost agreed with Ahmed's assessment that our music was indeed "too jaunty" at times. How I missed Ahmed: his stories, his lessons, his easy companionship. But he had departed for his long journey home more than a month before with promises of correspondence at whatever port he encountered next, and I eagerly awaited any letter from him. I hoped it would contain reports of adventure, exotic discoveries, and by the time he reached home, descriptions of how his city had changed in his absence. For now, I would have to content myself with imagining those foreign lands as I stood next to the extra braziers brought into the Great Hall. The orange glow illuminated the room as if it were the workshop of those craftsmen who forged Brisingamen, Freyja's golden necklace, in their land of Svartalfheim. But this was not some dwarven kingdom.

From the decorated hall, walls bearing shields, tapestries, and banners, Oleg wished it to be known as the land of warriors, a prosperous territory led by the strongest of them all.

I wore jewellery so fine many might have thought it was Lady Freyja's own. Around my neck, I wore the golden torc and several lengths of amber beads, all given to me by Kjarr. My Valkyrie pendant still lay in my small chest of ever-increasing jewels, and every time I looked at it, I felt a stab; I was turning away from what I was in favour of what I needed to be. Odrun made me look the part, my hair piled high in a crown of braids. She'd dressed me in a gown of green, trimmed, as ever, with silk that glittered in the firelight. My garment matched the tones of fabric draped from beams, and my ornaments, the warmth of the fire, telling one and all that here I belonged.

Our preparations ensured that every table, no matter how lowly, would receive plates piled high with the *Haustmanuthur* harvests. Roasted haunches of deer, steeped in rich herbaceous sauces accompanied by parsnips in butter and sage, along with thick barley stews flavoured with nutmeg and smoked pork. Kyiv's residents praised Oleg as a generous ruler that evening and, as their cups overflowed with ale and mead, they celebrated both his honour and his courage.

'To our Grand Prince, who will bring all the tribes of the Dnieper and beyond, under Rus' rule,' Sveineld the Younger toasted, raising his cup from the dais. He sat to the right of the Grand Prince with a vacant seat between, waiting to be filled with Boyar Oddrsson. On Oleg's left, as always, were Kjarr, Ellisif, and me.

Oleg nodded at Sveineld, and the court echoed the call. 'To our Grand Prince.'

Not one eyebrow arched in surprise towards the woman seated next to him. They were all accustomed to Ellisif's presence. She accompanied the Grand Prince wherever he went. For a ruler to have a woman was not unusual, but to bestow upon her the honour of sitting beside him at the high table would have been worthy of the whispers had she not been of high rank already.

Ellisif smiled at me, her round cheeks flushed with overflowing happiness.

Though Kjarr had expressed his concern about their relationship, the couple was deliriously happy. 'For once,' Kjarr explained, 'Oleg had the support he had been missing.' Not since his sister's death did Oleg have the soothing influence of a woman who loved him.

Ellisif inclined her head to me, and I did the same as I watched the Grand Prince squeeze her dainty hand under the table. Then they lifted their silver cups, each pair of lips curving into a smile as they sipped at the liquid.

Love, it seemed, made the court of Kyiv a vibrant place, and though it had been dreary for me at first, had become more than tolerable. Ellisif had been a major factor in that. She had proved a good friend, one I was fortunate to have, and a wealth of information on the intricacies of my new home. Earlier that day, Ellisif had been giving me a history lesson regarding the Polianians. She seemed interested in their gods and folk stories as she impressed me with their many iterations.

'The Polianians,' she advised, 'once were ruled by three brothers, Khoryv, Scheck, and Kyi. It was they who lived here before us and for whom Kyiv is named.'

'For Kyi?' I confirmed.

She nodded. 'When Oleg first came here, and rescued the city back from Igor's captors, he tried to name it something else, but it never stuck. Everyone still calls it Kyiv and it must be because the Polianians love these three brothers. I imagine they're heroes of some sort. People say their spirits inhabit that old space up on the rocky hill,' she explained. 'You know that sacred place where the boyars won't go?'

There was indeed a dark wooded area that bore a special flat-topped rock. Many believed it the home of the gods which the Polianians worshipped, and some knew it to be the grove of gods much older. Men fear that which they do not know, and though I was not particularly afraid of it, I kept a respectful distance. I wanted to ask Ellisif if we might ride near it some time, but she had already moved on.

'Apparently, the three brothers also had a sister named Lybid. But no one knows what happened to her,' she continued as she reached for her cup. 'She probably got married off,' she lamented.

Ellisif was a fount of knowledge about the Drevlians, Polianians, and even some tribes further away. Much of this came from her maid, Licinia, who had since become Sihtric's woman and left Ellisif's service. Ellisif had then come to live with Alfrunr, Oleg's niece, and the other young ladies preparing for marriage who were kept under an ever-watchful eye.

I sat back as my friend stopped talking, and we watched men and women weaving across the hall in each other's arms, dancing in time with the drum and pipes.

Upset turned in my guts, and I folded my arms around my middle. For the last couple of days, I had been unwell, and it was likely inflicted by my gorging on a bag load of fresh plums Ellisif and I had harvested on our morning ride two days prior. We had stuffed ourselves until the fruit's purple flesh stained our fingers and darkened our gums. Ellisif consumed just as many, and she seemed fine.

Kjarr noticed my discomfort and leaned towards me. 'Are you off your food again?' he asked, mumbling into my ear as he downed his cup of mead.

I had eaten some of the bread, and a fair few chunks of turnip, but hadn't touched the venison. 'Too many plums,' I groaned. 'I already told you that.'

'You did,' he acknowledged, 'but you've also missed your courses.'

'Only one,' I corrected him, though I was sure this belly ache resulted from nothing more than eating too much. It was too early to tell. If I was with child, I would be glad to know the awful dream where Gudrun had called her curse upon me had been just that, and would welcome our child who would hopefully fill the void I felt in Freyja's passing.

Kjarr was like a hound that could sniff out its prey on the barest of scents. 'Gods!' he whispered, nuzzling my shoulder. 'It would make me so happy.' That was almost all he thought about these days; impending conflict with the Drevlians, Oleg's relationship with Ellisif, and a child.

'I know you would,' I muttered in return. It would please me as well. That was no lie. If Kjarr and I had another child, it would heal so many wounds, but I could not shake the feeling that no matter how much either of us wished for it, hopes would not be enough. 'We must be patient,' I cautioned.

'A spring baby,' Kjarr beamed as he counted the months. 'A good time for a *barn* to be born. He'll be a strong one.' He waved at a thrall for a refill of his cup. 'We should celebrate.' Kjarr's eyes were twinkling, half-watered with drink as he looked at me, swaying offbeat to the music.

My stomach lurched again. 'I feel quite ill.' Perhaps I was not accustomed to the heavy food of court feasts.

Kjarr's mouth opened into a broad smile as he took my hand and held it to his chest. 'You may feel that way a while yet.' Kjarr made to stand, but the drink had the better of him and he stumbled, catching his arm on Oleg's tall chair and the Grand Prince guided him to his seat.

'Cousin,' Oleg roared with a laugh. 'It seems you've had your fill! But we have something to toast to this evening, I hear.' Oleg smiled at Ellisif, still seated beside him.

'Nothing that we can announce so soon,' Kjarr replied, settling back in his seat. He inspected the inside of his cup and when he saw it was still empty, he sank backwards and sighed.

I exhaled in exasperation. Kjarr was normally so reserved. To see him like this was alarming, but was becoming a more common occurrence. 'Perhaps you should eat some more,' I suggested, placing my hand over his cup.

He took the hint and nodded, shovelling a chunk of bread into his gob. 'It's usually I who cautions you against rash behaviour,' he said, mouth full. 'Do you remember that time you almost pummelled a fellow to death in the Skogarmaor?'

'To be fair, the man called me a litany of insulting names before my fist met his face,' I responded quickly to Oleg and Ellisif, who both looked at me with gaping mouths.

'Oh, he deserved it,' Kjarr put in, 'and lived, albeit with a broken nose and perhaps a few less teeth.'

Oleg laughed through his nose and shrugged. 'We were no better in our youth,' he began. 'There was that time you almost strangled yourself escaping the brew house after trying to pilfer a barrel of ale.'

'Only because you wanted it!' Kjarr added with a raucous laugh of his own.

Oleg nodded. 'We caused some trouble back in Holmgardr, didn't we? Rurik loved a good fight and a clever trick,' he remembered his now deceased brother in marriage. 'Though he was well older, he often encouraged our boyhood antics.'

'He did,' Kjarr agreed, and I saw his eyes lose focus as he lost himself to memories.

'Only because he thought we would be dutiful, eventually. Make a good match and further his plans,' Oleg went on.

'Hmm,' Kjarr mumbled.

'You know,' Oleg said, turning back to me, 'when Rurik first told Kjarr to take a wife, I'd expected he would find a beauty, wealthy and well-known. But he made it very clear that he was not interested in those attributes,' Oleg explained.

I furrowed my brow, unsure if he meant to insult me. 'How old were you when you were commanded to wed?' I asked Kjarr.

'Twenty-one summers,' he answered.

'And we gave him five more to find a suitable maid,' Oleg put in.

I counted on my fingers. Kjarr was approaching twenty-nine. We had been married more than two years before. So, that meant… 'You were running out of time,' I whispered, turning to scowl at him.

He grimaced and replied, 'I had only a few weeks.'

My eyes bulged, and I wasn't sure how I felt about the revelation.

'I asked because I loved you,' Kjarr said only loud enough for me to hear him, 'and we needed each other.'

Oleg continued with his explanation, looking towards me as he said, 'When Kjarr married you, my first thought was to expel him from my close circle because he married without my permission, but I recalled our promise. He was free to choose so long as he did so within the time frame. And, besides, he's my favourite cousin and I could never remain upset with him. When I met you, Signe, I knew at once that Rurik would have liked you. My sister, too, would have loved your company.'

Much mead and ale had been consumed and almost everyone at the high table had a loose tongue, but I thought he meant no malice by what he said. I could not say the same of Ellisif's family. Below the dais, I observed Estrid watching her daughter like a hawk. Her mouth pinched as if she chewed her lip inwards, and her eyes narrowed to the point she might have burrowed into Ellisif's mind. No doubt the woman was looking for an opportunity to exploit her daughter's proximity to the throne. Estrid's glare met mine, and she dipped her head in dutiful deference. Not so low as expected to honour the Grand Prince's kin, but just enough to acknowledge my presence. Her husband, Heilagr, stared at Oleg in between downing mugs of mead and stuffing his mouth with fat-glistened lumps of meat. Whether they approved of Oleg's relationship with their daughter was immaterial. Oleg could do just about anything he liked. And Ellisif had said they welcomed it, but I was concerned about how Hersir Heilagr and his sour wife, Estrid, might try to use their new position.

Runolf dragged my attention away, dressed as he always was, in court colours. He scurried through the crowd to whisper in the Grand Prince's ear, 'Knyaz, the Khazar Emissary has arrived.'

Oleg barely hid the surprise on his face. His nostrils flared and his shoulders pulled back. 'Were we informed one was being sent?' he asked. Oleg was ever aware that any failure of his advisors would be his to bear.

'The possibility was discussed months ago,' Runolf advised. 'It is most unusual to arrive without prior correspondence.' Sweat beaded on the man's sand-coloured brow as he pulled at the collar of his cream tunic.

Oleg breathed in deep. The voice he used for court business was deeper, more restrained than how he spoke in private, 'How can we be sure this man is Khazarian?'

Runolf nodded, agreeing that the question was one to be asked. 'He has the credentials. We have, of course, stripped him of his weapons and have every reason to believe the new Khagan sent him, Knyaz.'

'Very well, Runolf. I am trusting you with my life,' Oleg responded, apparently satisfied that his druzhina had tested the man. 'You may bring him in.' The Grand Prince's buoyant happiness withered before my eyes as he adopted the thick facade of leadership.

'Knyaz,' Runolf started, lowering his head, 'he has requested a private audience.'

'I bet he has and wishes to stab me in the guts with some concealed weapon,' Oleg grumbled, leaning forward to grasp his silver cup.

Runolf shook his head. 'Knyaz, he has no weapons. We took them all and only gave back that which was safe to do so.' He looked towards the great door where another guard stood waiting to open it. 'I, myself, inspected the man, Knyaz.'

'Then I am satisfied, Runolf,' Oleg answered. 'As for a private audience, he will have to wait upon my pleasure for that. Admit him to the hall.'

The messenger nodded and made to leave, but Oleg stopped him. 'Can you ask the kitchens for their food scraps, Runolf?'

'Food scraps, Knyaz?'

'So we might throw them at him,' Oleg finished, his smile tight and eyes much darker than usual.

The guard stared at him blankly, not sure how to answer.

'Oh, Runolf!' Oleg groaned, obviously disappointed that Runolf had not found this humorous. 'Clear the musicians and dancers, and have him come forward,' he instructed.

Runolf scampered down the hall, slinking in between the mass of feast attendees and, together with the second guard, pushed the great doors open. Every man and woman stilled, turning their attention to the man who stood on the threshold. He was clad in a brown leather coat, thick stitches along its seam, embroidered with whirling patterns in red thread. Under this, his long tunic of cream-coloured linen was also stitched with the same design. The Emissary's legs were wrapped with thin straps of browned leather below brown wool pants, and his feet wore short boots with slightly pointed toes. He was dark. Not of skin, but of eye and hair, both of which were deeper than the rich browns of the earth after rain, almost black. The Emissary's hair curled at the ends and shimmered like an oil slick. It surprised me he should be handsome. I'd heard little of his people, but somehow, I'd imagined them to be wild looking and sharp; nothing like the man who stood before us. His dark eyes looked directly at the dais, his broad nose, and high cheekbones covered only by his neatly trimmed moustache and short beard, did not betray any emotion. If he was stunned by the gathering, nothing about him showed it.

The man walked forward, leather creaking as he strode into the otherwise silent grand hall and bowed low before Oleg. 'Grand Prince,' he started, voice deep and inflection strange because of his accent.

'Address me by the title of khagan,' Oleg instructed, looking coolly at the man. 'It will be easier for your tongue and your mind.' Oleg was making it clear he considered himself on equal footing to this man's master, the Khazar Khagan, and by demanding to be referred to by the same title made him acknowledge it.

The man nodded as Oleg motioned for him to raise himself. 'My Khagan sends gifts,' the Emissary waved towards a guard who held a small box.

Oleg said nothing, waiting for further explanation.

The Emissary searched his mind for the translation, 'Dried bladder of the fish, Khagan.'

A few in the room recoiled, but others leaned in, straining to hear better and understand the benefit of such an item.

'Used for making clear liquids, for the bladder takes away the impurities. It is only made in Khazaria,' he explained. 'My Khagan also gives his greetings.'

Oleg's eyes did not move from the Emissary, even though I knew later tonight in his private dwelling we would be excitedly discussing this new thing's uses. The Grand Prince's face remained schooled. 'Do these greetings extend to submission to our rule and a cessation of his relentless insistence of his overlordship?'

At this, the Grand Prince stood. Even without him being raised on the dais, Oleg was head and shoulders taller than the Khazar Emissary, towering over him like the giants of Jotunheim.

The dark man sniggered and itched his nose with his knuckle. He knew at once this was not how he should have acted as the warriors lining the long tables squared their shoulders and the guards' hands went to the hilt of their swords.

The man stiffened. 'He does not, Khagan,' he admitted.

'Khagan Tarkhan sends you as emissary, yet I have not heard your name.' Oleg ran a ringed finger down the length of his jaw.

The Emissary swept another low bow and introduced himself. 'I am Tarkhan Tuvan, Khagan.'

Oleg's eyebrows knitted together. 'You have the same name as your lord?' he asked.

He nodded slowly. 'Tarkhan can be both a title and a given name, Khagan. The title I bear, "Tarkhan", is much like that of your boyars. I have been named Tuvan just as you are named Oleg, I believe,' Tuvan explained carefully.

'I was named Helgi at birth and now that I rule over Slav tribes, I have taken Oleg as my own,' he allowed. 'Why then, Tarkhan Tuvan, does the Khagan of all Khazaria send one man to meet me when most would send a retinue? Does it only take the intelligence of one Khazarian man to form an alliance? Or is it that the Khagan is simply seeking a wife and has sent you to gaze upon the maidens of Kyiv?'

Tuvan's mouth curved downwards. 'The Khagan is always looking for a wife,' he agreed. 'He has many from subjugated tribes, the most beautiful of each land. He would have one from you if you were to offer someone of appropriate standing.'

The court took in a collective sharp breath and the tension in the room was drawn tight as a bowstring. Sveineld, Harald, and Helgi shared an uneasy glance, no doubt thinking back to the discussions they'd had about this very scenario.

Oleg laughed mirthlessly, his icy-blue eyes glowing with the rage that simmered below. He beckoned Runolf forward and bent to speak in his ear, though he still looked at Tuvan. 'Perhaps I was too lenient when I requested kitchen waste to be thrown at your head. Might I suggest instead that we separate it from your shoulders altogether?' he spoke coldly, never taking his eyes from Tuvan's.

Tarkhan Tuvan did not appear to register the threat. It might have been a lack of understanding, but I thought he heard it well enough and chose not to react. From the few stories Ahmed had told me of the Khazar empire and their armies at Itil, I assumed this was not the first time the man had been threatened with execution.

'It was at the pleasure of my Khagan that I was sent and at his pleasure that I continue living. It is not for me to tell him the likely success of this mission, nor if I live or die, Khagan. I am here to deliver his message and to discuss our futures, and that is all.'

Oleg chuckled to himself. He stroked his chin with his forefinger while he observed Tuvan. 'I do not deny I am curious, Tarkhan Tuvan.'

*But that was all he would concede right now*, I thought.

'You are welcome at court and may keep your head,' Oleg announced magnanimously. 'Should you cause any trouble, we will not hesitate to end that arrangement.' The Grand Prince waved the Emissary away with an open hand.

Tarkhan Tuvan dipped his head low. 'Thank you, Khagan,' he replied and took his leave to join some very wary members on the bench at the end of the hall.

Grand Prince Oleg placed his hands on the arms of his seat, ready to resume his position, but Sveineld bent to Runolf as another message was brought forth.

'Grand Prince, a message from the Drevlians,' Sveineld murmured from his side. 'May we bring in the messenger?'

'An emissary from the Khazars and the Drevlians in one day,' Oleg boomed, chuckling as he allowed himself to sink into the chair.

Sveineld shook his sandy brown head. 'It is not good news, I am afraid.'

'Bring them to my rooms,' Oleg commanded, taking his cup and downing it in a single gulp. Ellisif refilled his cup silently and set the jug away from his place. He took her hand and called the high table to accompany him as he told all else to continue feasting until they had their fill, then bed down for the night. The promised entertainment would have to wait for another evening. Tonight was not the night for celebrations.

Runolf brought in a red-caped man, travel weary and dirt-covered, into the partitioned room that was Oleg's own. He bowed, stiff-jointed.

'Grand Prince,' the man began. He was gasping, as if he had ridden hard and without stopping. 'The Drevlians did not greet us at Iskorosten with honour, as they promised to do.'

'They stole from you?'

He shook his head.

Oleg guessed again, 'Did they dishonour the meeting place? Refused to discuss terms?'

The *huskarl* shook his head once more.

'Tell me, man!' Oleg cried, dropping the veneer of composure as he stalked the room full of his warriors and advisors, waiting for the messenger to reply.

'Their leader, Prince Mal, killed my lord and his warrior, Ulf. He left only me to return,' he explained.

Oleg dropped into his seat, stroking the carved arms as he thought.

Sveineld leaned across the table. 'We knew this was a possibility.'

Oleg nodded thoughtfully. 'I had hoped they would agree to our terms and pay us tribute without us having to woo them.'

Helgi and Harald tittered at the casual use of the word when all in the room knew that the method used would be far less gentle than a proposal of marriage.

'We will avenge the deaths of Boyar Oddrsson and his *huskarl*, Ulf,' Oleg announced. Before he could go on, his head snapped around to the woman standing by the partition, holding the hand of a small child dressed in the finest clothes I'd ever seen a young one wear. 'Knyaz,' the woman mumbled from her bowed head.

The Grand Prince held his hand out and summoned the small boy to his side. 'Igor, come.' He stood and raised the boy onto the seat he had vacated and turned to his men. Igor's nursemaid stood on his right, holding the small boy's hand.

'My nephew, Igor, who will one day be your grand prince,' he boomed. 'One day it will be he who will lead you. He has the blood of Rurik in his veins and will be, by the will of the gods, a great warrior lord. It is for Prince Igor, son of Rurik, that we fight,' he announced.

Igor's ruddy cheeks were flushed as his pale eyes darted around the room. Kjarr told me the long angular nose was like Oleg's sister, Igor's mother, but the boy's colouring had come from his father; light brown hair and the cool blue eyes that ran the family line.

'Knyaz,' Igor squeaked. At six, he was still considered a child, only to be attended by servants and tutors, and rarely would he come to court. But tonight, Oleg had deemed it necessary to show the men that which they bled for.

'Here and now, you will swear blood oaths to my nephew,' Oleg commanded. 'None of you shall do him harm, only honour, as his lineage demands.'

Igor stood as still as he could, though his eyes continued to travel around the room. He watched as a thrall brought in a plate of sweet cakes topped with lashings of golden honey. His mouth fell open as the men came forth to make their oaths, and as they concluded, Igor could contain himself no longer. He broke from his nursemaid and raced to the silver platter, snatching two of the small cakes and stuffing one into his mouth.

Old Odholf, the grey-streaked senior Boyar, chuckled. 'So like his father,' he remembered.

'He has his father's hunger, too,' Sveineld called with a laugh as the nursemaid tutted her royal charge, taking him from the hall back to his private rooms.

Many of the boyars laughed their approval at the young Prince's defiance.

'His father's hunger was for expansion,' Oleg continued. 'Our druzhina will have a wintertime campaign against Prince Mal. It is time I unleash my wolves amongst his sheep.'

Oleg's men stamped their feet on the floor and bellowed their assent to the announcement. Ellisif's hand slipped into mine. It was easy to be overcome by the clamour. Kjarr stood by his cousin, nodding. It had been too long between blooding swords and axes, and the Grand Prince's circle was thirsty for conflict. Each wanted to prove themselves to their ruler and their gods. Every man wanted to earn their place in Valhalla, where they would feast and fight forever more. Though they all fought for different things; wealth, women, honour, and some for the violence itself, they all fought for the same man. And, Oleg had ensured they all knew who would come after him, whether that was in truth or just for show, was yet to be proven.

# TWENTY-SIX

Oleg resumed the feast the very next evening.

He wanted to send to Iskorosten for Boyar Oddrsson's body. Few were optimistic enough to think the Drevlians would return it and even fewer volunteered to retrieve it. Likely, the old man's head sat on a spike outside the settlement's gates. Carrion for the crows and ravens. Still, Oleg had made offerings and lit a pyre, though there was no body to burn. The man had served two rulers well, and Oleg wanted Boyar Oddrsson in the hall of the slain.

The hall did not have the carefree air of the night before. After honouring the dead, Oleg turned to other matters.

'An appointment,' Oleg began, rising from his seat and gesturing with an open hand to Sveineld the Younger.

'Grand Prince,' the man replied.

Oleg turned to address the court. 'As you all know, it is essential we strengthen our territories. If we have learned anything from our recent dealings with the Drevlians, it's that we must post trusted posadniks to fringe territories to compel tributes and squeeze out violent tribal conflict. It is therefore my direction to you, Sveineld the Younger, that you shall be a boyar in your own right and become Posadnik of Pleskov.'

'You honour me, Grand Prince,' Sveineld replied dutifully, though he masked his actual response well.

To be sent there was to be given an arduous task of controlling tribes and settlers who might wish to live outside the law of the Rus'.

Oleg wasn't finished. 'Obviously, I will need you during our winter campaign against the Drevlians, but come the warmer weather, you shall depart for Pleskov.'

Sveineld bowed his head low, so much so I could not see his eyes. He sat down and raised a cup to his lips. The gesture said all that needed to be spoken. By the terse line of his lips and his lowered gaze, I could tell he was not overly pleased, but Oleg had moved on.

'And now, your entertainment. Tonight, in honour of our own Boyar Oddrsson, may I present to you.' Oleg motioned to the guards at the door. 'Thorbjorn Hornklofi, who has lately been at King Harald Fairhair's court in Norway and comes to regale us with the mighty deeds of their men abroad. Please, fill your cup, and enjoy the tales.'

Both Ellisif and I took up an ewer of mead and made sure all cups at the top table were filled. They all sat forward, anticipating the treat to come. Across the hall, I saw Tarkhan Tuvan sitting on the same long table as Sihtric, Sven, and Eskil, drowning himself in fine ale, and shovelling morsels into his moustached gob. My eyes lingered on Sven. These days his attention did not turn towards me but to that of the men he held company with, as it should have. I smiled for a moment, remembering my urging him to find joy in this place and somebody to share it with.

I sat, brushing my hand along Kjarr's forearm, dressed in the delicate weave of fine linen cuffed by bright and slippery silk. He covered my hand with his own and we looked ahead as the skald entered the Great Hall.

Thorbjorn was a man in his prime. Straight as an arrow, thin and well proportioned. He strode into the space before the dais and produced his lyre from a bag of leather slung over his arm.

'Thank you, Grand Prince,' he spoke clearly, his voice rising above the low hum of excitement. 'I have come from the home of King Fairhair, whose deeds are well known. He wishes you to receive my latest poem in his honour.' Thorbjorn's deep blue eyes looked over the crowd as he twiddled the small knobs at the top of each string of his lyre.

'What is it named, Thorbjorn?' Oleg asked from the high table.

'*Song of the Raven*, Grand Prince,' Thorbjorn replied with a nod before sitting on the stool brought forward by a young thrall boy. He set his hands over the lyre, fingertips touching the cords. 'I shall begin.'

He plucked, making a melody so gentle each listener was drawn forward, perching on the edge of their chair, ears open to receive well-woven words that only a master skald such as Thorbjorn Hornklofi could weave. Many knew of him. His renown had spread across the

Austmarr and down the rivers like blood to the heart. He had visited the courts of Uppsala, and much of the Kyivan court had once belonged to families of the Svears. To have such a man bring his craft to Kyiv showed Oleg's power and the respect he commanded from his fellow rulers.

Thorbjorn's hand stilled the quivering strings. 'Spear-shakers of Odin,' he began, his voice taking on an ethereal quality. 'Hear me tell of an edge meeting so bloody that only the reconciler of men, King Harald Fairhair, could have won. These deeds I heard from the maiden of the battle-slain, fresh from the corpse-road. On her shoulder sat Munin, the darkest memory of all.'

Men craned their heads and smiled to themselves as they deciphered kennings so sweet that Bragi himself could have crafted each line. All listened as Thorbjorn spun his story of the Battle of Hafrsfjord, so recently fought that none had heard of the conflict prior. The skald told of men gathering in innumerable quantities from lands, including Hordaland, Thelemark, Agder, and Rogaland, all set to defeat Harald's men. In the end, Thorbjorn sang, King Harald Fairhair stood victorious on top of the corpses of many rulers of the aforementioned lands, their brothers, and their sons.

'Many noble wolf-feeders fell that day, even men of the wolf-bane, those moon howlers of fury that know no fear of the apple of Hel,' Thorbjorn rasped into the space of the Great Hall. Then he fell silent, head drooped forward, chin on his chest. His hand was limp on his lyre as his fingers ceased their plucking, pink and calloused from their work. The thrall boy, who had earlier brought a stool for Thorbjorn to sit upon, now offered a cup of ale on a board, setting it on a small table. Thorbjorn sat motionless for a moment and then jerked alive, gulping the drink down in great mouthfuls.

'You swear all this is true?' someone bellowed from the crowd.

Grand Prince Oleg stood. 'You dare ask a skald if every kenning is exactly as it would be? Such is the permit of the trade. But if what Thorbjorn Hornklofi says is in essence truth, then King Harald Fairhair has indeed become king of all of Norway. Something we did not know was possible until now. May the gods continue to look upon him favourably,' Oleg praised the ruler with a raised cup. 'And we shall send gifts across the ocean to Harald and his wife, Ragnhild, to show our friendship.'

'And to make sure they don't set their gaze on our shores next,' Kjarr whispered into my ear.

I bit the edge of my lip as my mouth quivered into a smirk.

The poem had been long, but a skald was expected to deliver more than one fine set of word weavings. Thorbjorn took his lyre in hand again and looked towards the dais. 'Grand Prince, I have another for you this evening, if it would please?'

Oleg inclined his head. 'It would. What name have you given this one?'

Thorbjorn looked up at Oleg. 'It is yet to be named, Grand Prince. The kennings were born just this evening when inspiration took hold. You and your court will be the first to hear it.'

At that, the entire room gasped. A fresh, previously unheard piece was a treat. *Song of the Raven* had been new to our ears, but we were not its first audience. To witness neatly spun words from a wordsmith so renowned as Thorbjorn Hornklofi was a tale to tell one's grandchildren.

With refreshed fingers, Thorbjorn began plucking at the strings, rapidly at first, then slowing to a twinkle like stars in the night sky. 'In the wide awning of cloud-halls, a bolt flame illuminates.' His words wafted over the crowd, some closed their eyes to hear only his voice and others squinted, trying to make sense of the complicated layers of meaning.

'It is the downpour before the day fire that gives cause for appreci-ation,' Thorbjorn went on. 'Then comes life-halls so tender that even the ruler of men cannot look away. A smile sweet as dripping amber soothes the forest of the mind.' Thorbjorn's words boomed.

All sat still, glancing between the skald and their Grand Prince, wondering, just as I was, if this poem had been intended for him. The skald had referred to "the ruler of men," which was often used in place of king or prince and seemed to allude to this ruler's love of a fair maiden. If Oleg found offence in this, he made no show of it. He remained perched on his chair, Ellisif's arm draped over his, watching the storyteller continue his words.

The skald took a deep breath to deliver the last verse. 'A kingdom at war with the enemy of men cannot prosper,' his voice built until it was a roar. 'When the steerer of the carriage is more inclined to love than the gentle illuminator of duty. And, when the fruit comes from the union of close bed-friends, the field-reddeners will rise, and answer the unspoken question with their blood.'

I looked towards Kjarr, who sat blinking rapidly, taking it all in.

It was within a skald's purview to make fun of, tease, or rile their benefactor, but this bordered on a suicidal attempt of affront.

'Did he say what I think he said?' someone mumbled on the low tables.

'Who can be sure?' his friend replied. 'You can never understand these skalds and their word vomit. Perhaps it means this war with the Drevlians will be vicious and bloody.'

'Or perhaps it means just as Thorbjorn says it. The Grand Prince is planting his seed in that young garden and will take the throne for himself,' a rough voice from a lower table grumbled.

'You need your ears cleaned out, Begla. All he's saying is that there'll be a union soon enough and from that comes a child that will cause war. Hmmm. No. That doesn't sound too good.' The man went back to drinking instead of deciphering Thorbjorn's stories.

'But a skald is not a *völva*,' Begla pointed out.

His friend did not reply.

All eyes had turned to Oleg, who now stood. 'And, to whom does this poem address?' he asked the skald.

Thorbjorn stood and turned from his stool. 'Grand Prince, you know well that the source of inspiration should never be revealed. The mystery adds to the intrigue.'

Oleg nodded and raised his cup to the tale-weaver. 'To Thorbjorn Hornklofi, master skald,' he said as he motioned to a thrall to bring the man gifts. 'And, a suggestion, if I may, for the name of this poem.'

'Yes, Grand Prince.'

'The King's Battle-Road,' Oleg offered.

'Hmm,' Thorbjorn postulated. '*The King's Battle-Road*?' he mulled the words in his mouth like a foreign wine. 'For it is the path travelled on each ascension?' Thorbjorn clarified.

'I believe it is,' Oleg agreed, narrowing his eyes.

Thorbjorn shrank away. 'It will be given due consideration, Grand Prince. Thank you for honouring me with both your suggestions and your gifts.' He scraped the pouch and food from the offered platter and retired to a plate of cooling meats and barley stew.

I took the lapse in celebration to seek Sihtric and Sven. They had been here earlier. I had seen them before the skald started his stories. But the hall was crowded with people leaving, loitering, or lashing themselves with drink. Towards the back of the hall were several small alcoves that served as sleeping benches for visitors, or secret enough recesses which sufficed for lover's stolen moments. Tonight, though, they were being used for Kyiv's wives, who ground gossip like their thralls milled grain flour.

'She's tighter than my husband's fist,' a woman tittered from the dark alcove to my left.

I stopped. It almost always came to nothing, but sometimes pointless nattering was worth listening to. There were other voices too, all intent on spinning rumours.

'Oh, Aslaug,' Estrid's unmistakable pitch complained to the first woman. 'Who does she think she is, coming into Kyiv and taking over my trade?'

'Come, Estrid. Surely, she has not. After all, you concern yourself with cloth for gowns and I hear Signe is making sails,' a third, softer voice tried to reason with the Boyar's wife.

'Either way, I'm told she cannot satisfy her husband,' Estrid said and cackled into her cup as she slurped up her drink. 'Boyar Hrolfsson is yet to have an heir. Either he cannot bring himself to bed her, or she cannot bear his seed.'

The two other women giggled at Estrid's crass assessment, and I felt my cheeks flush with heat. I should have left. There was little to be gained from hearing them spit their venom, but I had promised Mirca we would discover Estrid's plans. So, despite my discomfort, I strained to listen to their whispered assault against my character.

'And, ladies,' Estrid began in a voice even more a whisper than before. 'I've had it from her household that Signe is barren.'

My body froze. Was this the method Estrid had chosen to bring me down with? It seemed she wanted to drive a wedge between Kjarr and me by spreading news of my inability to bear him an heir. Horror gripped my chest and twisted at my insides. There was only one person in my household with whom I had shared my fears and she had never given me cause to doubt her before.

*Odrun wouldn't disclose this without a reason*, I told myself.

'Well, that explains a few things, doesn't it, Estrid?' Aslaug, Old Odholf's wife, replied. 'She won't last long. Her husband will set her aside and take another wife, and then he'll have his heir and you'll be free of her.'

Estrid chuckled in agreement.

'And, speaking of heirs,' Aslaug began. 'What do you make of that poem, Estrid? It's rather sly of Thorbjorn to come in here and rattle off some riddles about children and war.'

'Is that what you think it was about?' the third voice asked innocently. 'If that's so, could it be a child of your dear daughter, Ellisif?'

'Don't be stupid,' Estrid dismissed.

'The Grand Prince is rather fond of your daughter,' Aslaug mentioned. 'And, if he were to make Ellisif his wife, his knyaginya, then their child might rule after him instead of Igor.'

'But I thought Igor was meant to take the throne after Oleg? It was Rurik's wish, and Oleg made the men swear blood oaths,' the third voice chimed in.

'Hush, Ranveg!' Estrid admonished. 'Yes, Aslaug, it was Rurik's will that Igor, his son, took the throne when he comes of age and strength. In the interim, Oleg rules. No one benefits from a child-king. Other tribes would come to feast on our bones and, in a generation, we would be no more.'

'If Oleg was to take the throne for himself and his heirs, it would be like the poem said. "The field-reddeners will rise and answer the unspoken question with their blood." Does that mean our druzhina would fight to decide the succession?' Ranveg asked.

'Where's my ale, woman?' a man across the hall beckoned to the alcove. He didn't look around, just impatiently lifted his cup.

'My husband wouldn't approve if Oleg was to usurp the throne,' mumbled Aslaug, fussing with something noisily. 'And, nor will the old boyars. They gave their oath to Rurik that Igor would be protected. That's why they came to take Kyiv from Haskold and Dir, those bastard brothers of Rurik's wife. No royal blood spilled there, just filth.' The woman spat on the floor.

'They were Oleg's half-brothers too,' Estrid mumbled, 'but don't call him a kin-slayer if you value your life.'

'No. And none of the druzhina would cheer at Oleg usurping Igor's crown. And, if he thinks to do it, he will have to answer to at least half of the boyars.'

Estrid gave a noncommittal sound that I imagined was accompanied by a complacent shrug. She wished her daughter was sitting on the low seat next to the throne. Estrid desired an heir that shared her blood, because she wanted the power she thought it would bring. But spreading rumours that Oleg also wanted this was a dangerous scheme, one that could unseat her plan, not to mention the entire dynasty.

'Ranveg!' the man waiting for ale bellowed across the space. 'Stop your senseless prattling, and bring me a drink, woman!'

Ranveg scuttled out of the dark place, paying no mind to me as she passed to serve her husband. Before she or Estrid could notice me, I abandoned my search for Sihtric and Sven, to rejoin my husband at the dais, smiling sweetly as if I had not witnessed the court rumbling towards civil war.

# TWENTY-SEVEN

*Vetrnaetr* was my favourite celebration of the year. It had been since I was a small girl.

The chill it ushered in shook leaves from their branches. Large piles of orange and red debris underfoot turned the same dull brown and greys as the changing weather. Howling winds spiralled through thinning forests, low hollow calls of the gods beckoning the woodland spirits and elves closer to the land of mortals. People grew wary. No longer did they traipse through the dark forest to gather herbs, mushrooms, and roots alone. We departed in company for added protection. I didn't mind. The woodland skeletons, with their naked boughs, might tower above me, but there was peace there. A sense of calm had settled after the frenzy of harvest.

Winter Nights, after all, welcomed the cold after abundance. Many dreaded its arrival, for it heralded a time of austerity; men sucked bones for the marrow, raided pantries to the last skerrick, and some shrivelled until the season's survivors resembled the empty grain-sacks they wished were full, just like their bellies. Before the lean season of winter arrived, the bounties were pickled, dried, and smoked. The key-carrying women of Kyiv would fuss until their shelves were overflowing. If they did not, their idleness could mean starvation. As a wife, these duties were also mine. Though as kin to the Grand Prince, we would not want for food for his larder was ours and, never did anyone hear of a king starving to death.

My approach to *Vetrnaetr* was not with apprehension. I loved this time, when the warmth had not yet seeped from my bones. Memories of summertime bathing, radiant sun, and the hopes of a new year were all fresh in my mind. None were yet marred by the long and brutal season to come. And, while others were too fearful to look up until

the hoar frost dusted the ground, there were always those who peered
at the dark skies, waiting for Odin's Wild Hunt. Once his warriors had
ridden through the night, it was safe to gaze at the stars once more, and,
on the first full moon after white ice covered the land, the celebration
would be held.

As his people shivered against those chilly winds that hailed from the
north, Grand Prince Oleg offered sacrifice to the winter deity Skadi,
a giant turned goddess after marrying Njord, god of the sea. To Ullr,
protector of oaths, he slaughtered a lamb, and at the altar of Odin,
Thor, and Freyr, he gave the blood of beasts. Oleg swore he would
defeat the Drevlians, and, though the climate was more temperate in
Kyiv than it had been in Aldeigjuborg or Karlstad, I felt the cold creep
down my spine like a spider crawling on my skin.

*Would the gods see? Would they listen? Were Odin and Freyja already handing
the list of names to the Valkyries so they may ride to snatch them from the
battlefield?* I shook the thought from my head as I listened to Oleg's
well-practised speech.

Besides the traditional *Vetrnaetr blót*, Oleg decreed a contest of games.
He declared the activity beneficial for both the druzhina's morale and
our readiness for the battle to come.

We all attended the sacrifice. Every one of us received a spattering
of a creature's blood. My brow still bore the bright red drops as I pored
over accounts in the warehouse in the mid-morning light. There was
no expectation for Mirca or any of our women to accompany me. In
fact, after the *blót*, they all headed to the festivities to watch the games
as would I once I finished my work.

My gaze fell on the packages of wool received in our last shipment.
They lay unwrapped on the sorting table and I counted them for the
fourth time. Everything was right, and relief flooded me as I reckoned
the sums their completed products would bring in. By the time the
*Bhobain* left in the springtime, I would have doubled my wealth, even
after paying Mirca and our women. Our warehouse was paid in full
from Kjarr's silver, and I would repay him in short order; that sum
would make it so. I reclined on the bench seat and tipped my head back,
smiling at the rafters. *All would be fine. The gods and the Norns loved me still.*

In the distance, I heard delighted screams from the banks of the river.
It must have been the running of the oars, a contest where men ran aft

to bow on oar shafts as other men rowed and tried to unbalance the runner. Only a man quick as a fox, and light on his feet, could succeed in such a sport and the winner had been promised gold. From the roar of the spectators, it sounded like the victor had just been decided.

I had hoped to conclude my work in time to watch the stone lifting. Eskil had declared himself the strongest of the druzhina and I wanted to see for myself, but the accounts had taken longer than I'd expected and that match had passed. But there was one contest I could not miss, so I locked the warehouse up and made haste along the dirt path to the open fields of Kyiv, where the throng was lining up for the next event. The crowd was thick, at least seven people deep around a central ring. Gaggles of men and women chanted the names of their chosen participants as I squeezed myself through the press of bodies.

The wrestling match had already begun.

Kjarr had asked me to stand by the sidelines so that he might see me, but I'd waited too long to come down and it was proving difficult to get to the front. I dived through the last two rows, my head popping through a gap between men's shoulders, as I forced my way in. My body slithered after and I grasped the small fence to stop myself from tumbling forward.

I stifled a laugh. To my surprise, this round's participants were mismatched.

In the centre of the space, Sven stood tall with his hands on his hips, his shirt untucked from his breeches. This had to be his first round. His clothing was dry, and no one was covered in mud. The crowd was eager, not yet baying for blood, and was calling out the name of the underdog.

'Frodi,' they cried.

The Sámi was crouched low before Sven, serpent eyes narrowed. He cast off his shirt and threw it to Björn, behind him, then slapped his naked arms causing them to redden. 'Come and get me, Sven,' he called to the larger man.

Sven stood aloof, a wry smile tilting his lips as he watched the *Bhobain's* steersman goading him. His gaze darted to the man walking into the ring, Oleg's messenger, Runolf, who today was acting as referee.

Runolf raised his hands, and all were quiet. 'Men,' he said, addressing Frodi and Sven, 'the contest continues until one of you yields.'

'Won't be me,' Frodi jeered as he flicked his grey-streaked dark hair from his eyes.

Runolf looked at him with bemusement, 'Or until one of you bleeds,' he added. 'If you hold a man down for the count of three and still he does not speak the words, he will be defeated. Is that clear?' Runolf asked, brushing his hand through the curls of hair on his chin.

Both men nodded.

The crowd erupted in whoops and cheers as they collectively leaned towards the ring, the fence sagging under the weight.

A sudden demand to irritate Sven as I did when we were children came over me. I couldn't help myself as I screamed, 'Go, Frodi!' from the sidelines.

Sven shot me the annoyed glare I'd wanted him to, and I grinned broadly.

Runolf whistled, starting the match.

Frodi launched first, wrapping his muscle-corded arms around Sven's middle with an agile charge that took the larger man off guard. Frodi's first mistake was tackling Sven to the ground. Once there, the larger man rolled on top of his opponent with very little effort and ceased Frodi's onslaught. Frodi bucked like a boar under the executioner's axe as he tried to slip out from Sven's bulk, but it was no use. My fair-haired friend twisted the smaller man's arms into the crooks of his elbows and looped his ankles around Frodi's thighs. He thrashed around, milling up the earth below, until all his strength withered and died. With a limp hand, Frodi patted the ground next to him, admitting defeat.

'You yield, Frodi?' Sven asked, a laugh escaping his throat as he no doubt recalled Frodi's earlier boasting.

Frodi mumbled something in response.

'Do you yield?' Sven repeated, pulling the man up by the arms, bending him backward.

'I do,' he yelped, furrowing his brow. 'You have won!'

Runolf scuttled back into the ring, unprepared for the match to have concluded as quickly as it had. He raised Sven from the ground, lifting his hand toward the sky. The crowd clapped and bellowed congratulations as the loser slipped onto the sidelines.

Björn offered Frodi a skin of ale and a chuckle over his misfortune.

Next to me, I felt a rough shove against my shoulder. 'Thank the gods we've found you, *bhana charaid*,' Sihtric spoke as he pulled a dark-haired woman beside him. 'You've met Licinia before?'

I nodded briefly. 'Only in that one lesson when you taught me the basics of your mother tongue,' I replied.

Licinia looked at me through the curtain of her dark lashes. Her heart-shaped face was beautiful, lit up by upturned eyes of spring green under thick dark eyebrows. She parted her full lips. 'Have you mastered it yet?'

I laughed. 'Is it possible to do so in such little time? It's so different from my tongue, but I like the sound and Kjarr is quite good. We practise together sometimes.'

She gave me a patient smile. '*Euphemia*, Lady Signe.'

It was easy to recognise her congratulations. At least I had learned that much.

Licinia turned back to the ring. 'Who are you hoping will win this next match?' she asked with an accent so lovely it made each word sound like a song.

'I believe my husband is next, and he wouldn't take kindly to my betting against him,' I replied with a laugh.

Licinia wrinkled her nose, so perfectly formed it might have been carved from stone. Ellisif had told me little of her previous maid. All I knew was that she was a thrall taken from a land near Miklagard. Now seeing her up close, I understood that any slaver would have snatched her without a second thought and I wondered what horrors she had been through to bring her to this place.

'It is your husband against the warrior Eskil, no?' she asked, and I realised I had been staring.

'Sorry,' I mumbled.

Licinia looked genuinely surprised at being apologised to.

'Yes, they are next.' Having witnessed Eskil's fighting first hand, I knew Kjarr was in for a tough match. I was glad my support of Kjarr required no financial endorsement. 'But you've missed Sven and Frodi,' I muttered to Sihtric.

It was Licinia who replied, 'Oh! I wanted to see that.'

I took her hand and drew her closer. 'Sven won it. That means he'll progress to the next round, though it's yet to be decided who he will go against.'

'Do you think he is strong enough to win?' she asked, turning her head towards me.

I hadn't thought about who Sven might wrestle against in the later rounds, but I had fought him often enough to know Sven was more than brawn. He also used his mind. 'We will wait and see,' I responded, looking at Sihtric as he gave me a pained smile. I released Licinia's arm and edged towards Sihtric. 'What's wrong?' I asked.

He shook his head and put himself between Licinia and me again. 'The real question,' he began, talking to both of us, 'is, do you think Kjarr has any hope of winning against Eskil?'

Licinia laughed lightly.

'I've seen Kjarr in a scrap or two,' Sihtric started, 'but the big man has brute strength on his side and is fully recovered after his injuries.' Sihtric leaned closer to speak in my ear, 'Kjarr tells me he feels invincible on the field today, after what you did last night, *bhana charaid.*'

My cheeks burned hot. 'Not to mention the time he's been spending at practice with Oleg preparing for the battle against the Drevlians,' I dismissed.

Sihtric cackled with laughter. 'Och! He didnae tell me anything. One look at your red face and that's all I need to ken.'

As he spoke, Kjarr entered the ring looking the most dishevelled I had ever seen him in public. Shirt untucked, trousers loose, and tawny hair wild. He leaned forward, arms out, preparing to fight Eskil, who was more than a head taller, and almost another man wide.

Runolf stumbled in to make his standard announcement, and both men nodded their ascent. 'Go!' he yelled, as he scuttled backwards into the roaring crowd.

This was more like it. The audience was eager to watch a senior boyar get pummelled by the lower-ranked powerful warrior, all in good fun. They screamed Eskil's name. Women pulled their scarves from their heads and waved them high, colourful banners to cheer on their chosen one. Their men placed loud bets on how long Kjarr might last, and how many of his bones would be broken by the end.

A groan fell from my lips as Eskil's hulking form launched forward, raging like a war stallion into enemy lines. I covered my eyes with my hands, peeking through as the crowd hissed. Eskil had stumbled, which left enough time for my husband to jump out of the way. I cheered.

Eskil cursed, and the audience seemed disappointed at the lack of blood so far. Kjarr rounded on the bigger man, trying to trip him. Eskil did not go down. Instead, he groped forward, trying to clasp Kjarr's limbs, but he, too, missed. Kjarr continued searching for an opening, but it was like watching a child throw stones at a bear. Eskil just flicked Kjarr's attacks away as if they were merely annoying. Eskil flung himself forward, bringing both men to the ground, and I thought my husband defeated as soon as Eskil straddled his torso.

To my surprise, Kjarr did not tap the ground. His shirt, now covered in dirt and sweat, stuck to him as he moved both his arms to Eskil's left side, creating a wedge. Kjarr used the leverage to shoulder the man off his balance as my husband rolled in the opposite direction. Eskil hit the ground before he knew what happened, evident from the stunned expression on his face. Dirt rose and spiralled into his open maw before he rolled onto his back, stupefied for a moment. Kjarr pounced, kneeling on Eskil's forearms, his face above the big man's belly, top to tail.

From between my hands, I watched. 'Eskil's down,' I said in shock.

'I blinked and missed the entire move,' Sihtric conceded, holding fast to Licinia as she shrieked excitedly.

Eskil flapped around in the dirt, coughing, and spluttering while he tried to kick Kjarr off. Kjarr grasped Eskil's leg and twisted it away from his body. The big man hollered and punched the ground with his pinned arm.

'Do you yield, Eskil?' Runolf asked from the sideline, not bothering to stand.

'No bloody chance!' he screamed back, still trying to buck my husband off. 'Owww!' he cried as Kjarr pulled his ankle with greater purchase. Eskil rocked side to side, gaining the momentum that would unseat his opponent.

In a move that was almost as swift as the first, Kjarr reefed Eskil's legs, bending them and pulling them towards himself. Kjarr's strength was astonishing.

'Ahhh!' the big man cried, 'you bastard!'

'I didn't know Eskil could fold like that,' I whispered to Sihtric.

'Dinnae think he did either,' Sihtric replied with a laugh.

'I yield! I yield,' Eskil repeated, turning to Runolf. 'Stop the bloody match. I yield!'

Runolf ran into the ring and ended the round by congratulating the winner. Eskil sulked, walking off with a limp, accepting a commiseration ale from Frodi on the sidelines.

Kjarr rushed to meet me.

'You beat Eskil,' I beamed, mopping the sweat from his face with a cloth.

He grinned wolfishly. 'You seem surprised.'

'I've never seen you do anything like that. I didn't know you could,' I admitted, still shocked at the outcome and wishing I had placed a wager on his success. *What odds would there have been? Enough to triple my bet, probably.*

He leaned in close. 'Does the display of my strength do something for you?' he asked, keeping his voice low. 'You don't need to wait, there are plenty of places…'

'Oh, stop,' I commanded, 'your blood is hot and you need a cool drink.'

He kissed my fingers. The exhilaration of winning the fight had gone straight to his head. Though he was right when he asked if seeing him in such command had awakened some desires.

'Who is next?' Licinia asked awkwardly from beside Sihtric as I pushed Kjarr's sweaty body from mine.

Cravings would have to wait because it was now the Grand Prince who entered the ring, and his opponent was the Khazar Emissary, Tarkhan Tuvan. I quickly realised that this match mattered more than any other. The outcome would determine the stronger man, yes, but that man also represented an empire. If the Rus' won over the Khazar, that might signal a future win in war. But if Oleg was to lose, it could undermine his strength as a ruler. And, if Oleg lost, would that be a sign from the gods that this conflict with the Drevlians was about to swallow Kyiv whole?

'I hope he knows what he is doing,' I mumbled to Kjarr.

Kjarr slipped his arm around my waist. 'He does.'

The crowd sucked in a sharp breath as Oleg came in, smiling and waving to his people. He was dressed in a sleeveless tunic, cropped at the hips, a tablet woven belt securing it around his middle, and loose trousers that sunk low in the crotch. Tuvan, by comparison, was hardly dressed at all. He wore firm-fitting breeches, no shoes, and no shirt. As he turned away, I saw the tanned skin of his back was criss-crossed with pink welts of long-borne wounds. His torso was also littered with healed war wounds. There were great gashes on his stomach, chest, and sides. It was a wonder a man could survive so many injuries and live. But Tuvan was strong, his scarred abdomen was also chiselled. Many eyes fell to that area as the man stretched in preparation. Across the space, Oleg, too, went through several motions to ready his body.

This fight would be well matched, and as Runolf indicated to begin, neither man gave anything that wasn't snatched up by the other. It took some time for them to find the ground, and when they did, it was many slight movements that had them slithering like serpents to entwine the other's limbs. It was no rough scramble, but an intricate game of strategic actions by those with many hours of wrestling practice between them. At one stage I thought Tuvan had the high ground, as he pressed the Grand Prince down, but he slipped, both men slick with sweat, and Oleg pinned him, twisting the Khazar's arm grotesquely behind his back.

Tuvan did not scream. He barely grunted when his arm popped from its socket, but he tapped the ground and yielded the match, before biting a piece of wood as the healer pushed his shoulder back into its place. If not for the dislocation of his arm, the match would have continued, and I felt Tuvan yielded when he otherwise might not have. Just long enough to make it a decent spectacle.

Tuvan sat on the bench, his dark features set as the Grand Prince approached him. 'Quite a fight, Tuvan,' Oleg congratulated, grasping Tuvan by the forearm.

Tuvan nodded and rolled his shoulders back with a crack, the skin of his righted arm red and the muscle swollen.

'You are a hard man to beat, Tarkhan Tuvan,' said the Grand Prince. 'A lesser man would have cried out at such an injury.'

The Emissary went to stand, but Oleg stilled him with his hand.

'Where I come from,' Tuvan began, 'it is a weakness to cry out. Only children and poor folk show pain, not men, Khagan.'

'Is this how you fight in Khazaria? In Itil?' Oleg wondered.

Tuvan shook his head. 'In Khazaria, we do not yield. It is not our decision to make. I would not have been released until the referee declared me beaten.'

'Is that so?'

Tuvan nodded and lowered his voice. 'By blood or by death, Khagan.'

The scars suddenly made sense. If one was not defeated until bleeding, it followed that their wrestling matches were bloodier and more violent. It crossed my mind that perhaps Tuvan could have gone much further in the fight, that he relented all too easily if he had taken part in many rounds in Khazaria and emerged the victor.

Oleg must have considered the same. He raised Tuvan and offered him a cup. 'It's a pity we were matched. I would have enjoyed seeing what you're capable of.'

The two men chuckled together in uneasy acceptance.

'Thank you, Khagan,' Tuvan replied and sipped from his cup.

The Grand Prince refilled Tuvan's cup. 'When the day is done, you shall eat at my table.'

Startled by the invitation, the Khazar Emissary bent from the waist and bowed. 'I am honoured.'

'We shall have to get that man's measure,' Kjarr spoke into my ear. Any time Oleg would spend with Tuvan, Kjarr would be right by his side.

But there was no more time for me to observe their conversation. The last round before the finals was about to begin and the crowd was tittering as the participants entered the ring.

'Look, Sihtric,' Licinia drew out the syllables of her lover's name until they were over annunciated. When she spoke, it sounded more like 'See-trick,' than the way others said it. 'Your friends,' she said, pointing towards the fighters. 'The handsome one and… the not handsome one.'

Sihtric chuckled and tucked Licinia's hand back under his on the fence.

Thorsten strode into the ring, already rid of his shirt and lustily kissing a fire-headed girl, several shades darker than his own, as he walked past.

'Looks like his wish came true,' I muttered to Kjarr. Thorsten had been ever vocal regarding his desire to meet a maid he could give his heart to.

Beside him was our short and crooked Björn, shipmaster, and part of the *Bhobain's* crew. At Runolf's signal, both Björn, and Thorsten charged forward in a comical collision. Thorsten fell straight on his back, legs into the air, having been busy laughing and enjoying the attention that he was not prepared for the onslaught. Thorsten flung his arms around like a sea creature, trying to capture Björn's surprisingly muscular body. He ensnared him, forcing the gap-toothed man to the ground. But Björn's fingers had worked their way to Thorsten's face and into the man's nostrils.

'His beautiful face,' Licinia cried, burrowing into Sihtric's shoulder.

Kjarr laughed at Licinia's outburst.

Sihtric patted her hand. 'Aye, but he'll be fine,' he said, trying to comfort her. 'Thorsten's a lanky lad. He'll have Björn on… Oh! Nae. Well, that was unexpected.'

And it was. The whole thing was over in moments. Thorsten had yielded to Björn's wiry strength but didn't seem too upset about it. He ran straight into the comforting arms of his bronze-headed love as Björn proceeded to the next round, which pitted him against the Grand Prince. Unwilling to give a proper fight to the Rus' ruler, Björn capitulated and Oleg progressed to the finals.

In the interval, Thorsten wandered through the gathered ladies offering his bone and antler combs for sale. So, too, did Gunnar. I saw him making his way through gaggles of wives, holding forth a small box of trinkets. As ever, his eyes roved over what he wanted, purses of coin, and the figures of the prettiest of women.

Only one round stood between the remaining competitors and the concluding match. As the fighters were summoned to the ring, Kjarr squeezed me tight and planted a heated kiss on my mouth before he slipped between the gap in the fence.

From the other direction, Sven marched in, shirtless and confident. He swung his arms, loosening up, and as he turned, I glimpsed the ink-work on his back, shoulder, and neck. On his right shoulder blade, a sea bird he'd had imprinted on his body for me. The last time I'd seen it was the night he held me on my hearth floor, lost in grief and almost devoid of our senses. I knew I shouldn't be looking at him as I did, knew I should release the breath I'd been holding. I told him it was too late. I was married; I loved Kjarr and there was nothing between us anymore.

'Oooh, I cannot be watching,' Licinia cried beside me, but she did not hide her face away as she had in earlier matches.

'Dinnae fret, lass,' Sihtric mumbled.

There was something about the way she watched Sven's movement that made my heart sink. Licinia's eyes were open, her lips parted as if she wanted to call to Sven, and in her hands she gripped some small wooden object. A ship. The same one I'd seen Sven carve weeks earlier.

Sihtric's gaze met mine, and he knew at once the realisation I was coming to.

The match had begun, and I turned in time to see Sven and Kjarr's arms wrapped around each other's waist, writhing and pushing. Kjarr grunted as he drove his feet into the dirt and angled his body down to drive the taller man backwards. Sven skidded. He had almost stepped over the line, which would cause instant disqualification, but he caught himself in time. With a monstrous bellow, Sven pumped his legs down and propelled Kjarr back, both losing their footing and tumbling onto the ground. Kjarr fell face forward, and Sven was on his side. They scrambled to their knees, Kjarr's face streaming with blood as his nose smashed into the earth. Sven was on one knee. Kjarr was on all fours as they made contact again, Sven screaming as he forced Kjarr to the ground by pushing on his shoulders.

'He fights like a bull,' Licinia whispered admiringly. Her chest rose and fell with deep breaths as colour flushed along her collarbones and cheeks. She bit her lip. Not the absent-minded chewing. It was a nip she might give a lover when their mouths met.

'Sven fights to prove something,' Sihtric said. 'This is but a game for Kjarr.'

'Do you think so?' I asked.

Blood continued to stream from Kjarr's face as Sven held him down. He was on his stomach, Sven's hand on the back of his head, knees on his back. Runolf edged into the ring, sensing the end of the match. Sven let out a howl, and I saw Kjarr had hold of Sven's fingers and was twisting them. The moment of hesitation gave Kjarr freedom to turn around, but Sven was nimble as he jerked his fingers from Kjarr's vice-like grip. Runolf stayed close, bending down to check that Kjarr wanted to proceed. Sven's knee ground into Kjarr's stomach, and Sven grasped my husband's left arm and twisted it like a knot of bread.

Kjarr tapped the ground beside him with his right hand.

'You yield?' Runolf asked, somewhat surprised.

'I yield to…' Kjarr began breathlessly, and I thanked the gods my husband did not have a wish to die today.

I looked at Sven. From the scowl on his face, he would have let the match proceed to tearing off Kjarr's limbs before he was sated. 'You yield to Sven Hakonsson of Karlstad!' Sven roared, to the adoration of the crowd.

Kjarr got to his feet, face bloodied and a smirk more malicious than I had ever seen him wear. They didn't shake hands, nor acknowledge one another as they walked in the same direction towards our group.

'This'll cause nae trouble, I'm sure, *bhana charaid*,' Sihtric said with humour. 'At least they didnae kill each other.'

'This time,' I added.

'You won!' Licinia exclaimed as Sven drew near and wrapped her arms around him. She pressed the small boat to his chest.

*He had made it for her*, and the comprehension hit me like an arrow to the chest.

Sven bent to kiss the top of her head before Sihtric pulled her away into his embrace.

I knew the hurt showed on my face. I'd never been any good at hiding it. Kjarr reached for me, pressing me against his sweat-soaked chest. 'That's the messiest I've come out of a wrestling match for some time,' Kjarr mumbled, wiping his face with a cloth.

'Hmm,' Sven grumbled in reply.

I clung to Kjarr, tighter than I might have had I not seen Sven's tenderness with Licinia. 'You fought well,' I offered dutifully to my husband as he finished cleaning himself up. No actual harm was done. The only wound he bore was that of his pride and even that was not much damaged after fighting so fiercely.

Before the final fight of the day occurred, there was entertainment. Masked players acted out the battle of Kyiv, where Oleg slayed Haskold and Dir, and freed his nephew, Igor. The audience jeered appropriately at the sly portrayal of the two bastard brothers and cheered for the man who portrayed Grand Prince Oleg. The crowned actor struck down the villains with a single blow of his great sword. As if it was that easy, as if anything was. Haskold and Dir crumbled to the ground, and Oleg stood victorious with Igor, his sister's child, at his side.

After Thorbjorn's poem the other night, Oleg was laying on the declaration of succession; there would be no question about it.

After ale and a rest, Oleg, and Sven re-entered the ring, encircled by hazel rods which, just as before, they were not permitted to step over. Runolf reminded them of the rules, to which they both nodded. Both men were stripped to their waists, sweaty, dirty, and ready to fight.

Runolf stood between them, holding each by the hand. 'You know the rules, Knyaz?' he asked.

The Grand Prince nodded.

'And Sven Hakonsson?'

Sven gave a curt nod and took a step back.

Licinia covered her mouth, stifling a cry.

Rage simmered inside me, a jealous rage I knew. So, I screwed up my face and chewed on my lip. Sven had every right to seek happiness, just as I had urged him to do so. I just did not understand why my guts twisted to see him show Licinia affection. Worse, why did I want to hate a woman who seemed so lovely and kind? Wasn't that exactly what I should want for my best friend? It would have been so easy to say I was upset because Sven was cuckolding Sihtric, but I knew it was a lie and I hated myself for it.

'Who do you think will win?' Kjarr asked, whispering the words against my neck.

'The Grand Prince, of course,' I tried to answer confidently. 'But Sven won't go down without a fight.'

'Oh, I know that well,' Kjarr replied, holding me close to the heat of his body. 'He seemed to have a particular vendetta against me.'

'Mmm,' I agreed, sinking into his embrace. Warm, comforting, and constant. *That was Kjarr*, I reminded myself. My dependable, loving husband for whom I should be more grateful.

'I didn't bear the man any ill will before, but I sense it doesn't run both ways,' he added. Kjarr was trying to draw me out. I could feel it.

'Sven is Sven. I never know what he is thinking,' I responded, watching the men fighting.

Sven pinned Oleg down, but slippery as an eel, Oleg slithered out of the hold and back to his feet.

'But I think you do,' Kjarr whispered, leaning in to kiss me.

I looked over at Licinia, her perfect chin resting on her hand as she watched her real lover fight the Grand Prince. I saw the way her eyes devoured him, raking over each muscled limb. Sven had looked at her with the same feverishness, and it wasn't hard to imagine the way his hands would trace her figure, the way he held her, or kissed her. My stomach flipped, and I turned to vomit on the ground, pushing Kjarr from me.

'I need to return to my room,' I said, wiping my face with the sleeve of my dress.

'Do you want me to come?' Kjarr asked, worry creasing his face.

'No. I'll be fine with Odrun. You stay and watch the rest of the match. Tell me who wins.' I requested as I backed away, slipping through the lines gathered around the ring.

I ran as if fleeing nightmares, hurrying back to the city gates where a constant stream of people were coming and going. They waved banners and cups in a joyous celebration of Winter Nights. My foot caught a rock, and I stumbled. A hand under my arm stopped me from falling.

'I've been looking everywhere for you,' Ellisif cooed with her soft voice and sweet smile. 'Did you see Oleg has made it to the finals of the wrestling? Of course he would. I never doubted it,' she went on.

'You're not going back to see it?' I asked as I brushed myself off and fell in line with her.

She waved her hand nonchalantly. 'Oh, he'll talk about it later, I'm sure. Do you want to take a walk?'

'I'm not feeling well,' I replied.

She loitered by the wall, obviously wanting to tell me something by the elfish way she grinned. The cold air had bit at her nose and cheeks until they were rosy. It suited her well and made the blue of her eyes more prominent than ever, though the blustering wind had darkened and chapped her lips.

'If we're being honest. I, too, have been unwell,' she announced, chewing on her dry lips. 'And, it's not the plums this time,' she whispered so low that no one around us would hear. 'I'm with child.'

'No!' I gasped and wrapped my arms around my middle. I doubled over again and retched into the weeds.

Ellisif recoiled and let go of my arm.

'I'm sorry, Ellisif. That's wonderful,' I lied. My hand reached into the pouch at my belt, my fingers found Freyja's small cap I always kept there and ran over the embroidery. It was fraying.

'Oleg is pleased,' she added, taking my arm again as we walked. 'You mustn't tell anyone, not yet. Of course, I've told Licinia and Alfrunr. I had to because I knew she would be so excited about a new babe to add to the nursery. Mother knows too. She could sense it before I even let it slip. You know what she is like.'

I attempted a smile, but the bile was rising again. 'Today has been a bit much,' I admitted.

'Isn't it funny that you've fought like most of these men, yet a little blood turns your stomach?' She giggled.

'Hmm,' I agreed, clutching my poor stomach. 'Please take me to Odrun,' I requested, leaning more heavily on Ellisif.

'Is that what ails you? Are you also bearing a child?' she wondered.

I groaned. Words escaped me. All I could think of was the skald's poem of foreboding. *When the fruit comes from the union of close bed-friends, the field-reddeners will rise, and answer the unspoken question with their blood.* A child to a boyar's daughter and an unwed grand prince was anything but wonderful. Between Ellisif's scheming mother, and the skald Thorbjorn's prediction of a baby to change the succession, it was as good as a declaration of war. And, as I had overheard, the boyar's wives of Kyiv were adamant their husbands would not fight for Oleg if he was perceived as usurping Igor's throne.

Ellisif left me at the door, as per my request. I stumbled forward, pushing the doors open and seeking my bed. Odrun found me lying on the furs.

'Are you all right?' she asked, lifting tendrils of my hair to peer at my expression below.

'Where have you been?' I questioned her. 'You weren't at the competitions. I thought you would be,' I said, straining to sit up. The queasiness had eased the further I went from Sven's presence.

Odrun helped me up. 'Someone has to creep around whilst the others are off enjoying themselves, don't they?' she replied. She tugged on her wadmal cape.

*She was always wearing that thick, stuffy, itchy, drab wadmal cape.*

'And that's part of the reason I came back,' I answered.

She eyed me with suspicion. 'So, you're not feeling ill?'

'I am. That was no lie, but I wanted to get out of there. Too much manly prowess,' I lied. 'What have you found?' I shifted to the end of the bed where she sat looking back at me.

'Estrid has someone watching you,' Odrun advised, as she handed me a cup of weak ale.

'Do we know who it is?' I took a drink. It was bitter, but it calmed my stomach.

'It's a man, that's all I know.'

My eyebrows rose. It wasn't like Odrun to give up. 'Information hard to come by?'

She nodded. 'Estrid keeps tight-lipped staff. You wouldn't like what I had to tell them to win their trust.'

'I think I know.'

Odrun blushed deeply. 'I had to give them something,' she began, reaching across to take hold of my hand.

I'd known it was Odrun who had spread the rumour of my inability to conceive, if only to make Estrid's thralls suspect she disliked me.

'You're not barren, Signe,' Odrun started, 'no matter what that grey old witch told you. And, besides, I'm a Christian and I don't believe crones can wield that sort of foretelling.'

I didn't mention that I trusted the words of a wise woman, such as Gudrun. 'Thank you. At least Estrid believes what you've told her thralls, and I suppose that's all that matters right now.'

'There is one more thing,' Odrun whispered, reaching into the pocket of her apron. From inside, she produced a carefully folded parchment. 'A response has arrived.' She traced her long finger across the red seal.

I met her amber gaze. 'What does it say?'

Odrun cracked the wax with her fingernail. 'I'll need Egbert to translate it. I never learned to read.'

# Twenty-Eight

We had been riding for a week.

Our first stop, the Drevlian ironworking heartland of Horodske, had taken three long days to reach. It was a land of rich forests and glittering lakes that were not yet covered in snow. Frost clung to the branches of oak and ash, sparkling like jewels against the muted winter backdrop. Scarce more than a dusting settled, but what fell through the dark hours and early morning melted in the still-warm midday sun and made the ground slick with mud. That night we camped on damp earth, snatching sleep in short bursts. No enemies came in stealth attacks and by the early rays of the sun the next morning, Oleg's forces were inside the barely defended trade settlement.

Horodske surrendered to the Grand Prince with little bloodshed. A few armed men resisted and things didn't end well for them. Their heads were skewered on spikes by the gates as a grim warning against further resistance. So it was that Oleg sauntered into Horodske with no losses of his own. The people of Horodske were pragmatic. Most were merchants for whom trade was life and so long as they could make money from their work, it didn't matter if the purchaser was Rus' or Slav. As a reward for their capitulation, Oleg's men gathered only the town's weapons as prizes of war, but left the jewellery, ironworking tools, and cooking pots as a promise of continuing commerce.

Oleg did not tarry long in Horodske. It was not his ultimate prize, though it was essential to pressure the Drevlian ruler, Prince Mal, into a confrontation that would end his obstinate refusal to acknowledge the Grand Prince's rule. Hersir Heilagr was left to hold the settlement. Heilagr had opened his mouth to protest, no doubt desiring the glory of battle and the need to slake his blood thirst. But one glance at Oleg's icy-blue stare stilled the Hersir's complaint with a twisted mouth and a bowed head. Heilagr could do nothing but watch as Oleg's force filed through the gates of Horodske and rode away. Oleg didn't look back. He knew Heilagr would be stalwart just as he knew the Drevlian Prince would hear of its capture and bring his full force to meet us soon enough.

Four days later, we had almost completed our journey. I thanked the gods Ellisif had taught me to ride. A week on Embla's back would have been intolerably uncomfortable if I had not grown accustomed to regular riding. Still, my backside ached, and my legs were stiff from their bent position in the stirrups. I slipped my right foot out and rolled my ankle around in the space between Embla's flank and the beast next to her. A week on the trail, eating stale bread and *grautr* of wheat and rye, had me missing the rich food of the court. Nothing compared to the hot meals prepared by Oleg's cooks. My hand clenched my rumbling stomach beneath my leather jerkin. I didn't want to eat, not now, not when I knew we would meet Prince Mal's forces this very day. Instead, my hand came to rest on the head of my axe, Forlog-Enda. It felt a little strange that Skara was gone, but Volundr had crafted a true masterpiece and she required her first taste of blood before the gods could truly bless her. I had taken her to the practice yard often, fighting others while a leather guard protected them from Forlog-Enda's blade. Her aim was true, the weight perfectly balanced, and above all, she felt right in my hand.

I'd sworn I was tired of battle after the conflict in Aldeigjuborg and I was, but this was unlike the threat faced by the Aldeigjuborg and Holmgardr troops at the Abandoned Paragon. That was a matter of defence. The Slavs had threatened our settlement and our people. Oleg reasoned the coming conflict with the Drevlians was also a matter of defence, this time proactive rather than reactive. The distinction seemed tenuous to me. *How could a pre-emptive strike be the same as defending one's home?*

'Hit them before they come for Kyiv in earnest.' Kjarr had relayed after one of his late night meetings with his cousin. 'The Drevlians think they can ambush us in the forests while they continue to pillage our Polianian allies. If we do nothing, we have no hope of standing against the Khazar and Pecheneg powers who seek to dominate the region.'

'If we cannot bring the Drevlians to heel...' I started.

'Just one small tribe,' Kjarr added scornfully, 'then we are nothing before those more powerful.'

We had to align ourselves with those tribes closest to us, even if we'd rather not. The threat of the Khazar homeland was many weeks away on horseback, far from the territories they sought to preside over. If the Rus' could subsume the lands of those who also wished to overthrow oppressive Khazar rule, then we might have a chance. But the Khazars had ruled the territory for some time and, I found, people were slow to accept change. Our job in this fight was to show the Drevlians what the Rus' were capable of. That our strength rivalled that of the famed Itil warriors and our ruler stood shoulder to shoulder with their Khazar master. Oleg wanted the Drevlian tribute. Desired their swords, and their deference. Then he would want the same from the other tribes. Only after that could we take on the Khazars. Before his dreams of dominance could be realised, the Drevlian capital, Iskorosten, had to be conquered.

Swathed by thick forests and fertile lands, it would be easy to hide the Drevlian army in the heavy scrub. So far, they left us unharried and, each time our scouts returned, they had nothing to report.

'They either have powers to hide themselves or they're not sending out advance parties,' one scout mumbled as he rejoined the file of warriors.

They walked four abreast, on foot or horseback. Only the senior nobility and a few of the druzhina had a mount. The rest of the force marched along all day, only stopping for brief rests and food, and at night, men slept under the canopy of trees with sentries posted every ten paces. Oleg rode at the head. He made no secret of our progress to Iskorosten. In fact, he used the march to intimidate the countryside. He drove the hovels' inhabitants into the forests but prohibited killing, for these might one day be his people. He ordered fires lit at night, both for the men's comfort and so Prince Mal might better judge how close we were to his doorstep. Oleg wanted Prince Mal to fear us and to know we did not fear him.

Over eighty well-trained fighting men made up our druzhina. More than most tribes could muster without the help of another. Oleg had commanded the entire druzhina and the boyars to accompany him to Iskorosten, leaving only Old Odholf and a third of Kyiv's guards to protect the city. And, at Horodske, he left Hersir Heilagr and ten of the Hersir's town guard.

Sheer numbers weighted victory on our side, but we all knew that the size of one's force was not the only determining factor and certainly not our aim. Grand Prince Oleg hoped to subdue the Drevlian Prince. He was young, Oleg's junior by perhaps a decade. As most newly crowned rulers did, Mal wanted to flex his muscles both in war and politics.

He would chafe and howl against us, but it was Oleg's ardent desire that it should be a show of force without bloodshed, though all were prepared for resistance if it came to that. Some thirsted for it, dreaming of a battle so glorious skalds would speak of it for years to come. I thought that was unlikely. Should we ever obliterate the Khazars, that would be the war of ages. Even the gods would take notice then and our friends in the north would receive travelling skalds to hear of Oleg's victory, just as we had hosted Thorbjorn Hornklofi.

Kjarr had not wanted me to ride out. He clung to the hope of me being with child even though we both knew I was not. In the end, he smiled and kissed my cheek before saying, 'Eskil insists you're his Valkyrie of the Field. If that's true, we may need you.'

When I had asked Eskil why he'd advocated for me, he replied, 'Because you ought to be there and I want to see what chaos you'll cause now that you're cursed by all the gods and the Norns.' His broad face had creased with a grin and his eyes sparkled as mischievously as ever.

I didn't feel cursed by the Norns, not by beseeching them at the place of offering. They wouldn't doom me to an ill fate if I'd been wrong in calling to them. Surely, they'd just kill me, sever my life thread. If anyone had damned me, it was Gudrun. *What did it feel like to be cursed, anyway?* I shuddered at the memory of that old grey crone speaking her evil words in her strangled voice.

Not once had Kjarr insisted I ride alongside him. He saw the boyars' sneers and understood they would accept no woman in their ranks. Nor did he insist I travel with the wives who followed the men, those who came to cook and clean and offer *other* services in the dark of night. So I rode in the middle file next to Eskil and Sven, who were awkward astride their borrowed mounts. The druzhina did not spurn me. Some of them had fought with women in the past, as rare as we were. And fewer still had witnessed their wives and daughters take up a weapon when the need arose and understood well what women were capable of. None of them would speak against me and, as a boyar's wife, even if it had crossed their mind, my status sealed their lips.

Embla stepped in time with my friends' horses, and I almost regretted my decision to ride with them. Neither had spoken a word all morning, and if I'd wanted to be alone with my thoughts, I would have ridden at the rear instead of being neither comfortable with the silence nor the constant stench of Eskil's horrible farting. It seemed this morning's *grautr* of beans and dried boar had not sat well in his stomach and, after another horrendous emission, I urged Embla ahead out of his cloud of offence. I gasped the clean air down in great mouthfuls as Sven joined me.

'He stinks,' Sven echoed my thoughts. He had been distant since I discovered his relationship with Licinia. From afar I watched him change as he adopted Oleg's colours, his insignia, as Sven had become one of the druzhina. Even now, sitting atop his dun mare dressed in a brown tunic and red cloak, he held himself surer than ever before.

I mumbled my ascent without looking towards him.

Sven cleared his throat before continuing. 'I will never marry her.'

'I don't care, so long as you are happy,' I responded.

We both knew it for the lie it was.

He gave a noncommittal shrug. 'Are you?'

'I'm too busy to know anything about happiness,' I replied. 'Between the business, life at court, and everything in between, life is good enough.' And it was. Business was progressing. We had orders to keep our women busy and all our wool accounted for.

'How is Kjarr's nose?' he asked. At the wrestling match, Sven had pounded Kjarr's face into the ground, causing it to stream with blood. He hadn't cared on the day enough to ask and we had not spoken of it until now. Most of the time spent in camp was by Kjarr's side, despite the disdain of the nobles, and when Sven and I had spoken, it had been nothing more than passing pleasantries.

I laughed through my nose. 'Not broken. Just a little bruising,' I replied.

'Pity.'

I glanced at Sven. 'I heard you fought well in the final match against the Grand Prince.'

His eyes caught mine. 'What sane man would go against the ruler of a land and try his best?'

'So, you would have won if you tried?' I asked, an amused smile dancing across my lips.

'Of course.' He flicked his dusty blonde hair out of his face. Like most of the druzhina, he travelled without wearing his helmet. Instead, Sven attached it to his saddle and would wear it when we met our quarry. That he was so well outfitted showed how high he had risen through the ranks. Earlier, Eskil had explained how Hersir Heilagr had honoured them with gifts of helms and weapons for their service, citing their distinguished abilities at arms and it caused me to wonder if either man would wish to remain in Kyiv's service when the crews departed.

'I could have won,' Sven repeated.

I chuckled to myself. 'Never change, Sven.'

Ahead, the line of men had grown silent. A wave of whispers rolled through the file as each warrior bent his head to another to hear the words spoken. Sven bent low over his horse's flank to receive the message.

'What did he say?' I asked as Sven straightened up.

'We're coming up on Iskorosten now and we are to form up around the perimeter,' he repeated. Those orders came directly from Grand Prince Oleg at the head of his men.

We rode a little further, and over a slight rise, we could see the settlement of Iskorosten built on an open plain, ringed by an old oak forest. It was a circular settlement formed of wood. Inside the tall oak palisade, we could make out a central area, above it a great hall, and many homes of the typical Drevlian dugout style with their almost entirely subterranean walls and roofs thatched with golden straw. Iskorosten's gates were flung open as if to welcome us, but Oleg refused to go further. Our force would not be fooled.

'Do they think us so stupid that we would all file inside and they can just lock the gates and slaughter the entire Kyivan army?' Sven asked in a whisper.

'Perhaps. Worth a try, right?' the man who had delivered the message replied.

Up ahead, warriors whispered sightings of Boyar Oddrsson's body on to the palisade wall. Two men were dispatched to retrieve it and to check there was truly no one left inside the town. The warriors returned with Oddrsson's corpse and placed it in a wagon to be taken back to Kyiv and given a proper send-off.

Behind the settlement, the lazy Uzh River flowed past rocks and fallen trunks. It was too peaceful, too undisturbed. We knew all too well that the Drevlians were close by, waiting for their moment to strike. They knew this terrain better than any of us; the forest was their home, and numbers mattered little if the enemy were woodland wraiths capable of slaughtering their enemy before they even stepped into the light.

Everyone was glancing around now, looking for any hint of the Drevlian forces. To our right, there was a gentle slope. Its bluff overlooked the river bend, but there was no sentry there. The land spilled into rich green as the field land returned to forests for as far as the eye could take in.

'Have they abandoned Iskorosten?' Sven asked, standing in his stirrups to get a better look.

'I doubt it,' I whispered back. 'They're here somewhere.'

A horn sounded in the distance. Low and steady, sending a chill through my blood. It was not a horn of our own. Instead of a single note filling the sky, it was a series of deep notes repeating as the last one ended. At the sounding of the tenth tone, a line of Drevlian warriors appeared from the tree-line ahead of us.

At first, it was a single row, but as they stepped into the midday light, we could see those ranks swelled to three men deep. They advanced no further, staying in their position where we could just make them out on the rise.

I guided my horse along our lines, reaching Kjarr's side and listening to his conversation with the Grand Prince. 'Have they been reinforced?' Oleg asked Kjarr.

Kjarr squinted forward and shifted in his leather-panelled saddle. 'It does not appear to be so, Grand Prince. They all wear Mal's colours.'

'Are we sure they did not send word to the Khazars?' he worried.

'Of that, we can never be sure,' Kjarr replied. He was being overly formal with his cousin, betraying his concern that this would not be the straightforward battle they had planned.

The Khazar Emissary, Tarkhan Tuvan, nudged his horse between my husband and the Grand Prince. Kjarr looked offended but said nothing. Oleg's personal guard edged closer, keeping his eyes on Tuvan's sword hand, which remained resting on his hilt.

'I apologise for the unwelcome interruption, Khagan, but I heard you discussing whether Prince Mal had received Khazar reinforcements.'

Helgi Heilagrsson nudged his mount's nose into the conversation. 'How would you know?' the younger Heilagrsson brother asked, not bothering to hide the scorn in his voice. 'You've been at the Kyiv court or travelling for months now. If they had planned something, it would have been during your absence.'

Tuvan exhaled slowly before speaking. 'And you don't think that Prince Mal would have sought my Khagan's aide as soon as Khagan Oleg took Kyiv?' he answered, just as seethingly. He turned back to Oleg, his face impassive. 'Khagan, in the spring, Prince Mal sent an envoy asking for reinforcements for a coming confrontation with your men.'

Oleg arched his neck and turned his head to the side. His eyes flickered closed for a moment as if wishing it all a bad dream, and when he opened them, he fixed Tuvan with a look that burned for answers.

The Khazar Emissary continued, 'They denied him, of course, Khagan. The Khazars do not care to involve themselves in the petty squabbles between tribes.'

'You insinuate that the Rus' is a mere tribe?' Oleg demanded, glaring at the Khazar Emissary.

Tuvan did not even shift under the Grand Prince's ire. 'The Khagan's words, not mine,' he clarified, mollifying the Grand Prince with open hands.

Oleg might have taken offence to the inference the Rus' were nothing but a small gang of miscreants, but I thought it more telling Tuvan had not referred to himself as Khazar. That he thought he was apart from them was a strange thing for an emissary to allude to.

Oleg's anger cooled. 'Your Khagan may have changed his mind.'

Tuvan's horse pawed the ground and lowered his neck to munch at the wet grass. Tuvan pulled the horse back to standing and patted its neck. 'The distance between Iskorosten and Itil is great, Khagan. It would take many weeks for their messenger to arrive with the request, and many more to march any reinforcements back to their aid,' he explained.

The Grand Prince's boyars crowded around him now, irked that their leader would speak of warfare with an enemy and, from the directness of their stares, many also dreamed of driving a seax into the man.

'Of course,' Oleg replied. 'But that is not a guarantee,' he added. 'The Khagan might have sent reinforcements from closer by, somewhere that did not require such a long journey.'

'It is possible,' Tuvan conceded, 'though unlikely.'

'Unlikely?' Oleg repeated, demanding further explanation.

'As you may be aware, Khagan. Emperor Basil of, how do you call it…' He paused, struggling to find the name. 'Ah…Mikellagardee,' he added. The word sounded brutish as he spat the syllables out.

The Heilagr brothers laughed at Tuvan's mispronunciation, but the Emissary was not ruffled.

'Miklagard,' Oleg corrected him.

'Yes, Basil of Miklagard,' Tuvan replied, 'his wife, Empress Eudokia Ingerina, died late last year.'

'I had heard,' Oleg added, casting a look into the distance to ensure the Drevlians stayed where they were. They too appeared to hold a conference, their ranks clustered together.

Tuvan scratched his horse's ear as he went on. 'There was a tradition with the previous dynasty, and the Khagan thought of offering one of his daughters as the next wife of the Emperor.'

Harald Heilagrsson, Ellisif's older brother, interrupted. 'I do not see how this information is related.' His dark honey-coloured beard could not hide the flush that overcame his face as he realised he had just admitted to being both poor at understanding politics and following a line of reasoning.

Tuvan sighed at the young man's intrusion. 'Just as you are now roughly wooing the Drevlians, my Khagan seeks to do with Miklagard.'

'I see,' Oleg replied, rubbing his nose with his knuckle and ignoring Harald's outburst. 'You mean to tell me that the Khazars will not send reinforcements because they are presently preoccupied with a conflict with Emperor Basil?'

Tuvan nodded. 'That is my understanding, Khagan.'

'Why are you telling me this, Tuvan?' Oleg asked, perhaps less sceptical than his senior boyars, who still clustered around him. 'Whose interests do you really represent?'

'My own, Khagan,' Tuvan replied, looking up with a blank expression. If he had inadvertently overstepped, he didn't show it and I thought nothing Tuvan did was without careful consideration.

Oleg seemed inclined to trust the Khazar Emissaries' disclosure. 'Here I was thinking that you were supposed to be advocating for your Khagan. I would not have my own representatives divulge secrets as you do unless they hope to bamboozle my enemies.'

Around him, his boyars cackled like a flock of ravens. He stopped them with a wave of his hand, and each man shifted his horse back a pace.

Tuvan gritted his teeth, before hiding the reaction behind his lips. 'I have personal experience with Khazar invasion techniques, Khagan. They are not kind to those whose land they take. Their warriors have cruel punishments for their hostages. The Drevlians, though they may not know it now, may find your rule preferable, even if they need some heavy guidance to that,' he explained.

Harald and Helgi's mouths fell open. Even Kjarr's eyebrows reached up towards his hairline, the same as Sveineld the Younger next to him. Ever unable to hide my feelings, my eyes grew large at Tuvan's confession.

'And heavy guidance they will receive,' Oleg agreed. 'Sveineld,' Oleg turned to the young Boyar. 'Take a message to Prince Mal. Tell him we have captured Horodske, though I believe he already knows. Tell him we intend to keep it as recompense for his unjust slaying of Boyar Oddrsson.'

Sveineld's steel-grey eyes worried beneath his brow, but he knew his duty. 'Yes, Grand Prince. I will deliver the message.'

'Take Harald and Helgi,' Oleg ordered.

The two brothers looked on with reluctance but obeyed the command and moved away with Sveineld. Once they had made room, Tuvan nudged his horse forward again.

'Striking at their trading centre is a powerful show of force, Khagan. The Drevlians fear little other than their gods, but they respect a true warrior prince.'

Oleg nodded as Tuvan guided his horse back to the lesser ranks. 'We shall talk later,' the Grand Prince advised, waving the Khazar away before his boyars tightened their circle around him to offer advice, but not before Sveineld, Harald, and Helgi cantered the distance between the Rus' and Drevlian forces.

We watched the tiny specks meet someway apart from the main Drevlian army where they spoke terms. Eyes darted about waiting for the flash of metal, a signal, or the approach of Prince Mal's forces but nothing gave away his reaction except for the speed with which the three men returned, galloping back to Oleg, breathless and heaving as they pulled up.

Sveineld retrieved his waterskin and drank deep before revealing the Drevlian Prince's response.

'He will not be dissuaded from the fight, Grand Prince.' Sveineld was twitchy. His hand pawed at his jaw-line, rubbing it aggressively with the heel of his palm while he spoke. 'The capture of Horodske angered him.'

Helgi and Harald appeared unable to form words at all, but their heads bobbed in agreement at everything Sveineld said.

'You told him his people were not put to the sword?' Oleg asked.

Sveineld nodded. 'I relayed your directive that should we come to terms, he may take possession of Horodske once more.' His hand fell to his side, and he busied it, stroking his horse's neck.

'And, still, he refused?' Oleg wanted to know.

With a swift nod, Sveineld confirmed, 'He did, Grand Prince. I suppose he did not take too kindly to us cutting off his principal trading town. Without ironwork, he will find it difficult to produce new weapons. He was most insistent that you would not live to see the end of the day, Grand Prince.'

Oleg scoffed at the war boast, 'We will see whose gods win the day.' He gestured to Sveineld to form up the men, and the young Boyar rode back along the lines to spread the word that it was time to prepare.

Men roared as they were given their orders, unsheathing weapons and giving them one last clean. Some drained ale skins to steel them for the fight to come and others uttered words to the gods so that they might watch and see how many lives he would take on this day. This, then, would not be just a show of force to intimidate the Drevlians. It would be a bloody battle fought shield-wall to shield-wall.

Our scouts informed us that the first line of Prince Mal's army were warriors, distinguished by their long cream tunics with buckthorn orange bands at the wrist, neck, and hem. Perhaps his professional force, if judging by the weapons they brandished. Each was armed with good blades and protected by long rectangular shields, quite similar to those of the rebels we fought at the Abandoned Paragon. Like us, Mal's men stood shoulder to shoulder, overlapping their shields to form a wall. But each of theirs was a large cumbersome board of wood, while ours was circular and much more manoeuvrable. The larger of the two might provide better defence at first, but as the two lines drew closer, I wondered if their abilities could withstand the furious onslaught of Grand Prince Oleg's infamous druzhina. Behind the Drevlian front line, a rabble clothed in rags and welding poor weapons such as sharpened rakes and sickles.

Our men were thirsting for blood. They required no encouragement to edge towards the enemy and, as the boyars who remained mounted assessed the opposition, they threw insults aplenty.

'They bring their farmers,' I heard someone say behind me.

His comment was met with mocking laughter, but even farmers could cause damage with a sharp enough edge. A man who ploughed the fields bore strength enough to sever a man's limbs. Grand Prince Oleg's boyars and druzhina felt smug in the knowledge he had brought only warriors with him, leaving the merchants and simple folk safe within the city walls.

'Labourers can still fight,' another of our number replied. 'Don't you recall you once grew barley in Svealand?'

'That was before I earned my rings,' the first man responded, jangling his many arm rings. He slipped in the slick mud, weighed down by his war gear. 'I hope it's drier out there where the sun is beating down,' he said with a laugh as his friend helped him to his feet.

Oleg raised his hands to still the advance. 'Dismount and tie the horses up at that copse,' he ordered, gesturing to the trunks close by. The youngest, all sons of the senior druzhina who were not yet skilled enough to use a spear, were instructed to guard the beasts. It was their job to stand, watch, and learn. They would fight one day, but it would hopefully not be today.

The Grand Prince turned back to his warlords, 'Keep the shield-wall strong. Hit them with full force and our fiercest warriors will break their line. Once the wall is open, pour in and send them to a bloody end.' He shoved his helmet onto his head, dome gleaming with high polish as his face disappeared behind the nose plate and cheek guards. He wore no crown embellishment, no engraving to give away his lofty status, but the sight of it marked him as an esteemed one, if only because few could afford such costly armaments.

I gaped at the figure he cut, tall, broad, and covered in metal.

'Tuvan, though I know you fight well, I will not have you beside me. Return to the horses and stay there until I send for you.'

The Khazar Emissary did as he was bade and said nothing in reply.

Kjarr grasped me by the arm and spoke breathlessly, 'I won't ask you to stay out of the fighting,' he began. He, too, was adorned in his war splendour; a helm just as fine as Oleg's, a chain shirt covering his torso, and at his hip, a pattern-welded sword with a decorated hilt. Kjarr had worn none of this when we took Horodske. I'd never seen him dressed for war before.

'Please, stay high,' he pleaded with me.

'And miss all the action?' I questioned coyly.

He narrowed his eyes, and I saw the corner of his mouth twitch. 'I didn't think Prince Mal would let this progress as it has. It will be bloody.'

I feigned shock. 'You mean we may have to fight? Lucky I didn't wear my silk court dress then.'

He shook his head. 'Stay high,' he instructed, his green gaze fixed on mine.

'In case you haven't noticed, there is no high ground here,' I gestured to the flat land around us.

'Stay back, then,' he countered.

'All right,' I agreed and, in my head, I added the caveat, *"back" means not in the front line.*

He chuckled, and I knew he read the defiance in my face. He drew me into his arms, pressing my face against the grate of metal. My leather jerkin creaked and my arms were stiff with thick bracers wrapped uncomfortably around him in a hug that felt little like affection.

'I love you,' he whispered, but I could only nod in response.

Kjarr didn't wait for me to find my words. Summoned by his cousin, he strode off, the picture of a warlord though I'd never imagined him that way. The man I knew years before in Aldeigjuborg was in stark contrast to the one who now stood at his royal cousin's side.

There was no time to dwell. Rolf, son of Old Odholf, beckoned me to bring my horse. Sven was there tying up his mount and took Embla's reins.

I glanced around for Kjarr, searching the men taking their position in the front line and I could just make him out, but then the druzhina filed in behind and he was lost to me. Oleg was walking before the first line, delivering a rousing speech.

'Did he tell you not to fight?' Sven inquired, after he'd finished securing Embla to a branch low enough that she might graze.

'Kjarr asked me to stay back, no more. He knows better than to demand an oath I would not keep,' I replied, turning away from Oleg's address and the gathered men. I unlashed my shield from Embla's saddle and slung it across my back, two cat heads emblazoned in white on the surface.

'I was just thinking,' Sven began, handing me an ale skin, and I took a swig. It was warm from being carried on his hip, but it took the edge off. 'Do you remember when we were creeping through the forest at Aldeigjuborg in the night, trying to surprise those rebels in the old fort?'

'Mmm,' I agreed, checking my belt, seax, and leather ties on each side.

'The night plays tricks with your mind,' he began.

In the dark, I had seen things that were not there, things the forest had sent to haunt me.

'Well, it's almost worse in the daylight. You can see what's coming,' he explained.

'I've fought enough to know that,' I replied tersely.

'But never like this,' he added, waving his hand towards the Drevlians who now stood in a straight line, twenty men across the field, two deep. '*Minn Svanr*,' he whispered. He hadn't called me that for a long time and I felt my breath hitch. 'It's a frightening place to fight in the shield-wall,' he warned.

'And you're worried about Kjarr's anger if I come to harm?' I teased, fussing with Forlog-Enda to make sure she sat comfortably on my hip. I tried to flip the loop off that held the axe head in place, so she could slide free of her sheath, but I struggled.

Sven came closer. 'If he hasn't killed me yet, I doubt he is going to.' He smirked, and he knew it irritated me.

'Is that what Sihtric told you? Seems you've got away with unmanning him, even if it is in private.'

He bristled at that. 'Sihtric doesn't mind, but he cautions me over my fondness for a particular boyar's wife.'

I felt my face flush, but I looked away as I pulled on the fastening over my axe. It still would not come free. 'Do you have any intention of curtailing this fondness?'

Sven's hand touched my waist. 'No,' he mumbled as his finger ran along the belt. 'Even if it was possible, I wouldn't want to.' He flicked the leather loop from the sheath, freeing Forlog-Enda, and I took a step back. 'Same deal as last time?' he asked.

I looked up at his mottled green-grey eyes with confusion. 'Huh?'

'If I can take a shot at the bastards, will you be my defence?' His hand, still perilously close to my hip, drew Forlog-Enda from her sheath and placed the weapon in my hands.

I took another step back. 'This time I refuse to nearly lose an eye for you.'

Sven strung his bow and drew it back, testing the flex in the sinew. His shoulders strained at his jerkin and he moved his arms to test his range of motion. 'I'm worth it, I promise.' He flung me a withering look.

I almost laughed at that, and a glance at Old Odholf's boy, Rolf, with his slack-jawed reaction to Sven's scandalous comment, made me snicker. Sven walked off, helmet under one arm and bow slung over his shoulder.

'If you haven't noticed, Sven,' I began as I caught up with my friend, 'the land here is flat. I don't think you'll be cresting any hill and raining down your arrows.'

Sven twisted his mouth. 'In a field, this thing is near useless,' he lamented.

'Then leave it with the horses and we can join the ranks,' I suggested.

'I might get a couple of good shots in, but it will be tight.' He looked at me with amusement. 'I thought you promised Kjarr you would stay back?'

I grinned to myself. 'If I'm not at the front, I'm back, aren't I?' I responded, grabbing him by the arm and dragging him into the lines of Rus' warriors. Sven slammed his helmet onto his head. He didn't argue, and, once we found Eskil, I had the big man on my left and Sven on my right. Without his bow and arrow, Sven would usually employ his sword, Hjarta-Gaddar, but the shield-wall was not the place for a sword. Instead, he drew his seax. I did the same, holding my seax in my left hand and Forlog-Enda in my right. My shield was still on my back.

Eskil snorted when he saw me. 'Ha! We'll have a riot today, Valkyrie,' he bellowed as the men before us hit their pommel or axe against their shield and roared out their battle songs to Odin and Thor. 'Cursed or no, Gudrun said you'd bring me luck.'

My eyebrows arched in surprise. Never would I have imagined Gudrun to speak favourably of me, not when I thought her words were an evil portend. I felt lighter hearing Eskil's admission.

'Let's hope she was right then,' I managed, touching my axe against his own; a sign of good luck shared between fighting partners. Sven followed the gesture, marking both mine and Eskil's blade with his own.

Across the field, Prince Mal must have delivered a moving speech of his own, for they too clamoured before beginning the slow march to meet us. My feet slipped as we shuffled forward, but my body did not slide. I was wedged between my friends and the surrounding bodies. We moved as one as the horn sounded again. This time it was ours, a single low note covering the entire battlefield, calling us to wet our blades with enemy blood. In response, the Drevlian horn tooted its strange ten-note reveille, and both sides sped up their pace.

They were close to us. We could hear the clank of their shields as they butted with each step, but I could not see, as most of the men before me blocked my view. It was not until the front line's shields clashed with those of the Drevlians that I knew our forces had met. Next came the press. A squeeze that forced the ranks together, stealing movement from limbs. Even if you desired escape, it wouldn't be possible.

The sun was strong above us, and I could feel the sweat drip between my shoulder blades and down my back. My boots churned up the mud underfoot like butter. Despite that, we pushed on.

'Forward,' I heard Oleg scream from the front line. I could just make him out from glimpses in the gaps between warriors in front. Kjarr was next to him, I knew, and I pleaded with the gods that it stayed that way.

Eskil turned to me, 'Shields and seax are what you need, Valkyrie. I know you want to blood her,' he said, nodding down at Forlog-Enda. 'But you'll be no bloody good to Sven and me if you can't run a man through.'

Reluctantly, I put my axe away and dragged my shield forward to cover the left side of my body, meeting the rounded line of the warrior's shield next to me. Eskil had seen the shield-wall before and, without my own experience to trust, I had to depend on his. There would be time enough to test Forlog-Enda.

'First time in this kind of battle?' Magnus asked from behind our butting shield, so close I could feel his breath on my neck.

I nodded.

'Hopefully, it won't be your last,' he replied, his tone a little too unkind for my liking.

'It won't be,' Sven growled back at the man and Eskil took a step back onto Magnus' toes for good measure. The warrior didn't respond except for a sharp wail as he extricated his foot from beneath Eskil's massive boot.

The battle went on. We lunged and pressed forward for what felt like long moments. As men tired, the ranks grew slack and drifted apart to allow room to swing their weapons. It was then I saw Kjarr as he roared and pushed his seax forward. A golden-haired man behind him, who looked like Ellisif's brother Helgi, but I couldn't be sure, stabbed a spear over Kjarr's head, straight through the eye of a Drevlian farmer in the second row.

I heard men dying. Their wild, painful howls swirled into the air as life fires were snuffed and their blood slicked the already sodden earth. A gap opened before me and Sven and Eskil pushed into it, forcing me behind their shields. Their iron bosses butted against the Drevlian defence, who snarled as they squinted into the blazing sun.

A spear glanced off Eskil's shield as he raised it to protect Sven's head, but left both men vulnerable from the waist down. I squatted and jabbed my seax forward, colliding with flesh in a squelching mess that told me my strike had caused fatal damage. I stabbed again, but this time met nothing. Frustrated, I edged in closer, desperate to break through the shields and finish my enemy. Sven held me back with his arm, still fighting his own battles.

'It's not your time to die, *minn Svanr*. Go no further,' he warned me as Eskil, in his fury and with enormous force, walloped Drevlian armoured heads with his axe.

Above the din, we heard Oleg scream a command, 'Pull back!'

As one, we took a step back and then another. Pressed firm against the enemy, I didn't understand why Oleg would command a retreat. But once there was a small corridor between the two groups, I could see the Drevlians had suffered the loss of a third of their number, which lay prone before us, slathered in mud and gore.

Grand Prince Oleg stepped out of line to call to Prince Mal, 'Surrender!' The Grand Prince was resplendent in his war gear and he roared at the Drevlian ruler as if he had not a fear in the world.

Prince Mal stepped forward. This was the first time most of us had seen the man up close. He was dressed in vivid woad blues and muted oranges from the buckthorn, with an ornate helm of well-polished iron that was etched with swirling patterns of nature's bounty. Prince Mal looked like a king, in stature and surety, as he carried himself with a confidence that came from his subject's ready obedience. He stepped toward Oleg and raised his sword to the sun at its highest peak.

'I will not,' he replied in our language. 'Prince Mal of the Drevlians will not surrender, for Khors is with us.' At this, he turned back to his army, who roared their agreement. 'See how brightly he honours this day?' Mal asked and again saluted the bright orb in the blue sky.

I wanted Oleg to challenge him, to see that smug grin wiped from Mal's sharp featured face, but he didn't, and the two leaders rejoined their lines. The Drevlian leader swung his sword with abandon, discarding his shield on the ground. He hacked at Helgi's shield and Mal almost had him on the ground until Helgi's brother, Harald, came to his aid. Men whispered the Prince had become battle-crazed and could not be beaten, but I saw a desperate man making a show of bravado.

Our ranks knitted back together and no longer could I see the wild Prince. Kjarr was engaged with one of the Drevlian nobles who was as well armed as my husband. Both had stepped out of the formation to give their swords space to swing. The sound of metal on metal rang out as they slashed and blocked.

Kjarr screamed Oleg's name, fighting for his cousin's glory, but his opponent bellowed something that sounded like 'Yan.' I couldn't be sure, but I recalled the druzhina's stories of the prized warrior of Iskorosten by the same name.

Kjarr struck hard but missed, then charged to the left and, in a move I could not fully observe, made the man stumble. Unsteady, the dark bearded Drevlian was late to parry the thrust to his side and Kjarr's sword pierced his jacket and the flesh beneath. Blood spread through the fabric, dying the cream tunic a deep red. The man touched his hand to that place and drew back his fingers, sticky with his lifeblood.

He roared, threw down his sword, and unsheathed a smaller blade from his belt. Quick as a wolf, Kjarr punched the man's arm with the pommel of his sword and struck him across the face with its tang. The Drevlian spun around in a daze and hit the ground like a sack of grain. Fighting all around seemed to slow as Kjarr raised his sword and drove it through the tribal warrior. The man screamed, gurgled, then choked as the blood simmered out of his mouth.

Prince Mal turned, a look of utter disbelief shadowed his face.

My husband unleashed a guttural growl as he pulled the blade out, the flesh squelching as it was removed. The gore of war splattered Kjarr from head to toe. 'For Oleg!' he roared, and the call echoed back to him.

For a moment, the Drevlians paused. All knew my husband's hand had slain a great warrior.

Magnus butted his shield against mine and I could no longer see through to the front ranks. I resumed my stabbing and lunging between Eskil and Sven as both men made their kills. They fought with a new discipline learned in the service of Kyiv's guard. But, as I jabbed my blade through gaps, I couldn't get the image of Kjarr the warlord out of my mind. I'd never seen him in battle before. I didn't even know he had any skill in it. He had never spoken of conflict, though I now knew he was well acquainted with weapon craft.

A deep voice screamed something in the Drevlian tongue and the fighting stilled. Men leaned on their neighbour to catch their breath. All gathered to watch Prince Mal run towards the man my husband had brought down. Grand Prince Oleg stepped forward, reading the hatred in Mal's eyes as he readied himself for single combat. But the world dimmed as the bright sun vanished behind a sphere of darkness.

The Drevlian Prince looked up in terror, his nose wrinkled as he muttered over and over, 'Khors.' It was the same word he had earlier used to describe the skies, but I still did not know what it meant.

His warriors glanced at each other, nostrils flared and eyes full of horror. They sank back from Oleg, his sword before him slathered with their brethren's blood.

'Khors,' they repeated as their leader commanded them to discard their weapons, which they did almost too willingly.

Oleg lowered his weapon. I turned and looked to the sky. Where the sun had been only moments before, now there was a ring of fire. The black orb had extinguished the sun god Sol.

Grand Prince Oleg's brow creased beneath his helm. 'You surrender?' he asked, looking at Mal's head hanging low with a pained expression.

His head shot up, and I saw he bit his lip so hard that it bled. 'My god demands it.'

'Khors,' they had said, and I remembered Ellisif telling me a story about the Drevlian sun god who bore the same name. Like us, it seemed the Drevlians could be deeply superstitious when it came to signs from the gods and, I hoped, whatever had caused Sol to slumber in the cornflower blue sky would last long enough to ensure the Drevlian capitulation.

Mal slumped onto his knees and looked up at Oleg from beneath his heavy eyebrows. Dark stains of enemy blood ruined his bright blue tunic. He hung his head again in a spiteful bow, teeth bared and white-knuckled fists as he offered forth his sword to the Grand Prince of the Rus'. It was a beautiful weapon, with an engraved pommel and leather-wrapped grip. Even the blade had etchings of woodland creatures dancing along its edge.

'I accept your surrender, Mal, Prince of the Drevlians,' Oleg announced, stepping towards him. 'Though, I wish you might have considered our terms previously, as they would have been more favourable to you. Now, however, we will not be as lenient.'

Mal spat a globule onto the dirt, tinged with bright red blood. 'The terms might not remain in your favour for long,' he forced the words out.

'And that is why we will have hostages from your noble houses; to ensure continued friendship between our people.' Oleg took the sword and inspected its beauty.

Prince Mal made to stand, but Sveineld forced him back to the ground. 'Stay, Prince,' Sveineld the Younger mumbled, dispensing deference as required, but not letting the defeated Drevlian run the show.

'You never mentioned hostages in our initial discussions,' Mal complained, Sveineld's hand still on his shoulder.

Oleg cleaned Mal's blade with a length of rough wool his attendant handed him before gesturing for Sveineld to take it. The Boyar released the Drevlian Prince's shoulder and wrapped the sword in the cloth.

'None of this would have been necessary if you were not so prideful,' Oleg went on. 'Is it so preferable to be ruled by that Khazar scum?' he demanded, spittle flying as he yelled the words. 'Fetch Tarkhan Tuvan.'

All eyes followed the Khazar Emissary as he came to stand before the Grand Prince. 'You have won the day, Khagan,' Tuvan congratulated the Rus' ruler.

'Their gods have turned from them,' Oleg replied.

Helgi, always waiting for a moment to bring attention to himself, spoke out, 'From here we could form an army large enough to overcome your lord, Tuvan,' he seethed.

His brother, Harald, put his hand on Helgi's chest to stop his prattling, but Tuvan did not even flinch at the mention of his homeland.

'I called you, Tuvan, so you might witness what we do to those who wrong us,' he began. Turning back to Prince Mal, he crouched down and growled, 'You slaughtered Boyar Oddrsson, my emissary to you, without cause to do so and that cannot go unpunished.'

'What will he do?' Sven whispered beside me, removing his helm. His sweat-plastered hair dripped down onto his collar.

'Men enraged are capable of anything,' was all I said in reply.

'Let me name the families, Grand Prince,' Mal pleaded, his expression softening.

'No,' Oleg cut him off. 'You have shown you cannot be trusted. We know enough about your people to know who your nobles are by their war gear. I will name the hostages.'

Mal cursed under his breath, but didn't move. He didn't dare look at anyone for fear of giving away those most valuable to him. 'Your man has killed my most treasured commander,' Prince Mal confessed, looking towards my husband who stood beside his cousin.

So, Kjarr had dispatched the fabled Yan. *The gods would favour him now*, I thought. Kjarr's eyes met mine and for a moment, he held my gaze. His jaw was set hard, as if he ground his teeth, and there was a storm of battle rage that thundered in his green eyes.

'Besides hostages, every month you shall offer one marten fur per house as an ongoing tribute, and in the spring, you will offer ten percent of your harvest until you have proven our alliance,' the Grand Prince detailed.

Prince Mal opened his mouth to interject, but Oleg was not finished. 'I will continue to monitor Horodske and its flow of trade for one year, or until you show us genuine friendship. Once you have done that, we can discuss terms and perhaps the release of your trusted advisors.'

Mal hung his head under the heavy penalty. There was a perverse joy in seeing an enemy brought so low.

'This agreement shall remain in place for our lifetime and you will sever your ties with Khazaria,' Oleg finished.

A hush fell over the gathered, all holding their breath in disbelief. The terms were harsh, but it could have been much worse if Oleg had put all the Drevlian survivors to the sword, and Mal knew this. Though there was rancour on his face, he understood if he disobeyed these terms, his tribe would cease to exist by the summer.

At last Prince Mal was drawn to his feet, and the two rulers grasped arms to seal their *agreement* as if honour still counted for something. Oleg roved through the lines of kneeling Drevlian warriors to extract five men who would be hostages. I knew Oleg had chosen correctly when a stocky man with dark hair was summoned from the ranks and an involuntary groan came from Mal's mouth.

When the man was asked to name himself, he announced, 'Niskinnin, first duke of the blood.' A man of perhaps twenty-five, with the same angular nose as Mal, and the same dark expression in his hollow brown eyes. A cousin then. Niskinnin was to Mal what Kjarr was to Oleg.

More were selected, bearing similar features to Niskinnin, and wearing fine swords at their belts. Kstianin and Ostromyr named themselves, and were taken into Oleg's keeping, and their weapons surrendered to their guards. Two more followed in their wake, and Oleg, now content with his five captives, ensured they were bound sufficiently, though, to his credit, provided them with water.

'I will also name an emissary to your court at Malyn, who will travel with you and relay our correspondences,' Grand Prince Oleg continued, looking behind him.

Malyn was Prince Mal's royal residence. Mal frequently travelled between Iskorosten and Malyn, as it was only a day's ride in either direction. The Rus' Emissary would be stuck to Mal like dung to a sheep's arse, and I didn't envy the man who would go there, nor his wife. Oleg's gaze raked over his boyars.

He stopped before Kjarr, who met his eye resolutely. I imagined life at the Drevlian court. From what I'd learned, they had little more than dugout homes and damp earthen floors. I could do it, I told myself. It wouldn't be forever, and with Kjarr there with his *huskarls*, I would be well protected. But to live surrounded by enemies was to be constantly looking over your shoulder, and as Oleg stepped forward a pace, I let go of my long-held breath.

'Helgi and Harald Heilagrsson,' Oleg began, addressing Ellisif's two older brothers. 'It is overdue that you both should step from your father's shadow and into the light. Together you will be the Emissary of the Rus' people to the court of Prince Mal of the Drevlians. You will receive three warriors to accompany you, and Runolf, my personal messenger, will come to you once every two months, so we may report on the progress of the Rus'-Drevlian alliance.'

Both men knelt to the Grand Prince. 'It is an honour,' they said in unison, and they meant it.

Neither man had shied away from the ferocity of battle, and their tunics displayed the evidence of their work. They would need that fearlessness in their new appointment if they were to survive it.

After this, Oleg went to each of his warriors to see that all was well. He had lost only four men that day, and a few others had injuries that would heal in time. The druzhina was commanded to depart and save for a few men who served as Oleg's bodyguard; most had moved on to their tasks.

Oleg stopped by us and demanded Eskil and Sven number the men they killed.

It was Eskil that answered, 'Two a piece, and the Lady Signe felled one.' He was evidently proud of both Sven and me.

'Well done,' Oleg replied, 'even the Heilagrssons only managed one each.' He turned to look at Helgi and Harald, who, splattered with red gore, seemed pleased with the day's effort. 'You're right, Eskil,' the Grand Prince said, turning to the big man, 'to have called her a Valkyrie. For she comes for men's souls quite ruthlessly. And Signe,' he addressed me, 'you're even with your husband.'

At the mention of his name, Kjarr appeared. Oleg laughed then, but I knew the man who Kjarr had downed was worth at least three of the type I had jabbed my seax into.

'Strip the dead. Take what you want and know that you have your Grand Prince's gratitude.'

There was no higher praise and both Sven and Eskil beamed with their Grand Prince's esteem. In the short time they'd been in his service, they had distinguished themselves above others, and I knew they would be marked for greater duties in time. Eskil and Sven approached the fallen warriors and took anything of value, leaving me alone with my husband.

'You're safe,' he said, pulling me towards him. He lowered his head and kissed me fully. I tasted the salty sweat on his lips as he drew his arm around my waist. The heat of his body seeped through my leathers and onto my skin.

'You sound surprised,' I replied as I returned his kiss.

He drew back, looking down at my face. 'Do you have to be a rebel in all things?' His mouth twisted into a wolfish grin. 'Sometimes I wonder if you do it just for the sake of defiance.'

I shrugged. 'You said to stay back, and I never made it to the front, so I'd say I kept my word this time.'

'This time,' he agreed.

'You killed Yan.'

He nodded mutely.

'I didn't know you could fight like that.'

He grinned again. 'Now you do. It is seldom enough to be just a merchant, especially when one travels with silver, as I do. Oleg needs warriors to protect him and Prince Igor. If Oleg was to fall before Igor became a man, who would the people look to assume the position? And if Igor was to perish, gods forbid, they may look to me and my heirs,' Kjarr explained.

*My heirs.* What he meant was any children born of our union and that was why he felt such pressure. That was the reason he ran his hands over my belly when we were in bed, why he worried every time I was feeling ill, or pushed away my plate. He was Oleg's backup plan.

I opened my mouth to speak, but Oleg had returned to speak with Prince Mal. In earshot of their conversation, we went silent. Kjarr turned toward his cousin, draping his arm around my shoulders and keeping me close.

Mal, now standing, had a Rus' guard on both sides, though they didn't lay a hand on him.

'Pity you are unmarried and yet without children,' the Grand Prince began.

'A marriage alliance might forge better bonds between our people,' Mal added, hopefully. He rubbed his fingers through the full wiry beard that connected with his moustache.

Oleg laughed. 'I would not offer my niece to you, Mal! Would you have me send her into the maw of a bear? Alfrunr would not be safe where the wolf readily prowls at her door. No, I say it's a pity you are unmarried because if you had a son, I would have taken him to raise at my court, mould him into the man his father could never be. Then we might have known a better, more secure peace.'

Sol returned to brighten the sky. Mal looked up into the glare. Even now, the sun's beauty was dimmed by the intercession of earlier darkness. All her warmth had disappeared.

Mal bared his teeth. 'May I live a life long enough to see it,' he replied begrudgingly, probably praying that his god granted him many years to outlive Oleg and overthrow his dynasty.

# TWENTY-NINE

Oleg was in an ebullient mood after defeating the Drevlians. The smile could not be wiped from his face as he clapped his hand on each of his advisor's backs in greeting. The Grand Prince was a man buoyed by his success in war and, in private, his lover Ellisif pleased him with the news of the baby that grew within her.

In the weeks that followed the battle at Iskorosten, Hersir Heilagr had growled at Oleg as if he were a mere farm boy and demanded the Grand Prince marry his daughter.

'The man needs to back down,' Oleg seethed as he finished dressing behind the partition at the end of the hall after the altercation.

Kjarr helped him fasten his silk cloak with a gold brooch. 'You have been with his daughter rather publicly, Cousin. Perhaps he feels dishonoured and in need of recompense?' Kjarr's comment was venturing into impertinence, but my husband knew how far he could push his kin.

'Cousin!' Oleg pretended to be abashed as Kjarr flicked off some fluff that had made its way to Oleg's shoulder. 'He was pleased enough for me to court her. Now she is with child, his demands are endless. "A position for my sons. More land for our family",' he said, mimicking the older man. 'When does it end?' he complained, turning away to grab his cap from the bench at the side. 'The man practically shoved her into my bed.'

Kjarr coughed. 'I wouldn't say that. Was it Inga who you found in your bed the other night? I wonder who put her there?' he asked wryly.

'No, it wasn't Inga. Sveineld would never compromise his sister's union with Harald Heilagrsson. It was a slave girl, put there by Hakon's wife. Gods know what they intended by it, but it distressed Ellisif. It took me the rest of the evening to talk her down from her jealousy.' He laughed to himself. 'Heilagr has no cause to complain. I've given the girl many gifts. He has expanded his land holdings, and his sons have been sent to Malyn. What more can he desire?'

I came forward with a cup of mead. Oleg took it, but stared straight ahead.

'Will you acknowledge the child?' Kjarr asked his cousin.

Oleg shoved his fur-lined cap onto his blonde head. 'On one hand, I welcome the babe, on the other I dread its arrival. A girl would be fine enough, but if Ellisif bears a son… urgh, such a mess I've made of this.' He drained his cup and slumped into his high-backed chair. 'I can't send her away. I'd be heartsick.'

Kjarr raised his eyebrows.

'Don't look at me like that!' Oleg chastised my husband, 'and don't you dare repeat those words.'

'I'd never dream of it,' Kjarr replied, waving the idea away.

In the shadows, I crushed a few white buds and their seeds into a pestle before scooping the mixture into a cup of hot water to steep.

Oleg massaged his brow. 'How can I take the child to my knee without creating a succession crisis?' He beckoned to me for more mead. Again, he swallowed it in one gulp. He stood and smoothed out the ruffled fabric of his silk-trimmed tunic. 'I'm surrounded by enemies; the Severians and Radimichs are prowling on the left bank of the Dnieper. The Drevlians are barely to heel, and the only group that supports us are the Polianians, and only because they would rather ply us with food than cleave us with weapons.'

Kjarr tried to soothe his cousin. 'They'll keep our food stores full, and, in time, the rest of the tribes will capitulate.'

'Mmm,' Oleg groaned and rubbed his temples with his fingertips.

'Drink this,' I said, holding out a small earthenware vessel. The steam rose pleasantly in curling whisps. 'A featherfew tisane for your headache.'

He took the brew without question and sipped. 'A warrior, wife, merchant, and a healer.'

'I'm no healer. I know a few herbs for common ailments, that's all.' I dismissed, taking his empty cup and leaving it on my preparation table. Oleg watched me as I went about my work, though I did not know if his half-glazed expression saw me or imagined the future he might have with Ellisif.

He smiled to himself. 'The gods bless you, Kjarr.'

'I am indeed blessed,' my husband replied.

Oleg blinked himself back to reality. 'If only there was a potion to sort out this situation.'

Kjarr chuckled as he stood by me. I scrutinised the lay of his tunic, pulling it to the right, and found a small hole that would need mending before the week was out.

'I'm afraid even if there was, it wouldn't work as desired,' Kjarr replied and kissed me on the cheek. 'Thank you,' he whispered in my ear before turning back to his cousin. 'Are you ready?'

Oleg nodded.

Runolf, the Grand Prince's messenger, entered the room silently, always tactfully waiting for his moment to appear. 'Your boyars are gathered, Knyaz.'

'Thank you, Runolf.'

Kjarr grasped Oleg by the shoulders and steadied him.

'Rurik would have been pleased, don't you think?' he asked Kjarr. 'This was his dream; to unite the Slav tribes and drive back the Khazars. Now, we are bringing that vision to life.'

Kjarr nodded. 'You are the man to see it done.'

Oleg took a deep breath and waved Runolf away to announce his entry.

'Knyaz Oleg,' Runolf bellowed in his deep and steady voice.

Kjarr shot me a weary look as he followed Oleg to the Great Hall, joining the other boyars standing before the dais. I stayed behind the screen, ostensibly to serve when needed. This gathering was for the men only, but I was ever Kjarr's eyes, watching for the things he could not, and his ears listening in case he missed something. It was always easier to observe when people didn't think anyone was paying attention.

Oleg took to the high seat and assumed the mask he wore when duties demanded it. His posture was rigid, every muscle drawn tight, his head was held high, and his icy-blue stare pierced through the farce of court manners.

I watched as Hersir Heilagr looked up at the Grand Prince with a smugness I wished I could wipe away with excessive violence. With his sons posted to the Drevlian court, he was master of his nest, eagerly waiting to snatch at a fat worm. It was ever a wonder that such a baleful man and his wife could produce the shining star that was their daughter Ellisif.

Beside him, Sveineld the Younger twisted a silver bead around a lock of his golden beard hair, twiddling it between his fingers. He waited for the Grand Prince to speak, looking at him through dark-rimmed eyes.

Kjarr was tense, too. Since returning from Iskorosten, there was an irritability in him that had not been there before. His temper rose easily, and, thankfully, ebbed just as fast. For the first time, I'd seen him kill as if it were second nature to him and now, though his hostility had never turned towards me, I was wary of the beast within. Kjarr glanced at the partition, exactly where I stood. A smirk curled at the edges of his mouth, and he cuffed his nose; a sign that I should listen closely.

'With the Drevlians now our allies,' the Grand Prince began, and I thought *allies* might be too sure of a term to describe the uneasy peace that existed between our people, 'we can now turn our attention to the left bank of the Dnieper, and a treaty with the Severians.'

It was to be expected. Oleg's mission was to unite the Slav tribes, and his men hungered for more battle.

'Come spring, we shall look to our eastern neighbours for tribute. Sveineld has visited their settlement at Chernihiv. The Severians are open to discussions,' Oleg continued.

I pushed my face against the screen to see Tarkhan Tuvan standing against the wall, arms folded across his chest. In the days since the Drevlian conflict, he had spent much time with the Grand Prince, and, I suspected, there was more to the Khazar than his well-composed countenance betrayed.

'Sveineld?' Oleg called.

The young Boyar stepped forward and turned around to address his peers. 'My men returned with reports favourable to a bloodless acquisition. The battle at Iskorosten has removed the Severian's desire to contest our rule. It would be my recommendation, because of their early acceptance, that we impose on them a lighter tribute,' Sveineld suggested.

Oleg nodded. 'They shall have it. I will have to appoint someone as emissary to the Severians, as you will soon leave us for Pleskov.' He rubbed his jaw-line with his thumb. 'The Radimichs might not be so easily cowed,' Oleg continued, 'but that shall be a matter for next winter's campaign. Perhaps, upon hearing of the Severian's surrender, they too will bend the knee. Only then will we secure the river road and our trade will flow unhindered. The Radimichs, though they may be the key to it all, as they sit at the confluence of the Desna and Upper Dnieper Rivers, shall not be allowed to leverage that fact.'

The boyars chuckled at Oleg's cunning.

Tarkhan Tuvan's dark eyebrows arched as he unfolded his arms. 'Khagan.' He stepped forward. It took courage for a man, foreign to our ways, to speak when not called to do so. 'The Khazars will attempt to stop the flow of silver if you do this,' he warned. Many a boyar shot him a scornful look that he did not allow to intimidate him.

'Of course they will,' the Grand Prince replied. 'Which is why we must make overtures to the remaining tribes. Once united, we will be too many to be oppressed by them.'

I was so absorbed by the discussions that I had not heard Ellisif's slipper-clad feet tiptoeing to stand next to me.

'Did I miss much?' she asked, one of her dainty hands resting on the swell of her belly as she leaned forward to kiss my cheek.

I backed away from the wall, careful our voices did not travel to the hall. 'More war, and so many names,' I whispered back.

'Oleg's always repeating them, over and over,' she lamented.

Kjarr and I did the same. Even putting Egbert to the task of recording each one and the important details about every man.

Ellisif shuffled to the bench against the wall and flopped down. 'I can't keep track of them all! And why is it always about war? Can't they discuss something more exciting?'

Leaving her to rest on the bench, I turned back to the gathering. Oleg had since moved on to sending emissaries to tribes more far-flung. 'Duke Siemowit of the Western Polans has a newborn son who I believe they have named Leszek?' Oleg clarified with Runolf. 'Hmm, yes. We will send gifts and good tidings. They will not bow to us, but their territory has access to river systems leading to the Austmarr. We may have need of that in the days to come.'

'How is business going, Signe?' Ellisif asked rather too loudly.

'Shh,' I whispered, 'I was trying to listen.'

Ellisif threw her head back and groaned. 'I don't know why you bother. Kjarr will tell you all later. Until then, come and sit with me.' She patted the seat next to her.

'I've got a sail panel I need to put on the drying rack and do a last inspection,' I explained, as I walked over to sit beside her. 'It will have to wait a few days.'

'You can't go tomorrow. That's when the Jol celebrations will begin,' she responded through a mouthful of cold barley pottage, her latest food fixation. 'You'll miss out on the fun. Oooh,' she moaned and clutched her stomach.

I took the bowl from her hands. 'What's wrong?'

She laughed, taking my hand and guiding it to the left side of her swollen middle. 'It was just a kick. He is so strong now, you can feel it if you put your hand right there…do you feel it?'

Beneath her layers, I felt the fluttering movements of the child within her womb. I nodded and felt tears prick at my eyes. Sometimes I wanted a baby so badly I could think of nothing else, and other times I thought my heart could not love another child. She pressed my hand harder, and I again felt the stirring.

'When will he come?'

She put her feet up on a low stool, reclining against the wall as I removed my hand. 'By the end of winter. Mother says I'm more than halfway done. Alfrunr and Inga have been counting the days and they both agree that he should arrive by the month after *Disablót*.'

Estrid, Ellisif's mother, had retreated from her vicious assault against my character since her daughter's pregnancy. With something better to focus her ambitions on, she had left me alone. For that, I was very grateful.

My ears pricked at the Grand Prince's voice. I got to my feet and shuffled back to the partition.

Ellisif called to me, 'Could you grab me…'

'Shh. They're talking about Alfrunr,' I replied over my shoulder.

This concerned us both, as we counted Alfrunr as a friend. Ellisif padded across the screened room and poured herself a cup of mead. 'Poor girl. So young to be a token of peace.'

I looked back at my friend with amusement. It was not too long ago that Ellisif's marriage was a similar topic of speculation. Since her relationship with Oleg, that had ceased, and now, whispers in the hall postulated whether he would take her to wife or cast her aside. Ellisif didn't seem bothered by the rumours in the least.

'My niece will marry next year,' Oleg decreed, raising his voice against the bickering senior boyars.

'Will you offer her to the leader of the Radimichs?' Hersir Heilagr asked.

'A prize so great as my niece, Alfrunr, cannot be wasted. I intend to seal her with someone who may bring the Rus' great pride, and a wealth of information,' Oleg replied.

'Have we ruled out an alliance with the Khazar Khagan?' Boyar Odholf demanded. Among the Grand Prince's most trusted advisors and having been so close to his brother by marriage, Oleg always considered Old Odholf's counsel.

Oleg brushed his hand across his knee as if there was a stubborn stain. 'I believe it would bring us no value,' he replied, glancing at Tuvan at the back of the room. The Khazar maintained his blank, uninterested stare.

'Could she make peace between us and Miklagard?' The Boyar pushed further.

The Grand Prince folded his hands in his lap and leaned forward. 'That, Odholf, would be a supreme goal. As you all know, we are yet to establish favourable trade terms with Miklagard. Alas, if that was to happen, Basil would insist on Alfrunr's conversion to the Christian God. I fear he would also insist on converting the Rus' people. That is a step I am unprepared to take. I will not abandon our gods, not when my very oath to rule is sworn to them.'

At that, the boyars nodded enthusiastically. Our people held fast to Odin. The very doors of Kyiv's Great Hall were decorated in his honour. Likenesses of the gods stood proud within the city's walls and all gave offerings at their effigies. That could not be undone so that a Rus' princess might marry the aged Emperor, whose days were surely numbered.

'Are they finished yet?' Ellisif whined behind me. 'I'm hungry and I haven't seen Oleg all day. He'll want to know how violently his son has been thrashing around.' She looked down at the empty bowl that had contained her pottage with longing.

'Almost.'

'Your *huskarls* must continue their training for the fights to come,' Oleg commanded. 'You all know your duty, and do them well. Tonight, please enjoy the meal in your honour. Boyar Hrolfsson, Tarkhan Tuvan, with me,' he called the two men forward, and the three of them walked behind the separating wall while the rest of the hall's attendees scattered.

The doors to the Great Hall opened, and through them streamed the prettiest of thralls who came to arrange the tables and benches, and place their platters of food before the boyars for consumption. Tonight, Grand Prince Oleg's advisors would feast, getting drunk on well-brewed ale. But the Grand Prince had tired of the pageantry and desired respite.

Inside Oleg's private rooms, Ellisif and I sat at a small table away from the men. I rubbed her ankles and swollen feet as she nibbled on some winter berries brought in from the kitchens. Oleg came to greet his lover, taking a berry from the bowl and feeding it to Ellisif. He delighted in experiencing the powerful movements of his son within her womb, planting a kiss on her forehead as he went to sit at the table with Tuvan and Kjarr.

'Grand Prince, you sent for me?' a meek voice questioned. Alfrunr stepped into the room, her burnished bronze hair streaming unbound behind her. Much shorter than her uncle, Alfrunr looked up at him with her sky-blue eyes full of wonder. She bowed low, holding out the sides of her forest green gown. 'Would you like me to serve you, Grand Prince?'

'We are friends here, Alfrunr. Please call me uncle,' he advised. 'Ellisif needs to rest and I would have you serve tonight so that we might honour our guest Tarkhan Tuvan.'

Alfrunr's cheeks flushed. She lowered her head and dipped. 'Yes, Uncle.' The shake in her voice gave away her nerves. 'I would be honoured.' She glanced at Tuvan through a veil of golden lashes. 'It is good to see you well.'

Tuvan's lips parted slightly as he watched Alfrunr fill the cups on the table. Tuvan's hand grasped the base, and he thanked the girl with a nod of his head. Once dismissed, Alfrunr joined Ellisif and me at the small table as Tuvan, Kjarr, and Oleg began a game of dice.

'You said you weren't born in Itil, Tuvan?' Kjarr prompted as he rolled the dice across the table.

'That is true,' Tuvan replied.

Oleg leaned towards the man. 'So, Tuvan, where was your home?'

Tuvan took a deep breath and answered, 'I was born on the banks of the Kama River.'

'And your parents?' Oleg pressed, not taking his eyes off the dice as Kjarr rolled.

'Were of the Mari people.'

Kjarr grimaced at his result and pushed the pieces towards Oleg. 'Mari? I heard the Khazars all but destroyed them.'

Tuvan stiffened and, to appear controlled, lifted his bronze cup to swirl its contents before draining the dregs into his mouth.

Alfrunr leapt from her seat to pour him more ale, her sleeve brushing against the dark man's hand.

'Thank you,' he whispered, looking at her. She slunk back, face as red as the winter berries in our bowl.

'Was it the Khazars that killed your parents?' Oleg asked. This time, he allowed his eyes to meet Tuvan's.

'It was, Khagan,' Tuvan agreed. 'Those who escaped the slaughter fled to the forests or the mountains, but some, mostly the children, were taken for slaves.'

There was an unspoken admission in that. With his parents killed, and likely a child at the time, Tuvan had all but confessed himself as a thrall.

'How long have you *served* the empire?' Oleg asked, tactfully ignoring Tuvan's status. He picked up the dice for his turn.

Tuvan watched the Grand Prince roll and, when he saw the total of the symbols, shrugged indifferently. 'Some twenty winters.'

'Basically a Khazar then,' Oleg added, glancing at the man as he handed him the die.

Tuvan took a sip while he contemplated his answer. 'Could someone who is not permitted to marry or sire offspring be considered a Khazar? Even if he was born to the Mari Chieftain before his capture.'

'Such a man, a warrior of renown, would garner some respect, no?' Kjarr interjected.

Tuvan's lips had disappeared into a thin line. 'Perhaps in your court, but to the Khazars, a man is worth only that which he can leave to his heirs.'

'I see,' Oleg mumbled, passing the dice to Kjarr. 'They wish to keep you expendable?'

Tuvan did not answer, but they all knew Oleg had voiced the truth.

Kjarr leaned forward as he took his turn. 'Then you were not named Tarkhan Tuvan at birth?'

'It is a Khazar name,' Tuvan agreed with a nod. His deep brown eyes appeared almost black in the firelight. 'It was intended to mock me, for it means "gift" in the Khazar language.'

Ellisif and Alfrunr beside me listened while they darned holes in tunics for the men of the hall.

'My father named me after the moon god Tolze. On the night of my birth, the moon was at its brightest. This is the only thing I remember of my mother, for it was she who told me this.'

His honesty disarmed the room. Oleg put the dice down, removed one of his armrings and laid it on the table between himself and Tuvan.

'You told me at Iskorosten that the Khagan was trying to tempt Emperor Basil of Miklagard with a Khazar bride. Do I take it that relations have cooled between your nations?'

'If I disclosed that, I would do the Khazars a disservice,' Tuvan replied, glancing down at the silver ring.

'Alfrunr, Ellisif,' Oleg called, 'you may retire. It is late and I am sure you desire your rest.' He kissed Ellisif's hand and he walked the two ladies to the door.

'Should I go, Grand Prince?' I asked, wondering if he had forgotten my presence, but he shook his head and suggested that I stay.

'You will repeat nothing you hear tonight,' he instructed, levelling me with one of his chilling gazes.

I lowered my head and spoke, 'I am a vault, Grand Prince.' With an unsteady hand, I refilled each of their cups and took my place at the side of the room.

'I wonder, Tolze,' Oleg started, making a point of using the Emissary's Mari name, 'if you might find a better life here, within Kyiv's walls?'

Tolze's eyes widened, but it was clear he did not know how to respond. 'I would fear for my life, Khagan.'

'As I fear for my own daily,' Oleg confessed. He stood and crossed the table to where Tolze sat. 'Show me your arm. How does it feel?'

Tolze dragged up the sleeve of his tunic, exposing his bandaged arm. 'It is much better, Khagan. My thanks to your niece for tending to my wounds with such skill.'

'It will please her to hear that though it grieves me you were stabbed in my hall when you were under my protection,' Oleg seethed. 'The assailant killed my man Magnus before he came for you in your alcove.'

Magnus, the man who I had stood shield to shield with, in the fight against the Drevlians.

Tolze nodded. 'I am fortunate the men of your druzhina came to my aid.'

'The murderer was a nobody. We don't even know where he came from. Which means he was working for someone else, a nameless lord, it seems. He divulged none of it before he was executed,' Oleg explained. It had all happened so quickly. Oleg and those closest to him did their best to keep the news contained. The assailant was spirited to confinement where he was interrogated until his fate was decided. Then, after being found guilty of the murder of Magnus, and the wounding of Tolze, was dispatched privately.

Oleg stopped and tilted his head to the side. 'Tell me, why do you think someone wanted you dead?' He asked as he traced the pattern of the armring, lingering over the snarling beasts at both nodes.

Kjarr sat back but said nothing. It was best to let this play out without interruption.

Under the table, Tolze's hands balled into fists. 'I betrayed my Khagan,' he admitted.

'How so?' Oleg backed away, resuming his seat. 'Tell me all. You have my word that it will go no further than us.'

Tolze's eyes darted around the room. 'The Khagan believes I have grown too close to you.'

'How would he know?' Oleg scoffed.

Tolze took a moment to sip from his cup. 'He is not aware, not yet, but his agents are. They see how much time I spend in your presence.'

'Is that not the role of an emissary?' Oleg pointed out.

But Kjarr had heard the insinuation in Tolze's confession. 'You mean to tell me the Khazar Khagan has men within my cousin's court?'

Kjarr asked, covering for Oleg's surprise lest Tolze would consider Oleg callow.

Oleg looked at Kjarr with concern. 'How many?'

Tolze swallowed hard. 'Two.'

Oleg continued. He gripped the base of his cup so hard I thought it might shatter. 'Including yourself?'

Tolze shook his head. 'No, Khagan. I am, of course, expected to report on all your dealings to my Khagan, but there are also men here who watch me to make sure I do not stray from the path I am instructed to follow.' He pushed his knuckle into the side of his neck.

Oleg gritted his teeth. 'Who are they?'

Tolze's chest rose and fell with a deep breath. 'I do not know.'

'You expect us to believe you?' Kjarr demanded, his anger quick to bubble to the surface.

Tolze raised his palms. 'I swear it on my gods and yours. I have never seen these men. They only appear behind screens at designated times. Please understand that I have attempted to catch them out. I have tried to place their voices but, as yet, I have not heard them among your men.'

'Then tell me how you meet them? When is your next meeting? We could lay a trap,' Kjarr suggested, reaching for the jug I had left on the table.

Tolze shook his head again, this time his shoulders hunched forward, and I saw his composure crumbling. 'Khagan, they have abandoned me. They are ghosts now.'

'You lie!' Kjarr raged.

'Cousin,' Oleg clipped. 'How do you know they will not communicate with you? Surely you have a method of getting messages to each other,' he wondered, as he turned away from Kjarr.

'They always came to me. I had nothing in writing,' Tolze answered. 'The last time I heard one of them speak, it was only to say that I was no longer welcome back in Khazaria and that my life was forfeit.'

'How long after were you stabbed?' Oleg asked. He took the armring in hand and flipped it over and over.

'The next day.'

Kjarr crossed his arms over his chest, calming down. 'They're efficient bastards.'

'Now, you are on your own.' Oleg ran his fingers over his jaw-line. 'Will they come for you again?'

Tolze chewed on his lip. 'I don't doubt it, Khagan.' He looked at the ring in Oleg's other palm. 'Unless you draw them out, Khagan, or you feed the Khazars what you want them to know. There are men in your court who would be useful to you.'

'Speak, Tolze,' Oleg agreed, placing the armring back between them.

'Two of the men you've taken as hostage report to Khazaria, Niskinnin, and Ostromyr,' he disclosed the names of Prince Mal's relatives.

'Of course they do,' Kjarr put in. 'Though they've been disarmed.'

Tolze considered this. 'But they will still send messages to Prince Mal and information flows freely from Malyn.'

'What are you suggesting, Tolze?' Kjarr wondered. Interest piqued, he put his elbows on the table.

'You would tell them only that which you wanted to be spread through their network, but you would also need a man to infiltrate them. A double spy.' Tolze's fingers gripped the edge of the table.

'You're proposing yourself?' Kjarr asked sceptically.

Tolze shook his head. 'They would not trust me. Not now.'

Kjarr narrowed his eyes. 'Yet you ask us to do so.'

'I do not want to return to the Khazar lands,' Tolze vowed. 'I was taken when I was small, humiliated, tortured, and until now, the opportunity to escape had never arisen,' he explained.

Oleg did not comment on Tolze's ordeal. His mind was already a step ahead. 'What man would you appoint to the position?'

Tolze shrugged. 'I know of no man who might fill the role, Khagan.'

I stepped from the shadows. 'Grand Prince, I know of someone who might be suitable.'

Kjarr shot me a quizzical expression.

I tugged at the hem of my sleeve. 'Though I may not like him, his cover is ideal. He is a merchant,' I detailed.

All three men turned to look at me. 'A merchant would be the perfect guise,' Oleg agreed. 'He could visit each place without arousing suspicion.'

'He speaks the language,' I added.

'You know this for sure?' Oleg asked, grasping his cup and bringing it to his mouth.

'I believe he does. He seemed able to communicate with the Khazar scouts that tried to take Eskil on our way here to Kyiv.'

Kjarr squinted as he ran through the names of every member of the *Bhobain's* crew silently as he counted on his fingers.

Oleg went back to stroking his jaw. 'Will he be amenable to the cause?'

'If there is money involved, I think he will,' I responded.

Oleg and Kjarr exchanged a knowing glance. Even Tolze seemed moved by the information. The Grand Prince picked up the jug from the table, gracefully poured the gleaming liquid into a fourth cup and handed it to me. 'What is the man's name?'

I took it and tasted its honey-sweet savour before I replied, 'Gunnar.'

# THIRTY

Exhausted and bleary-eyed, I flopped onto my bed. Kjarr remained with Tolze and Oleg, discussing their plans for uncovering the Khazar agents within Kyiv, but I could not stay awake any longer. They'd asked me where they might find Gunnar, but in all honesty, if he wasn't selling his cheap trinkets at the market, I did not know where he spent his days. I hated suggesting the man for any advancement. It felt like a betrayal of Odrun, and I hoped she would understand I did it for the good of my people and not because I valued Gunnar.

Fully dressed, I flopped onto my bed and considered if I had enough energy to disrobe before falling asleep.

'You're in late,' Odrun mumbled as she sat down next to me. In her hands was the new dress I had suggested she sew for herself, made from fine woven wool from my collection. 'Are you alone?' I asked her as I closed my eyes against the warm golden light of the brazier.

She took my hand. 'Egbert is here too.'

Normally Egbert would be asleep by now. He wasn't in the habit of waiting up for me as Odrun liked to. I opened my eyes and sat up. Our rooms were fastidiously tidy, as if Odrun had busied herself all afternoon and evening. The chests had been dusted and squared away. The rods on the wall were bare, and all the tapestries and pillows looked as if a frustrated hand had beaten them clean.

'What's going on?' I asked. 'Is everything all right?'

Odrun smiled a secret smile as she lay down her work and handed me the unsealed letter that had arrived weeks before. 'Better than all right.'

The parchment was creased in many places. Odrun must have opened and refolded it a hundred times, waiting for Egbert to read it to her. She gave it to me. It smelled like her, a simple fragrance of lavender. I looked back at Odrun's face, lined with excitement as she ran her fingers over the broken seal.

'What does it say?' I asked, inspecting the letter, but the writing was imperceptible to me.

Egbert joined us, retrieving another unfolded piece of parchment from a small chest at his scribe table. 'I've translated it for you so you might experience the impact of the words more greatly.'

'So dramatic,' I replied, grinning at him.

Since arriving in Kyiv, Egbert had taken to our language, culture, and gods with an enthusiasm I had witnessed other Christians apply to their own religion, but never the Old Gods. He had learned our staves and spoke basic phrases in several of the Slav dialects.

Egbert smiled benevolently. His brown curls were groomed for this moment of importance. 'Read it, Signe.'

Odrun's hands, now free of their charge, picked up the fabric once more and wrung it in her clenched fists. She let out a small squeak.

'Are you crying, Odrun?' I asked, looking towards her.

She wiped away a tear, eyes glittering amber in the brazier's light. 'A little,' she allowed. 'For so long, I prayed for this.'

I took the parchment from Egbert's hands. 'Bring me a light, please, Egbert,' I requested, and my Frankish monk-turned-scribe brought the brazier forward, careful not to burn himself or his handsome clothing. The glowing flames illuminated his deep-coloured eyes, and the smile that covered his face almost outshone its light.

I lingered over each word as both Egbert and Odrun watched me so intently I thought neither took a breath. My gasp was loud as I took in the last line and suddenly the seal and signature made sense.

My throat was dry as week-old bread and my heart hammered in my chest, but I could not find the words for what I had read.

'I'm not ready for Grand Prince Oleg and the court to know yet,' Odrun whispered.

She gripped my arm, and I looked at her fine angular features and amber eyes like I was noticing each for the first time. I sniffed back the tears and let the letter fall into my lap.

I shook my head in disbelief. 'You are free now.'

She gazed at me with affection, tears beaded on her fair lashes as they streamed down her smooth cheeks. 'And you will have your reward.'

# PART THREE
## INTO THE FLAMES

# THIRTY-ONE

'Her thread is long and fine, spun by her fair hand,' I sang to myself as I tidied the warehouse. It was a pretty ditty one of my warehouse ladies, Frida, had taught me, though I was not very good at recalling the words. 'Round and round the spindle goes, dropping to the ground,' I continued. 'Don't break the thread, for it is life, and…' I stopped.

The next line escaped me. *Was it the verse about the Norns? Or was it the part about the husband's shirt?* I couldn't remember. It didn't matter, with no one else to remind me I could sing whatever words I liked.

Earlier that day, Mirca and I had farewelled our women as they left, handing each a piece of silver as their Jol gift from us. Their smiles had been broad. I thought of them now, all sitting by their warm hearth fires sharing a meal with their loved ones, and felt a pang that I was not doing the same. Kjarr was where he always was; with his cousin, and I was where I was most needed; in my warehouse, attending to business. It did not bother me so much that I was alone. There was some peace in that. What rankled me was the impression that, although Kjarr insisted he needed me by his side, I never saw the truth of it. He seemed to do a fine job without my presence.

My teeth chattered in my head, and I pulled my fur-lined cloak around my shoulders. I had contemplated lighting a fire, but did not plan to be away as long as I had. The sails had to be hauled in from the drying racks and that had taken longer than expected. I'd wandered down to the shipyard, calling some stragglers to help me bring the enormous pieces of cloth. They were too heavy for me to manage on my own. Once that was done, those friendly men waved their goodbyes and trudged up the hill into the lightly falling snow. Those few were the last to go, deserting the shipyard skeletons of new builds and the hulls of those ships waiting for repairs. All would wait until Jol had passed and work would begin again.

The cold, damp weather could not diminish Kyiv's spirit as its inhabitants prepared to celebrate. Many of the boyar's wives were busy decorating the grand hall with garlands of winter greens or brewing copious amounts of ale for the feasts to come. I had no skill in brewing and took no joy in floral embellishment as Ellisif and her mother Estrid did. And they had Alfrunr, Inga, and a bevy of other women to help them with those tasks. If I hadn't retrieved the two sails before the snowfall, they might have become sodden, warping beyond rescue. We couldn't afford to lose the product, much less the money they would bring in with their eventual sale.

I took a deep inhale, ready to belt out the next line of the song, but caught the faint whiff of something burning on the breeze. A bonfire. Jol revellers were always lighting something on fire.

I knelt on the cold ground, dragging one edge of the sail to meet the other as I folded it in half over and over until it was a manageable square of fabric. A small, dark shape caught my eye from across the room. A mouse squeaked as it clawed through the soil at the base of the wood construction.

'Where do you think you're going, little one?' I asked, walking over to see what all the fuss was about.

The small creature issued another high-pitched squeal and burrowed under the bottom section of the wood where the planks were dark with rot. I pushed on them with my foot to test their strength and they gave in. I groaned and touched my hand to the golden torc that I wore around my neck.

'That will need to be fixed come summer,' I said, more to myself than the mouse, but it stopped and looked up as if it were listening.

My hand went to my belt where my seax usually lay. I wanted to take a scraping of the wood rot, but I found my blade missing.

'Odin's beard!'

I'd leant it to Odrun this morning as she was keeping up the pretence of being a slave and I had not thought to ask for it back before I left.

I kicked the rotting wood, and it bowed out. The mouse, seeing the gap I made, escaped through the opening.

'Good luck surviving out there,' I uttered as I turned back to the folded sail on the ground.

Its weight was cumbersome as I scooped it up and walked towards the tables. I feared it would slink out of my grasp and I would have to start the entire process again. But it didn't. The sail flopped onto the bench and I stood back to admire it beside its twin. Two sails. They would bring in a healthy sum, and each of my ladies would count on the payment.

Almost everything else was in order, save for a few loom weights that Branka, our chief weaver, had left out when she had returned home to nurse her sick daughter. Clay weights that usually hung from the warp threads of the standing loom, but having been cut off, lay discarded on the ground. Next to it, I lifted the lid of the weights box and slotted each of the round discs into their spot. My fingers traced each row, organised according to weight and size, just as Mirca liked them to be. There was a simple comfort in the way she did things.

*That bonfire must be huge*, I thought as its acrid stench filled my nostrils. Oleg had said nothing about sanctioning one of this size, but if it was as big as it smelled, I should have been able to see it from the hilltop. When I tried the warehouse doors, I found they were barred from the outside.

'Hey! I'm in here,' I called out in case someone had thought to do me a favour by locking the door and thus protecting the contents within.

No one answered.

I threw my weight against the door. My shoulder burned as I hurled myself on its unyielding barrier and the wood rattled on the pivot. It did not budge.

Then I caught a stronger smell. Not the far off a trail of ash on the breeze but of swirling smoke which now entered the warehouse. Through the planks of the eastern side, I saw flames licking the edge of the outside wall. They reached higher as I watched and felt their heat pricking at my skin.

I gasped, aware of the limited air within. Fire raced along the eastern wall. Wool, hanging from hooks, caught fire. The threads shrank back from the flames but caught alight. Heat blazed the beams with an awful crackling as the warehouse filled with smoke. My eyes were watering, my throat felt scraped and raw. I had to escape. It was clear the door was not an option. Someone had barred it to commit this offence.

I looked up through the haze. It would not be long before the beams faltered. I recalled the rotten wood. I scrambled, crawling on my hands and knees as I gasped through the choking smoke. My hands prodded the damp section of wood on the western wall. I thumped it and it yielded a small gap. If I had Forlog-Enda or my seax, I might have been able to leverage the planks out of place, but all I had was my strength and each inhalation of the noxious fumes weakened me.

'This cannot be my fate.' I moaned as I drove the heel of my palm against a plank. It cracked and fell away. 'Thank the gods.'

Again, I hit the wood with my hand, sending smarting pain through my wrist and arm, but that would be nothing compared to the agony of burning alive. I pulled away three small sections of planks and I tried to ease myself through the hole. It was wet, muddy, and I knew I was ruining my cloak, but the will to survive preceded my desire to preserve my fine clothing. My head managed easily enough through the gap, my shoulder struggled as my fabric snagged on the uneven wood. A loud tear sounded as I dragged myself further. I knew not if I ripped through my cloak or dress. I just kept going. My hips passed painfully, pinched by the unforgiving dry wood surrounding the rotting portion. I pulled my legs out as I came free of the burning wreck and sat in the mire, gasping for cleaner air.

I sobbed, I couldn't help myself as I half-crawled, half-stumbled away, watching everything I'd worked so hard for go up in flames.

'Help,' I cried, but there was no force in my voice and it came out as a strangled moan.

Fire engulfed the building now. Two of the four walls were invisible behind the blaze, but the roof had not yet collapsed. From the outside, it seemed to burn more slowly than it did when I was trapped. Maybe there was time to alert the town and bring help to extinguish it.

On unsteady legs, I ran through the long grass. The afternoon sun was waning and my eyes felt clouded with smoke, making it difficult to see. I dragged my disobedient feet through the sludge but managed only a dozen steps before my ankle struck an object and I fell to my knees. Something had snagged me and would not let go.

A hand slithered across my face and covered my mouth.

'Do not scream,' the voice cautioned me.

My eyes searched for the speaker, but the way they held my head made it impossible to turn towards them. Try as I might, I couldn't cry out, not even if my voice hadn't been muffled by their hand. The person took me by the shoulders and spun me around so fast I hit the ground, flat on my back.

'Stop thrashing,' he growled, and I realised the man who restrained me was Gunnar.

I scrambled back onto my knees. He was never a friend, and I knew he had not come to help me now. His weight bore down as he pushed me onto the ground.

'I didn't think you'd be inside, but it's a welcome bonus.'

My blood ran cold despite the heat of the uncontrolled fire. Heart thudding in my chest, blood rushing to pulse in my ears; it all drowned out his words. His mouth moved, but I couldn't hear him, though I could see the same malicious glint in his eyes as he had when Odrun struggled against his unwelcome advances.

With a groaning *crack*, the fire consumed the warehouse. Its complete collapse was imminent.

'Help,' I rasped, but he only laughed as he pressed me harder onto the ground. *It's so cold*, I thought as I twisted under Gunnar's bulk.

Then he forced something sharp against my throat, *a knife*. I summoned my remaining strength, driving my foot into his shin and jabbed my elbow upwards, sending the weapon in his hand ricocheting across the stone-studded ground.

Gunnar looked down at me in surprise. 'Stupid bitch,' he cursed as he reached for the knife. Grasping it, he raised it above my head and drove it into the ground there.

I looked above me, thinking how I might reach it.

'Don't get any ideas,' Gunnar warned me, flicking his tongue along his teeth.

He fumbled for something at his waist and, taking advantage of his distraction, I jerked my arms out of his grip and sent my fist into the side of his head. He drew back in a stupor, but it gave me enough time to land another blow. Reeling from the impact, he fell backwards, and I stumbled to my feet, limping away as quickly as I could. Gunnar launched himself towards me and tackled me to the ground. With a sickening thud, my jaw met the frostbitten soil. I moaned in pain as the fire roared behind us and I knew at once that the roof must have given way. Acrid char of cinder and smoke filled my lungs. I coughed on the choking fumes.

Gunnar pulled his cloak over his mouth and dragged me by the legs, to the place we were before. I clawed at the ground as he tugged me, but he was taking no chances. Gunnar bound my hands with rope, lifting them above my head and looping them around the knife still in the ground.

'I curse you, Gunnar,' I growled and levelled him with an evil glare, though terror ran through my veins like ice.

He laughed, kneeling in the haze, looking down at me. 'Curse me all you like, but you'll not escape again,' he promised as he crawled over me and pressed his body onto mine.

I tried to kick out, but his weight crushed me.

'When I'm done with you, I'll drag you back to the fire so you can burn with your beloved textiles; you've got Estrid to thank for that.' His urgent fingers gathered up the length of my silk-trimmed dress.

'No,' I cried as my feet scrambled in the dirt, striking rocks and clumps of earth. Even bound, my fingers scraped at the ground, fumbling with the knots and trying to pry the knife from the frosty earth. Nothing would budge. I wanted to shut my eyes, to pretend like none of this was happening.

The flames were high now. I hoped to all the gods that someone would see the fire and not wrongly assume it was a bonfire, as I had earlier that night.

'If you could have kept your mouth shut, I might have let you go, seeing as you preferred to escape so badly,' he whispered against my ear as he sank his teeth into my lobe.

'Stop!' I tried to buck his body from mine.

Gunnar slapped me across the face. 'And if my man had done his job right, we wouldn't need to be in this mess,' he continued, his knee forcing my legs to part. 'If we had just killed the Khazar.'

I twisted to my side, squeezing my thighs together, and Gunnar howled in frustration. His ash-smelling fingers crawled over my breasts and clasped the gold torc around my neck. He pushed the solid metal against my windpipe.

'But you had to suggest me as a spy for the Grand Prince. "Speaks the language, a merchant, and is motivated by money." I believe that's what you said.' He didn't look for a reply as he forced my torc back harder and my eyes bulged. I futilely gasped for breath as I felt my body chill where it lay on the frozen ground. 'I'm assuming it was just a lucky guess. I wouldn't have thought you were smart enough to figure out I was already operating as an informant,' he said with a chuckle as he fumbled with his belt. 'Not so fortunate for me, because unlike you they realised and came looking for me, but I have time for one more job before I need to leave,' he prattled.

The sky dimmed, and Gunnar parted my legs without my resistance. Gunnar's words faded into a *whooshing* noise as his hand pressed harder on the torc at my throat.

I didn't want to die, not like this, but I did not wish to live through this either.

The last thing I saw was Gunnar, sweat dripping streaks through his dirt-stained face as he groped between my legs. His hazy form grew larger in my blurred vision, darker, and more malevolent, until my body was lost to me, and my mind rose from the terror inflicted in that field.

I blinked my eyes open. My throat was as rough as gravel, but I was alive. I shivered, frozen from laying on the cold earth. The pungent odour of smoke was thick in the air, and I still lay in the grass but my dress covered my legs, soiled though it was. I found my arms were unbound, but my wrists bore the welts to prove they had been. Every movement was agony as I forced myself to my knees.

The warehouse was smouldering.

'Pass another bucket,' I heard someone call ahead of me.

I squinted towards them and could just about make out the shapes of a few people.

To my left, I heard the deep growl of a man's voice. 'Get up,' I heard him say. 'Get to your feet.'

Not sure if he was speaking to me, I stumbled towards the voice. All was a blur in the dwindling early evening light. My chest rose and fell with heavy breaths as I sucked in the fire-fowled air. It was bitter and harsh, and I vomited black on the ground.

'You're a coward,' the voice seethed, and I knew it to be Sven. His towering frame stood over a smaller figure cowering in the grass.

Unsteadily, I continued towards him.

'Who asked you to do this?' Sven demanded. 'Why did you kill her?' His voice broke as he said those words.

Gunnar cackled, a laugh rasped by the smoke. 'I'll never tell.'

I tried to clear my throat, but it was so raw, still strangled by his invisible hand. 'Estrid,' I choked out.

Neither of them heard me. So I staggered closer and groped for Sven's arm.

'It was Estrid,' I managed.

Sven caught me as I faltered and I wished I could have seen Gunnar's expression as he saw me standing. I hoped he looked upon me as if I were a spectre of his worst nightmare, a *draugr* that lurked in the forest and stole the newborn children of the city.

'I thought...' Sven stammered, then shook himself. 'Eskil,' Sven bellowed, calling the big man towards us. 'Take this piece of filth straight to the Grand Prince.'

'Why not Hersir Heilagr?' Eskil questioned.

'Because the Hersir's wife is named as the instructor of his evil deeds and the Grand Prince will want to interrogate this one before anyone else finds out. Make sure it is so.'

Eskil grunted and dragged the merchant away as Gunnar wailed and pleaded for his life.

When we were alone, Sven turned to me, still holding me tight under the arms. 'Are you all right?' he asked.

'I can't see much,' I replied, though my throat hurt to speak. I ignored the deeper question. 'Was anything salvaged?'

He released me but kept hold of my hand and led me towards the smoking ruins. 'Some things might still be found, but the building and the textiles are lost.'

I stifled a cry. It hurt too much to sob. It pained me to think of Mirca and our women who had needed the funds that would come from the purchase of our sails. I retched.

'Where is Kjarr?' Sven asked. There was no softness to his voice. It was harsh, angry, and brutal.

I tried to focus on the outline of his face and wondered what he saw when he looked at me, what Kjarr would see. *Scarred, cursed, broken; was that who I was now?*

'With Oleg,' I replied.

Sven ran the tip of his finger along the battle scar near my eye, then to the mark on my neck. 'I'll take you to Odrun, then I'll find your husband. There are some things I need to say to him.'

# THIRTY-TWO

By evening Odrun sat by me in the bathhouse, scrubbing the dirt from beneath my nails with a stiff bristled brush. Steam billowed around us as she looked at me. Not with pity, for she knew well the damage Gunnar could inflict, and the strength required to endure it.

'Can I wash you?' she asked, her voice a whisper, and I nodded my reply.

Odrun took a length of soft linen and dunked it into the hot water, dragging it over my skin. Dirt swirled in the bucket as every cut was wiped clean.

'You are safe here, Signe,' Odrun said, reaching out to touch my hand.

I drew back, I couldn't help it.

She offered me a knowing smile.

'You are safe here,' she repeated and continued her work, but didn't take my hand again. Her touch, as she washed me, was so gentle and I was so exhausted that I fell asleep. But the dream world is not a place one should dwell when they have suffered living nightmares. Realm spirits waited to feast on my misfortune and agony. I jolted awake.

'The bad dreams will lessen in time,' Odrun promised, her amber eyes downcast. 'Lavender oil?' She held a small vial of the stuff for me to smell but, with nostrils filled with the scent of burned wool and charred wood, it was impossible.

'Anything to take away the odour of smoke,' I ground out in my hoarse voice.

Odrun's hands smoothed the slick ointment across my skin, soothing burns, scrapes, and bruises. When she was done, I was dressed in a clean garment, and supporting my weight on her slim shoulders, she helped me back to my rooms. Before we'd even mounted the stairs, we heard the raised voices inside.

'You do not protect her,' Sven yelled at Kjarr.

*Had Sven been here the entire time Odrun, and I were at the bathhouse?* I wondered. After delivering me to Odrun, he had set out to locate Kjarr, who, as usual, was with Oleg.

'And don't tell me she doesn't need your protection, that she is strong enough!' Sven raged. 'She is still a woman and, yes, she can defend herself, but not like this.'

Kjarr did not respond.

Sven continued his tirade. 'This court is full of scheming players, as you are well aware. You were born to this life, and she was not. As her *husband*, it is your job to keep her safe.'

Kjarr's voice screamed back. 'And you need to remember that it is *me* she married, and not *you*!'

Sven was silent for a moment before he clapped back. 'If she had married me, none of this would have happened.'

'If you are not more careful…' Kjarr growled.

'You threaten me? The man who found your wife so close to death that I thought she was gone,' Sven shouted. His voice hitched when he recalled finding me in the long grass. 'You should have protected your wife, that which you should hold the most dear.'

'Don't speak to me in this way, Sven!' Kjarr screamed indignantly. 'One word from me and I would have your head severed from your neck. Don't think I wouldn't do it.'

Sven scoffed. 'You don't think I could do the same? Except I wouldn't need to command anyone else to do my dirty work, Boyar Hrolfsson,' Sven sneered. 'It would take but a slash from my sword to do the job.'

'How dare you!' Kjarr shouted.

Sven was not one to be intimidated. 'You can threaten by virtue of your position, yet you do not protect those you claim to love.'

Odrun glanced at me, and I shook my head. I wasn't ready to go in yet, and Kjarr and Sven needed to finish what they had started.

There was quiet. Maybe Sven was telling Kjarr what really happened up on the hill, or perhaps their argument turned bitter. We couldn't hear. My fingers twisted at the strands of my hair. It still reeked of smoke despite Odrun having washed it three times and dousing me in her sweet-scented lavender oil.

More silence followed until the door creaked open and Sven stepped out, his face contorted in an angry crumple. He shot me a fleeting look and bolted down the stairs towards Sihtric's home. Odrun led me inside, tactfully excusing herself to find Egbert in the Great Hall.

Kjarr sat in a high-backed chair by the brazier, one leg over the arm. In his hand was a mug of some inebriating substance. He watched me as I entered and as I winced when I sat in the chair beside him.

His eyes fluttered closed. 'How are you?' he asked as his eyes flickered open and he tried to stand.

I gestured my hand, and he resumed his seat.

'As well as expected, I suppose,' he answered his own question. His gaze swept over me and I knew it was a grim sight; bloodshot eyes, bruised, scraped, and battered. He hung his head. 'I'm sorry, Astrid. Sorry, I was not there.'

I nodded. 'Will you fight Heilagr in the hazel rods?' My voice was thick and grating.

Kjarr looked across at me. 'If I could, but Oleg has forbidden it for fear of a blood feud between Heilagr's house and his own. He will not allow it. Gunnar, though, will pay for what he has done.'

It was not our way to ignore the wrongs of others. Blood was repaid in kind, and I was infuriated that Kjarr would allow me to be so dishonoured by another member of the court and permit them to go unpunished.

*Always what Oleg wanted, never what I needed.*

'Our gods demand revenge, Kjarr,' I reminded him as forcefully as I could manage. 'Heilagr, too, must pay. It was his wife that commissioned the ill deed.'

Kjarr's hand rose to stop me from speaking. 'I will hear no more about this. Oleg has prohibited Heilagr's death by my blade, and that is the end of it.'

I folded my arms across my chest and seethed. I would have argued more, but it pained me to speak both the words and with a throat so raspy.

Kjarr gnawed on his lower lip as his gaze settled on my neck. He saw the marks Gunnar had left there when he choked me with the torc Kjarr had gifted me. For as long as I lived, I would never wear the thing again.

Kjarr filled his cup and swirled it slowly. 'What is he to you?' he asked without looking up.

My brow furrowed as I tried to understand. 'Do you mean Gunnar? He was on the *Bhobain* with me from Aldeigjuborg. There is nothing more than that.' Every word was like swallowing clay shards.

Kjarr shook his head and downed the remaining liquid in his cup before he levelled me with a frosty glare. 'You know who I mean.'

*Sven, then.* There was no one else. 'He is my friend.'

'Hmm,' he mumbled as he rose from his seat to pour another cup for himself. 'I guess he should be thanked for finding you,' he conceded.

'Did you?'

He sculled his cup and set it down. 'Of course. You are the most precious person to me in all the nine worlds, and it pains me greatly that I have failed you.'

Yet he had.

'It tortures me that there is a man who would step into my shoes should you give him the faintest of nods,' he said, turning to look at me.

I opened my mouth, too shocked at his insinuation. 'I have not and would not.'

Kjarr slumped into his chair, legs splayed as he chewed on his lip. 'Have not?' he questioned, raising an eyebrow.

Heat rose in me. Not because he knew about my past with Sven, including the time in Aldeigjuborg when I nearly broke my vows to Kjarr, but that he sought to question me at a time like this.

'You know all there is to know,' I responded. 'Do not act as if a man who has been nothing but honest offends you more than the man who tried to rape and kill your wife this night.'

Kjarr appeared taken aback. 'You are right. I'm sorry. I'm not sure what…'

'You should be,' I replied curtly, and looked away from him, hiding my tears.

Kjarr knelt before me on the floor. 'Astrid, I have not been the husband you deserve,' he lamented, taking my hand. 'I should have protected you, even if you have been capable of doing that yourself in the past.' Forlorn, he hung his head. 'Sometimes you need me and I have not seen that. I should have done better.' He rubbed his hand along his jaw-line. 'We will right the wrongs done and, Astrid, I promise I will be a better husband to you,' he said as his gaze lifted to meet mine, 'if you will give me more time.'

# THIRTY-THREE

The next few days were a blur.

In the aftermath of the warehouse burning, Gunnar was proclaimed a would-be murderer and rapist, as well as destructor of property by arson, and sentenced to death. There could be no lesser penalty for a man who had threatened the Grand Prince's kin.

Oleg's men had interrogated Gunnar relentlessly, even though the merchant had disclosed his master's identity. It was no small matter to bring down the Hersir of Kyiv and his wife. Oleg wanted to be sure Gunnar was not boasting.

Evidence of Estrid's earlier contriving to ruin my business did no good to her claim of innocence. It shocked no one to hear the rumours she had spread, but her machinations for murder and destruction sent ripples through the court. Even I struggled to believe she had plotted my death.

*Perhaps Gunnar had taken that upon himself, along with his desire to humiliate me.* I shuddered. The thought of his creeping hands on my skin, and the scent of burning lanolin still present in my nose and mouth, caused my stomach to turn.

Ellisif clung to my arm as Oleg declared her parents guilty of their crimes. She sobbed as Estrid and Heilagr bowed under Oleg's judgement, hearing themselves outlawed from the Rus' lands. They would be banished to Svealand, or wherever they deigned to go, so long as they never stepped foot in Oleg's territories ever again; on pain of death. Then the final twist of the knife came.

Oleg drew himself up to his considerable height, glaring down at the cowed Hersir and his spiteful wife. 'All lands and titles are henceforth forfeited to the wronged party. Boyar Hrolfsson will have this as recompense for the offences committed against his honour.'

*Against his wife,* Oleg meant, but the compensation was due to my husband, not to me. I did not doubt Kjarr would hand part of it to me for my use, but the declaration still stung.

Heilagr snarled and Estrid's lip curled, but neither dared to glance at Oleg, Kjarr, or me. With their sons away at the Drevlian court in Malyn, the couple could do little more than grieve for the loss their children would suffer. For my part, I didn't want their land or wealth. None of it would undo the harm. I wanted retribution, but Oleg had denied it and instead, I would receive goods spoiled by Estrid and Heilagr's poisonous touch.

I shifted from one foot to another, my bruises sending waves of fresh pain throughout my body. Ellisif squeezed my arm tighter as the Grand Prince broached the matter of her brothers.

'I trust your entire family is not tainted?' He directed the question at the Hersir.

'They do not know of this,' Heilagr agreed, still looking at his feet.

Oleg stroked the arm of his high-backed chair, tracing a notch in the wood. 'Harald and Helgi will keep their position as emissaries to the Drevlian ruler. I will not deny them a chance to make their way on their own merits. This will not be a blood feud, Heilagr. I forbid it. Too many good men are lost to that rage and it only ends when entire lines are extinguished. Take this allowance as a gift, Heilagr, for all the years you served both me and Rurik, but do not mistake my mercy for weakness, for if you return I will not be so kind,' he warned.

Heilagr and Estrid bowed even lower. Their knees shook from holding the position.

Only Ellisif, their daughter, had gone unmentioned. By rights, as an unmarried daughter she, too, should have been sent away, but I sensed Oleg would not do it. Ellisif hung off my arm, tears falling soundlessly onto her round cheeks as her other hand cradled the child within her womb. Selfish or not, Oleg took one look at his woman and I knew he refused to cast her out. Hastily, he declared Ellisif in his charge and left it at that.

Guards came forward to take Estrid and Heilagr from the Great Hall.

'Father, I, I...' she stuttered as her parents were led away.

No one had given her time to say farewell and even if they had, her parents were more concerned with pleading and bargaining.

Estrid called to her friends, Aslaug, and Ranveg, beseeching them to intercede on her behalf, but without wealth or the Grand Prince's favour she had nothing left to offer. Both women turned their back on their one-time friend.

'Mother,' Ellisif called and, for the briefest of moments, Estrid turned. Without acknowledging her daughter, Estrid whipped her head back to the doors.

I knew Ellisif wanted to intervene, to stop Oleg from sending her parents away. There was nothing she could say that would excuse their actions. She gaped at me, opening and closing her mouth like a fish out of water.

Her shoulders slumped, and she turned to me. 'Why did they do it?' she asked. 'They had so much wealth and power. Why did they reach for more?'

I didn't answer. Nothing I said would make it any better. I just held her as she cried bitter tears.

Once I put Ellisif to bed, I joined Kjarr in Oleg's rooms where the Grand Prince paced about the space. I often did the same when I searched for a solution. Sitting idle did nothing for the racing mind.

'Scheming weasels,' he seethed, walking a faster lap towards the far wall. 'They've put me in an impossible position. And, if that was not enough, we have failed to locate the Khazar spies. All of this will reach our enemies. The Drevlian hostages will make sure of that. Nor have we found a suitable candidate to serve as our spy in the Khazar court, not now that Gunnar has proved inappropriate.'

*That was an understatement.* Kjarr and I exchanged a concerned glance.

'What about Ellisif? How can I keep her here at court without looking like I'm handing out concessions?' He rounded the table and kept going. 'Helgi and Harald serve a purpose, so long as they do their duty. If Prince Mal kills them, that might solve any concerns that they would seek revenge for their parents' ousting… but Ellisif. Urgh!' he groaned. 'I can't just keep her here because she is my mistress. Most of the senior boyars have already voiced their discontent. They want her sent away with her parents and do not think she can be trusted. She couldn't have been involved. Could she?'

I stepped in front of him, 'Grand Prince.'

He looked down at me, his eyes a hollow icy-blue. 'Oh! Signe.' Oleg looked to Kjarr for an explanation, but my husband only shrugged.

'Would all be solved if Ellisif were married?' I asked. I didn't add *to you,* but I believed he would come to that conclusion himself. 'Then she would no longer belong to Heilagr and Estrid but to her new husband's family.'

'True,' he mused as he rubbed his chin and resumed his pacing.

'If you…' I began, but stopped when I caught the brief shake of Kjarr's head. *Not the right time to suggest their union,* I reminded myself, *maybe after Jol.*

Oleg stopped abruptly before Kjarr. 'Is it vengeance enough that I sent them away, Cousin?'

Kjarr took Oleg by the shoulders, and they looked each other in the eye. 'It will never be enough. My wife has been grievously offended.'

'We have already discussed this,' Oleg responded, shaking off Kjarr's grasp. 'You would not win against Heilagr and I cannot lose you.'

Yet Kjarr had fought against the renowned Drevlian champion, Yan, and won. It seemed Kjarr was on the verge of reminding his cousin of this before the Grand Prince slammed his fist on the game table. 'I forbid it.'

Kjarr picked at some imperceptible speck of dirt on his silk tunic. 'I would have liked to draw blood, Cousin, however, you have determined otherwise. I will obey.' His voice was as cold as the room and I crept towards the brazier for its warmth.

Oleg stood back from the table. 'You would have done it differently?'

Kjarr walked towards me, his eyes fixed on the small flame that flickered within the metal container. 'I would have slain Estrid and Heilagr. As for Gunnar, the repulsive pig, for him, I would reserve only the most painful of deaths,' he snarled.

Since the fire, Kjarr never left me alone. He had me follow him everywhere, his little tag-along. If I stepped from his sight for a moment, he worried, snatching me back as if I were a pouch of gold he thought would be stolen. It was one extreme to another, and I did not know if he did it to punish himself or me.

'Receiving their lands and silver goes some way to reparation,' Oleg tried to argue.

Kjarr turned, a low growl from his throat. 'Reparation?' he yelled. 'I don't want reparation. I want that man, if one calls such a creature that, to burn a hundred times over and even then, it still would not right the wrongs,' Kjarr screamed, red-faced. Spittle landed on the Grand Prince's cheek.

Oleg stepped back, his hand brushing away Kjarr's saliva. 'I understand your anger, Cousin,' Oleg replied soothingly, patting Kjarr on the back. 'But the man is sentenced to die, and it will be an inglorious death.'

Kjarr took a great inhale and calmed down.

I stepped past the table, close to Kjarr and Oleg. 'It should be my right to kill him.' My eyes were still blood-red, and to look upon my face was frightful.

Kjarr shook his head slowly. 'If this was Aldeigjuborg, you might have had your revenge.'

Oleg took my hand. 'He is not worth the time you take to lift your blade.'

'And certainly not the first blood Forlog-Enda should taste,' Kjarr added.

'His end will come soon,' Oleg explained. 'Justice must be done in the light, Signe. Gunnar will be executed, and everyone will know how traitors are punished in my lands.'

# THIRTY-FOUR

Smoke billowed from bonfires arranged outside the walls of Kyiv, tainting the crisp scent of freshly fallen snow. Acrid fumes rekindled memories of my burning warehouse, which was still so raw to my mind. The stain of ash was not long gone from my skin, nor the stink from my mouth and nose. But tonight, the rising pillars of smog ushered in the auspices of the Midwinter Solstice, not the harbinger of more trials. This was the night of the *blót*.

In the groves above the city, high on the plateaus to the west, we would honour our gods in the sacred place once inhabited by the Polianian gods. A site of towering oaks where they would relish in their blood offerings. Gunnar's life was to be sacrificed at their altars, and, though I doubted any of the Aesir would desire such a detestable soul, the Old Gods demanded blood to command their favour. And death was coming for Gunnar.

Early evening cloaked the land in shadows, ghastly silhouettes moving in the bonfire light. The walk from my rooms had me shivering. My teeth chattered in my head, but as we approached the pyres, the warmth of their flames brought the feeling back to my extremities. I wriggled each of my toes in my boots and remained at the front of the gathered crowd, waiting for my attacker to be led beneath the greatest of the oaks. There the snow had been cleared and the dormant undergrowth lay stiff and brown. Two guards stood alert, occasionally glancing at the hemp rope slung over a bough above their heads.

Odrun, wearing a heavy cape and deep hood, clasped my arm. She said nothing. Neither of us had spoken as we dressed in our warmest winter clothing. No words were exchanged as we made the slow march to the grove with the baying crowd. There was nothing to say. We both knew what was about to happen.

We heard him before we saw him. His howls seared the night as he was dragged around the thick oak trunk. Eskil and Sven hauled him by the arms through the white snow, his feet trailing behind him. He did not try to stand, or walk, but attempted to cling to anything and anyone as he passed by, hoping that it would spare him from this fate. People shrank away from his clawing grasp as Gunnar screamed and pleaded for mercy like a man with no shame. A criminal could harbour no hope of reaching Valhalla. All he would find was the crooked finger of the half-dead Lady Hel, beckoning him to her realm of darkness.

Neither Sven nor Eskil looked towards me as they held Gunnar in place, and I was glad for it. All that was left of me was my lightening blood-red eyes underlined by dark rings, a neck bearing the imprint of Kjarr's torc, and the bruises that still coloured my face. I knew Odrun's expression would have been as bland as mine, but I dared not drag my stare from Gunnar's pathetic begging as the men stopped below the length of rope. This is what Kyiv's court had gathered to see, a villain dangle. A death dance to Hel's jaunty tune as she summoned him to the shadowlands of Helheim. Life extinguished under the guise of giving to the gods. But all understood the message Oleg now sent; *go against me and mine, and you forfeit your life.*

Odrun's hand slipped into mine, and she squeezed. For a moment, I thought Ellisif would take my left hand, but she would not join us. Since her parents' banishment, she'd taken to her bed, weeping for their transgressions. It was Kjarr who brushed his fingers along the back of my hand as he strode to take his place beside his cousin.

Grand Prince Oleg presided over the gruesome show. He would allow none of his men to place the noose around Gunnar's neck. Oleg would do that.

Gunnar sobbed. He spoke no words as he fought against Oleg's touch. The ruler nodded to Sven and Eskil, and both held fast to Gunnar as Oleg looped the rope around his head. Gunnar jerked against them, thrashing until Eskil tied his hands behind his back, and the two of them stood back with the other guards. A better man might have accepted his fate and faced it with bravery, which at that last moment, might have put Gunnar in better stead with the gods. They liked to be entertained, after all. Gunnar was not such a man. His cowardice was detestable, a stain that could not be easily expunged. He snivelled horrendously as the hemp rope tightened. Tears streaked his beet-red face and the snot that flowed from his nose made him appear almost as disgustingly vile as he was inside. Gunnar's cries slowed to gasps and Odrun almost crushed my hand as we watched Oleg and Eskil pull on the rope, lifting Gunnar into the air. This, then, was not to be a quick dispatch. No one would kick a stool from under his feet, his neck would not swiftly crack. Gunnar would suffer.

Odrun spat on the ground, and I cursed his name. And still, we clasped hands. Our suffering flowed from one to the other, shared. Both of us were stronger now.

Gunnar dangled from the rope. Eyes bulging as he gasped for the night air. He twisted and thrashed. A wild kick. He tried to point his toes to reach the ground. Every movement, every attempt, was futile. He lifted his arms away from his back, ripping at the bindings, but the knot was stronger than his will to live. The rope dug deep into the skin of his neck, grinding against the soft flesh and drawing blood. It trickled onto his soiled tunic collar. Gunnar's shoulders sagged, and he bellowed like a beast to slaughter. Then he pissed himself.

Laughter rippled through the crowd as they watched the liquid trickle down his naked feet and drip onto the earth. But Odrun and I were not moved. I did not want to laugh. My eyes bored into those evil blue orbs, the same eyes that had enjoyed my fear as he pinned me to the ground. That same icy glare drank in Odrun's bare body when he kept her as a slave. No, I would not look away even when he garbled and dribbled.

Spittle pooled on his lips and trickled down his toad-like face. Gunnar searched the crowd with terrified eyes until they rested on Odrun and then me. He glanced between us, panic rising as if the hatred in our souls could cause him more pain. His mouth fell open, a rattling noise escaped his lips.

I felt my heart leap, and I bit the inside of my lip to stop the smile that curled at the edges of my mouth. I would not look away and, I knew, from her tightening grip, that Odrun felt the same. This was it. We would stay to watch his final breath. All the damage, all the pain Gunnar had caused, would die with him.

He jerked and spluttered. Blood moon eyes fixed on our faces. His bound hands went slack against his back and his legs kicked one last time. As his eyes glazed over, his pupils became full and black.

And Gunnar finally got what he deserved.

# THIRTY-FIVE

Runolf jolted me from my slumber.

My first thought was of the Khazar spies. 'Have they been caught?' I asked him, but as I became more alert, it made no sense why he would rouse only me to tell this news.

Runolf shook his head.

Kjarr startled, staring at Runolf's silhouette in the dark room. He reached for his sword. Nightmares plagued both of us. Kjarr tortured himself with *what-ifs* and I relived the flames of that incendiary night.

Runolf swore and backed away, holding his hands before him. 'It is only Lady Signe who is required, Boyar Hrolfsson,' Oleg's messenger whispered as he wiped the sweat on his brow. He explained himself in time to ease Kjarr's wrath and I gripped my husband's arm moments before he slashed out with the weapon.

'You should not go alone.' Kjarr put his blade down and reached for me as I threw a thick dress of wool over my head.

'She will not be alone,' Runolf asserted.

My husband rubbed the sleep from his eyes with his free hand. 'But this court has proved itself untrustworthy with one so precious as my wife.' He did not release his grip on my forearm.

'Runolf will assure my safety,' I said, as I extracted myself from his grasp.

The messenger nodded. 'This is a woman's matter, Boyar Hrolfsson. I suggest you seek Knyaz Oleg. He may have need of you.'

'At this time of night?' Kjarr asked. 'What could he possibly…'

I wrapped my cloak around my shoulders.

'We must go, Lady Signe.'

Runolf hadn't told me anything else as he led me into the frigid air. My bare feet padded along the cold ground and I wished I'd taken the time to put on shoes. It was dark as tar. Only the light from the sentries on the wall and the ensconced lights hanging from doorways lit the way. Black figures watching a flutter of fabric pass by in the immense gloom. I glanced up at the doors to the Great Hall. The Odin who looked down on me tonight seemed to know what I was walking into. The waves under the warships raged harder than before. I heard them roar along with the wind. Only it wasn't the wind, I realised as Runolf pushed the double doors open. Screams pierced the void. A woman, Ellisif, was experiencing a pain that could not be escaped.

In the hall, men who bunked in their alcoves were awake and gathered, discussing which tavern they should take themselves to as I walked by. Oleg's guards stood uneasy, helpless in the battle with the invisible force that caused Ellisif's suffering. Their swords and shields were useless to ease her pain, and their faces bore the consternation of their impotence. This was the women's world, where patience, calm, and quiet wisdom reigned.

Aware of the urgency, I raced past the dais and through to the partitioned room where I'd spent many nights hearing my husband counsel the Grand Prince. Ellisif's agony took on a distinct tone, a low bellow as she lost herself to her labours. The sound transported me to a memory I wished to never recall, the night Neflaug called upon my oath to bring her child into the world. My Freyja. I pushed away the thought, too painful to recall when Ellisif would need my mind whole to help her. Ellisif's wailing turned my blood cold as I pressed my hand to Oleg's chamber door.

'Frigg protect her,' I beseeched the goddess and stepped through the doorway and nodded to Runolf to take his leave.

Inside, the room was warm, the light and heat coming from the two braziers in opposite corners. Over one, an older woman recited the chants of birthing. *The Song of the Mother.* Words I had taught Helga before I left Aldeigjuborg. A tune I hoped had played a part in keeping her safe during the delivery of her twins.

Ellisif lay on the bed, panting.

A woman stuffing rags into a bucket by the wall spoke, 'It's too early.' She clicked her tongue as she squeezed the steaming excess water from a cloth.

Alfrunr was standing next to her, looking at me. She was already weeping. 'The Norns weave what they will,' she said. It was glib, but in a moment such as this, what more could she say?

The woman beside her rocked back and forth as she wrung the cloth again, though it was almost parched. 'It's too early,' she repeated. She sucked in her lips and tried not to cry. 'Why must the gods take them from us?'

Behind me, the door opened, and Licinia stepped over the threshold. 'Ellisif?' she called, taking long strides to the girl's bedside. 'I'm here.' She took Ellisif's hand in hers.

'My mother?' Ellisif managed between sobs.

Licinia shook her head, jet hair loose over her plum-coloured dress. 'Gone,' she replied, sliding her hands to Ellisif's elbow.

Poor Ellisif would not know the comfort of her mother again. Even if their relationship had been terse, there were times when a woman needed her mother, and this was one of them.

Licinia turned to beckon me over. 'Let's get you up.'

I took one arm and Licinia took the other, and together we guided Ellisif to the end of the bed, where Alfrunr had tied a rope from the post.

'Take the rope, just like the reins of your beautiful horse,' Licinia instructed. Ellisif wrapped the cord around her fist and sank back, pulling down on them as she cried out.

I took a bowl of water from the table next to the woman over the bucket, obviously grieving for her own lost children. She was too far in remembrance to be of any use to anyone. Over Ellisif's glistening brow, I sponged the cool water and let it drip down to soak her *serkr*. She opened her mouth, and I pushed the cloth to it as she bit down and sucked out the moisture. My hand massaged her sacrum, the bony space at the top of her backside that often ached when women laboured. Ellisif let out a guttural moan.

'That's it, my love,' Licinia cooed. She looked at me, tears beading on her long lashes. 'Not much longer.' We rubbed her back together, hands passing over one another's as the old woman chanted her song by the bedside.

Alfrunr brought more water.

'How long has she been like this?' I asked, keeping my voice low.

The girl was stunned, but tried to help as best she could. 'It began after the … ah… event,' she replied.

She almost certainly meant Ellisif's parents being declared outlaws. What else would cause such a reaction? 'Two days?' I clarified.

Alfrunr shook her head. 'At first, we thought it was something she ate. The pain was less intense, a slight cramping. But it got worse this evening, and that is when we sent for both of you.'

'The poor girl,' Licinia whispered. 'Sometimes women have pain and it passes if they rest, then they can keep the baby inside.'

Alfrunr shook her head again and led me by the arm to the brazier. 'Just before we sent Runolf to fetch you and Licinia, Ellisif's waters broke,' she explained.

I covered my mouth. Suddenly, I felt ill. 'We will need a lot of cloth,' I instructed Alfrunr, and sent her to gather the supplies we would need.

Alfrunr nodded at each item, then squeezed my hand. 'We must do our best for Ellisif,' she whispered. 'She hasn't had the chance to make any offerings or have the wise woman attend for the rituals. That's why I brought my mother's old nursemaid to sing the songs,' she finished, turning towards the stooping crone singing through all Ellisif's cries.

'Lady Signe. Please come. Something is happening,' Licinia called from the ground where she crouched, looking up Ellisif's dress. Licinia's gaze met mine, and she blinked slowly.

'More bowls and cloth,' I told Alfrunr, and she ran to grab them, shaking the other woman from her stupor. Together, they rushed to place them on the floor.

'Ellisif, you are so close now.' My voice was gentle as I reached up to rub her lower back. 'That's it. Breathe deep.'

Ellisif's moan was low as she sank her chin onto her chest and bore down. Her face grew red with each push. I looked between her legs. Where I expected the child's head, a foot emerged. I looked to Licinia and felt the panic rise.

'You must push. Harder, Ellisif. As hard as you can,' I urged her.

Alfrunr looked down at me. She saw the dread there. She tilted Ellisif forward, allowing the girl to fall back into her arms for support. 'Breathe now,' she told her friend.

Ellisif screamed, the sound fracturing the night as the baby's body was delivered, but the head was yet to appear.

'Again,' I called to her. 'You must push again.'

The child was stuck from the chest up, its arms, neck, and head had not yet emerged.

'Gods!' Licinia exclaimed, looking to me for guidance. She could entreat all the gods of our world if it meant Ellisif and her baby lived.

My teeth bit into my cheek as I considered what I would say. 'Ellisif, I must do something that will cause you pain,' I said, staring into her tear-stained face. 'Get something for her to bite on,' I instructed Alfrunr.

All she had was an old spindle, but it would do well enough to stop Ellisif from grinding or breaking her teeth.

'Keep her still,' I cautioned the women, and each took a leg or arm.

When I was much younger, my mother helped a woman birthing her fourth child. By the time a mother had that many children they knew what to expect but, just like Ellisif's baby, her's had come out by the feet. I had been a young girl assisting my mother then, but I recalled standing aside, in shock, watching as my mother first slipped the child's arm out before she rotated to do the same on the other side. After that, the shoulders emerged with some coaxing, and then the head, which had to be delivered quickly or else the child might suffocate. This was knowledge passed to my mother from her own mother, a woman who had delivered one of her babies in the same manner, though that child had not lived. The child my mother had brought into the world had survived and it was that success which now gave me hope as I performed the movements.

Both the arms and shoulders came free by my hand. 'Push, push, push!' I called to Ellisif. 'It's just the head to come.'

Licinia held what was exposed of the child's body in her outstretched hands. It was tiny. And it was a boy. An heir for the Grand Prince.

Ellisif pushed with a mighty effort, and her son dropped free of her. There was a collective sigh as Alfrunr wiped Ellisif's brow and the old woman came forward to cut the cord with a knife of jet. Licinia and I sat with the child between us on a pile of clean fabric.

Ellisif lay back on the bed. 'Why doesn't he cry?' she asked once her sobs had slowed.

'Because he does not breathe,' I responded, my mouth dry as I formed the words. 'The cord has wrapped around his neck and strangled him before he could take a breath.' I couldn't lie to her. There was nothing to be gained from delaying the truth.

Licinia held the boy's small hand. His body was the colour of bilberries. So tiny. Almost skeletal. The child's eyes were closed, mouth puckered as if to stifle his first cry. Gently, I unloosed his fragile neck from the cord that encircled it and laid him, sleeping, in Licinia's hands.

'Elli,' she began, addressing her young charge like a child once more. 'He will not live. I'm so sorry.'

Ellisif pushed herself from the bed. 'Give him to me,' she snapped, holding out her hands.

We wrapped her baby in a square of soft linen, swaddling him as newborns often liked to be. His mother snatched him into her arms and began rubbing him all over, breathing over his exposed face. She held him as she lowered herself onto the bed.

'Child of Oleg,' she spoke to him. 'Olegsson,' she began, but shook herself. 'Not Oleg, for that was the name he took to rule his people. If the gods are to know you, they must know your father by his name.' Ellisif looked towards me, and I nodded reassuringly. 'Child of Helgi. Helgisson,' she commanded, tucking her finger beneath the linen and stroking the translucent skin of her son. 'Helgisson, you will live!' Ellisif peered up, desperation clouding her eyes. Her lip quivered and her eyes darted between her attending ladies. 'I forbid you to die!' she cried, holding the child tight.

Licinia came to stand by her. 'He is gone, Elli.'

'I refuse to acknowledge it. This is the son of the mighty warlord, Oleg. Warrior and ruler of our people. His child cannot die,' she commanded, ignoring her previous maid. 'Signe!' Ellisif called. 'Go to Oleg, and bring him to me. His son will live if his father demands it. Run!'

I didn't know what to do. The child was gone; he was unmoving in her arms. Nothing I did now was going to change that, but I wanted some way to bring Ellisif comfort and if bringing Oleg to tell her the same would do that, I would gladly go. Alfrunr and Licinia stared at me, knowing this errand was madness.

'Run!' Ellisif screamed.

I sprinted from the rooms and ran to the only place I thought Oleg would be. He had left the use of his rooms to Ellisif and cleared his halls. Once Kjarr had found him, I knew he would have brought him back to our lodgings. Up the stairs, I raced, flinging the door open with such strength I expected it to splinter. Oleg was there, sitting beside Kjarr, slumped in his chair.

'Grand Prince,' I said as I caught my breath. I sank low before him. 'Ellisif is asking for you.'

'How is she?' Kjarr asked in a monotonous tone.

'Well enough.'

Oleg didn't look at me. His eyes stared fixedly into the flames of the glowing brazier. His jaw was set as he bit his lower lip. I glanced at Kjarr, sitting beside his cousin, and the blank expression he wore told me the Grand Prince was unreachable. Instead of the Grand Prince, I turned my attention to Kjarr.

'Husband, Ellisif has delivered a boy,' I informed him.

'A boy?' Kjarr asked, glancing at Oleg. 'A boy, Cousin. Do you hear? How is the child?'

'He does not cry,' I said, hoping they would both understand what I meant by the comment. 'She asks that the Grand Prince comes to see his son.'

'Does not cry?' Kjarr queried. His eyes widened as the comprehension set in.

'Ellisif asks you to come and command your son to live, Grand Prince,' I spluttered. All this repetition was wasting time. Ellisif would be frenzied with worry, and I was terrified of the state she would be in upon my return.

I prostrated myself before the Grand Prince. 'Oleg, please come. Ellisif is beside herself with grief. Perhaps if you…' I begged.

Oleg swallowed hard as he raised his hand and looked at me. 'No, Signe.'

'No?' I repeated, brow furrowed as I lifted my head.

Kjarr helped me to my feet. 'Cousin, it might bring her some comfort to see you. Would you not see your son?'

Oleg cleared his throat. 'Living or dead, I cannot have a child; no less a son.'

I stared disbelievingly at those vacant blue eyes, lighter and icier than ever. 'You do not need to acknowledge the child to go to her.

Ellisif needs…' I trailed off, too shocked at his insistence to deny my friend any comfort.

'I cannot,' he repeated, looking back into the flames. They danced over his face, casting long shadows.

'What should I tell her?' I managed, clinging to my husband's arm. He gripped me as if his life depended on it.

'Whatever you will,' he responded coldly, and I was relieved his piercing eyes were no longer upon me. 'If you need to tell her anything, tell her the Grand Prince wishes her good health soon.'

I gaped at him, uncomprehending of his callousness. 'And of your son?'

His lengthy silence made me think he would not answer. Oleg's hand clasped his knee, and he flicked his eyes to mine for an instant. In them, I saw the caring, love-fond man I had come to know, and then he blinked and all of that was gone, replaced by a frozen heart and a ruthless mind.

'May the gods ease her suffering,' he replied.

'Grand Prince,' I uttered, sinking low and biting my tongue. Oh! How I wanted to scold him. To shake him from this insensibility. Instead, I turned on my heel and retraced my steps back to Ellisif at the Great Hall. It felt like a much longer journey than it had in the middle of the night. The sun was rising. A splash of colour drenched the sky with its amber hues, but it didn't seem beautiful in the least. Back at the hall, I looked up at Odin, atop the intricate carving on the doors, and snarled at the Allfather.

*How could Oleg, who said he loved Ellisif so completely, deny her in her time of need?* Would he be punished for it? Only the Norns would determine that.

I braced myself as I entered the room. Alfrunr and Licinia knew as soon as I stepped through the door that I was alone. They looked to Ellisif.

'Where is he?' she demanded, still holding her son as she reclined against the bedhead.

'He could not come,' I replied. *How could I tell her Oleg's true reaction?*

Ellisif glared, waiting for further explanation. Her golden hair matted against her skull, her dress drenched in sweat. She seemed to have aged in one night, much older than her fifteen years. 'Did you tell him I bore him a son?' she asked, as if that would make any difference.

I nodded and said the only thing of value Oleg had spoken. 'The Grand Prince wishes you to be well and prays the gods will ease your suffering soon.'

'My suffering? It is our suffering. His son! HIS SON!' she raged, sitting up and holding the bundled child against her chest. 'You told him it is his son, didn't you?'

My heart hammered. 'Of course, Ellisif.'

She howled.

Give me blood and battle, that I could face with resolve, but the devastated cries of my friend distraught at the loss of her first baby and spurned by her lover were too much to bear.

'I'm sorry, Ellisif,' I mumbled feebly.

There was an inescapable sinking sensation as she screamed, 'Why?' over and over. A voice inside told me I already knew the answer, and the realisation made me sick.

# Thirty-Six

## Jol 883 CE

'Are you sure you're ready to do this?' I asked Odrun as I fixed her golden-brown braids into place with thread and bone pins. She smoothed her hand over the arrangement and looked at herself in the palm-sized piece of polished bronze she'd purchased from an itinerant merchant.

'Are you?' she responded, setting the reflective surface on the table.

Her amber eyes glowed in the brazier light as if they contained the golden gemstone. I held her gaze. My pale blue eyes were no longer marred by veins of blood. My appearance had returned to normal, though the scar on my right temple would always be there. The marks may have faded, but the hurt I carried inside had not. Since Ellisif lost her son, she had shut me out. I wasn't the only one. She excluded everyone from her presence, and I felt it keenly, since I had delivered Oleg's harsh rebuff.

'Of course,' I tried to sound undaunted.

Odrun stood, the deep green fabric of her dress unfurling to the floor. Around the neckline, she had painstakingly embroidered petals and leaves in costly gold thread. She took my hand.

'Boyar Hrolfsson's assurances that the Grand Prince is content with the arrangement is my only concern,' she spoke formally, 'though it is your happiness that matters more.'

I squeezed her hand. A stronger bond had formed between us since the warehouse fire, and even more so after Gunnar's hanging.

'I will be happy when I leave this place,' I replied.

She beamed. 'You and me both.'

Odrun wrapped one of my marten fur-lined cloaks around her shoulders and headed towards the door.

'Wait. I have something for you.' My hands shook as I picked up the golden torc Kjarr had gifted me when I'd first arrived in Kyiv. I passed it to her.

She took it. 'I thought you said it would go to the gods.'

I pressed her fingers around the band. 'They will understand.'

Odrun looked up at me. 'But will your husband?'

These days, Kjarr kept me closer than his shadow and, for all the attention he gave me, none of it felt like the closeness we previously enjoyed. Worse, he seemed to believe that instead of continuing with my journey to Miklagard with Sihtric, I would be safer staying with him in Kyiv. Still, he had accepted my promise never to wear the thing again. He knew it represented too much suffering for me to keep it.

'I hope you don't take offence at the gift, given what Gunnar did with it.' I didn't think that made it cursed, just filled with painful memories. 'Aside from beads, which are commonplace, it's the only piece of jewellery that would be worthy of you tonight.'

Odrun loosed her cape, exposing the welts around her neck from her time in chains. 'It will cover the scars I have long hidden with that hideous wadmal cape.'

'Perhaps we should burn it,' I suggested.

A genuine laugh rang out from her. 'What a pagan thing to say.'

I shrugged. 'It might help you forget Gunnar and what he did.'

Her eyes went cold, the smile left her lips. 'I do not fear Gunnar, Signe, nor his spirit. He does not haunt my dreams anymore and he cannot hurt me, though this,' she said, holding the metal to the light, 'will hide the marks he left on my body.' She wrapped the torc around her neck. It hid the scars well.

She made to turn away, but hesitated. 'I'll have it blessed by a priest. Just in case,' she added, stroking a finger along the swirling pattern.

I laughed. 'What a Christian thing to say.'

Odrun reached for my hand. I felt her tremble. 'Are you scared?'

Her free hand pulled her deep hood over her head, careful to avoid messing the pile of braids there.

'I'm here. I won't leave you until we reach the Great Hall,' I promised.

She nodded. 'And then I must do this on my own.'

On the threshold of the Great Hall, Odrun's hooded figure stood gazing up at the carvings surrounding the double doors. She turned to the guard and gestured for them to be opened. Light streamed out into the night, illuminating her outline. She untied my cape from around her shoulders.

'Enjoy this,' I whispered, as I took the fur-lined garment in my arms. She nodded without turning and stepped into the warm orange glow.

The people at the back of the hall were the first to notice her, gaping at Odrun's crown of golden hair. Where her wadmal cape had once covered her collarbones, now a torc of gold lay, the mark of the wealthy and honoured. It sparkled in the firelight, catching the glowing flames in its metal.

If anyone recognised her, they did not voice it. All seemed too shocked by the stunningly angular features of the foreign beauty before them. Taking advantage of the crowd's distraction, I slipped into the hall and made my way past the alcoves as I moved toward the dais. I glanced over my shoulder in time to see Odrun assessing the room. She inclined her head to Runolf, who stood inside the main doors at the bottom of the aisle.

He made the announcement I had been waiting to hear since Egbert handed me the translated letter with its strange seal of red wax.

'Knyaz. Court of Kyiv. I present to you Princess Gerberga of the Western Franks.'

Everyone gasped. Ranveg gawped like a fish out of water. Eskil's eyes were wider than the width of his belly. Sihtric's hand went to his chest, as if the very sight of the Princess would stop his heart from beating. I wished I could have seen Björn and Frodi's reaction but could not find them among the crowd. The noble Drevlian hostages, Niskinnin, Kstianin, and Ostromyr, barely raised their dark eyebrows as they schooled their faces blank. No one imagined Odrun... *No! Not*

*Odrun,* I reminded myself, *Gerberga.* No one imagined Gerberga was anything other than Odrun, the slave girl.

My eyes searched the hall for Egbert, and I found him on the lower benches with the other servants. He was beaming, a smile from ear to ear as he watched his friend stride gracefully into the hall. She was resplendent in her gown of deep nettle green and curtseyed before the Grand Prince. Oleg played his part brilliantly. He walked forward, holding his hands out to her as he looked her over with nothing but pure joy on his face. She bowed to him again before he spoke.

'We are pleased to receive word from King Carloman that come spring, a ransom will be sent for his cousin's freedom. Upon the laws of war, they will deliver this handsome sum to Boyar Hrolfsson's wife, Signe, for the protection she gave you all those months on the river road and ever since. Princess Gerberga will discharge her debt.'

I almost scoffed as I took my place next to Kjarr. Gerberga never owed me anything. Not in her present form, nor her previous life as Odrun. I would have done it all for free because it was right. But Gerberga had been insistent that I be rewarded for liberating her from the malicious Gunnar.

'I will be forever grateful,' she told me. 'You have kept my secrets, even when you didn't understand what they really meant. Even if they might have cost you more than you were willing to pay.'

Soon, I would have a friend in the Frankish court but, more importantly, Gerberga was free and would go home.

'Come and sit by me as my guest of honour, Princess,' Oleg invited Gerberga to the high table.

Gerberga's eyes twinkled as she rose from her low bow. She took the steps up the dais with such grace as she was born to display. She passed by Ellisif, seated at the low table below the raised platform. The young woman glowered at Princess Gerberga with an expression that bore a distinct resemblance to the one her mother often wore.

Oleg offered his hand as Gerberga took her seat. She turned to the Grand Prince and granted him her sweetest smile. 'It pleases me greatly to be here, Grand Prince.'

# Thirty-Seven

Jol wasn't quite as merry as it should have been. With the Drevlian peace holding thanks to the noble captives, and missives arriving from other tribes open to negotiations, the court, and the Grand Prince ought to have been elated. But the buoyant happiness Oleg experienced during his relationship with Ellisif had vanished when they severed ties. He waded through melancholy in the days since the loss of their child, though tonight's observers would think it all a distant memory as he chatted merrily with Princess Gerberga. He poured cups of mead for them both and waved to attendants to begin the dancing. Ellisif continued to play the part of the adoring subject, covering her shattered self with a mask of contentment, despite her earlier scowling. She tried to catch the Grand Prince's eye. That much was clear from the way her golden locks bounced as she danced with a young man in red. Her gown of vibrant green, her favourite colour, was belted high to disguise the bulge that remained and might not subside for some time.

Oleg refused to be ensnared, busying himself in discussion with various boyars as he drank himself around the room. He pointedly looked in the opposite direction. Although it was clear from his posture, he felt the pull of his previous lover's presence. I chewed on my bottom lip as I watched the farce. Ellisif twirled and wove through the other women before clasping hands with her partner once more. Her movements belied the discomfort she must have felt being out of bed so soon.

'Some women heal faster,' Alfrunr had said, but I saw the grimace Ellisif made when she thought she was unobserved.

It hurt her to be here, emotionally and physically. Even more so when she watched Grand Prince Oleg take Princess Gerberga's hand

and lead her into a dance. When the music faded into the next tune, Gerberga excused herself. She was ill at ease with such attentiveness.

The Great Hall brimmed with people gathered for the Jol feast and, I suspected, more came to see the truth of the rumours that flowed through Kyiv's social circles. From the connections Gerberga made in other households, who now whispered news to me for a fee, I'd learned some spoke of a secret marriage between Oleg and Ellisif. A dangerous untruth to repeat. Estrid's repurposed thralls also disclosed reports that Ellisif was dead or grievously ill following the stillbirth. Her appearance tonight set eyes wide with wonder as the court questioned whether they imagined the relationship and pregnancy. They would never know the weight of keeping up appearances like Ellisif did. Much too young for such pain, I wondered how deep those scars would run and what grip they would hold on her life.

I watched as Ellisif tipped her head back and laughed. Not her usual, unbridled laughter, but a false chuckle forced from her throat. She was carried off in a swirl of fabric as she joined hands with a chain of ladies, winding their way through the hall in a dance. They wove around tables, past the hearths, as smoke wafted upwards in tendrils of grey. The smell still reminded me of the warehouse fire, though the cinders had been swept away, and rebuilding had begun, but the memories were burned into me like a brand against the skin.

Kjarr sensed my discomfort and slid his hand under the table to clasp mine. 'Do you want to dance?' he asked.

I shook my head. 'I'm happy sitting here.'

Kjarr gripped my hand tighter than a dying warrior, in search of Valhalla, would cling to his blade. 'Ellisif is putting on quite a show,' he mumbled under his breath.

I didn't reply. The heat from the braziers and hearth fires burning made the room stifling, and with so many people packed into the hall, there were hardly enough places at the benches. I suddenly felt as if I could not breathe. Kjarr refilled his cup and watched the dancers. Ellisif and her chain of beautiful ladies snaked their way through the press of bodies as if they had not a care in the world. Sveineld the Younger, with an uncharacteristic amount of gaiety, joined hands with Ellisif and another woman, linking the line of dancers into a circle. His sandy-brown hair whipped as he sidestepped with them. A celebration such as this would not be had when he became Pleskov's Posadnik and he appeared eager to enjoy it while he could. Alfrunr was also enjoying the night's festivities. She had excelled in her position as lady of the hall. As Oleg's kin, she oversaw the decorations, kitchen, and the night's entertainment.

An extraordinary number of shields were displayed on the walls. Some I recognised with the colours and emblems of Kyiv's prominent families, others were unknown to me and may have come from the stores held at the armoury. Alfrunr had selected lengths of fabric in shades of green, red, and gold, to hang between the columns. For her, this night marked her official entry into the court. Her uncle, Oleg, had determined she had reached an appropriate age to be presented, and she radiated with pride as she twirled alongside Ellisif. Alfrunr broke off from the chain, as the next steps in the dance were taken in couplings. Each pair held hands, as other couples wove, under and over, with their neighbours. Tolze took her for a dance partner and stooped to pass under Boyar Leifr and his wife, Ranveg. The men passed through first, pulling their woman along after them. Tolze looked back over his shoulder at Alfrunr and gave her a beaming smile. Kjarr must have noticed, too, and he squeezed my hand once more. His scent of amber and moss grew stronger as he kissed me on the cheek. I believed it when he said he would be a better husband to me. At least I wanted it to be true.

In the days after the fire, and even more so since Ellisif's sorrow, Kjarr had been by my side. He'd come to prepare the site of the warehouse fire, scavenging through the wreck to discover anything that could be salvaged. He made excuses with the Grand Prince, begging leave to walk with me outside the city walls. Yesterday, we strolled through the fresh snow to the grassy hill that overlooked the shipyard and selected a place to rebuild. Try as he did, I could not shake off the feeling that he had often chosen to stand by Oleg instead of me, and it caused me to doubt him.

Grand Prince Oleg, who had resumed his seat at the high table, rose. His silk finery threw different shades of red in the flame-light as he raised a hand to address the gathering. At once, the music ceased, and the dancers stilled. Those with seats left to find them, all breathless and full of joy. My stomach grumbled as I smelled the food that streamed in. Oleg said nothing as he watched the procession. Plates, that before arriving in Kyiv, I would have believed only the gods could have conjured. Glistening joints of meat and porridges of pork and onion sprinkled with green herbs came in the first wave. Thralls were laden with enormous plates that were placed at the high table first before they lay platters of lesser cuts on the lower trestle planks. Next came the piles of flatbread, warm and inviting. I slid one off the heap and chewed into the pillowy dough. Whoever milled the flour so fine had patience I couldn't dream of, and whichever cook had griddled each round had done so with a skilful hand. Small bowls of dried fruit followed, another of nuts, and all washed down with copious amounts of mead. The sweet aroma of honey tangled with the delicious scent of the newest platter placed before me, a stew of venison.

For days I had been avoiding food, because of the nausea from the fire, or the despair growing in the pit of my stomach. Kjarr had warned me about visiting Ellisif as Oleg pulled away from her. But it didn't sit right with me. Ellisif had done nothing wrong. She was simply a girl used and discarded by a powerful man who decided that it was the time to do so. No longer favoured by the Grand Prince, Ellisif took her seat at a lower table while Princess Gerberga sat in Ellisif's usual seat by Oleg's side. Ellisif chatted with a boyar and his wife, passing a flatbread to the brown-haired woman. She nestled her chin on her shoulder, glancing at the high table. I caught her eye and offered a sympathetic smile, which she returned, scrunching her nose with feigned mischief.

Next to my husband, Oleg's shoulders were tense, and I would have bet my last piece of silver his teeth were gritted inside that noble mouth of his. For days, I'd wanted to shake him, wake him up, and remind him of how much he needed Ellisif. It was no use. Where he was once receptive to my suggestions, he was now lost to his plotting and planning. *At least he allowed Ellisif to remain at court.* I tried to comfort myself with the thought. Where she went next was anyone's guess. Her brothers might find her a husband when they returned from Prince Mal's court.

'Stop worrying. I don't think your brow can furrow any more than it is,' Kjarr whispered, running his thumb along the back of my hand.

I smoothed the lines of my forehead and scooped some venison stew into my bowl, breathing its heady aroma. It was the only thing I found comforting about the night.

Kjarr returned to his discussion with Oleg. Tolze leaned back to speak with Oleg and Kjarr, as Alfrunr leaned forward to examine Gerberga's intricate embroidered neckline. Across the room, Sven's gaze blazed a path through the crowd. I'd been all too aware of him tonight, more so with Licinia seated next to him, her arm draped over his as she laughed at one of Sihtric's jokes. My friend had disliked my husband before they had even met, and now that they had exchanged words, he hated him all the more. Sven was convinced Kjarr could not protect me and was undeserving of my loyalty. I knew it was not a lack of ability that prevented Kjarr's retaliation. That much was clear when I'd seen him kill Yan in the battle against the Drevlians. It all came down to where Kjarr placed regard, and until now, that had not been with me.

Pretty, dark-haired, Licinia leaned across the table to pick up a pitcher of ale. Sven looked away as she whispered something in his ear and filled his cup. He turned back, raising it towards me with a grin that was both leering and deliberate. In return, I offered a scowl that failed to offend. Licinia, unable to distract Sven, returned to her conversation with Sihtric, cackling much too loudly at a joke I would wager was not that funny. Sven tapped two fingers against his chest in some gesture I didn't understand. *Already drunk, no doubt.*

Kjarr shifted in his seat. 'What was that about?' he asked, motioning to Sven, who had dropped his eyes to the food before him.

'I don't know,' I answered, and I reached for one more flatbread. This time, I dipped it into the rich venison stew.

'I'm not sure I like him,' he replied, nodding towards Sven, who was engaged in a drinking game with Eskil.

'A mutual feeling, I suspect.'

Kjarr poured me another cup. By court etiquette, it should have been me serving him, but he was putting in an effort. 'Would you agree if I asked you to stay away from the man?'

'No,' I answered. 'He'll be with us when we go to Miklagard and you have no reason to question his fealty, as he's sworn to Oleg and has served him these many months.'

Kjarr grasped his face with his hand, leaning his elbow on the table. 'Isn't that woman,' he began, pointing to Licinia, 'Sihtric's woman? She seems more interested in Sven.' He said my friend's name with a hiss.

'I thought you would have discussed it with Sihtric by now.'

Kjarr shook his head.

'You've been too busy, I suppose,' I added.

'Am I that predictable?' he asked, pouring me another cup after I downed the first.

'You're asking the wrong questions, Husband,' I replied dryly.

He stared across the room for a while, watching Sihtric banter with the men and women around him. It had been hard for Sihtric, too. Before we left Aldeigjuborg, he warned me I might not like it here, and for him, Kyiv would never be home. He liked the freedom and distance that Aldeigjuborg provided.

Kjarr's mind was working overtime to understand. 'Sihtric doesn't even like…'

'Hush,' I cautioned him as he came to the realisation. 'Sven and Licinia took a liking to each other and Sihtric permitted it,' I explained, and for once, I did not feel the sting of jealousy. Sven had been a good friend, and he deserved to be happy.

Kjarr sat back, more relaxed than before, and slid an arm around my waist. He drew me closer. 'I should visit Sihtric,' he began. 'I've neglected my friends for too long.'

Kjarr planted a soft kiss on my cheek before releasing me.

Beside us, Oleg cleared his throat. I thought he might reprimand Kjarr's display of affection, but his eyes were not on us. He was looking out to the crowd as four kitchen thralls carried a heavy platter into the hall. On top of the gleaming metal was the Jol boar, billowing steam emanated from it as it was delivered fresh from the kitchen fires. Its crackling skin was parched from roasting, and rivulets of liquid fat ran down the sides of the beast. The thralls puffed as they struggled to the high table, where a space had been cleared for the pig. Oleg let it rest there while he stood to address his court.

'Before we swear oaths on the Jol boar, I have some announcements to make,' he began, voice filling the hall and quieting the din.

Everyone filled their cups, anticipating the toasts to come.

'As it is the time for gifts and celebrations, let me begin with this; to honour his alliance with us, and the wealth of knowledge he brings from the Khazar court, Tolze, previously Tarkhan Tuvan, will be henceforth known as Boyar Tolze.'

At first, the crowd was silent. Wives pushed cups toward their husband's mouths to stop them from objecting.

'Boyar Tolze will be instrumental in overthrowing the Khazars and seeking tribute from other Slavic tribes. He will be appointed as my advisor in the matter and forsake any allegiance he has with the Khazar people. To seal this, I give him the title of boyar with lands of his own, and the hand of my niece, Alfrunr, who he will wed in the spring,' he finished.

A ripple of discontent ran along the tables. Many of the senior boyars had harboured hopes of the Princess marrying their son. Oleg hinted at this weeks ago, and I had seen the smiles between the pair which told me they too had warning. Alfrunr, along the high table, lowered her gaze, a soft smile upon her mouth, and even in the low light of the evening, I saw the pretty blush on her cheeks. Seated next to her, between herself and Gerberga, was Tolze. I had to remind myself of his Mari name after calling him Tuvan since he arrived. Tolze sat straight-backed, proud, and beneath it, happy. For them, this would be a love match, and a springtime wedding would be the lift the court needed before they began their campaign against the Radimichs.

Well wishes rang out until Oleg raised his hand. 'There has been much speculation regarding me taking a wife.'

Ellisif's head shot up. Her lips twitched as if she wanted to smile for the first time in weeks and, in her eyes, I saw a glimmer of hope.

'With my niece marrying Boyar Tolze, the Great Hall, and the people will have a Lady of Kyiv. As you see,' Oleg said, gesturing to the room's decorations, 'Alfrunr has done an exemplary job of tonight's event, and as my closest kin she will maintain this position until Prince Igor marries and assumes the throne.'

I couldn't bear to look at the disappointment on Ellisif's face.

'Sveineld Sveineldsson, please stand,' Oleg commanded, and the young Boyar did as he was bid. 'As you all know, Sveineld Sveineldsson leaves us for Pleskov in the spring, but I could not let you leave for that outpost without a suitable partner. A gem of the court.' Oleg cleared his throat. His gaze settled for a moment beyond my eyeline, but he moved on. 'Sveineld will take Ellisif Heilagrsdottir to wife,' he added, almost so fast I couldn't take it in. 'It will be a double wedding. My niece, Alfrunr, to Tolze. Ellisif to Sveineld,' he clarified with a clap of his hands.

Sveineld nodded in thanks, clearly advised ahead of time of his impending nuptials, but Ellisif was incredulous, eyes boiling vats of hatred. She was his ward, without parents to object on her behalf. Her brothers, the only ones who might rally against the union, were far away in Malyn. As an unwed woman, she could do nothing more than express her unwillingness, but who knew where that would get her? With a family who were declared outcasts, her options would be limited and a marriage to Sveineld was a lofty match for a woman in her position. It was a clear declaration from Oleg that he was unilaterally ending their relationship.

'You all agree with these unions?' he asked, as if anyone had a say.

Tolze and Alfrunr agreed readily, as did Sveineld. When Oleg's gaze settled on his previous mistress, she frowned, her bottom lip quivering as she held back the tears.

'Knyaz,' she began, schooling both her face and her voice, 'you honour me with this union,' she lied. 'But…'

The court held its breath. The Grand Prince drew back as if he anticipated her saying something that would shame them both.

'May I make a request?' she asked, sweeping her gleaming hair off her shoulder.

Oleg inclined his head, but his eyes were wary.

'I ask my Knyaz for Licinia, my previous maid. Would you consider returning her to me so that she will bring me comfort in my new life as Pleskov's lady?'

Relieved, Oleg nodded, 'Of course,' he agreed and clapped his hands together again before reaching for his cup. 'Congratulations.' Oleg raised his drink, toasting the couple, and opened the oath giving for the night.

I excused myself from the high table's company and raced to intercept Ellisif as she burned a path to the doors of the Great Hall. She was oblivious to my presence until I grabbed her arm and she spun around to glower at me.

'Oh, it's you,' she gasped as her shoulders relaxed. 'Looks like I'm being sent off to the wilderness,' she complained as she pushed through a group standing by some roast deer. 'After everything that has happened, I would not have expected him to be so cold.'

I followed her as she collected another jug of mead from a passing thrall. She drank from the spout.

There was nothing I could say. Such was the whim of a ruler.

'How could he do this to me?' she demanded, dragging me into a dark alcove.

People along the tables drank and feasted, ignoring Ellisif and me behind them. I looked around as if the faces in the crowd would be of some help. No one could make this right. My heart thudded, and in my ears a stark whooshing sound like the tide sucking waves back to the ocean.

'I never imagined he would do this.' My voice cracked as my heart broke for her. Barely up from her childbed and so poorly treated that I thought she might not survive the night. 'When I discussed your marriage with Oleg, he made me think it would be you he wed.'

Ellisif's eyes blazed, lip snarling, and nostrils flared. 'What did you do?' she seethed as she set the jug down on a shelf and turned to face me.

I stepped back. 'Didn't you want to marry him?' I asked, but as I voiced the question, I realised how ridiculous the notion was. Grand Prince Oleg would never have married Ellisif. She knew that.

She shook her head. 'How would marrying me solve anything? You're new to court, Signe, but even you should have understood that he could not take a bride.'

I stuttered some unintelligible sounds.

Ellisif continued as if I had not tried to speak. 'If Oleg did that,' she hissed, trying to keep her words from being overheard, 'his people would think he was usurping the throne from Igor.'

'I didn't think,' I replied. All I had imagined were two people uniting in love.

Ellisif softened, turning her head and taking a deep inhale. When she spoke again, her voice was tight but had lost its harshness. 'I was content to live by his side and bear his bastard children. It's all I wanted.'

That I understood. But in her innocence, she hadn't appreciated that the choice was not hers to make. It was his, unfair as that was. 'That's not all your parents wanted,' I replied. 'Once their schemes were unearthed, he had no choice,' I added, then scowled when I heard myself defending him. 'The alternative was to exile you with your parents.'

'That might have been preferable,' she snapped at me. Ellisif shrugged off my placating hand.

'Perhaps I can speak with Kjarr, and maybe he can…'

'You've done enough,' she replied, shaking her head as she backed into the shadows. Her face was a mask again. 'Leave me alone, Signe.' Ellisif strode off, picking up the jug from the shelf and resuming her place by Sveineld, expertly filling his cup to the brim. Her features were still, eyes downcast as if shy. *The perfect player.* Her eyes flicked up, and Ellisif glared at me across the room, turning my blood to ice in my veins. She was not a woman I wanted as an enemy, and I wished to all the gods that I'd never said a word to Oleg, never put the thought into his head.

At the high table, Oleg ate, ignorant of Ellisif's suffering as he served Princess Gerberga. I hated him for what he did to Ellisif. He finished his mouthful and stood before the long line of men who waited to touch their hands to the beast on the platter before the Grand Prince and make their New Year promises. Oleg went first. Kjarr handed me another cup of mead as I resumed my seat, and I downed it to dampen my regret.

'My Jol oath,' Oleg began, 'is this. In order to fulfil the oath I swore to Rurik, Grand Prince before me, I shall never take a bride. I will acknowledge no child, never take one to my knee as my own, so long as I shall live. This, I do for the good of our people, and the safe accession of the heir, Igor,' he said, waving an open hand in the child's direction. Igor's nursemaids trotted the young child out whenever his presence was required.

Oleg stepped aside and let Kjarr approach the boar. Kjarr placed a hand on its backside. 'I, Kjarr Hrolfsson, swear to be Oleg's kinsman all my days, to never desert him, to be forever stalwart in my support.' He sent a grin towards his cousin and bowed his head to cement the promise.

Other senior boyars followed, promising this and that, inconsequential to me as I continued drowning my sorrows with cups of mead. Then Sven stepped up to the dais, Sihtric pulling at his sleeve as if to stop him, but failed when the larger man brushed him aside.

'I, Sven Hakonsson, swear by the gods that the Norns wove together Astrid of Karlstad and me,' he began.

My breath caught. Kjarr's eyes bore into Sven's profile, but my friend kept his head down, hand upon the pig.

He continued, 'I will be hers until the end of time, past Ragnarok, when all things are dark, there I will remain by her side.'

From her position at one of the low tables, Licinia watched Sven with unease before a realisation dawned on her face and her gaze flicked to me. My cheeks burned. Listeners were confused, all unaware of the object of Sven's affection. All but Kjarr, who looked at me in outrage. Most of the audience would have believed Sven left some pretty girl in Svealand and was heartsick over her absence. They weren't entirely wrong.

Bile rose in my throat as I excused myself from the bench. I couldn't stand this place for a moment longer; the pretence or the deception. Kjarr's hand caught mine as I passed him. 'We go together,' he warned, and we headed for the main doors.

Sveineld was making his oath as we walked the length of the aisle, something about being an exemplary Posadnik of Pleskov and honouring his new wife and his lord. Sven disappeared. Likely sensing a poor reception to his oath. Kjarr was incandescent in his wake. He stormed ahead and dropped my hand as he pushed out of the hall without looking back.

Licinia pulled me towards her. She studied me with her gemstone-green eyes. Her dark hair was fixed in braids, some up, some down, and her dress of red was belted tight to accentuate her small waist. She blinked, considering her words before she spoke. 'It almost makes sense, Lady Signe,' she began. 'Sven was forever looking toward the shipyards. Did you know you can see them from Sihtric's residence? When I asked him about it, he told me he liked to watch the swans sometimes. I gave it no mind until now, *Svanr.*' Licinia said the name in my mother tongue and offered me a knowing smile.

*Sven be damned. Why did he have to be so dramatic?*

Swearing on the Jol boar was considered unbreakable. Men died for leaving them unfulfilled, even if they were made from the bottom of an ale jug. Some even exiled themselves rather than complete a promise sworn to steal a woman or win a kingdom. It was not to be done lightly. An oath to support one's lord, to win glory on the battlefield, that was what I had expected. Not a declaration of fate.

Licinia wasn't holding her hand forth waiting for payment for her silence, nor was she trying to intimidate me. She told me this because Sven had jilted her just as Oleg had done with Ellisif, I realised, and Licinia wanted to make sense of it. Too much pain had been caused in one night.

'It's not fair that he hurt you, Licinia.'

She shrugged as if none of it mattered. 'Who am I to have feelings?' she asked, 'I'm a thrall. I'm not free to do as I please. Even if Sven wanted me, I'm Ellisif's possession to be carted off to Pleskov.'

'I'm sorry,' I managed.

'I don't want your apology, Lady Signe. You have done no wrong in this. You bear no blame, though I suspect Kjarr's days are numbered while Sven waits in the shadows to claim you.'

'Licinia, no!' I cried, reaching for her. 'That's not what's happening here.'

She stepped back from me. 'I don't wish you ill, Lady Signe. If anything, you need luck. Elli holds a grudge as well as her mother and while I don't wish you harm, I caution you to keep your distance.' Licinia's dark features twisted in anguish. 'Go, and *kalateehee.*' She wished me luck and faded into the throng, her dark hair disappearing behind a sea of fair-haired revellers.

Pushing through the doors, I stalked into the night, searching for Kjarr, who no doubt had found Sven by now. It was only a matter of time before one threw a challenge to the other and they came to blows. Kjarr was drawn tight as a bowstring, an arrow seeking a target, and Sven was the canvas, stretched unyielding across the frame, waiting for the first strike to land. I found them by the southern gate. With most of the druzhina at the feast, there were few around to stop them, and fewer still willing to intercede in a dispute with the Grand Prince's cousin.

'I would have protected her at all costs, no matter the consequence!' Sven yelled as I found them, though neither took notice of my presence.

Kjarr growled.

'Failing her time and again. You are not a good husband,' Sven seethed, as he waved an exasperated hand.

'Yet, I am her husband, and you would do well to remember it,' Kjarr threatened, though Sven stood taller than my husband.

Sven stepped forward. 'Why? Because you are some boyar that demands respect?' Sven stooped his head over Kjarr's smaller frame.

Kjarr tipped his head back and laughed mirthlessly. 'You think you can steal her from me?'

Sven leaned in to whisper, 'I'll just wait for her to realise you're the lesser man, or for you to die. I have a feeling you don't have much longer.' He leaned back again and brushed something from his cloak.

Having collected his weapons upon exiting the halls, Kjarr half-drew his sword, and Sven's hand went to the hilt of Heart-Piercer while they glowered at each other.

'No one is dying tonight,' I vowed with an annoyed exhale. 'I forbid the both of you from declaring a duel, swear on it,' I demanded as I stepped out of the shadow and into the light of a torch by the gate.

Kjarr was the first to glance at me, face full of anguish. 'Everyone witnessed the oath he made!' He gestured at the taller man.

Sven dropped his hand from his weapon and rubbed his temples. 'And what of your oath?' he questioned Kjarr. 'What kind of man reaffirms an oath he's already made? A pointless promise.'

'Pointless? You think swearing my allegiance to the Grand Prince is a pointless promise?' Kjarr demanded indignantly. 'I am loyal to the Grand Prince.'

Sven shook his head. 'Why not swear to avenge the hurt to your wife's honour? To right all the wrongs committed against her?'

'You know Oleg prohibited the blood debt. He executed Gunnar and gave Heilagr's lands to us. What more…?'

'You would be bound by that feeble agreement?' Sven challenged, shaking his head.

Kjarr turned back to Sven, his brow creased with consternation. 'I am oath-bound by many things, and I am not a man to break it. To do so would be worse than death.'

'We can agree on that,' Sven replied. 'I too am no oath-breaker.'

'But you would be a seducer of men's wives,' Kjarr growled. 'Making an oath like the one you did this night is a challenge to me and my union with...' he looked at me and hesitated.

'No one knows who Astrid is,' I pointed out. 'She might as well not exist.'

'But she does!' Sven interjected, rounding on me, 'and she deserves more than this.' He gestured to Kjarr in frustration.

Kjarr's sword hissed as it came free of its scabbard and Sven, surprised at facing the gleaming weapon, stumbled backward. 'You may have *known* her in the past, Sven, but the woman who stands here now is not the same girl you dishonoured and forsook years ago.' Kjarr spat at the ground by Sven's boot.

Sven pulled Heart-Piercer free and braced himself.

'I asked both of you to swear you wouldn't duel,' I yelled at them.

'Yet neither of us agreed,' Sven replied without looking at me. He kept his piercing gaze on Kjarr.

'Sheath your swords!' I commanded.

Sven stopped, plainly intending to heed my warning, but Kjarr would not lower his blade. Instead, my husband smiled wolfishly and said, 'Then let us go to bed, Wife, so I may put my sword away somewhere secure.'

My mouth fell open as I took in Kjarr's meaning. It was the crassest thing I'd ever heard him say, and I was certain he said it for the benefit of inducing Sven's rage. And it worked. Sven produced his sword again and took up a fighting stance.

'Are you going to threaten me with the blade of your lackeys, or will you fight me this time?' Sven taunted.

'Stop it!' I screamed, trying to push between them, but they wouldn't allow my interference.

Sven bared his teeth. 'He will never be able to protect you.'

'I am not a prize to be won by the last man standing,' I shrieked as I tried to shove Kjarr back with my shoulder.

Kjarr pushed me out of the way. 'But I will protect you now.' He smirked at Sven. And the way they sized each other up made my skin crawl.

'Neither of you is protecting me. Kjarr, you are guarding your honour because you think Sven has offended you. That is a very different thing,' I pointed out, gathering my cloak around myself.

'Go home, Wife,' Kjarr growled.

I turned my head; I didn't want them to see the rage that simmered within. 'If either of you survive this stupid fight, don't come looking for me. I've had enough of the relentless bickering. It makes you no better than children squabbling over toys.'

Neither man replied as I trudged back to the hall.

In the night, I meandered, I didn't know where to go. The Great Hall was not a place I wanted to be. I had no desire to experience Ellisif's rage again. Nor did I want to see Oleg strut around, declaring his grand plans for the empire. I was tired, and I desired the freedom of the river road to nourish me, the clean breeze against my skin.

In the distance, Sven, and Kjarr were hurling insults at one another, piercing the night with their sonorous voices. Dogs barked, upset by the shouting, and a small crowd made their way out of the hall, standing under awnings to see what all the fuss was about. Two guards ran past me, seeking their master. They stopped to give me an obsequious nod.

'Boyar Hrolfsson is that way,' I said, pointing to the southern gate. 'He has quarrelled with Sven Hakonsson. Please make sure they don't kill each other. The fault lies equally between them, and Sven is not to be punished because of my husband's displeasure.'

They nodded briefly and shuffled off into the darkness, where the men's wild shrieks continued, their words indecipherable.

Either could kill the other. Sven could overpower Kjarr owing to his enormous size, but Kjarr had the court and resources behind him, besides the fact he could wield his sword with a fast-paced accuracy.

For a moment, I considered returning.

The wind howled as the snow lashed the streets. I could hear no screaming, no clash of weapons; it was done. All was silent except for the crunching footsteps that followed me.

# Thirty-Eight

'So, you didn't kill each other?' I demanded as the presence closed in behind me. I could tell who it was by their gait, the purposeful stride of a man sure of his station.

'Not this time,' Kjarr agreed, taking a longer step to meet my pace.

'Where is he then?' I asked, letting out a steady exhale. 'Did you order the guards to take him away?'

Kjarr stopped. 'Do you think so little of me now?'

'I don't know what to think,' I replied, and we started walking towards our rooms.

'As much as I find the man infuriating…' Kjarr began.

I glanced at him. 'He provokes you, but you have the option of ignoring it.'

He ignored the jibe. 'Despite my dislike of him, Sven is a warrior of Oleg's retinue. My cousin also tells me he has earmarked him and Eskil for higher duty,' Kjarr explained as we wandered side by side.

*Interesting. It seemed Kjarr harboured a small kernel of respect for Sven, even though he was wary of him.*

'But he is infuriating,' my husband added as he tried to take my hand.

I allowed it, linking my fingers with his. 'Oh, I know.'

Our pace slowed, and we lingered by the market square. 'He appears to know just what to say to get under my skin.'

'Hmm,' I mumbled. Sven had been under mine for years. I'd chafed against that presence before, but now I understood I needed it. Sven made me want to be better, stronger, and to follow the strings of fate.

'I may not have hurt him,' Kjarr said, breaking me from my thoughts, 'but I wanted to.'

I laughed through my nose. 'We should celebrate your restraint,' I replied caustically.

Kjarr snorted as he scratched his neck with his free hand. 'You're angry at me, I can tell.'

'And here I was thinking I'd unlocked the ability to hide my feelings.'

He pulled on my hand as he stopped. 'It's not just the fight with Sven. I saw Ellisif berating you earlier.'

'Don't distract me,' I seethed, 'it's you I'm angry with. Your closeness with Oleg has cost me everything. First, he takes my husband from me, then my business suffers because of jealousy. This has almost cost me my life. Now, Oleg's actions have exacted their price yet again, my only friend at court!'

'Being close to the throne has its disadvantages,' Kjarr agreed, 'but there are benefits too.'

'Not that I can see. Ellisif hates me because Oleg cast her aside and commands her to be Sveineld's wife. Sometimes I think Kyiv is a cursed land, either that or it is me the gods curse.'

'All because Ellisif is angry with you?' he questioned.

'The fire, Gunnar, and Ellisif, too.'

'Why would Ellisif's marriage be on you?' he wondered.

I let him come closer, desperately wanting to feel someone was on my side. 'When Oleg was conflicted, I suggested he wed Ellisif.'

Kjarr dropped his arm, reaching for my hand. I didn't pull away, I just allowed him to hold my limp hand. 'Oleg had been brooding over it for months. Ellisif's marriage had been in consideration before you even came to Kyiv, but once she was visibly pregnant, Oleg couldn't bring himself to announce it. After the child was lost, he saw it as a sign from the gods. Once he had decided it was an indication, there was no talking him out of it. And, I can tell you this for certain; your comment had nothing to do with that outcome.'

I melted into his arms, relieved and miserable all at once. Tears fell from my eyes, and I wished I could tell Ellisif all of it. Though it would make no difference to her now.

'That old witch in Gnezdovo cursed me.'

Kjarr scoffed, taking my hand and placing it on my chest. 'I don't believe that, not for one moment. Who would want to curse you, my love?'

I felt his heartbeat steadily under my palm. 'She told me I was barren.'

'And you think it's true because we are yet to conceive?' he asked, looking down at my tear-stained face. 'Astrid,' he whispered, 'you're not.'

Whether it was the cold or the shiver that ran through me as I admitted the fears that had plagued me for so long, I let him hold me. Vexed as I was at his obstinance, he was mine and though he supported Oleg, sometimes blindly, he never gave me cause to wonder if there was anyone else.

'I wish I never came here,' I confessed for the first time.

Snow was falling while Kjarr kept his arms around me, my head leaning against his chest and listening to the dependable beat within. The pace quickened as he drew a breath. 'I wish we could go together to Miklagard in the spring, but Oleg needs me.'

Another delay, hardly a revelation; almost too predictable. A new promise broken because of Kjarr's obedience to his kin. I pulled away from his embrace. 'But Oleg doesn't need me.' I wiped my nose on my sleeve.

'But I do,' Kjarr whispered. His eyes pleaded, and his hands tightened around my waist. 'I need you, Astrid,' he repeated, 'and if you stayed another year, we might have a child, then both of us would feel more secure.'

My lip trembled as much in sorrow as in anger as I imagined the beautiful babe that we might produce. 'Are you sure it's me you need? It seems all you want is someone who will wait for you at night and warm your bed. Occasionally, you might need a woman who will listen to you, and perhaps guide and support you. Is one wife not as good as another?'

'What are you saying?' he urged, his voice shaking as much as my hands.

'Where were you when I needed you these past years?' I demanded. 'When you should have been by my side, you were by his!'

Kjarr grimaced. When he left Aldeigjuborg, Oleg had commanded him to his side, just as he did now. We both knew he could have disobeyed the order, we also understood what it would have cost him to do so. For that, we both paid the price. 'You don't think I would change it if I could?' he asked.

'Oh, I'm sure you *think* you want to change it all, but I also think if time repeated, you'd make the same decisions. Oleg needs you now, just as he always will. You'll never be free and that means…'

He reached out for me, but I shrank back. 'I have no right to demand anything from you,' he began. 'I'd hoped you would want to stay with me.'

*Guilt.* He would try to lure me in by making this about my commitment to him. 'In this awful place?' I asked. 'Full of shadows that haunt me? You mean to say that my fate is to follow you? That's…' I hesitated.

'The reason you never wanted to marry again,' he finished for me. His shoulders slumped forward, and he bit his lower lip. Kjarr offered his hands, but this time I didn't take them. 'You have your own fate, Astrid Tarbensdottir, one the Norns have woven with golden thread,' he began, and frozen in anger, I let him tuck a piece of hair behind my ear. He stared at the scar marking my temple. 'If you wait one more year, we can go together as honoured emissaries to the Emperor of Miklagard and I'll make sure we are never parted again.'

*More promises he wouldn't keep.*

I opened my mouth to say as much and shook my head, unable to comprehend yet another betrayal. It wasn't fury that burned deep inside me anymore, it was disappointment. I let it drip off me, fill my eyes, and harden my spirit.

'You stay where you're needed,' I mumbled.

He searched my face for meaning, but I wouldn't let him see the dagger he'd buried in my heart.

I walked away, gathering my cloak around me as if it could stop the foreboding that seeped into my skin.

# THIRTY-NINE

## SPRING 884 CE

'Are you sure you cannot mend the rift?' Alfrunr asked as she turned her pale face to the spring sun above us. 'What happened to her was cruel,' she continued, 'but I wish Ellisif had not refused our gifts and farewells.'

The snub hurt Alfrunr especially. Inga, Alfrunr, and Ellisif had been friends since childhood. Inga was now Ellisif's sister by marriage and would be twice over once Inga married Ellisif's brother Harald when he returned from Malyn.

Alfrunr had brought a sweet-smelling bouquet of fresh flowers, which Ellisif cast into the harbour without a glance at her friend. And the gift of herbs and carefully selected tinctures I'd created for common ailments, she'd *accidentally* dropped on the deck of the merchant's vessel carrying them to Pleskov. Ellisif would not release this grudge unless her life depended on it, and even then, I was not sure she would give up her pride before she surrendered her life.

In the weeks before her departure, Ellisif had stalked the halls of Kyiv. She snapped at anyone in her way and glared at me any chance she got. Many times, I'd tried to fix our broken bond but, as her journey drew nearer, she grew more resolved to punish me with silence. Only one woman remained to attend Ellisif, Licinia, who had little choice in the matter. Her mistress would drag her to Pleskov, where Ellisif would no doubt rely heavily on the woman. I feared for Ellisif in her new life as Sveineld's wife whilst she overflowed with anger, but Kjarr assured me Pleskov's women, eager to pander to their new lady, would soon soothe Ellisif's wounds.

I took my place by Alfrunr's side on the rocky outcrop, watching tall-masted ships fade into the distance.

'Mend the damage between us? I harbour no hope of that,' I replied. 'I believe Ellisif's exact words were, "If you ever set foot in the halls of Pleskov, I'll burn them down around you." She was quite explicit about it.'

Alfrunr stifled a nervous laugh. 'I'm sure she didn't mean it. In time, her anger will cool,' she hoped, 'and then she'll answer our letters and we can put this terrible period behind us.'

There was no point in spoiling Alfrunr's optimism. Ellisif now covered herself with an armour of rage to protect her broken heart, just as I wore a leather jerkin in battle. Women did what they had to in order to survive and when Ellisif warned me, "Do not speak my name." I'd had enough of curses to tempt her promise. I would stay well clear of her, and of Pleskov, if I could help it.

I pulled my hair over my shoulder and started braiding it. 'Oh, I think Ellisif has made it very apparent she never wants to hear from me again.' If I had kept my mouth shut on the night of the Jol feast, we might have salvaged our friendship. But telling Ellisif I had suggested her union to Oleg had been the death knell, fatal to a beautiful, joy-filled closeness that I missed dearly.

Alfrunr blew out a held breath, her eyes as puffy and red as mine, for we had both shed many tears. 'Such a pity,' she mumbled. 'Sveineld is a good man. She might just come to like him.' Her cheeks were aglow from the day's heat, though there was a cool wind to take the sting out of the sun. 'I'm not used to wearing this yet,' she explained as she pulled at the cloth over her shimmering bronze hair.

'Why not take it off? No one is watching you here,' I suggested as I tucked the end of my plait into the neckline of my gown to keep it from whipping in the wind.

She tugged on the head covering again. 'I just need to get used to it. Now that I'm married, I must do what is expected of me.'

Alfrunr excelled at the rigid court rules. She was sweet and kind, but sometimes I wanted to shake her and remind her that some rules were meant to be bent and that blind obedience did not make you a better wife.

'Does Boyar Tolze expect it of you?' I asked with a smirk.

Alfrunr blushed, deepening the colour on her already flushed cheeks. 'He likes my hair unbound,' she confessed, her hands toying with a bronze strand as she wound it wistfully around her finger.

Since her marriage to Tolze, Alfrunr was aglow with a contented calm. She was at ease in the company of her new husband, and Tolze had taken to Kyivan court life like a bird takes to flying. He was by the Grand Prince's side at every council. A veritable fount of knowledge regarding the Khazars, and instrumental in preparing Oleg's forces to wrest the tribal vassals from the Khazar Khagan.

I wrapped my arm around her and hugged her sideways. 'It's good to see you happy.'

'I am,' she replied, smiling to herself. 'And Princess Gerberga?' Alfrunr asked as she pulled off her kerchief and lay it in her lap, her uncovered hair ruffled in the breeze like glowing metal as she leaned back on the rock.

'She left this morning,' I responded, reclining next to her, leaning on the heel of my palm.

'I was sorry I could not come to say farewell to her,' Alfrunr lamented. 'We were late to rise this morning.'

I laughed but did not turn to see whether she spoke with embarrassment.

'That reminds me,' she said, 'that I was in the middle of embroidering Tolze's new tunic.' She left then to meet her husband, leaving me to enjoy the waning sunlight on my own, and went with such cheer that I knew at least one of us was satisfied with our fate.

In the days before the river flowed freely, Gerberga (*how that name sounded so sweet after she shed her thrall name*) had felt free to walk outside the walls and to ride with Alfrunr, Tolze, Kjarr, and I. Gerberga truly seemed to enjoy her final weeks in Kyiv, and though she was glad to be returning to her homeland, she understood her new-found freedom would be short-lived. She was bound to be married off as soon as a suitable match was selected. We had grown so close in the past year and came to rely on one another. Many a night we sat by the brazier, sipping expensive drinks from far-away lands and discussing Gerberga's past and the future she hoped for.

'Why didn't you reveal yourself to me earlier?' I wondered one night as we drank an entire ewer of spiced mead.

She looked at me with her rich amber eyes and scrunched her nose. 'I wanted to. Once when we swam at that lake before we arrived in Kyiv and many times since, but who would have believed me?' she asked seriously. 'A slave girl who deigned to declare herself a princess. Ha! Gunnar would have beaten me for my arrogance and made my life even more miserable.'

'You're not wrong,' I agreed, refilling both of our cups. 'What will you tell your cousin when you reach the shores of Frankia?'

'What I need to,' Gerberga began, swirling the liquid that resembled her eye colour around in her cup. 'If I must maintain the lies, then I will. That is between God and me.'

I tapped the side of my mug, thinking back to Father Niall's Christian teachings. 'Is it not a sin to lie? Isn't that one pillar of your faith?'

Gerberga pursed her lips as she took a sip and looked deep into the flames. 'I've been to the depths of hell, Signe. I've seen the deprivation of humanity. It's fearful and frightening.' She leaned forward, holding her cup between her hands as her elbows rested on her knees. 'Every day, I pray for deliverance, and I know the Lord will forgive me for the untruths I need to tell. It's a funny thing,' she started, chuckling to herself.

'Funny?' I pressed.

'He,' she began gesturing to the ceiling, 'brought a heathen to free me.' Gerberga laughed then and looked at me, a single tear rolling down her cheek. 'He works in mysterious ways, indeed. In my life I have prayed for so many things, Signe. Yet this is the only thing I have truly longed for. Now that I have experienced the darkness, I will be a stronger wife to my husband and a lady to my people. I will always look for the light in a person, no matter where they come from or which god they follow.'

I reached for her hand. 'I will miss you, Gerberga,' I managed, though the lump in my throat grew larger.

The next morning, our tears did not cease. I sobbed when Gerberga boarded her cousin's ship. Even Egbert wept as Gerberga's few belongings were loaded onto the vessel. The Princess' lip quivered as she hugged us in turn, her cousin's men hurrying her so they could leave with the tide. She departed with promises to have her court scribe write to us of her safe arrival, and at least one message a year. In return, she demanded the same. I just smiled and nodded towards Egbert, who swore effusively that he would send word more often than that. He bowed to her, almost prostrating himself on the ground, and when she raised him, he kissed her hand with a sad reverence. Egbert was sorry to see her go, no matter how glad he was that Gerberga was free. I watched him wipe the tears away as the crew made their preparations and, spurred by a sudden whim, urged him to go with Princess Gerberga.

He furrowed his brow. 'Nothing in the world would cause me to leave your side,' he told me solemnly. 'My home is with you.' Egbert stared at the water and shuddered. 'I have no desire to go back to that dingy monastery where I didn't even know what living was. Sometimes it seems my life did not begin until the raiders took me. Well, after Eskil purchased me at the markets of Holmgardr and then you did and…I never felt the freedom to reach for more until I found you.' Egbert offered me a wide smile.

I couldn't help but grin at his persistent optimism.

'And I'm glad that you did,' I replied as we waved farewell to Gerberga's ship, watching it drift from sight.

'I hope, soon, the *Bhobain* will carry us to our new adventure,' Egbert said, 'though, I know, things are still uncertain,' he added hastily.

No sooner had our friend's ship vanished did Egbert produce a folio, and he ran a finger over the entries. 'We need another loom,' he advised. 'Mirca has directed that it needs to be wider than the last as our latest commission is for a sail larger than we've produced in the past,' he explained, passing me a scrap showing the size.

'Oh, this is unexpected.'

'Your business did not end just because the warehouse burned. Mirca has been quick about reestablishing work, even before the building was completed. Now, if we return to the sail,' he went on, gesturing to the paper, 'with the new loom, we need only fabricate three panels before sewing them together.' Egbert and I sat on the rocks, listening to the gentle sound of water on the shore.

'How much time will it save?' I asked, holding the scrap in my hand, and going through calculations in my head.

'Hmm,' he mused, running his ink-stained fingers along his chin. 'Branka and Mirca wouldn't need to remove and rehang weights, nor rethread anything. I'm not sure of the exact amount of days it would save, but once they get going on the loom, their speed is quite unfathomable.' His voice was full of awe at their skill.

I ran my finger over the dent of my scar and grinned at him, at the man he had become. Once he had worn his robes long, his hair lank, and his form was spindly and unnourished, now his dark hair was voluminous, eyes bright, and perhaps the greatest change of all was his faith. It was a curiosity at first, but he had fanned that flame until the desire to know our gods burned within him. Around his neck, he proudly displayed a harp pendant, the emblem of Bragi, the god of word and wisdom. I thought the selection was very fitting for a man who was brought up reading the word of the Christian God.

'How many days, Egbert?' I repeated.

'Four at least…perhaps,' he mumbled, and realising I wanted his decisiveness, straightened up and added, 'yes, four days by my calculations.' He tapped his folio and nodded, but tilted his head to the side when I fixed my gaze on the distance. 'What is it, Signe?' Egbert asked.

I gripped his arm. 'Nothing terrible, I promise. I was just remembering the day I found you and Gerberga in the forest. Do you recall when I caught you drawing letters in the dirt?'

He chuckled. 'Of course. I didn't know what to make of you then, but I felt I could trust you.'

My heart felt lighter because of his comment, something I hadn't felt in the weeks since my fallout with Ellisif.

'And you never suspected Gerberga was a princess?' he questioned, patting the hand that grasped his forearm.

'Not in my wildest, fever-ridden dreams,' I answered. 'I knew she was haughty, and I loved her for it, but a princess? No!'

'She's a princess that has left you a small fortune with her ransom,' he added, tapping the pages before him. 'What will you do with it all?'

I'd been thinking about it since Gerberga told me of the sum she'd demanded from her cousin. It was a staggeringly large amount and King Carloman had not bargained in the least. Of course, Egbert had crafted the correspondence so Princess Gerberga seemed an honourable hostage, well-treated, and ignorant of the communications. Of the three of us, it was only I who had been oblivious to it all.

'First, we need to make sure Mirca has everything she needs for the business to run smoothly. We'll do the same with Mila in Gnezdovo, and Hilde and Helga in Aldeigjuborg.'

Egbert clicked his tongue. 'Already attended to.'

I turned to look at him beside me, releasing my grip on his arm. 'You are brilliant,' I beamed. 'We will also require funds to set us up in Miklagard if we ever get there,' I said, waving a hand towards the city. I'd had enough of Kyiv to last a lifetime.

Egbert pulled at his collar, and I knew that meant an uncomfortable conversation was soon to follow.

'Oleg's council was this morning, wasn't it?' I queried.

Egbert attended all the important meetings, ostensibly as my husband's scribe, but he always reported back to me. I got more information from Egbert than I did from Kjarr these days. Kjarr and I took our meals together, when possible, but we no longer lived in each other's shadows. Oleg's inner circle had tightened, and he'd decided that women no longer had a place in it.

'The Grand Prince officially prohibited Boyar Hrolfsson from leaving until the campaigns against the Radimichs and Severians are concluded.'

'Of course he did.' I pulled at a blade of grass that tufted between the rocks, running my fingernail along its length, and cleaving it in two. The greenery caught in the breeze and blew away. I fixed my eyes on the water, watching the surface and trying to calm myself. It shouldn't have come as a surprise. It was hardly a revelation that Oleg would prevent his cousin from leaving Kyiv. There were signs earlier than at Jol that the Grand Prince wanted Kjarr at his side rather than send him to Miklagard, as he had promised. Perhaps a small part of me had known I would always take this journey without him.

Egbert scraped his bottom lip with his teeth. 'What will you do?'

'You mean will I stay with my husband or go alone?' I grabbed another green spear from the ground. 'Undecided,' I replied tersely.

Egbert leaned towards me and plucked a small flower from the earth. 'You know I will be with you whether you stay or choose to go.' He twirled the blossom between his fingers.

'Thank you, Egbert,' I responded numbly, but I couldn't meet his eye. The anger in me threatened to spill. 'Did Oleg say anything else?'

He cleared his throat. 'Surprisingly, yes. He has named Eskil and Sven as, hmm… What did he call it?' He closed his eyes, trying to recall what he had heard. 'I believe he said they were to be sent, "as military gifts to the Emperor of Miklagard for a term of three years." Neither man appeared surprised by the announcement.'

My brows almost reached my hairline with shock.

'It's a clever move. The Grand Prince has few things to trade that the Emperor does not yet have access to, but warriors, and northern warriors at that, are a commodity worth exploring. With this offering, he shows his respect and his hopes for a future alliance,' Egbert continued.

'How did Eskil and Sven take it?' I asked, staring at the flower still in Egbert's grasp.

'They both intended to go anyway,' Egbert started. 'At least they have financial backing and a purpose for going.' He shrugged. We both knew Eskil would enjoy the appointment, but Sven was about as keen on someone else deciding his fate as I was. 'There was one other thing.' He stopped and gritted his teeth, obviously unsure how he should proceed.

'Yes?' I stared at him blankly.

'There was a comment made…about you. I have debated whether to tell you, but I feel you should know.' Egbert sounded as if he would rather not divulge it at all. 'It was something the Grand Prince said. It might have meant nothing but…' he trailed off.

'Get to the point, Egbert,' I answered, perhaps a little too rudely as I balled my hands into fists.

He looked away, gazing at the river. 'When Kjarr complained to the Grand Prince that you would not appreciate the delay in going to Miklagard, the Grand Prince said, "Perhaps you should have married someone with less personal ambition, Cousin. A merchant is not a wife to settle." Boyar Hrolfsson appeared quite stunned by the remark.'

'What did Kjarr say?' His was the only opinion I cared about.

Egbert looked conflicted. 'What could he say?'

With Oleg in his present melancholy, it was better to ignore the jibe than stoke his ire.

'There is nothing to worry about, Egbert,' I lied, trying to soothe him as much as myself. That comment would burn for a long time, but I wouldn't let it roil me now. 'Anything else?'

Egbert perked up. 'In fact, there is.' He sat a little taller.

'Tell me it's something good,' I groaned whilst I massaged my temples with my fingertips.

'It is,' he added quickly, 'a letter from Ahmed Ibn Rashti.' From his bag, he produced a parchment scribbled in the tongue Ahmed taught me.

I took it from his hands and marvelled at the script. 'I'm not sure I ever expected to hear from him again,' I said as I read the simple language of the correspondence. 'It certainly is good news.'

Egbert looked at me and twisted his mouth. 'I could find someone to help us translate it if you haven't kept up with your studies,' he suggested.

'No need. Ahmed has kept it basic enough. He says if we make it to Miklagard, he will give us introductions for accommodations in the city,' I advised as I deciphered each word. Even though I stumbled with some of the trickier phrases, I was pleased with my efforts. I folded the letter and flicked some dirt from my apron dress. 'We shall write and thank him.'

'He will journey for a while before he reaches his homeland, but our response will probably make it there before he does. Messengers travel faster than the caravans,' Egbert explained. 'In the meantime, we have work to do, and you,' he began, looking pointedly at me, 'have a decision to make.'

# FORTY

All morning, I contemplated my choices.

There were benefits to staying in Kyiv, I could see that. Besides remaining in my husband's company, I could assist Mirca in expanding the business, but I couldn't escape the feeling my welcome had run out. On the other hand, leaving would offer adventure. The journey to Miklagard would provide much-needed freedom and would stop that itching sensation crawling beneath my skin as I recalled my father's insistence that I go there. It wasn't the advantages that frightened me, but the cost. One way or another, there would be uncomfortable conversations and I'd had enough of those to last a lifetime.

Just before sunset, with only a kernel of decisiveness, I meandered to Sihtric's residence. My strides were not long and purposeful, but trudging along as an angry child might. The plodding walk of someone sent from the hall to a task they didn't want to complete. And that's exactly how I felt. For months since my argument with Kjarr, I had flopped between staying and leaving. Sihtric, holding a meeting this evening for the *Bhobain's* crew, had been told not to expect my attendance.

As I continued through the empty Kyiv streets, my determination grew, and by the time I reached Sihtric's room, I knew what my answer was going to be.

*Kjarr has forced me to make this decision*, I told myself as I placed my hand against Sihtric's door and heard the voices within.

It wasn't until Eskil's deep belly-laugh emanated from the room and the echo of amusement that I realised what I missed was simple comradery.

Fury simmered in me. An outrage that my husband would keep me in Kyiv because he did not want us to be parted, though he knew it crushed my soul to be here. I pushed open the door and sent it into the wall with a deafening clatter.

'That's it!' I announced to a sea of surprised faces.

Sihtric opened his mouth, but before he spoke, some reason returned to me.

'Sorry about the door,' I apologised, shutting it behind me and striding to the table where they all sat on stools around it.

Eskil cuffed his dripping nose and chuckled. He wore stacks of brilliant gold and silver armrings given to him by the Grand Prince. In his service he had set himself apart, his valour only matched by Sven, and the two of them appeared every bit the part. 'Told you she'd bloody be here. Good to see you returned to your senses, Valkyrie.'

Sihtric stared at me expectantly. Björn and Frodi, taking advantage of everyone's distraction, poured themselves a cup of ale. Kari, Sihtric's thrall pottered about by the far wall, only glancing at his master for instruction. Sven still hadn't looked up from his hands.

I stood behind a vacant stool between Eskil and Frodi, yet to sit down. 'I'm leaving Signe behind,' I declared, clutching the edge of the table. In my gown of costly silk, I was out of place. Instead of comfortable travelling clothes, court garments were adornments for my position at court. The outfit made it difficult to manoeuvre in, and after donning my belt and weapons, the coarse grain of the leather rubbed through the thin fabric and sat uncomfortably on my hip.

Sven examined his nails.

Björn shrugged. He was the first to call me by the name Signe, unbeknownst to him. The day I had escaped Sven's proposal and found myself on Björn's merchant ship bound for Aldeigjuborg had been the first day in the life of Signe. Now, almost four years later, that life was ending. Signe would die so that Astrid could live again.

Frodi peered up from his mug. 'Are we missing something?' he asked, flicking his greying hair from his face.

I ignored his question and spoke to Sihtric, the only one who seemed both interested and informed. 'From now on I am Astrid.'

Frodi and Björn glanced at each other as if the name was familiar, but they could not put the pieces together. It was Björn who offered the first comment. 'One name is as good as any other, eh? But if you keep changing it, I'll have to call you "Girl" lest I forget it altogether.'

Sihtric looked at me but said nothing. I guessed by now he had worked out my identity. Eskil was the only one who seemed genuinely agog with the realisation that I was Astrid, the object of Sven's Jol declaration. Sihtric slid an earthenware cup across the table-board, and I filled it with the bitter amber liquid from a jug in the centre. Only then did Sven look up from his fascinating fingernails.

'I refuse to dwell in my husband's shadow,' I continued. Sven squinted as he listened. 'The Norns, who have not cursed me!' I shot that remark at Eskil and Sven, who both shrugged indifferently as if neither had suggested the notion. 'The Norns lead me to Miklagard, where my father also guides me. This, I know, is my fate.' I finally sat on the stool and as I did, a splinter from the wood caught my gown and pulled a thread. There was a loud sound as the tear became a run in the silk.

'That's an omen, Valkyrie,' Eskil said.

I shot him a reproachful glare. 'It's just a sign that this dress will not be coming to Miklagard with us.'

Eskil nodded. 'A sign to leave this bloody place? Maybe.'

'What about Kjarr, *bhana charaid*?' Sihtric asked me.

'I am yet to tell him my final decision, but he will not deny me. He understands what I need. Besides, Oleg tells me Kjarr will be released as soon as they have suppressed the Radimichs, and I hope he will join us next year,' I explained. 'I am a merchant in my own right, by my authority,' I continued, taking a break to down the contents of my cup. 'I want to go to Miklagard on the *Bhobain* with you all.' At this, I raised my drink to salute my friends.

They copied the gesture and offered small grins in reply.

'I do not want to wait another year only to find out the Grand Prince will not release Kjarr to be emissary to Miklagard. I will not be stuck in Kyiv indefinitely.'

Sihtric cleared his throat. 'There is little else to say.' His way of telling me to wrap up my rambling. 'Of course, we are pleased to have you aboard.' He sipped on his ale. 'It's your decision,' Sihtric replied, 'though I'll nae deny it'll be a benefit to have someone who speaks a bit of the language.'

I arched my brow as I asked, 'You never learned?'

He shook his head. 'Just cannae get my mouth around the sounds. People think I'm choking.'

'Astrid the Far-Travelled,' Sven murmured, his gaze unwaveringly intense, 'just as Ahmed said.'

'Speaking of Ahmed,' Egbert spoke from behind me.

I'd been so absorbed in my passionate declaration that I had not realised he had entered the room.

'Am I permitted to divulge the contents of his letter?' Egbert asked me.

I gave a swift nod, and he took the remaining seat on Sven's right, leaning his elbows on the table as he eased himself into position.

Egbert proceeded, 'Ahmed has offered to make introductions for our housing in the Great City.'

Eskil shoved Sven with his shoulder and Björn and Frodi hooted with delight, but it was Sihtric who spoke. 'Between his men and mine, we'll find a place because…'

'You ken someone,' the group finished for him and chortled in unison.

'Fine, fine,' Sihtric groaned, waving away the prods and pokes from the men. 'Och! I should box your ears in, you *braw reivers*.' His face went a splotchy red, though, from the way he hid the smile on his lips, I knew he enjoyed the jest. 'One year ago, we began our journey to Miklagard, and, minus a couple of people, we will see it through.' Sihtric raised his voice as he stood up.

The rest of us got to our feet, and each raised a full cup.

'To Sven and me, who go to Miklagard to show Emperor Basil what us northerners are made of,' Eskil toasted. 'What the rest of you'll do, I don't bloody know; trade or something,' he added.

I cleared my voice. 'Do you recall the witch Gudrun in Gnezdovo?' I asked, as all remained standing.

There were nods, and I swore, a few shudders as they recalled the wise woman. Eskil was the only one who smiled at the memory. He had spent three days and nights in her company, and when he left, he was besotted with a young woman and healed of his injury.

'It was her that foretold my fate,' I began. 'She told me to be considered worthy I must find the Queen of Cities, whoever that may be. My hunch is that the answer lies in Miklagard.'

Sihtric raked his fingernails through the stubble on his neck. 'Queen of Cities, you say?'

He waited for me to nod.

'It's nae a woman, *bhana charaid*. Once it was named Nova Roma, to some, they ken it as Byzantium, others call it Constantinople, but in our tongue, it is Miklagard, and it just so happens to be where we are headed.'

# EPILOGUE

## SPRING 884 CE

The *Bhobain* lurched forward with each well-timed stroke. Sven's prow-beast glared, open-mouthed over the waterway, as we rowed away from Kyiv. Its curved neck forced its gigantic eyes down, staring into the depths as if it could see the fish within, straight down to the rocky riverbed. Sven had spent all his free time carving it and, aside from the off-centre nature of its features, he'd done an excellent job. Sihtric named the wooden beast *Nathair-Sgiathach*, after the winged snake-like creature that had once roamed his mother's homeland. This was *Nathair-Sgiathach's* maiden voyage, and we displayed her only briefly for fear of scaring the friendly spirits who would bring us a lucky journey. We would mount the carved creature again once we left the Grand Prince's territory.

My shoulders ached already, though the pain could not tug the smile from my face as I shipped the smooth oak handles into the rowlock to turn my gaze up to the bright sun.

'Stop your daydreaming, Valkyrie,' Eskil teased from the bench in front of me. He shot me a grin.

I rolled my shoulders before grasping the oars again. The skin had already broken on my palms, a discomfort that nudged me out of my long months of drudgery. I was back in the blazing spring sun, where its reflection on the river caused our faces to leather and brown. Days of spinning, weaving, and practising with Forlog-Enda were fine, but there was something about a crisp breeze and the sound of water lapping against the *Bhobain's* strakes that made me feel free. What I really wanted to do was stand at the prow as Sihtric often did, wind in my hair and on my face, but from Eskil's earlier comment, now was not the time. We had many weeks of travel ahead, and my moment would come. Until then, I could only dream.

When I had told Kjarr about my leaving, I expected he would be sour. He didn't know if a year would be sufficient to bring the Severians and Radimichs to heel, but had promised to depart as soon as Oleg released him. If my suspicions were correct, Oleg would set his sights on yet another tribe and further expansion before he let his cousin leave, emissary or not. Perhaps it would be I who would return to Kyiv before Kjarr ever left it.

My cheek tingled where Kjarr had kissed me in parting. He had presented me with gifts which now lay in a chest under my bench with my neatly folded silk-trimmed dresses. They were the wonders of wealth; a lampwork glass whorl for my spindle in the prettiest shade of blue. It reminded me of the River Volkhov in the winter when ice crystals formed on the surface. White shards amongst the bluest of blue hues. Along the Volkhov's banks, I had wandered for so many months waiting for Kjarr to return to Aldeigjuborg, a place I might never see again, though I wished I might someday. There were also bolts of fine woven linens and wool that I almost felt bad for accepting. The lengths came from Estrid's suppliers and would have been Ellisif's inheritance if she had been entitled to anything after her parents were outlawed. Kjarr also gave me another gold torc that I didn't dare wear on the river road. Instead, I'd put on my old Valkyrie pendant and tucked it under the neck of my dress. Thieves were plentiful and that kind of wealth was best left hidden. It was only after I'd given him a new tunic spun, woven, and sewn by my hand, and decorated with Kyiv's colours that he'd held forth his final offering; a set of new leather arm bracers stamped with the bident of the Rurikids on the smooth space of the forearm. He wanted all to know that I belonged with them, even if I did not feel it yet. My needlework on the decorated tunic was unrefined, a poor display of skill compared to the leatherwork of the bracers. But Kjarr still clutched it, running his fingers over the stitches that were tied messily on the backing. He pulled me into his arms, thanking me with a kiss so deep I thought it would suck my soul straight from my stomach.

It felt strange to leave him when all the previous times it was Kjarr saying goodbye as I stood on the docks. He didn't stay to watch the *Bhobain* fade into the distance. I'd asked him not to. We had said what we needed to in private, and I knew myself well enough that in parting I could not hide the sadness from my face if he was there. Mirca had gathered the women outside our new warehouse to watch us depart. I saw her on the bluff and knew my business was under good command. No one else had come to wish me well, for Kyiv had been a lonely place. The more I thought about it, the more I realised this journey was mine and whether Kjarr accepted my leaving begrudgingly or with understanding, it didn't matter. This was my fate. Ordained by my father. Divined by the Norns. Desired independently. Gudrun the Grey of Gnezdovo had said as much, though it had taken me far too long to figure that out. I chuckled to myself, remembering how I'd believed the Queen of Cities to be a person rather than a place.

'What are you laughing at?' Frodi grumbled from behind me on the steering oar. He scrunched his face into a horrible sneer.

'Get out of the wrong side of the bedroll this morning, Frodi?' Sven threw back at the Sámi.

Eskil tossed his head to the side, indicating to the ship gliding along next to us. 'Laugh at the *River-Raven* when we beat them to Vytechev,' he commanded using his best hersir voice.

Sihtric struck his forearm with a clenched fist in a rude gesture as the *River-Raven* surged ahead of the *Bhobain*.

'Pull!' he yelled, and the competitive spirit he often kept hidden inside crept forward. A wide smile spread across his handsome face, and he leaned into the wind, beckoning us to increase our speed. 'Faster! Dinnae *haver*. Or the bastards will get the better of us through the firth.' Sihtric waved his hands for emphasis, conjuring some spirit to spur us on.

The *River-Raven's* captain Vrangi cackled as he too urged his crew on. It was all in good fun. Vrangi and Sihtric knew each other from journeys past and the games we now played lightened the often uneventful voyage.

'Vrangi! Looks like the *River-Raven* has seen better days. Did you nae put her in for repairs this season?' Sihtric goaded.

Vrangi gnawed on the edge of a loaf that looked rather stale. He flung the rest into the waiting hand of an oarsman with yellow hair who caught it and launched the bread directly at the *Bhobain*.

'Duck,' Sihtric warned through raucous laughter, but the loaf caught Frodi on the shoulder before it bounced into his hand. 'Breakfast!' the Sámi exclaimed, as he gummed on the dry crust.

Vrangi clapped the blonde man around the head but laughed all the same.

Björn took hold of the loaf, now discarded by his friend, and stood at the aft. 'Pull ahead,' he ordered, drawing his arm back. He hurled the rye missile towards the *River-Raven*, which had gained a few strokes on the *Bhobain*, and hit the yellow-haired crewman in the back of the head.

He turned and shook his fist at Björn, trying to hide his amusement.

'A lucky shot,' the man called back.

Egbert shook his head on the bench opposite me, but his shoulders shook with laughter, just like the rest of us.

Such foolery had been the morning's sport. Had Thorsten been here, he would have enjoyed the rivalries, but he had stayed in Kyiv with his red-haired lover. I did not doubt that he would do well there, where his bone combs and hairpins were in high demand. I was proud to say I owned several of his creations. The *Bhobain's* crew were sad to lose him, not least the music he played on those campfire nights where we enjoyed warm meals and pleasant company. Sven had tried his best to convince him to come, but nothing would tear Thorsten away from his beloved lady of the flame.

Sven gestured ahead as Vrangi shouted a challenge at Sihtric that was just out of my hearing. From Sihtric's amused chuckle, it was clear Vrangi meant to engage us in a contest once again. Frodi leaned against the steering oar to veer right off the small island ahead. Numerous land masses dotted the Dnieper River from Kyiv, making it difficult for those unfamiliar with the waterways to navigate them. The *Bhobain* drew so near the *River-Raven* that I braced for impact. But Frodi knew the *Bhobain's* lines so well that he kept aside our rival's ship, forcing them away from the more favourable path where the inlet was wider and deeper. Vrangi pushed back, testing our commitment, surely hoping the *Bhobain* would be the first to back off and allow the *River-Raven* to glide ahead.

'Not bloody likely,' Eskil shouted back to Vrangi as he grasped the oar tighter and wrenched it back with all the force his sizable forearms could muster.

Sven's back muscles tightened as he, too, pulled the oar harder in front of me. The *Bhobain* listed for a moment before righting, then we hauled, leaping ahead into the flow before the *River-Raven* had a chance to take it from us. Vrangi angled left at the last moment and took the narrow route around the low island, just missing a sandbank.

Once we made it through the forking river, the two streams met once more. Vrangi gestured obscenely at our leader, his mirth betrayed by the grin he wore. He'd been bettered today, but he didn't seem to mind too much.

After our race, we sailed alongside the *River-Raven* towards the gathering point of Vytechev. The outpost had been initially controlled by the Polianians, however, when they allied with our people, Grand Prince Oleg brought it under his control and stationed guards there. A small community had sprung up around it, extending the original Polianian settlement. It was close to Kyiv. A morning's walk was all it took to breach the gap between the two places, faster still on horseback. The ride would not see the sun move a single mark in the sky, though I had never been there on my morning rides. By the river, it was less than half a day's jaunt, which made it the ideal place for sea travellers on their way to Miklagard. It kept them out of the ever-expanding city of Kyiv and out of trouble. There we were to congregate in great numbers as we organised our ships, compiled our resources, and made our final offerings, and, when all were prepared, we would set off as one.

The dangers we would face were many. Rapids bubbled along the way to Miklagard like cauldrons. Their relentless waters drew men under their foam, wrecking ships, and destroying precious trade cargo. Joining with other crews meant there were more hands to do the unloading and carting of goods across land whilst the others guided ships through the rapids. More eyes to act as lookouts, watching for the Pechenegs who especially liked to prey on groups at the perilous crossing. The vicious tribes of the lower Dnieper would think twice before attacking such a fleet. Like most opportunists, they searched for easy pickings.

If the Pechenegs were anything like the Khazar scouts we had encountered before Gnezdovo, I would give my new gold torc to the gods to keep them away. Tales of their brutality were frequently repeated. The dominant fear was that they might appear with a larger force than our own. If that happened, they could overwhelm us and take whoever and whatever they wanted. A realisation that dwelled uncomfortably in my mind.

'There!' Sihtric called as he pointed to Vytechev, which, just like Kyiv, was of wood construction.

We knew Oleg had plans to fortify both sites as he tightened his control on the region and, as we rowed into the deep natural harbour, sheltered by its many islands, it was easy to see why he was keen to strengthen it.

The semicircle inlet protected the settlement's inhabitants from two directions, leaving a partial land wall to enclose the rear approach. From its position above the water, overlooking a dramatic bend in the Dnieper, it was clear no ship could pass without being noticed. It was the kind of advantage that any ruler would look for, and Oleg was driven by the need to expand the lands Rurik had left him.

Frodi, Björn, and Sihtric expertly guided the *Bhobain* into a narrow space between two wide-bellied ships. Using a plank, we reached land by climbing over each vessel.

Sven grasped my arm and gestured across the many hulls, where three men inspected a newly unfurled sail. 'Isn't that one of yours?' he asked, unable to hide his excitement.

'That's Folcmarr's ship,' I replied, 'with one of our sails.' It was made by our Gnezdovo warehouse, led by Mila. Our Kyiv operation had only produced one since the fire. 'And so is that one.' I pointed to another, 'but it's an Aldeigjuborg production.' It was daubed with the crude image of a black raven.

Sven nudged me with his shoulder as we waded through the ankle-deep water towards the camp-ground. As far as the eye could see, pitched tents of thick linens and wool were stretched over poles. Fires were already lit, and some men fussed with sustenance on the boil above the flames. Slavers confined their chained-up chattels in makeshift pens on the periphery and shoved the meagerest of rations through the cage. Too hungry to be proud, the captives scooped the vittles from the ground and consumed them in haste.

This was the trade that made the northern nations rich. Winter was the time for capture and spring was the time to sell the poor souls at market. At the height of the season when people were plentiful, a pretty female thrall might be a fifth of the value of her counterpart in the colder months when her like was scarce. Regardless of the season, rich men were almost always up for buying them. Soon the markets would teem with slaves, and in their eyes, I saw the fear that Gerberga and Egbert had held when they were both enslaved.

My scribe caught up with me and I saw him grimace in the captives' direction. Doubtlessly pleased his fate was now to live free but sorrowful for the plight of those he saw penned. Unless we planned on buying them all, there was no way to help. Even as a wealthy woman, it would cost tenfold the gold I possessed to release every one of them. I'd heard that in the markets of Miklagard one might buy any person, in any combination of colours and proportions. Though the concept of variety impressed me, the reality of it horrified me considerably more.

'Don't stand there gawking,' Eskil grumbled as he lumbered past, 'or they'll start thinking you want to steal the bloody wretches.' He meant it kindly, though Eskil was always rough with his sympathy.

I looked away.

Sihtric strode ahead carrying bedrolls and sacks, along with his man Kari. Both trudged towards a patch of ground we would call home for the next few nights before Sihtric left to speak to Vrangi, who was standing by a campfire, prodding something in his cooking pot. They spoke of other crews to come, those who would travel with us, and guard against the menacing Pechenegs. Men like Björn, Frodi, and Sihtric, who had traversed these rivers before and were aware of their dangers. These were acquaintances from Holmgardr, and across the sea in Kaupang and Dyflin. *Good men,* Sihtric told me. Traders who shunned the slavers, toting crafts, and other goods far from their homes where they might fetch a higher price.

When the planning was done, and the warm afternoon light faded into nightfall, each crew made their sacrifice, something of value for protection and favour. Three tall carvings stood amongst the trees where those who came before us had laid offerings at their feet. As always, Odin was one of those who was represented. He who needed blood and spoils to cast his sole eye over a man's life. It was Odin, too, who had the greatest hoard of gifts; animal carcasses, food, and small silver coins had been laid at the statue's base. Those who hoped their strength would preserve their life enriched Thor. For the men who beseeched the god of merchants, they placed their humble bounties beneath Njord. It was here that I placed my offering of cinnabar-coloured fabric, so beautifully woven that even the goddess Frigg would be honoured to wear it. Njord should have been pleased with such a gift, for it was costly and fine and, I prayed, it would ensure our safety on the road ahead.

Once the individual offerings were made, a goat was slain. Its blood drenched the earth under the effigies. Before its ordeal, the animal drank a brew of calm. It did not fight the knife that dragged across its neck. With a solemn bleat, its legs folded under its body and fell to the ground. Four more goats were slaughtered that night, all brought from Kyiv's market so their flesh could fill our bellies. For some of us, it would be the last time we ate fresh meat and a warm meal until we reached a major port, or, worse still, Miklagard itself. By the time our meals were eaten, darkness cloaked the land. Everyone who was not on watch loitered fireside, drinking and telling stories. Those who already felt exhaustion had made their way to their tents or bedrolls, some snoring louder than a wolf's growl. Sihtric and Kari had retired. Frodi and Björn were drinking with Vrangi at his camp. Egbert had found some learned men travelling with a group of merchants to converse with, and who knew where Eskil was.

'I hope you're not going to snore like that all night,' Sven said in jest as he gestured to the tent next to us, its occupant loudly snoring.

I shoved him with my shoulder. 'Even if I did, there is no way you'll hear it over Eskil. He sounds like someone sawing down a tree.'

He cackled, throwing his head back.

The moment was disturbed as a man walked past us toward the ships. We all monitored our vessels. Some crews left men aboard to protect their goods.

*That's where Eskil is*, I remembered. *It's his turn to guard the* Bhobain.

The man walking past, stopped, and looked around, perhaps disorientated in the darkness. His pockmarked face appeared hideous in the low light. He walked on, disappearing into the inky night. I was conscious of my own scars and ran my thumb along the rift at my temple.

'Do you know him?' Sven asked, tossing his head in the direction of the man marred by childhood illness.

'Just looks like someone I used to know,' I replied, thinking of Auden's youngest son, Gorm.

Sven squinted into the dark. 'How could you tell?'

I shook my head. 'I can't. It's too dark and there are many men with faces destroyed by disease.'

'Have you forgiven me for Jol yet?' Sven asked, flame-light dancing on his face where it drew long shadows beneath his nose and eyes. His skin looked yellow and glossy.

I glared at him. 'No.'

We had exchanged very few words since winter. With Kjarr's temper to soothe, I had kept well away to cloak my anger over his Jol oath. A promise he was honour bound to keep or die trying.

'And don't say you're sorry because I know you're not!' I warned icily.

He turned his head, and the shadows on his face moved, draping his profile in pitch.

'It put me in a very difficult position,' I continued, remembering the many nights Kjarr had tried to read the meaning of that vow. With every touch and kiss my husband had analysed both my love for him, and the probability of a hidden relationship between Sven and me.

Sven huffed as he picked up a twig and threw it into the fire. 'I never meant to do that,' he conceded.

'Kjarr told me you said as much,' I replied.

He looked towards me; the flickering flames captured in the dark orbs of his eyes. 'Though I am sworn to be by your side, he also made me swear to protect you.'

'Of course he did,' I responded caustically, 'and how much is he paying you for that service?'

'Nothing,' Sven answered, looking offended. 'I would have done it anyway, whether he asked me to or not.'

'I'm still annoyed with you,' I mumbled.

'Good. Then at least you're thinking of me.' Sven smirked in the gloom, shifting on the log under his backside. 'And, if you recall correctly, I swore nothing more than to be by your side.'

'You're infuriating,' I growled. The ground crunched as I twisted my foot into the loose topsoil.

He shrugged. 'I can't pretend to be what I'm not.' Sven ran his hand through his dusty blonde hair, then along his short-bearded jaw-line. His wrists sparkled with the gifts of the Grand Prince, several intricate bands of precious metal to mark his status as a distinguished warrior of the druzhina.

'You mean to tell me you planned that oath? It wasn't some ale-drenched promise made in the heat of the moment?' I stifled a yawn.

'It was considered,' he admitted as his hand went back to stroking the short hair on his neck. 'It was my way of telling you there was no one else,' he said, glancing toward me, 'even if there have been others.'

I cursed myself for the extra beat my heart took.

'We've been the best of friends for such a long time,' he added.

'There have been a couple of interruptions,' I pointed out as I slid from my position on the log onto the ground and reclined back.

Sven threw another stick into the fire. 'Those aside, I would like to be by your side for the rest of our lives,' he spoke slowly, his tone serious and his gaze unflinching as it moved to my face.

It was I who broke eye contact first, leaning forward and looking away to poke the flames with a branch I'd picked up from the ground. 'That's a promise I can also make,' I agreed.

'Can you make one more?' he asked as he finally looked away. 'Could you go through just one season without a serious injury or being involved in a catastrophic event?'

'I suppose I could try,' I teased, tapping the earth with my stick.

He smiled then. I studied the lines that spread from the corners of his eyes, and he looked every bit of his twenty-four years. 'Whether I serve another, you are the worthiest of them all.'

'Why?' I questioned. Suddenly I felt like a youth again, always demanding an explanation from wise old Sven who was barely two winters older but seemed infinitely more knowledgeable when I was nothing more than a young farm girl.

His grin grew faint as he answered, 'Because you're honest, even when the truth is hard to tell. You support others, and the gods love you! The Norns, too,' he added.

I threw my head back and laughed at the stars. 'Oh, so you admit I'm not cursed after all?'

He leaned forward, elbows on knees. 'How could anyone curse you, *minn Svanr*?'

I turned towards him, watching him as he watched me. The branch I'd been holding caught alight, and I released it to the heat. It smouldered and burned while I thought of the promise Ellisif made that should I ever walk the halls of Pleskov, she would raze it to the ground. I'd been close enough to dying in a fire to know I didn't want to repeat the experience.

The campfire crackled and hissed as the wood became ash. Even so, I did not look away.

'Our fates are intertwined, just as I've always said,' Sven went on, 'no matter where this journey takes us.' I knew not if he meant in life or our plans for Miklagard.

I swallowed as I formed the words, 'Of that, only the Norns may know.'

# THE RURIKID DYNASTY

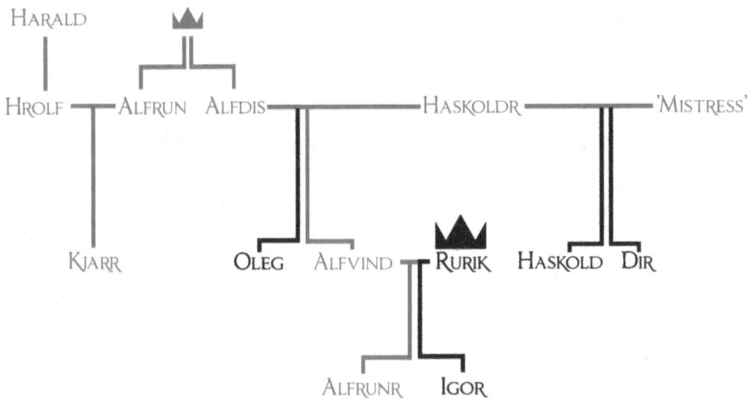



⚜ : Royal lineage from Scandinavia.

Names in grey are are the author's invention. Parents, wives, and mistresses of those semi-legendary historical figures such as Oleg and Rurik existed, however their names have been lost to history.

# AUTHOR'S NOTE

When I set out to write *Serve the Worthy*, I knew Astrid would encounter some big, and historically well-known, characters on her journey. This book tackles a large geographical region with many cultural groups, religions, and languages - it was a big change from the smaller cast of *Oath Undo Me* and *No One's Viking*. That's a large part of the reason behind including both the list of characters and the family tree. With historical names so similar, and the interconnectedness of the court, I wanted to add these for readers to refer to.

Some readers will be familiar with the semi-legendary Grand Prince Oleg, who assumed the throne after the first recorded Rus' leader Rurik, for whom the dynasty is named (the Rurikids). As I mentioned in the Author's note of *No One's Viking*, Oleg's genealogy is vague. No one seems to agree where he came from or how he was related to Rurik. Not much is known about Oleg's early life either. He had not yet attained the epithet "The Prophet" and would not rage into Byzantine history for another twenty years, but he was very busy in the background.

As I researched the Grand Prince, he seemed to be a man driven by duty and sworn oaths, a protector of his nephew Igor, and a deeply conflicted man. In this book, we see all the above and the difficult decisions he makes in order to secure the future of the Rurikids. Whilst this book takes place in the initial years of his reign, future instalments will explore both the origins of his sobriquet and what kind of man he would become. The same can be said of young Prince Igor, who will eventually marry the vengeful princess turned to saint, Olga. His wife appears in the records without so much as a backstory, with no mention of her birth or her parents (not wholly uncommon for a woman during the Medieval period). In this book, I have made some educated estimations, though sometimes one must resort to the ever-convenient (though historically inconvenient) narrative freedom when evidence is lacking.

There are many issues with the recorded history of the Rus' in the 9th century. Besides a staggeringly sparse amount of it, what we do have (especially when it comes to births, deaths, and marriages) are usually considered estimations. For example, Alfvind, who in *Serve the Worthy* is the full sister of Oleg, half-sister of Haskold (also known as Askold) and Dir, and mother to Alfrunr and Igor, in historical sources she is recorded as Askold and Dir's mother, even though she would not have been born at the time of their births. Both Haskold's and Dir's dates of birth are listed 10 years before Alfvind's and therefore could not possibly be related in this manner. It was common, however, that daughters were named after their mothers either similarly or exactly. For ease of distinction, I have changed Oleg's mother's name to Alfdis and, because of the disdain with which Askold and Dir are treated, I have written them in as bastard children from the same father (Haskoldr) and another woman, namely his mistress and therefore are not treated with the same reverence and do not have the same 'royal blood' as Oleg, Rurik, or Alfdis.

Kyiv is also somewhat of a mystery. By the 10th century, some written sources give excellent descriptions and even some sketches of the city, but the Kyiv of the 9th century is somewhat of an enigma. As always, I turned to archaeology, particularly the work of Dr Johan Callmer. It would have been incredibly difficult for me to understand the region's topography without his amazing work, specifically his article, *The Archaeology of Kiev, to the End of the Earliest Urban Phase: Harvard Ukrainian Studies*. From Callmer's work, I could "see" Kyiv. It is also important to understand that Kyiv did not exist in a vacuum, rather it was a settlement (later a town) that was surrounded by many Slavic powers, many of which are referred to in this novel and almost all gave tribute to the dominant power of the time, the Khazars. Before beginning the *Viking Trading Lands Series*, I knew precious little about the Slavic world, its gods, cities, and leaders. On this front, my thanks to Dr Leszek Gardela for his exemplary work on the Viking Age, many of his scholarly works and books have been seminal to my understanding of the broader world in which the Rurikid dynasty operated, particularly the Slavic powers of the time. If you have not heard Dr

Leszek speak, I recommend beginning with his appearance on the *Nordic Mythology Podcast* (Episodes 71 *Sheild Maidens and Warrior Women,* 159: *Slavic Mythology*) or *The History of the Vikings Podcast* (*Viking Warrior Women: Vikings in Poland*). I also recommend his books, *Women and Weapons of the Viking Age: Amazons of the North* and *The Norse Sorceress: Mind and Materiality of the Viking World.*

The major conflict of *Serve the Worthy,* the Drevlian battle, is based on the 883 extraction of tribute by the Rus'. It is not recorded whether this was given willingly or by force. Given the Drevlians' warlike nature and constant conflict with their Polianian neighbours, I could not see them bending the knee to Oleg without a fight. There must have been some show of strength to encourage the Drevlians to capitulate, hence the battle at Iskorosten. Towards the end of this fight, Prince Mal surrenders after the world goes dark. Though there is no record of what occurred on that day, as deeply spiritual people, signs from the gods spoke volumes. When the sun disappeared, a type of eclipse, the Drevlians must have seen this as a sign from Khors (their second most important god) that they would not be victorious. Just as King Darius III of Persia saw the blood moon, on the eve of the Battle of Gaugamela against Alexander of Macedon, as the end of his reign, so too Prince Mal may have interpreted the eclipse as the end of the Drevlians if he continued to fight. Instead, he surrenders for now and continues as the ruler of his people. This *peace* that follows, if we can call it that, would remain tenuous for years and, by the end of Prince Mal's life, tensions had come to a head. This tipping point would be an interesting topic to explore, and I would like to do so in a standalone novel from a different perspective. It is simply too good to remain unexplored. Until then, Prince Mal, and the noble hostages held in Kyiv, will remain a thorn in Grand Prince Oleg's side.

This brings me to the other important player in Oleg's court. Ellisif, who brings us much of the region's knowledge, was such a fun character to write. In the beginning of *Serve the Worthy,* she is effervescent and optimistic, though through her circumstances she exits the book as Astrid's enemy, a sad decline of their once beautiful friendship. Ellisif is a strategic invention, although her position, connections, and events of her life are inspired by the women of this time and she represents quite a significant woman, though that must remain undisclosed until it is revealed in a future novel. Her story will continue in future books and her eventual children will become the stuff of legends.

In chapter 26 we meet Thorbjorn Hornkolfi, a real-life 9th-century skald (Þórbjǫrn Hornklofi, I have anglicised his name for easier reading). *Song of the Ravens,* as his work is titled in this book, combines elements of both of his surviving poems Glymdrápa and Hrafnsmál, and are heavily influenced by the events of the Battle of Hafrsfjord and the imagery of a Valkyrie speaking with a raven about the deeds of Harald Fairhair, the first king of all Norway. I have reworked the stanza using kennings, which would have been understandable to the 9th-century ear, but hopefully not too complicated for the modern readers to decipher. Kennings, for those who are not familiar, were a way of referencing something else by using a particular phrase. For example, my use of the phrase, "Maiden of the Corpse-Road," was a common reference for a Valkyrie. It's not too dissimilar to the more modern cockney slang of London, though kennings may have been invented for the use in skaldic verse rather than everyday communication, my comparison would probably offend a great skald like Thorbjorn deeply (apologies to Thorbjorn, though perhaps he would forgive me a little poetic licence there in the name of art).

I would also be remiss if I failed to thank Dr Cat Jarman for her brilliant book, *River Kings,* which (luckily for me) follows much of the trading route that Astrid and her friends travel. This work has been infinitely useful in my understanding of trade goods and merchantry during the Viking Age. Further to my understanding of trade was the complex river systems that the Vikings and the crew of the *Bhobain* would have navigated on their journey between Aldeigjuborg and Kyiv. If you've ever witnessed a flood, you might comprehend how powerful water can be. It has the strength to move earth, carve out new routes, and move large amounts of debris and silt - thus changing the entire course of a river and the rivers they connect to. When considering which rivers crews took, and the point at which they would portage their vessel (take it out of the water to walk it overland) it is made even more difficult when you take into consideration that rivers change over time. Here I want to thank the authors (Marytnov, Subetto, and Brylkun et al.) of a study titled, *The Route from the Varangians to the Greeks: Truth or Fiction* in Economic Geography. The bathymetry work saved my bacon! Historical sources say things like, "they (the Vikings) took their boat out and put it in the XX river" giving no additional description or pinpointing the location. Plotting points on river systems to find these portages would have been tortuous without their work.

Finally, and as always, I would like to thank my family who always listen to my latest ideas, *fascinating* (to me) new research, and yet another Viking Age *fact* whether or not they want to. Thank you also to my fantastic BETA and ARC/street team, who always provide valuable feedback. Thanks to my editors, map maker, cover designer, and formatter who make these books look so beautiful. Without you all, I may have wallowed in self-doubt much longer than I did this time around. We all have our moments.

And, thank you to you, wonderful reader.

Astrid's adventures will continue in book four of the *Viking Trading Lands Series*.

# Contact

You can join my newsletter, *The Merchant Viking*, where I share the latest Viking Age archaeological news, freebies, and series updates.

You can sign-up at:
www.meganformanek.com/free

Want to discuss sources, talk about who your favourite character is, or connect on the modern trading route (social networks)? Follow me:

| | |
|---|---|
| Facebook: | /MeganFormanekAuthor |
| Instagram: | /megan.formanek.author |
| X (Twitter): | /MFormanekAuthor |
| Goodreads: | /MeganFormanek |

If you enjoyed this book, I'd appreciate a brief review. Sharing your thoughts can help new readers find this book and make a big difference.

# Also by Megan Formanek

## The Viking Trading Lands Series

Oath Undo Me

No One's Viking

Serve the Worthy